DEATH OF A RENAISSANCE MAN

DEATH OF A RENAISSANCE MAN

LINDA UCCELLO

St. Martin's Press • New York

THE DEATH OF A RENAISSANCE MAN. Copyright © 1986 by Linda Uccello. All rights reserved. Printed in the United States of America. No part of this book may be used or reproduced in any manner whatsoever without written permission except in the case of brief quotations embodied in critical articles or reviews. For information, address St. Martin's Press, 175 Fifth Avenue, New York, N.Y. 10010.

Design by Laura Hough

Library of Congress Cataloging in Publication Data

Uccello, Linda.
    Death of a Renaissance man.

    I. Title.
PS3571.C24D4   1986   813'.54   85-25171
ISBN 0-312-18801-3

First Edition

10 9 8 7 6 5 4 3 2 1

To Athanasia (Stacey) Tsaboukas,
whose birth began my Renaissance.

ACKNOWLEDGMENTS

I wish to express my deepest gratitude to all those friends and relatives who have encouraged my writing, in particular to Joan Diehl, Terri Matteo, Karen Martorano, Katherine Matteo, A. Heath Jarrett, Samantha Hart, and Linda Shaw. Thanks also to Max Von Fromm of the Ambrose-Mar Elia real-estate firm. And to Karen Matteo for all the copies.

DEATH OF A RENAISSANCE MAN

"Woe is me, to have seen what I have seen, to see what I see."
—Ophelia in *Hamlet*,
William Shakespeare

"All my sins are mortal."
—Caravaggio

1

The last time I saw Joe Savanah, it was a gorgeous bright spring afternoon in Manhattan, and we were whiling away all those beautiful sunlit hours in his apartment. He had a terrific apartment; light and airy and big. It was almost as good as being outside. I think New Yorkers mostly feel guilty when they're inside on a beautiful day. I mean it's so rare to have a beautiful day in New York that people generally feel they should be outside, making the most of it.

Well, Joe and I were making the most of that beautiful day, you can be sure. We were in bed together, naturally. I say *naturally* because whenever Joe and I were together, it was most likely in bed. What I mean is, we didn't do a hell of a lot of socializing with each other otherwise.

I personally found his conversation quite boring. The assumption was that he found me boring too. But I don't really think that was it, now that I think about it. What it was, I think, was that he was a little bit afraid of me. Afraid I was going to sum up his whole character in one unflattering sentence or something, if he gave me half the chance. So he made sure he didn't give me half the chance. Anyway, whatever the reason, we didn't talk all that much to each other. But we got along fine in bed. Really fine, twins-in-the-womb fine. I mean close. No problem communicating AT ALL.

Anyway, so there we were, in his big, airy, top-floor apartment, in bed together, doing whatever we were doing, when all of a sudden he got out of bed and said, "Excuse me for a minute." Which cracked me up no end. I mean, it sounded so formal. One minute we were doing this and that to each other, and the next, he pops up with this *Excuse me for a minute.* I said, "You're excused," and he walked out of the bedroom and into the living room, closing the door behind him. He didn't have any clothes on, so this next part really puzzled me.

I heard him open the front door of the apartment and start talking to somebody. This is the part the police had trouble believing. I can't say I blame them. A naked man opens his apartment door and strikes up a conversation with somebody in the hallway. Even for New York, it sounds peculiar.

But, anyway, that's what happened. I could hear him talking by the front door. I couldn't hear exactly what he was saying, but I know it was his voice, and I couldn't hear the other person at all. Then I heard the outside door close. And it sounded like whoever was outside came in. Came into the living room, that is, and the conversation resumed from there. But I still couldn't make out this other voice. Things got quiet for a while.

Then something strange happened. I heard them leave the apartment and go upstairs to the roof. Joe didn't have a regular old tar roof. He had a roof garden. It was fixed up really nice up there, with patio furniture and strung lights and bamboo shades you could roll up and down for privacy.

Actually, Joe owned the whole building. He bought it as a tax write-off or something: I wasn't really paying attention when he explained it to me. See what I mean about him being a boring conversationalist? Anyway, he lived in the top-floor apartment and was the only one with access to the roof.

Now I was just lying in bed, relaxing and staring up at the ceiling. In fact, I almost drifted off once or twice, which pleased me no end. Usually, I was much too hyper around Joe to ever fall asleep after we made love. He said he couldn't fall asleep with me around because he didn't know how to sleep with one eye open. So I was glad that at least I was feeling so mellow I was actually capable of falling asleep. I thought, maybe this signifies a new plateau in our relationship. Like trust!

Either I had just drifted off or I was just about to when something brought me full awake again. It was the weirdest sound. A loud *whooooooshing* sound, coming from outside. Then a real loud BANG! So help me, the whole room bounced at the same moment as that bang. And we were four flights up! What the hell was *that*? I thought. It sounded like someone threw something big out of a window. Something really big, like a piano or a safe, for God's sake. It struck me as odd that people should be throwing things out of windows in this classy neighborhood. I mean where I live, people do stuff like that all the time—but here? On the Upper East Side?

I waited a little longer for Joe to come back. I don't know how long. I mean, I wasn't lying there, timing the guy. I was just staring up at the ceiling and waiting.

Then I heard the front door open again and footsteps in the living room. I called out, "Joe?" There was no answer. I called out again, but there was still no answer.

Finally, I got out of bed myself and put on his robe.

I opened the bedroom door a little bit and peeked into the living room. I didn't want to be embarrassed in front of strangers in my robe. Or his robe. I probably called him a few more times, too. Then I went out of the bedroom and looked around the apartment. It was empty, except for me. So I went up to the roof garden, but nobody was there either. So I stood around feeling stupid for a while. I mean how far could a naked man go in New York City? Then I walked over to the ledge of the roof garden, rolled up one of those shades, and looked out into the streets. The city looked beautiful. It was so warm and balmy, without that spring chill there sometimes is. Everybody was already in Central Park, like they were saying, "Come on, summer! We're ready for you!"

I don't know why I happened to look out into the streets. This also gets the cops. What made me look out precisely then? How do I know? Maybe I expected to see Joe walking down the street, naked and all. All I know is, I looked *out*, and then I looked *down*, and there he was. Sprawled out naked in the alley, lying on the pavement, face up.

His eyes were still open, and so help me, it looked like he was looking straight up at me. There was this uneven puddle of blood under his head and the blood was spreading out slowly from this puddle and farther on down the pavement.

And there I was, leaning out over the railing, half-undressed, with my boobs hanging out, and screaming! It couldn't have looked more incriminating if the guy still had a hard-on.

This next part I don't remember all that well. I do remember running down the stairs. I don't know why I didn't take the elevator. All I know is I remember running down the stairs. And I remember this loud *turkey* sound echoing in the staircase. Like a turkey gobble, but very loud. Like, "OOOODLE, OOOODLE, OOOODLE." Somewhere along the way, it struck me that this sound was coming out of *me*. I don't know *what* I was screaming. Certainly not, "OOOODLE, OOOODLE, OOOODLE," but something turkey-sounding. Probably I was just screaming "*Oh*," but it came out all wobbly.

Then I remember being in the alley where Joe was and wondering why everybody got so stupid all of a sudden. I remember sitting on the pavement and pulling Joe onto my lap and saying, "It's all right, Joey. Don't you worry. This is nothing. It's going to be all right. Don't you worry, Joey," and all these real stupid people just standing around and looking at me like I was *crazy*. There was this little crowd down there by then, and I couldn't understand how they could *all* be so stupid at the same time. Nobody was running for an ambulance or to call 911 or anything. They were just standing around like they had all the time in the world. Didn't they know he had to have help right away? Didn't they know that time was of the essence, so to speak?

But it turns out this crowd of people wasn't so stupid after all. It turns out they already knew Joe was dead. And I was the only dope who didn't.

2

Now, for this next part, I'd like to explain something. Which is that I was not all that hysterical. I mean, maybe I was a little bit hysterical. All right, but I wasn't so hysterical that I didn't know what I was doing. The point is, what I was doing made perfect sense—I don't care how crazy I looked. I am referring to my behavior after the police arrived.

What happened, after I got it through my thick skull that Joe was dead, was that I screamed a good deal. Also, I did not want to leave him alone in that alley. So what happened was, I was sitting there on the ground, holding on to Joe and screaming my fool head off and not wanting to let him go, and these various helpful types kept coming over and trying to pry me off him, and I sort of fought back a little bit. Nothing very violent, mind you, just a few well-aimed punches, and then these various helpful types finally decided to leave me alone, saying stuff like, "All right, wait till the police come. They'll handle it." Which was fine with me, because right then, I didn't want anybody touching him or touching me or touching anything. I just wanted everybody to leave us the fuck alone. I knew he was dead already, but so what? I mean he still bore a striking resemblance to the Joe I was quite fond of and I just didn't want anybody touching him. What was I supposed to do, just stand up and say, "Oh, well. I guess he's dead. I might as well go home"? I needed a few minutes to get it all straight in my mind. I know we're all supposed to be efficient robots in this society, but give me a break!

As it turned out, when the police did finally get there, I still wasn't inclined to let go of Joe. I sort of fought them off, too. I guess my mind still wasn't ready to adjust to the situation. But they were real determined to get me away from him, and in the end, they did. So there I was, being practically carried, kicking and screaming, back into the building by these big two bazookas.

They took me into the concierge's office, which was on the first floor, and I sat in there for a while, worrying about what they were doing to Joe's body out in the alley. I know I wasn't being too rational. A few times I tried to get up and run out there again, but they stopped me. They weren't being nasty about it or anything. In fact, they were being very nice. But they were definitely being forceful. I was not above taking a few swings at them too, but they were just wild crazy swings, because I felt so wild and crazy inside. What they were mostly trying to do was subdue me, I guess. Then what happened was that just as I was about to haul off and hit one of those cops— the older one, about fifty, I guess—I happened to look at his eyes for a minute and I saw they were all teary-looking and that just finished me off but good.

I realized that everybody knew this was a terrible thing and it wasn't just me and even this cop was crying over it, and it suddenly made me realize they weren't the enemy and that nobody was going to hurt Joe because it was already too late. So I just collapsed against this cop's chest and started to cry like I never cried in my life. Just these terrible hideous moans and wails that sounded really grotesque and strange, even to my own ears. And he just kept patting me on the back and saying, "There, there. There, there." And then after a while, I finally stopped crying and just sat down in a chair, trembling and shaking from head to foot and feeling *sooo* cold. I sat there quietly for a while. My mind was still in chaos, but at least I stopped ranting and raving. I lost all track of time.

Anyway, as I sat there, I started thinking about how this whole crazy thing started, about how Joe had been alive one minute and dead the next and one thing seemed crystal clear to me. Somebody killed Joe. Somebody went up to the roof with him and pushed him off. I can't tell you how clear that was to me. Somebody killed Joe, and now that somebody was walking around, free as a bird, like it never happened.

I mean, on one hand, what the hell was the difference? What did it matter who did it and why? It wouldn't change anything. So, I thought, the hell with that. Don't even pay this low-life animal bastard the honor of thinking of him. He'll rot in hell for all eternity. But then I just couldn't get my mind off it. And the longer I sat there, the more I thought of it. I just couldn't get my mind *off* it. I started getting *obsessed* with it.

Maybe that's because I'm a Libra. I'm not only a Libra but I have five planets in Libra—all the important ones. And you know what Libra's thing is? Justice. So maybe that's why I was getting so obsessed with this business of somebody walking around free after doing this horrible thing.

So I mentioned it to a cop. "Somebody did this, you know?" I said.

"If you'll just wait a few minutes," he said. "Lieutenant Morrisey from Homicide will be in here and you can—"

"Somebody did this to him, you know? Somebody who right now is walking around free. Free and alive, while Joe is— Somebody did this. They're probably still right around here. Maybe they're outside, watching, in the crowd."

"Lieutenant Morrisey will be right with you. If you'll just hold on for a few more minutes."

"I think I should tell somebody about this right away. Before that low-life fucking bastard has a chance to get away altogether. I think I should talk to somebody right away."

"Just a minute," he said. Then he went out of the office I was sitting in and came back with another cop. A young guy in plainclothes. So I told this plainclothes cop all about what happened. He listened to it all, but he told me I'd have to repeat the whole thing to Lieutenant Morrisey in a few minutes. I told him, fine. By then the whole place was crawling with cops. Blue was everywhere. Some of my acquaintances refer to the police as *bulls*. Talk about your essence of bull. I couldn't wait to see them all spring into action and go out there and catch the low-life bastard that did this. Maybe I'd still be there when they dragged the bum in. He'd wish *he* fell off a building by the time I got through with him.

Finally, this Morrisey came in to talk to me, which was a surprise because Morrisey turned out to be a woman. I figured she must be twice as good as a man to have gotten this job in the first place. So I was glad there'd be somebody really good working on this case.

Her general appearance wasn't impressive, though. She looked a little plain. You know how nuns dress now? Now that they don't wear the habit anymore? Kind of plain, but efficient and clean looking. Her face went along with that idea, too. Nothing dazzling.

She reminded me of somebody. Was it some old nun I had at St. Agatha's grammar school? Then I knew who. Did you ever see the movie *It's a Wonderful Life* with James Stewart? She looked like the angel in the movie, Clarence. But there was a difference. She looked like a version of him that had been hardboiled. I know everybody says that about cops—*hardboiled*. But in her case, it was true. She had the same kind of cherubic, befuddled face that actor had, but hers wasn't so fluffy and pliable looking. Hers looked tougher, less movable.

I started to tell her what happened, but she cut me off. She said it would be more helpful if she just asked the questions and I answered them. She seemed very nervous about all of this, very red in the face, and there was perspiration over her top lip. I figured she was worried about handling this right, and I certainly didn't want to gum up the works, so I nodded and said fine. She was very nice about it all, not nasty or anything. Almost respectful.

"Could you tell me your name please?"

"Nikki Andrews. Nicole, really."

"Address?" She was writing this stuff down in her little book.

"106 Avenue B. Manhattan."

"Are you employed, Ms. Andrews?"

"Uh . . . yes. In a way. I'm an artist. A free-lance artist. I work on different projects. I don't have a steady employer."

"I see. An artist." She put it in her book and looked up and smiled at me. "Like Mr. Savanah," she said.

"Well, he was a lot more successful at it than I was."

"Marital status?"

"Single. Divorced, really."

"Uh-huh. Could you tell me your relationship to Mr. Savanah?"

"We were . . . uh . . . friends, I guess you could say." I had a raincoat on by then. Someone had given it to me a while back, back when I was shaking and trembling to beat the band. Beneath it I was wearing Joe's robe, which had bloodstains. Now Morrisey glanced at my attire and said, "Friends?"

"Yes."

"How long have you known Mr. Savanah?"

"Years. Years and years."

"How many years?"

"Uh—about fifteen? I don't know. I'm very bad with numbers. Since college. Let's see. Sixty-eight? About fifteen or sixteen years."

"I see. And you've been friends all during that time?"

"On and off. Except when he was married. He was married a few times in between."

"And you weren't friends when he was married?"

"Well, we were friends, but we didn't stay in touch that much."

"But Mr. Savanah is married now, as I understand it. You were friends now, weren't you?"

"He was separated now. They were getting divorced."

"Did he tell you that, Ms. Andrews? Or was that something you deduced on your own?"

"Listen, I don't want to be rude or anything, but could we go into all of this later? You see, I think whoever did this might still be around, so if I could just tell you what happened, maybe you could go outside and . . ."

"Yes, Sergeant Caputo told me all about what you related to him. We'll get to the events of this afternoon in a moment, if you'll just be patient. We treat all suicide cases as possible murders, and our investigation—"

"No, you see, that's what you have to understand right off. This was no suicide. You gotta eliminate that possibility right off. This wasn't a suicide. This was a murder. Somebody came to the apartment, and he was talking to them, and they went up to the roof and—"

"Ms. Andrews, please. I assure you all possibilities will be investigated. Please stay calm."

"The thing was he was naked. So it had to be somebody he knew. Really well. Even if it was somebody he knew really well, it's strange that he should open the door to them, naked and all. He—"

"Did Mr. Savanah say anything this afternoon that led you to believe he was depressed? Or feeling desperate?"

I couldn't believe this! She wasn't listening to me at all. In fact, she was making it very clear that this was going to be done her way or not done at all. I took a deep breath and tried to stay calm.

"No, he didn't say anything that sounded desperate."

"Did he seem worried about anything?"

"No. He didn't seem worried. He has happy and chipper and—" Clean. He was also clean, as we had just taken a shower together. But I didn't think I had to mention that.

"*Unduly* happy and chipper?" she said. "Unusually happy and chipper?"

"No, just his regular self. Listen, it must have been a woman, because he was naked and all. It must have been a woman he knew very well. Somebody he had already . . . been intimate with. Somebody . . ."

She ignored me. "Did you notice anything missing from the apartment when you went into the living room, after Mr. Savanah . . ."

"Missing? Now you think it was a robbery? This wasn't a robbery! This was a personal call! Somebody he knows! Maybe some jealous broad, who was mad about finding him with somebody else. Joe slept around a lot and maybe she—Hey! Where was Ann Pender when all this was happening? I think you should find out where Ann Pender was when this was happening because—"

"Ms. Andrews. If you're going to get hysterical again, we're not going to accomplish anything."

All right. So my voice was a little shrill. And I probably looked a little nutsy, too. But I was excited, not hysterical! You think she would have known the difference. She was supposed to be a cop, wasn't she?

"Now," she continued. "To establish the time of the death."

While she was busy establishing the time of death, the murderer was probably on a flight to Argentina.

"What time did you arrive at Mr. Savanah's apartment?"

I felt like screaming. "About noon," I said.

"And how long afterward did—"

"Listen. Half the city saw him fall. Somebody'll know the time. Right now I think I should be telling you about—"

"About noon." She wrote in her little book. "Was Mr. Savanah alone when you arrived?"

"Yes."

"Did he mention expecting anyone else later in the afternoon?"

"He wasn't expecting anybody."

"Did you and Mr. Savanah have any sort of an argument during the afternoon?"

"An argument? No, no. We didn't have any argument. We—Hey, wait a minute! Now you think *I* did it? Oh, God!"

Morrisey was getting annoyed. "As I have already explained, Ms. Andrews, every possibility must be investigated. If you will just answer the questions."

I hate when I'm excited and people tell me to stay calm. "Listen," I said. "I didn't push him off the roof. But somebody did. And it was no robber. It was a female. Some jealous female. Ann Pender, I'll bet. Because they were getting a divorce and she was crazy-nuts with jealousy. That would be her style, the spoiled brat! Where was Ann Pender while all this happened? That's what I want to know. WHERE WAS ANN PENDER?"

So help me, if I was still Catholic, I'd believe in miracles. Because who should come walking through the lobby doors at that precise minute but Ann Pender, with an Elizabeth Arden shopping bag in one hand and a Gucci box in the other. Through the open door of the concierge's office, I could see her standing in the lobby, looking around, confused. I sat down again and sighed deeply. Morrisey slammed her book shut. The young plainclothes cop came over and spoke to Morrisey.

"Mrs. Savanah is here," he said. "She'd like to speak to you."

"I'll be right there," she said to him. To me, she said, "Excuse me for a moment. Mr. Savanah's wife has arrived."

I nodded. Did she come to confess? I wondered. It didn't matter. She was here now. Maybe justice would be done after all!

3

I sat there by myself for a while.

I could see through the little slits in the venetian blinds that it was already starting to get dark outside. I wondered when I could go upstairs to Joe's apartment and get my clothes.

Things seemed to have quieted down considerably in the lobby. Something had given me the impression of a lot of noise. But when I stopped to listen I noticed it wasn't all that noisy in the lobby. So where was the noise coming from? Probably from outside. But, as far as I was concerned, I didn't ever want to go look out a window again. I'd never get over that shock I had when I looked down at the alley and saw Joe down there.

A cop opened the door and peeked in at me. "Can I get you anything? Coffee?"

"No, that's all right. Thanks."

"Okay. She'll be right back, don't worry. You can go home soon."

I nodded, then I remembered my clothes.

"Do you think I could get my clothes? They're still upstairs, in the apartment."

He stepped into the room. "Well, you can't go up there just yet. They're dusting for prints and stuff. In fact, they're going to need a set of your prints, too. Your fingerprints. Did they tell you about that yet?"

"No."

"Oh. Well, they'll tell you about that soon. You'll probably have to stop by the precinct tomorrow or something, so they can get a set of your prints. So they can eliminate your prints from whatever other prints they find up there. Don't worry about it though. It's no big deal. The ink comes right off with soap and water."

"Oh."

"Well, I'll go ask about your clothes. Maybe they'll let me bring them down here and you could change in the john or something."

"Okay." I wasn't that anxious to go back upstairs anyway. Come to think of it, I wasn't even that anxious to put on those same clothes again. Things were so different now, different from when I had taken them off. I felt like crying again.

The cop picked up on it right away. "I guess this waiting around isn't doing you any good. I'll go see what's keeping her. And to ask about the clothes."

"Thanks."

I was left alone again in the room. I just sat there, doing nothing. It must have been only a few minutes, but the next time I looked up, I saw it was really dark outside now. And it sounded noisier than ever out there. I started pacing around, wishing she would hurry up back so I could go home. Without even realizing it, I went over to the window and fiddled with the venetian blinds so the slats opened and I could see out. I couldn't believe my eyes!

I never saw so many people on one block before. Not even at the San Gennaro feast. The office window faced right out on to Sixty-eighth Street, across the street from Central Park, just off Fifth Avenue. The whole street was barricaded off. Talk about your sea of humanity! It really did look like a sea, with the people ebbing and flowing against barricades set up against Fifth Avenue.

I had forgotten about how fucking *famous* Joe was. I guess you figure if you know someone famous, you're always more or less aware that they're famous. But that's not how it was, not with me and Joe, anyway—maybe because I knew him before he got famous, so I always kept on thinking of him in the same old way.

That's why it was such a shock to look out that window now and see that mob! God! I hadn't seen anything like that since John Lennon died! But that was a stunned, solemn crowd but here there was happy chaos and razzle dazzle.

It was really dark outside now, but everything was all lit up. There were police cars parked catty-corner here and there along the curb, and they had their red revolving lights going. And there were some remote-control units, or whatever you call them, from ABC or NBC or whatever. There were some mounted policemen ambling back and forth on the fringes of the crowd.

To tell you the truth, the whole thing looked quite pretty. Very Toulouse-Lautrec. The crowd looked like it was having a fine old time, and there were flashbulbs going off every couple of seconds, like they were so pleased with themselves they were taking their *own* picture.

This was just the kind of thing Joe loved.

For one crazy minute, I wanted to run upstairs and say, "Hey, Joey! You should see what's going on out there! You wouldn't believe it! And all for *you!*" But then I remembered, of course Joe wasn't upstairs anymore.

I closed the blinds and walked away from the window. Morrisey came back. She brought me my clothes, and I changed in the john.

Apparently Ann Pender hadn't confessed to anything. But I wasn't going to argue about it anymore. Let the police do whatever they damn pleased. I just wanted to go home, crawl into bed with my head under the covers, and never come out again. Let the whole world hang!

Morrisey told me about going to the precinct the following day, so they could take my fingerprints. First, of course, she asked me if I had ever been fingerprinted. What did she think, I had a record? I was sorry to disappoint her. She gave me a card with the address of the precinct and stuff on it and told me to stop by the following day at my convenience.

"How did you intend to get home?" she asked.

"I thought I'd walk."

"That may be a little difficult," she said, gesturing outside. "Do you know what's going on out there?"

"I saw."

"It doesn't even make sense to try to call a cab. I suppose I could have a squad car take you home."

"I'd still rather walk." Let her keep her damn favors.

"Okay. You'll have to go out the back way."

"Fine."

We came out of the concierge's office together.

"Donnen. Walk her to the back door in the basement. She wants to walk home."

The street in the rear of the building was nearly deserted. I guess everybody was out around the front. I went out the basement door and walked toward Madison. On Madison, I started my trek downtown. A clock in a deli told me it was 8:17.

I started to feel really exhausted at around Twenty-Seventh Street, so I walked back to Fifth to catch a bus for the rest of the trip home.

Well, this was one beautiful spring day that had certainly turned to shit. The city looked rusted out, corroded. The people looked like tired ghouls. My own reflection in the bus window told me I looked like the biggest ghoul of all.

I felt like crying, and I did, sitting right there on the bus. Listen, in New York, you could do almost anything anywhere and nobody would pay you any mind. You could shoot up in a doorway, you could fornicate on a park bench, you could expose your genitalia in the subway, or you could clean your teeth at a Chock Full O' Nuts lunch counter, and nobody would bat an eye. (Not that I've ever done *any* of those things.) Anyway, crying on a bus is small potatoes, so I sat there and cried.

Where had all the beauty gone? The beauty of the city? My

beauty? The beauty of life? Right into the grave was where it went, with Joe.

Back in my own apartment, I sat, blank-eyed and slightly drunk, staring at my silent TV set. I didn't want the sound on. I wasn't really watching it.

I had drunk a goodly amount of brandy, smoked an enormous amount of cigarettes, and cried a copious amount of tears. The cigarettes now tasted lousy, my eyelids were puffed into water-logged pillows, and there was something wrong with the brandy if it couldn't get me drunker than this.

The phone was ringing on and off all night, and I was ignoring it. Instead, I sat on the floor and stared at my silent TV. The Eleven O'Clock News came on, and I got up and changed the channel. I watched "The Honeymooners" instead. When it was over, I flicked back to the other channel, figuring the news was over by now.

"—sky-rocket rise to fame began in the early seventies, when the art world was forced to sit up and take notice of this intense, prolific young man in their midst. At first dismissing his work as inconsequential, they were soon forced to revise that opinion, recognizing the depth and richness that lay beneath the deceptive simplicity of his paintings. No sooner had he conquered the art world than he took on the literary world as well. His books became commercial successes as well as artistic triumphs. Two were nominated for the American Book Award; *Passions and Winnings* in 1976 and *The Color of Shadow* in 1980. A jack-of-all-trades is a dilettante, a master of all trades is a Renaissance Man.

"Yet, despite his enormous artistic accomplishments, Joe Savanah didn't live in the ivory tower of elitism. He referred to himself as 'a regular working stiff.' It was that lack of pretension that endeared him to so many. Intellectuals, Establishment society and Joe Six-Pack felt an affinity with Joe Savanah."

The anchorman went into all the stuff about Joe's "philanthropic activities."

Then he lowered his voice to an even more solemn level and said, "And now, at the zenith of his multifaceted career, when his star shown brightest in the night sky, it has been snuffed out. The reasons don't seem important now." (Didn't they?) "All that remains is the fact: Joe Savanah has been taken from us. His artistic achievements will survive to enrich the world forever. But his loss as a human being will leave the world poorer. Or, as Joe might have preferred to hear me phrase it, 'So long, Joe. It's been good to know you.'"

I felt like throwing up, I swear to God. Did you ever hear such drivel in your life? That didn't tell *beans* about what Joe was really like. I mean, from hearing that, would you get the impression of an Indian in the wilderness? Because that's what the man was. Not that he was really an Indian or anything. Beautiful—God, so beautiful—and superior and strong and madly, crazy-nuts, in love with everything that happened and everything that existed, and part of the earth but part of the sky, too, and gentle and brutal and mysterious and an open book and passionate and SO-FUCKIN' INTELLIGENT and vulnerable and CAPABLE and sweet!

A wild Indian, that's what the man was.

The phone rang again while I was taking another swallow of brandy, and this time I answered it. I felt like bitching to somebody. Anybody.

"Nikki? At last! Where the hell were you?"

It was Brendan. Brendan Marsh. A friend of mine. A good friend. Platonic. Really.

"I was right here."

"That's what I figured. Why didn't you answer the phone?"

"I was busy."

"Doing what?"

"Feeling sorry for myself."

Brendan was silent for the briefest moment, then he said, "It was you there today, right?"

"*Yooouuuu* got it!"

"Shit! I was hoping that maybe at the last minute, you changed your plans or something. I was hoping that you canceled out, or he canceled out, or *somebody* canceled out. When they said 'an unidentified female companion,' I said, maybe it's not her."

"It was me."

"Shit!" He was silent another minute. "What happened?"

"What'd they say happened?"

"On the news?"

"Yeah."

"They said he jumped out of a window."

"It was the roof."

"All right, the roof. Whatever." More silence. "Is that what happened?"

"More or less. They said he jumped?"

"They said it looks like suicide."

"The fucks."

"Nikki? Did you see . . .? Were you there when he . . .?"

"I didn't see anything. He was on the roof. I was downstairs in his apartment."

He sighed. "Well, thank God."

"I just heard."

"Shit! I'm coming over."

"No. Don't bother. I'm all right. Really."

"I'm coming over anyway."

"No. Really. Don't."

"I'm leaving right now."

"No. Don't, Brendan. Really. I mean it."

"Why? You really want to be alone?"

"Yeah."

"To do what? Wallow in angst?"

"Yeah."

"So I could be there for that."

"You'll ruin it. You'll keep trying to cheer me up."

"Or worse."

We both laughed. He meant he might make a pass at me, so to speak.

"Or worse," I agreed.

"That might be the best thing for you right now."

"It might at that."

"I heard sometimes people feel very horny after something like this."

"Did you, now?"

"Yeah. Is it true?"

"Yeah, it's true."

"Don't worry about it. It's just the life force reaffirming itself in the presence of death."

"Oh."

"Were you worried about it?"

"A little."

"Well, don't."

"Okay."

More silence. "Are you *sure* you don't want me to come over now?" We both laughed again.

"I'm sure."

"Seriously. It might help."

I started to feel weepy again over Brendan offering his body as a means of consolation. I was moved.

"I don't want anything to help."

"Okay. So talk to me for a while."

"About what? Did you hear what they said about him on television? I just heard this goddamn eulogy that made me want to puke! They made him sound like a fuckin' politician!"

"Well, you have to be prepared for a goodly amount of bullshit."

"Still! All about how he was a friend of the Common Man! About how statesmen were crazy about him. And illiterates. Which is probably the same thing."

"Yeah, well."

"You shoulda heard it!"

"I did hear it, as a matter of fact. Well, don't worry. In a couple of weeks, they'll be saying a whole different story. You know how those things are. They'll uncover all kinds of scandals about him and then they'll be yelling, 'We were duped! He wasn't such a saint after all!'"

"Uncover what? He was an open book. Everybody knows everything already about him. He didn't hide anything."

"Who knows? They'll come up with something. Hey, listen. You want to really get aggravated? Did you hear what she said about it?"

"Who? Pender?"

"Yeah."

"I don't know if I want to get that aggravated."

"Come on. It'll do you good."

"What'd she say? I don't know. I don't want to hear it. Oh, all right. What'd she say?"

"Get ready. She said, 'I hope and pray he found the peace that eluded him so long in life.'"

"Bitch! Bitch! Bitch! Bitch! Bitch!"

"I knew that'd get a rise out of you. I bet the color even came back to your cheeks."

"'Hope and pray.' Don't make me laugh. If that bitch ever prayed for anything, it was absolute power. 'Dear God, please make me absolute ruler of the world. Amen.' And what peace did she ever bring him? I'd like to know. She drove him crazy. She was out to destroy him from day one. That self-righteous prig!"

"Yeah, well . . ."

"Can I tell you something? Huh? I think she did it. I think she killed him."

"Yeah, well . . ."

"I don't mean symbolically, emotionally, or whatever. I mean she really killed him."

"What are you talking about?"

"I didn't want to get into this again. I've been talking about it all day and everybody looks at me like I got two heads, but there was somebody else there. When he went off the roof,

I heard him talking to somebody. There was somebody there, and they killed him."

"And you told the police this?"

"Yeah. Of course."

"What'd they say?"

"Nothing. I don't think they believed me. I don't know what the hell is their problem."

"Their problem is a famous man died and it's easier to call it a suicide than anything else."

"Yeah, well, that's too bad, because it wasn't."

"Tell me what happened. Exactly."

I told him.

When I finished telling him, he said, "And you told the police all this?"

"Yes. Of course."

"Not a cool move, Nikki. Not a cool move at all."

"Why not? I just told them the truth about—"

"Hey, listen. You didn't happen to mention that you thought it was Ann Pender who—"

"I most certainly *did* happen to mention that."

"Oh, Nikki! No, no, no, no."

"Why not? If she's the one who—"

"Are you kidding me? Ann Pender? Ann Pender's family owns everything! Including the President of these United States! Are you crazy? Implicating her in a murder?"

I didn't say anything and he went on. "First of all, you handled it all wrong. But don't worry. It's all right. Tomorrow you change your whole story. You were hysterical. You didn't know what you were talking about. There was nobody else there. He was depressed and dejected."

"But he wasn't—"

"Play it up big. Not *too* big. Say something about how he was saying that fame was really a very hollow thing. Go along with what *she* said. About how he told you he couldn't find peace anywhere."

"Brendan, that's crazy. I already told them that he was

happy as a lark. For one thing, they'll know I'm lying. And for another, I'm not going to—"

"They won't care if you're lying, you idiot! They'll be so overjoyed to hear your new version, they'll kiss you on both cheeks and give you a medal. That's what you should have done in the first place—*lie!*"

"That's a very cynical attitude, if you don't mind my saying so."

"It is not. It's just realistic. Look. You told the truth and what happened?"

"Nothing happened. They're still investigating it. They'll get around to listening to my story and they'll—"

"They think you're lying, right? They think you're some crazy broad who made up this ridiculous story for God knows what reason. They think you're lying! That's because most people that the police deal with *are* lying. They are *used* to people lying to them. They expect it. And they're right to expect it, because most people lie to them. They're just being realistic."

"No. They'll know the difference if I tell—"

"Don't you know what happens when you talk to the police? They listen very nicely to what you're saying, they nod and say, 'Yes, yes, go on.' And meanwhile, all they're thinking is, why is this person making up this particular story? What does this person have to gain by making up this particular story for us? That's all they're thinking. They're not even listening to what you're saying. They're too busy trying to figure out what you're trying to hide with this story."

"A very cynical, paranoid attitude."

"It's the truth, Nikki, I swear. You'll see. But, hey, listen, I don't want you to see. I don't want it to get that far."

"Maybe it's because you studied law?" Brendan had a law degree, but he wasn't a practicing lawyer. He sweated out three years of law school, then discovered he didn't really want to be a lawyer. He wanted to be an investment counselor on Wall Street. So that's what he became. He loved money. I mean loved it! Passionately, sensually loved it. When he wasn't wheeling and dealing on paper, he was drooling over his coin collection. "Isn't that beautiful? I swear, money is so fuckin' beautiful." Brendan was a corker sometimes.

"It's made you paranoid and cynical," I said.

"You change the whole fuckin' story tomorrow, Nikki. And you do not mention Ann Pender again, except in reverential tones. Maybe you should even apologize for the wild accusation you made. Tell them you didn't know what you were saying. But don't even bring her up again if they don't. Remember, if you don't make trouble for the police, they won't make trouble for you."

"Nobody's making trouble. I mean, maybe they weren't paying too much attention to what I was saying, but they were being very nice."

"That's only because they don't know who you *are.*"

"What's that supposed to mean? Who am I? Jack the Ripper?"

"I don't want to be brutal, Nikki."

"Go ahead. Be brutal. 'Close your eyes and be brutal.' Guess who said that?"

"Who?"

"Hitler!"

"Very interesting."

"So? Go ahead. Who am I?"

"You're some half-baked flake of an artist from the Lower East Side. Who is barely, *barely* solvent. I'm just looking at it from their point of view, Nikki."

"So? What is that, a crime?"

"All I'm saying is that earlier today they didn't know who you are. For all they knew, you were about to become the next Mrs. Joe Savanah. So they had the kid gloves on today with you. But now they'll check around a little bit. And by tomorrow, they'll know you're not all that well connected, and the gloves will be off."

"It really is a very sick attitude you have. Almost as if you believe we live in Russia or something."

"Wise up, you moron."

"Good night, Brendan."

"Call me before you go, or I'll call you. In the morning. Around ten. I'm going to call a lawyer friend of mine first. Find out exactly where you stand on this. Meanwhile, DO NOTHING TILL YOU HEAR FROM ME."

"Shhhhh! The phone may be tapped."

"Keep kidding around, jerk."

"Hehehehehe. I'm sorry. I know you're only trying to help. I appreciate it. I really do. I love you for it."

"Really? You love me?"

"Yes."

"So how come you don't put out for me?"

"Because I want you to respect my mind."

"It's too late. I already know you're severely retarded."

"Good night, honey. Sleep tight."

"You too."

4

It is two mornings later, and I am lying in bed with Joe. Our limbs entwined, I feel him enter me. So warm, his magical, throbbing cock. So deep inside me. I come, again and again. I can't seem to stop. He keeps me coming. We have all the time in the world for this. We have eternity. And then a chill runs through me, remembering the nightmare. "It felt so *real*," I tell him. "Unbelievably real. Horrible. You were dead. In an alley. You were lying, dead. It was awful." I start to cry.

"No, no." He clicks his tongue, like, what a shame you had such a terrible dream. "I'm here," he says. "It's now. Inside you." "But it was so *real*." He licks the tears from my face, then kisses me, his tongue deep in my mouth. I am filled with him.

A loud blast fills the room. It makes my brain jump. I hold on tighter to him. I don't want our bodies to unlock. It's always painful, a wrenching away, when he pulls out. No matter how many climaxes, no matter how long we've been permeated with each other. It's ALWAYS painful to feel him pull out. I don't want it to happen now. "I love your cock," I tell him. "I LOVE your COCK!" "I know." He laughs.

Another loud blast rips through the air. Somehow, our bodies are separated. It didn't hurt this time. But how . . . ?

"Wait a minute," I whisper to him. "Okay," he says. I sit bolt upright in bed and scream out, "WHAT!"

And suddenly, he's gone. Vanished into thin air. I am alone

in bed. But how?`. . . Was I dreaming? . . . No, no, see? I am all wet. My crotch is all wet. He—

Oh. It was a dream. The wetness is only mine. It was only a dream. And it is the door buzzer that shatters the air again like machine-gun fire.

"WHAT!" I yell out again, only really waking up now. "Who is it? Just a minute!"

It wasn't anybody. At least not anybody outside my apartment door. It was the downstairs buzzer that was ringing. And the intercom was broken. I could only buzz back and let whoever it was into the building, without talking to them. But I wasn't in the mood for company. Who the hell could it be anyway? I looked at the clock. I definitely was not expecting anybody at 7:35 in the morning.

The events of the previous day had been uneventful, if you could ever call getting fingerprinted by the police uneventful. Lieutenant Morrisey wasn't there and someone else did the honors. Other than my jaunt to the precinct, I stayed alone in the house all day. Brendan had called with his usual cautions. "Keep your mouth shut. Say only what they want you to say. Wise up." I wanted to stay alone in the house even though I felt mostly cried out.

I decided not to buzz back and let the intruder in. If it was important, the police or something, God forbid, they could ring the super's bell to let them in.

I went to the window to see who had left. It was Shelly. Shelly Donat. I watched her familiar waddle carry her down the street to the corner. From the back, she almost looked like an old woman. Her short, gray, frizzy hair clung around her head. She had the hair of an ancient African.

I watched her departure, a little bit sorry to see her go. I would have liked to talk to her. Later, maybe.

It wasn't the first time I had watched Shelly from the back. I seemed forever privileged to rear-view images of the girl.

Woman, now. The first time was in kindergarten, out in the wilds of Bensonhurst, where we both grew up.

"You want to see somebody who looks just like Huey Duck?" another five-year-old asked me. A boy. I didn't want to see anybody who looked like Huey Duck. Kindergarten was weird enough. I wanted to go home. I shook my head no to the boy. "Huey Duck!" he persisted, disbelieving my reluctance to avail myself of this opportunity. He clarified. "You know Donald Duck's nephews? Huey, Louie, and Dewey? That girl over there looks just like one of his nephews." Why Huey? I wondered. All his nephews looked identical to me. I assumed the boy was some sort of connoisseur of Donald Duck-ia. "Go look at her. She looks just like Huey."

I recoiled in horror. Oh, God, how grotesque kindergarten was! I missed my mother. Even from the back, that girl looked like Huey. Her hair was white-blond and kinkier than any hair I'd ever seen. It was cut short and brushed back across her head.

When I finally did get a gander at the duck lookalike, I was relieved. She wasn't nearly so grotesque as I imagined. But there was definitely a resemblance. Her eyebrows and lashes were so light that they all but disappeared from her small, bird-like face—newborn chick, downy looking. But her face was saved from undue fragility by the sharpness of her features. Was this a baby chick or a hawk not yet completely formed? I didn't think I liked her.

By junior high her hair was brown, and we talked to each other more. Busty but otherwise thin, with her hair beaten into submission, in a style that kept it clamped around her head like cement, she looked like one of our teachers.

In high school she discovered straightening. She used to go up to Harlem to have it done. "I'd go to hell and back for it. I feel like I joined the human race the day I got straight hair."

Summer came, the one between our junior and senior years. Shelly went to Manhattan Beach for a tan. She went everyday for a week. The chemicals they used up in Harlem to straighten her hair reacted with the sun, and Shelly was transformed. A lion's mane of glistening, golden hair enveloped her face. The goldest gold! Thick and shimmering, it lovingly framed her, delicately curling in front of her ample breasts.

I walked behind her down the street one day, unwitting. Boys in convertibles called out to her. "Hey, beautiful! Want a lift? Hey! Gorgeous! You can say hello, can't you? Just hello? Aw, come on. A little smile?" Boy, some girls really were blessed. It didn't seem fair. My pace quickened, and I nearly passed her when I heard the familiar voice.

"Nikki?"

I turned, reasonably sure I didn't know anyone who looked like that, even from the back.

"Yes? Shelly? Shelly! Is that you?"

She giggled shyly. "Yeah."

"What happened?!"

"My hair. It turned blond in the sun."

"Oh, my God! It's gorgeous." The ugly duckling had turned into a beautiful swan, all right. Even her eyes looked different. No longer merely blue, they were blue-green now, with flecks of gold in them. Large, lagoon-looking eyes; misty and beautiful.

"Thank you. I know." Her small slender fingers reached up and pulled some golden strands of it down in front of her face, where she studied it, cross-eyed and up close. "I didn't expect this to happen. It's the straightening stuff that does it. Isn't it amazing?"

"My God!"

Such was her condition of gorgeousness when we began at Cooper Union a year later. We were going to be artists. Cooper Union was, and is, divided in half; half of it is an art school, the other half is an engineering school. Joe was an engineering student then. He thought he wanted to be an architect. Looking as she did, it wasn't long before Shelly caught Joe's eye. To hear her tell it, they were going together. Marriage was about five minutes away. She already considered herself unofficially engaged. Also, to hear her tell it, he was the most noble, ethical, kindest man who ever drew breath. She bored me silly with tales of his nobility. There was only one little problem. His ex.

Twenty-three years old, Joe already had one ex—Leticia Hassel. Tish. Who wouldn't let go.

"What's the matter with her?" Shelly demanded of me. "It's over! Can't she get that through her thick head? How dense *is* she, for God's sake? Why does she think he got the divorce? Because he *loves* her? But she just keeps hanging on. She's such a leech!"

Tish Hassel was from Texas. She met Joe three years before, in New York. She wanted to marry him. He didn't want to marry her. He had his career to worry about. Tish came up with an idea. If they got married, she'd support him through school. Joe didn't think it was a good idea, but Tish persisted. What was the problem? Her family, the Hassels of Dallas, was loaded. Besides, it was just a matter of time before he would be a successful architect. He could pay her back, every penny, if that's what he was worried about.

It began to sound like not such a bad idea after all. As Tish kept saying, what was the problem? Joe registered at Cooper Union and Tish brought her intended home to Dallas for a visit. Suddenly, it was a problem.

Joe was an orphan. Tish had always been something of a problem to her parents. An only child, they spoiled her rotten. And what was their reward? As soon as she hit her teens, she became flighty, irresponsible, even openly rebellious. They hoped she'd grow out of it. Maybe letting her go to school in New York would straighten her out. Instead, she comes back with this orphan in tow. And says they're getting married.

The Dallas Hassels did not cotton to the idea of having possibly brown, or even, God forbid, black grandchildren. Joe's lineage was a mystery. Sure, he *looked* white, but who knew for sure? This, as far as they were concerned, took the cake. They nixed the marriage. Tish didn't care. She'd marry him anyway. They said they'd disown her. Tish still didn't care. She'd marry him and support him through school, even if it meant waiting tables.

That's what it turned out to mean. Joe vowed a million times he'd make it up to her. He'd pay her back every penny, *plus*. Even if they got divorced someday, her three years of waitressing would guarantee her a life of leisure thereafter.

Tish didn't care about that. She only cared about Joe. If he was happy, she was happy. But he wasn't happy. Two years into the marriage, he couldn't stand it anymore. He wanted a divorce. He'd put himself through the last year of school some-how. *But*, he assured her, this didn't change his original prom-ise. As soon as he was on his own two feet, he'd take care of her forever. As for Tish, if only she could remain part of his life, she'd be happy. She remained part of his life.

After his divorce, Joe did not lead a celibate life. He was up for grabs, and everybody was grabbing. When he was "seeing" Shelly, he was also "seeing" Tish. Then he met me and he was "seeing" me, too, much to Shelly's annoyance. ("How *could* you? You're supposed to be my friend! You're just a traitor, that's all. Tish, I could understand. They were married. But you! He made a pass at Lois, too, did you know that? And she turned him down because of our friendship. And I hardly know her at all, compared to *you*.")

But how could I not? He was so beautiful and exciting and dynamic. He was so . . . oh, how could I not?

Joe's love life developed a geometrical progression to it. Girls kept getting multiplied and nobody got subtracted. And we were all so *friendly* to each other. All us girls, I mean. Of course, times were different then, the hippies and whatnot. All very free-flowing and liquid. Nobody wanted to be uptight about fidelity. Also, nobody wanted to issue him an ultimatum and have it rejected and be out of the picture altogether.

Sometimes our paths would cross, coming in and going out of his apartment (a hovel on East Third and Avenue B).

"Tish! How *are* you?" "Fine, Nikki. How about you?" "Barbara!" "Lois!" "Nikki!" "Shelly!"

And Joe, the happy pasha, sitting back, pleased by the peace and good will of it all. Until we all started to bitch— privately, to him.

"What was *she* doing here?" "Nothing. We're just friends." "I'll just bet!" "No, really."

Eventually, he had to be more careful about the flow of traffic. We never saw each other anymore. Who knew who he was still seeing and who he wasn't? He knew, but of course he wasn't talking.

Shelly and I resumed our friendship, if only to commiserate with each other over the others. Also, Shelly began to realize it wasn't so much a question of who saw Joe first as who he saw last.

Shelly and I shared confidences, swapped stories. Until I put a stop to it. "Let's not talk about Joe any more, all right? We can talk about anything else, but just let's not talk about Joe any more."

"Why not?"

"I just don't want to, all right?"

"Okay, but I think you're being very silly. He is clearly the most interesting topic to either of us and . . ."

"Shelly, please!"

"Okay!"

And now she was here to talk about Joe again, but I didn't let her in. I was a little sorry, as I watched her old gray head turn the corner, disappearing out of sight.

I debated going back to bed or staying up and facing the day. The thought of a cup of coffee seduced me into staying up. I had just finished making the coffee when the phone rang.

"Nikki? You're there?"

"Yeah, Shelly. Sorry. I just missed you. The intercom is broken and you were already out of the building by the time I . . ."

32

"Listen, I have to talk to you. I have to talk to somebody before I go crazy. You've heard, I'm sure."

"About Joe? Yeah."

"I feel like I'm cracking up."

"Come on up."

"Are you sure it's all right?"

"Yes. Come back."

"I have to talk to somebody about this. I mean who do I really have to talk to? No one! My mother? Nikki, my mother has gotten so senile, you just wouldn't believe it. If I talk about him to people that didn't know him, it sounds like I'm name-dropping, for God's sakes. Can you imagine now? Telling people what his death is doing to me? I'll sound like those screwy women who threw themselves on Valentino's *grave* or something. Or Elvis fans. You know what I mean?"

"Yeah."

"At least you knew him, too. You know what I'm saying?"

"Yes. Come on back."

"Okay. I really need a sympathetic ear."

I told myself it would be therapeutic, that I really needed a sympathetic ear, too, but all of a sudden, I didn't want it to be Shelly's. God! We had to share him enough in life. Did we have to share him in this, too? I was sorry I told her to come back. I vowed I would just listen to her and keep my own mouth shut.

She looked like hell when she arrived a few minutes later. A little like van Gogh. Scraggly, bug-eyed, dangerously at wit's end. "I think I'm cracking up," she said, as I opened the door to her. "When did you hear about it?"

I told her I was there, and it took a moment for the shock to register; then, at the precise moment her ass hit my kitchen chair, she gasped, "Oh, my God! This, I cannot handle. No. I'm sorry. I don't want to hear about how it happened, or what the body looked like or any such thing, all right?"

"All right."

"I just don't think I could handle it right now."

"Okay."

"Boy, this is a switch, isn't it? Usually, it's you, shutting me up about him. And now I'm shutting you up. That's a switch."

She turned down coffee but accepted tea. "Anyway," she said, "I was on the highway when I heard it. Driving back from Florida. I drove down to see my mother last week. So I'm driving along and they announce it on the radio. I could not believe my ears. I nearly drove right off the goddamned highway, I swear. Finally, I just pulled off to the side of the road, and I just sat there screaming and crying. It was awful."

"I can imagine."

"So then I wanted to drive straight home. I pulled off to the side of the road once or twice for a quick nap, only because I thought I would pass out from exhaustion, but believe me, I haven't slept more than two hours in toto.

"As soon as I got back here, I realized how absurd I was being. What was my big hurry? There was nothing to *do* for him. There was nowhere to go. I did *not* want to go back to my apartment. With all those memories there? How can I face that now? I still have one of his manuscripts on my desk! His work-in-progress." (Shelly always refered to Joe's work in the most formal terms, as if to do less was a sign of disrespect.) "I hadn't even finished typing the first draft yet. Oh, my God! I just remembered something else. I still have his passport in my bureau drawer! I was going to bring it to be renewed for him. And now . . . How can I go back to my apartment, I ask you. Anyway, I just drove around the city for a while, then I thought of coming here. I hope you don't mind."

"It's okay," I said. But it wasn't okay. Or okey-dokey or copasetic or hunky-dory. I didn't want her here, telling me about his manuscript on her desk or his passport in her drawer or his heart in her pocket or whatever the hell else she planned on telling me about. I wanted her to finish her goddamn tea and get the hell out.

5

"*So you've been driving* all night? You must be exhausted."

"I've been driving since the night before last!" Her blood-shot gaze reached beyond the haphazard row of greenery that separated my kitchen from my living room—bedroom and on to my still unmade bed. Oh God, I thought, don't tell me she wants to fall out here? "I'm just totally exhausted," she said. The time was ripe for me to offer her the use of my domain to crash. I let it overripen and fall off the tree. She let out a weary sigh.

"Whoever thought he'd kill himself?" she said. "Whoever, ever, thought . . ."

"He didn't kill himself."

"What are you talking about? That's what they said on the radio. The radio said . . ."

"The radio was talking through its ass. Somebody killed him."

She stared at me blankly. "What are you saying?"

"I'm saying what I'm saying! Somebody killed him. A woman."

"Why a woman?" she asked, almost pleasantly. It was clear she didn't believe any of this. Especially the part about it being a woman. You know, it's really aggravating when people don't believe what you tell them. It's infuriating enough when you're lying and they don't believe you. But when you're telling the truth besides, it could really drive you crazy. Now I was the one who sighed wearily.

"He let somebody into the apartment right before it happened. They went up to the roof together. It had to be a woman because he was naked."

Her bellow was gratifying. "*NAKED?!*" she screamed. Then, "*Naked?*" more softly.

"Yes. Thank you. My point exactly. You know how modest he was. He wouldn't have been standing around naked in front of a man."

Active as his libido was, it was only activated by the opposite sex. He was against homosexuality, not on any moral or religious grounds, but because it offended his aesthetics. Two tops and no bottom, so to speak. Gays came on to him all the time because he was so beauteous of face and form, but their interest quickly waned as he bored them silly with a lecture on the intrinsic balance of the universe, the yin and yang of sexuality. "He wouldn't have been standing around naked," I reiterated to Shelly. "He even slept with his pajamas on, for God's sake."

"We were so alike, I swear. I sleep in pajamas, too." (It was starting. I was determined to ignore it.) "We were *so much* alike! It was like we were the same person! How can I mourn for him? How can I grieve for him?" she demanded, commencing to mourn and grieve, "when we were the same person?"

And thus the game was under way. The game of Who Loved Him More. Who Understood Him Better. Culminating no doubt in a robust round of Whom Did He Really Love? I remembered my vow to not play this time. Even though here was a dandy opportunity for me to score points. Did Shelly know why Joe didn't like to hang around naked? *Why* he slept in his pajamas?

I knew: Because at one of the idyllic foster homes he was in, the father of the family was a drunken bastard who would return from an evening's carousing with an overwhelming desire to beat his wife senseless. She would, on occasion, have to

36

rouse Joe and her other charges from a sound sleep and hustle them out to the safety of the street. After a while, Joe learned that, no matter how hot it was at night, you slept with your pajamas on. Even as an adult, he couldn't get over the lesson. He was afraid a fire would break out during the night, and he didn't want to ever again find himself in the ridiculous position of being naked on a city street.

Did Shelly know this, too? Had he confided that to her, the bastard? After telling me mine were the only ears to receive this information?

"I wonder why he always slept in his pajamas," I said.

"Because that's how he *was*," she told me with authority. "He was just a naturally modest person." Thank you Joe, I prayed silently, for that crumb.

My opponent meanwhile was caught up in the game, mistakenly thinking she'd just scored a victory, though a minor one. She was greedy for bigger gains.

"Basically, he really did believe in the old-fashioned values."

Yeah, like fidelity, I thought with an inner smirk. Joe's idea of fidelity was not sleeping with more than one girl at a time.

"Did you know that about him?" she asked.

"No."

"Yes, well . . ." I–knew–him–so–much–better–than–you remained unsaid but implied. "The thing is, we were such good *friends* above and beyond whatever else was going on in our relationship."

"Mmmm," I agreed. I was not going to get caught up in this.

"Let's face it, in *fifteen years*, our friendship had certainly been tested to the fullest. God, through three failed marriages on his part, we always remained friends. In fact, I was even fond of some wives. Well, Tish, of course, I always hated. She just had no gumph at all! Totally passive. Totally dependent. No man likes that for long. But the second one—did you know her, Lorraine Rice?" I shook my head. "Oh, she was a doll. With that little button nose and that perky chin. I liked her, I really did."

My eyes started to glaze over. The bad thing about listening to somebody else's bullshit is that, after a while, it starts sounding true. I mean if you don't confront it—every step of the way—gradually you kind of get hypnotized by it and you start believing it. It was so pleasant, listening to Shelly tell about how much she liked Lorraine Rice. It went completely out of my head that she used to call Lorraine The Gnome or The Midget.

"But of course, that marriage didn't last too long," Shelly continued educating me. "And then of course there's Ann. Ann and I are very close. Very close. Did you know that?"

"No."

"Well, by now, I was so involved in every aspect of Joe's life that it was inevitable that Ann and I should become friends."

"Oh."

"Well, of course! You take his writing, for instance. Look, the books would have been written with or without me. But I do think I was a big help to him. He said so often enough. Ever since school, I did all his typing. Did he ever tell you that?"

"Yes. He mentioned it once." ("How come Shelly still does all your typing? Can't you hire a secretary, you cheapskate?" "I got *two* secretaries. They can't read my writing. I write my books in longhand first. Nobody can read it but Shelly." "Humph!" "What are you complaining about? *You* want to do it?" "Yeah, Joe. I live to type your manuscripts. That's my raison d'etre. Better yet, why don't I do it in calligraphy for you? On parchment paper. Like the monks with the Bible. I'll just dedicate my life to—" "You don't have to get *sarcastic*." "What are you getting so *touchy* about? I just asked." "So now you know. Listen. She just types my manuscripts. She doesn't blow my cock or ... she just types my goddamn manuscripts!" "Oh, who gives a shit!" "Well, you, obviously, if you're getting all excited about an old friend who still does me the life-saving favor of typing my manuscripts. She's a big help to me." "Oh, go fuck yourself, you conceited bastard!" "She's just a friend!" "Drop dead!")

"He did mention it to you?" Shelly asked.

"Yes."

"What did he say, exactly?"

"He said you typed all his manuscripts. He said it was a big help to him."

She smiled. "See? He was never one to take favors as his due."

The longer Shelly sat there talking, the more etched in granite her relationship with Joe became. By default, my relationship with him became all the sleazier. I didn't type his manuscripts. I didn't wash his socks. I just screwed him.

"Plus, he used me as his sounding board for a lot of his ideas," Shelly said. (It was understood what he used *me* for.) "Did you ever even *read* any of his books?"

("Why don't you ever read any of my books? Don't you really want to know me?" "I already know you. And I don't like you that much." "Sometimes it's hard to tell when you're kidding." "I'm not kidding.")

"No, I never read any of them."

Shelly leaned back in her chair, consolation replacing some of the grief in her face. It was such a comfort to her to know that my relationship with Joe was as bad as she always imagined it.

"Well, they are a little deep. But you really should. You might get *something* out of them." Shelly grew in stature with every word. I, on the other hand, was quickly being turned into an ad for Frederick's of Hollywood. Too bad I was still wearing the ratty robe I had thrown on at the start of this visit. It would have been so much more appropriate if I had been sitting there in a little nylon tricot number. In red, with the strategic parts cut out.

Shelly would have appreciated that. In addition to being

Joe's helpmate and bosom buddy, she did have a full time profession. Shelly designed matronly looking clothes for matronly people, Margaret Dumont types. The ladies were wealthy and the dresses were expensive, so Shelly did all right financially. She had a reputation for reliability among her clients. They knew they could count on her to never come up with anything post-1935.

"And even with his artwork," she droned on hypnotically, "I was a big help. Handling all the details with the galleries and the museums. Doing all the things he couldn't count on anyone else to do. To do right, at any rate. Did you like his artwork?"

The straws she had so gaily been heaping on my back began to weigh heavy. If anybody ever understood his artwork, it was I! I understood what made him great years before any asshole critics caught on to what he was doing. What's more, they never did catch on to what he was doing. But he foxed them. He knew how to brown up to gallery owners and art critics, and he beat them at their own crooked game. And it was just like Picasso said, when he said, "In the beginning, only a handful of people really understood my work. And now, all these years later, after all the fame and the praise and the millions, who understands my work? The same small handful. The same!" Was Shelly going to tell me about Joe's artwork now? I went berserk.

"I am so sick of this," I growled like a surly trapped animal. "I AM SO GODDAMNED SICK OF THIS!"

Her head shot up like a jack-in-the-box.

"Nikki! What's the matter?"

"I CAN'T TAKE THIS ANYMORE."

"What? What'd I say?"

"Ohhhhh, I could wring your neck! It's always the same old story."

"What same old story? Would you calm down please?"

If you ever want to drive someone off the deep end, what you do is stir them up real good, *real* good, and then tell them to lower their voice and calm down. "Who do you think you're kidding with this bullshit?" I yelled. " 'We were the same person,' " I mimicked. " 'He counted on me so much for everything.' Do you think I don't know what you're saying? What you have *always* been saying, with all your little reports? That he loved you; that, to him, I was just an inconsequential piece of ass. A quick roll in the hay. But YOU. Oh, you were the *real* thing!"

"I never said that," she said earnestly, shaking her head from side to side, the wrongly accused.

"How stupid do you think I am anyway? Do you really believe that I am such a chippy at heart that I would have an affair with a man for upwards of fifteen years without believing he really loved me? Or do you believe your own bullshit by now?"

"I never said . . ."

"His precious gem!" I spat out in disgust. "Do you remember that?"

"That still sticks in your craw, doesn't it?" she said. (That's another thing I've discovered. When you're recounting old hurts to someone, old crimes they've committed against you, they know *instantly* what you're talking about. In fact, they can go back *even further* and tell you what a shithead you were to them on occasion.)

" 'He called me his precious gem.' Honestly!"

"First of all, it wasn't *precious gem*! Precious gem is from a comic strip. *Peanuts*. But then, your whole life is a comic strip, so I can understand you getting confused. Just to set the record straight, he referred to me as his *priceless jewel!*"

"Big shit."

"And, second of all, if your own relationship with him looked shoddy when you compared it with mine, wellllll . . . is that my fault? If you were forced to come to certain conclusions because of the things you heard from me . . ."

"Ahhh, you were just a better bullshit artist than I was,

that's all. I could have done the same thing, but I wouldn't lower myself."

She looked dubious. I went on.

"You know, I read about two characters like us once. In a short story. An old married couple. They hated each other. Years before, the husband had killed the wife's pet cat. In retaliation, she killed his parrot. Or vice versa. Anyway, now they were two old people, still married, but they hadn't exchanged a word in years. But what they did was pass notes back and forth to each other once in a while. And the notes always said the same thing. Hers said *Your parrot!* And his said *Your cat!* That's going to be us someday. Yours will say *Priceless jewel!* And mine will say . . .'" I had to stop and think. The time dragged on. Shelly started to titter. I did, too, even though I still felt mad as hell.

"Can't think of anything, huh?" she said at last.

"Not at the moment!" My humor disappeared as quickly as it came. "Besides which, what are you bragging about anyway? Just because he wasn't hot for your body doesn't mean he really loved you! Didn't you ever hear that joke? 'Just because you had trouble in school doesn't mean you're a genius.' Well, just because he wasn't hot for your . . .'"

"HA!" She had a look of genuine surprise on her face. "*What* ever gave you that idea? That he wasn't, as you so characteristically crudely put it, hot for my body? HA!"

You mean he lied to me? Of course. How stupid I was!

"Not that it's any of your business," she said, "but it just so happens that Joe and I had a very wonderful sex life. Yes! Did you think you had the franchise on that? Sorry to disappoint you."

Maybe she was lying. I watched her through narrowed eyes. She continued.

"I assure you, Joe and I were compatible in every way. In EVERY way. Do you find it so hard to believe a man can have an emotional and mental rapport with a woman, in addition to a physical one? Well, they say all is yellow to the jaundiced eye. If that's been your experience . . ."

Compatible, eh? What did she mean, *compatible*? *Compatible* could mean almost anything.

"So now you're going to start bragging about your sex life with him too. I knew something was missing. What's next? Slides? I hope you have some tangible proof of this, because you don't think I'm going to take your word for it! Let's hear it, anyway. Let's really share some confidences. How many times in one night? For what duration?"

She looked puzzled. She didn't know if I was kidding or not. Neither did I.

"Oh, Nikki, stop it. You're being ridiculous."

"Am I? We've compared notes on everything else. Why not this?"

"All right. Suffice it to say that I found Joe to be an extremely caring and tender lover. Considerate and supremely satisfying in every way." That certainly sounded like my boy. "And he found me to be the same way," she said. "He said so often."

I rolled my eyes.

"What's the matter?" she said. "Not good enough? I'm afraid it'll have to do. I don't have any slides."

We had movies. Videotapes actually, that we made for the Beta-Max. It occurred to Joe one steamy and passion-filled night that, pleasurable as it was to have me doing such-and-such to him, there was yet room for embellishment. If he could watch a tape of me doing such-and-such, *while* I was doing it, so much the better. It certainly sounded like a good idea to me. So he taped *me* doing such-and-such, and then we taped *him* doing such-and-such, and then we ran the tape while we did it in real life.

It turned out to be a wonderful case of sensory overload. It knocked our sexual world off its axis, and we both went careening into outer space for hours thereafter. The man was Homeric.

We also had Polaroid snapshots, which we one day intended to commit to canvas and oil. (It always seemed a terrible shame to me that the Polaroid people couldn't really advertise that aspect of their camera. I mean, could you imagine James Garner looking full into the TV camera and saying, "Nobody gets to see these pictures but you, folks. No lab technician, no processor, no drugstore guy. Just you and"—he gestures with his head toward Mariette Hartley—"your friend." God knows what it would do for sales.)

Remembering my own tangible evidence of our exploits made me feel better about Shelly's allegations. After all, *compatible* didn't sound that terrific. And she was not one given to understatement, especially not where Joe was concerned. I cheered up.

"Does this strike you as a little bit disgusting?"

"What?"

"The two of us talking like this. Fighting over him. Even now. Like two dogs fighting over a bone."

"That's very good," she said. "That's a very good description. That's exactly what it's like. Two dogs, fighting over a bone."

There had been a sense of shame gnawing at me right from the start of this conversation, but I had told my sense of shame to take a walk. That was one conversation I was going to have or bust. So we had the conversation and I felt ashamed of myself now for having it.

Shelly looked at me and laughed a little bit. "I don't believe you. You're too much. What are you blushing about? One minute, you're demanding pictures of me and Joe having sex and the next you're blushing like a ten-year-old. What's with you?"

"I just don't think it's right for us to be fighting over him like this. I think it's disgusting."

"You're embarrassed by this?"

"Aren't you?"

"Not in the slightest! Nikki. I'm a realist! This is life. This is how people are. What is there to get embarrassed about? So we're fighting over him. Big deal."

"Even now."

"Especially now. We both want to keep our memories intact. Our versions of what it was like. We're more competitive than ever, *now*. So, we're two dogs fighting over a bone. What of it? Such is the way of the world. Very few people are altruists. Joe was. But that's the exception to the rule. The rest of us are all out for numero uno. You, me, and everybody else in the world.

"That's some world view."

"It's an accurate one. A true one. *Truth is beauty*. Isn't that what the poet said?"

"That doesn't sound like such a beautiful world view to me."

"What are you telling me? Are you telling me we can't talk about Joe anymore?"

"Yes."

She sighed. "Okay. Have it your way."

There she sat, looking like Huey Duck–van Gogh. And there I sat—Gauguin—cranky, angular, a bastard, spoiling her feeble good time. Bullying the innocent one who thought she knew it all, but didn't really.

I was the one who knew it all. All the hard stuff. For instance, I knew Shelly never loved Joe. And I never loved him either. Nobody did. Not ever. That's what I found out when I looked over the ledge and saw him lying in that alley, dead. I knew, suddenly and incontrovertibly, that no one anywhere ever loved him. Because if somebody somewhere loved him, even once, he would not be dead.

Oh, I know it didn't make any kind of real sense. But that didn't stop it from being true.

"You want to sleep here?" I said to Shelly.

"I don't want to go home. And I'm really exhausted."

"Sleep here."

"Would you mind?"

"Not at all. I'll change the sheets."

"Thanks."

The sheets changed, she was about to crawl into bed when I called to her from the kitchen.

"Shelly? Why don't you bleach your hair anymore? You had the most glorious . . ."

"I *never* bleached it. It was the straightening stuff that turned it blond. In the sun."

"Oh, yeah, that's right. Well, why don't you straighten it anymore?"

"Because it's gray now. It wouldn't turn blond anymore. It would just stay gray. What's the point in having straight gray hair? I'd just as soon leave it like this. Why? What's the matter? You think it looks funny like this? Don't you like it?"

"No, no. That isn't it. It looks fine. I was just wondering."

"Oh."

I heard the bed creak as she climbed in. Then she said, "Those days are gone forever, Nikki. We'd better face it. All those glorious, golden days . . ." I heard her voice crack. "I'm afraid they're gone for good."

I carried the dishes to the sink. I heard her crying softly. I turned on the water, so she wouldn't hear me.

A half-hour later, dressed, and dry-eyed, I tiptoed out of the apartment. It was Saturday. Brendan would be home. I'd go over there. I'd buy bagels for our lunch. Sesame seed for him, onion for me. With tons of cream cheese and lox and tomatoes.

6

"*Bring a knife,*" I told Brendan, when I called him from a pay phone on his corner. It was always a good idea to call Brendan before popping in. He occasionally had female guests. "Bring two knives. A butter one and a serrated one." Brendan didn't want me to come over. He wanted to have our bagels in the park. It promised to be uncomfortable, but I was in no mood to argue with him. I knew what he was really worried about—the police. He was afraid I was being followed or some such nonsense. I didn't see a hell of a lot of difference between my being followed to his apartment and my being followed to meet him in the park, but Brendan seemed to think we would look more innocent if we ate in the park. But, of course, I wasn't being followed in the first place. "And a big thermos of coffee."

"Of course coffee. Ten minutes. Less."

"Now, isn't this much more pleasant?" he said, as we sat uncomfortably on a grassy knoll in Central Park.

"Paradise," I told him.

"Oh, relax and enjoy yourself. It's a beautiful day."

"I hate beautiful days. Beautiful days suck."

"Oh, that's what you wanted the knife for," he said, watching me uncomfortably slice a tomato. "Why tomatoes?"

"Because I didn't want lox, but I wanted something orange on my bagel."

"What is this, some kind of new diet? Eat by color? I've

heard of paint by number, but eat by—which *reminds* me, Nikki! There's something I wanted to ask you about, but I didn't ask sooner because I knew you'd bite my head off. Do you happen to own any Savanahs?"

"Savanahs? You mean paintings?"

"Yeah."

I understood why he feared for his head. "That's probably the first thing you thought of, isn't it? The paintings. When you heard he was dead. Isn't it? What the painting would be worth now."

He munched happily on his bagels and lox. "No, it's the second thing I thought of. The first thing was, oh, God, that moron was going there today. She'll probably be found standing over him with a smoking pistol. *Then* I thought of the paintings. So? Are you rich or what?"

"Or what. I don't own any Savanahs."

"Crap! Why not? You were his friend, weren't you? Didn't he ever give you any?"

"He gave me one once. I gave it back."

He nearly choked. A crumb flew from his mouth when he spoke.

"You gave it *back*? WHY?"

"I got mad at him. We had a little falling out when he married Pender. I sent him back his painting."

"Oh, Nikki, Nikki, Nikki. Do you know what your little gesture probably cost you? Was it a big painting? A large canvas?"

"One of his biggest."

"Oh, God! Half a mil AT LEAST. Conservatively speaking! And it's only going to go up. Pass me that knife. I want to slit your throat."

Eros. The painting was called *Eros.* It *was Eros.* An abstract, spaced out, mysterious, beautiful, unpredictable, and outrageous. But ultimately frightening, because it was infinite.

It didn't scare me at first. At first I just marveled at how well he got it down. Just oil on canvas, yet he got it down.

Captured it. Elusive Eros. You could stand there and stare at it. A miracle!

It only scared me after that night. That strange and timeless night we spent together. We barely said a word all night. A silent night. A holy night? Can something that frightening be holy? Or is holiness always frightening?

All I knew was I'd do anything for him after that. Anything he asked me. I didn't own me anymore. He did. All I could do was hope he was a good man and would never ask me to do anything evil. Because now I would do whatever he wanted. There was no choice anymore. I was his.

I was terrified after he left. Terrified. And there was the painting, telling me I didn't belong to me anymore.

It'll pass, I thought. Whatever this terror was, it would pass. I'd tell him about it. He would laugh. He would laugh at me for overreacting to everything, as usual. But he didn't call that day. Or the next. And when I called him, there was no answer.

Two weeks later he married Ann Pender and I sent back the picture. I told myself it was all for the best, that something freaky was going on between us and it was better to let it end like this. Maybe I wasn't the only one who got scared shitless by that night. Maybe he was doing me a favor.

But I didn't believe it for a minute. We could have worked it out. Nothing really sick had gone on between us. No S&M, for God's sake. Just this feeling that I could suddenly see out of his eyes, that when his lips moved they were my lips too. I was inside his body, making love to myself. Only he was real. I had evaporated.

Was that just love?

"You sent it back." Brendan was weeping into his thermos lid. "Maybe by rights it's still yours. It was a gift, after all. Can you get it back? What am I saying, half a mil? At least a million! It was a really big canvas?"

I laughed.

"Do you see why you get nowhere in life, Nikki? Every-

49

thing's a big joke to you. Go 'head. Yak it up. A million dollars? Big deal! Who needs it? Not you, right, Nicole?"

I had never seen Brendan in such despair before. And so angry about it too. It was hysterical.

"For instance," he went on, "say, sometime during the course of this present difficulty, you should require the services of the legal profession. Do you have any money for that? No? I thought not. I hope you're not counting on *my* legal expertise. I know corporate law. I know almost nothing about criminal cases. I hope you're not counting on *me* to . . ."

"I'm not counting on you, Brendan."

"And as for lending you any money—well, now, won't *that* look suspicious. I mean if the police suspect you of withholding evidence and then a friend of yours lends you money for your defense, a male friend at that, well . . ."

"Huh?"

"It's like Nixon's pardon."

"I'm lost."

"Listen. Here's what my lawyer friend explained to me. He said your biggest risk is that they'll think you're withholding evidence. That you saw who it was in the apartment with Joe and you're not saying. Because it was someone connected with *you*. You get it? A jealous lover of *yours*. Whom you're now protecting."

"That's ridiculous! They don't even *believe* me about this other person there. Why should I be insisting there was someone else there if I want to protect this person?"

"Because *you* don't want to get blamed for it. At the same time, you want to protect this other person, so you just say there was someone else there, but you don't know who."

"And it was you."

Brendan looked at me with an absolutely stupefied expression on his face. I reiterated.

"If you lend me money, the police will think it was you in Joe's apartment."

The stupefied look disappeared. "Right," he said.

"Oh"

Brendan leaned back on the grass, his hands crossed under his head. "I could go for a smoke now."

He did not mean one of my low-tar mentholated cigarettes.

"Here? In the park?" I said. "In the open?"

He raised himself onto his elbows and looked at me.

"You're really funny," he said. "You're up to your eyebrows in a murder case and you're worried about a drug raid? Here? In Central Park? Where the whole park is stoned? Hahahahahaha."

"The whole park is not stoned. Look at all those healthy people jogging. They're not stoned."

"Not yet. First they run, then they go home and snort coke. They're very health conscious." He reached into his pocket and pulled out an anemic-looking cigarette.

"Want some?"

"Brendan! Please! Not here." I looked around, expecting a SWAT team to descend momentarily. For somebody that was worried about me being followed by the police, he sure was relaxed about drugs.

"Okay, okay, take it easy. Want to take it home? For later?" He was only asking to be polite. Brendan knew I didn't smoke marijuana. He knew about the time I had tried it years before. What happened was, I was wearing my hair in this topknot. And I had all these fake skinny braids twisted around the topknot. So I took a few puffs of one of these funny looking cigarettes and nothing happened. But that night, all night, I dreamed my fake braids came loose and were trying to choke me. I kept waking up in a cold sweat. Brendan said I was the only person he ever heard of that had a real bad LSD trip on a half joint.

"It'd be better for you than all the brandy you've been swilling the last couple of days."

"I'm on the wagon," I told him.

"Really? Why? What happened? Now, tell me you drank a

little bit and went through the d.t.s" He laughed. I didn't. "What happened?" he asked again.

"I had a hallucination this morning."

"What are you talking about?"

"A real hallucination. I thought he was there. My eyes were open, I swear. And I saw him."

"You were probably dreaming."

"My eyes were open and I *saw* him."

"You were dreaming. Plus, you were probably still a little drunk."

"It was a real hallucination. It was awful."

"Don't worry about it. You miss him. So you saw him. It probably won't happen again."

"I hope not. It was terrible. When I realized again he wasn't really there . . ."

"You react to everything so damn strongly," he said with mock anger. "Reefer, liquor! God knows what you must carry on with sex!" He was trying to cheer me up. I let myself be cheered.

"You're a real wild woman in bed, I bet, huh?" He grinned at me licentiously, the Big Bad Wolf talking things over with Little Red.

"Me?" I said in shock. "I'll tell you the truth, I've never had an orgasm." He laughed so loud some people sitting nearby turned to look at him.

"Who do you think you're kidding?" he said. "It's always the quiet-looking ones. The ones who look like school teachers who . . ."

"I look like a school teacher?"

"It's always the ones who look a little shy and subdued . . ."

"I LOOK LIKE A SCHOOL TEACHER??!"

"A little bit," he said defensively. "Beautiful, yes, this we know. A sphinx. Subtle. But if somebody didn't know how to look, you could look a little . . ."

"I LOOK LIKE A SCHOOL TEACHER?"

"Nikki! Stop kidding around! I mean it. Don't hit! Nikki! Is there still a tomato in that bag? If you get tomato guck on this shirt . . . Nikki! You see? Are you happy now? STOP IT. All right, that's enough. We have to talk. This is serious. We have things to discuss. NIKKI! Oh, shit! Now you did it. Now I'm going to mop the floor with you."

The running helped. The moving of muscles, the pumping of blood through the veins. Was my body mine, after all? Reaching, straining, gasping for air: his ghost loosened its grip on my body. On me. Was that all it took? A sprint in the park? Was that why all those people were running, too? To exorcise ghosts? To take back what used to be theirs?

Brendan caught up with me and latched on to my arm, pulling me down on a bench beside him. "Damn cigarettes," he heaved between pants.

We finally caught our breaths. "What do you have to talk to me about?" I said. "What's serious?"

"Your situation."

"Fuck my situation. There is no situation. The police didn't believe me and . . ."

"You don't know that. Could be they believed you and they're investigating it on their own first."

"Oh. So?"

"So you could be in a lot of trouble. What I told you about withholding evidence. That's what they'll suspect. If you're lucky."

"And if I'm not lucky?"

"They'll think you did it."

"Oh." I got up from the bench.

"Where are you going?"

"Let's go back and get our belongings. I have a feeling the picnic is over."

7

Brendan and I continued our walk through the park.

I still say it could have just been a random person. A comparative stranger that maybe he had business dealings with or something."

"He wouldn't have stood there naked talking to them."

"Oh, that's right. I forgot. Saint Joe."

"He wasn't a saint. He was just a little shy. He didn't walk around like Nature Boy."

"Okay. So it was somebody he knew. A female, you say. Who are the females in his life?"

"It's a long list."

"Think of his will. Think of anybody he might have left money to. Who would profit by his death? That's another thing the police are going to consider."

"Okay. First of all there's Tish Hassel. His first wife."

"How is she fixed financially?"

"Okay, I guess. He still supported her."

"What do you mean supported her? Alimony?"

"I don't know if it was anything *legal* like that. I kind of doubt it. I think it was just their own arrangement. They made it years ago. She supported him through school and he promised to always take care of her after that."

"You mean she had nothing on paper?"

"I doubt it. She's not the type to want something in writing from him. She'd rather just take his word for it. It'd be more friendly like that. She mostly wanted to stay on good terms with him. Emotionally. I don't think she'd really care that much about the money."

"This girl has all her marbles?"

I laughed. "Yeah. More or less. Why? Is that unusual?"

"Are you kidding? In this day and age? When people are drawing up prenuptial agreements after the first date? *Before* the first date, even?"

"Well, she's just an old-fashioned girl, I guess."

"What does she do for a living? On her own, I mean."

"Mmmm. Nothing, I guess. She used to be an artist. Taught art at a yeshiva for a while. Before that, she was a waitress while she put Joe through school. But when he started to make big money, she retired from everything."

"So he really has been taking care of her?"

"Yes. He promised to always support her and he did."

"For how long?"

"I don't know. About fifteen, sixteen years, I guess."

"Maybe he was getting tired of supporting her."

"I don't think so. Why should he get tired of supporting her now? When he had more money than ever?"

"Sometimes, the richer people get, the stingier they get. I know from the bastards I work with. They'll drive you crazy over a nickel!"

"He wasn't like that. He wouldn't mind taking care of her forever."

"Saint Joe again. So you say. You don't know for sure. It's possible he told her it was time she pulled her own weight."

"So she killed him? Never happen! She wouldn't care about the money, I'm telling you. She would care more about staying on good terms with him. That was the most important thing to her. That they should remain close."

"What was this guy, enormous or something?"

"Brendan!"

"Sorry. Go ahead."

"Why would she kill him if he was going to stop supporting her? For what he'd leave her in his will? That doesn't make sense. If he was going to stop supporting her, he'd take her out of his will, too."

"Oh, yeah, that's right. Okay, but what about the emotional reasons? The woman scorned and all that. If he wanted to break all ties with her?"

I shook my head. "She'd be devastated all right, but she wouldn't kill him. She'd waste away over in her apartment on the Mews."

"The Mews? In the Village?"

"Yeah."

"Expensive address."

"He took good care of her."

"It had to get on her nerves. It had to bother her that it depended on his good mood to support her. That she had to be so dependent on him."

"Tish? Are you kidding? She couldn't have been happier about their arrangement. He was like a doting father to her. And she was his good little girl. He was better than a father. At least he would never disown her."

"Her father disowned her?"

"Yes. For marrying Joe. So, you see, she didn't care about money. She didn't care about her parents, she didn't care about money, she just cared about . . ."

"What about her parents? Did she ever make it up with them? After the divorce?"

"No. They wanted to, but she didn't want any part of them. *Or* their money. She blamed them for the divorce a little bit. A lot. She thought that maybe if they had helped her and Joe out a little bit, they would have stayed married."

"How do you know all this?"

"She told me. We were friends. She said her parents wanted to patch things up now with her. And she said, 'Sure. Now that I'm not sleeping with any big bad *man* anymore. Maybe they think I'm going to be their little virginal daughter again. Well, fuck them!'"

56

"So she never made up with them?"

"No."

"Sounds like she could hold a pretty good *grudge,* if you ask me."

"Would you stop making her sound like Lady Macbeth? You should see her. She always has a perpetual cough. Very tubercular sounding. She's tall and thin. Like an overgrown waif, sort of. Pathetic. Long stringy brown hair. She's always got a cold or something. Watery eyes. A perpetual tissue in her hands."

"Sounds delightful."

"She's nice though."

Brendan stopped walking on the path. "Wait a minute. Wait a minute! The paintings. I have to keep coming back to the paintings. Did she have any Savanahs?"

"Ohhh, tons of them. All his early stuff. When they split up, I think he thought the least he could do was leave her his paintings. She's got dozens of them."

Brendan whistled low.

"Hers, outright?" he said.

"Hers, outright."

"Well, Tish Hassel is now one very rich little waif. There's her motive."

I started to shake my head again.

"Listen to me," Bren said. "Just say for the sake of argument he was going to break the ties that bind. Stop supporting her. Cut her out of his will. If he dies and she still has his paintings, she's set for life."

"What if he never told her that?"

"Okay, even so. Maybe she'd heard of women's lib somewhere along the line. Maybe she doesn't like being so dependent on him anymore. Maybe she wants her own money. That would really stick it to her parents. She'd really be independently wealthy now. Independent from them. Independent from him."

"She wouldn't *want* that. She still makes him Texas chili!

She *lived* for a compliment from him, a friendly pat on the head once in a while, a kind word. That's all she wanted from him. It was like Joe replaced her parents for her. So maybe he was a little distant sometimes. She could handle that, as long as she knew he was always going to take care of her. And he *was*."

"I can't wait to see that will, that's all I know. Okay, next."

"The wives, or the girlfriends, too?"

"The wives."

"Okay. Lorraine Rice. She lives in California. I doubt she had anything to do with this because she's hardly ever even in New York and . . ."

"Lorraine Rice? That wouldn't be any relation to Samuel Rice, would it?" (Samuel Rice being one of the grand old men of the theater.)

"Yeah, it's his daughter."

"He married Samuel Rice's daughter? I never knew that."

"It was a brief marriage."

"You notice how this guy always married *up*? Samuel Rice's daughter. Johnathan Pender's daughter. No wonder he didn't marry you. Your father's a welder in Brooklyn."

"Do you want to hear this or not?"

"Yeah, go ahead."

"Lorraine Rice. She's an agent now in California. A talent agent. Movie stars and such. She's also a born-again Christian. Very much a born-again Christian." He looked at me surprised. "Listen," I said. "She'd need something like that after Joe. He could leave people very fucked up. I'm surprised she didn't become a Moonie after being *married* to him."

"This guy sounds so wonderful, I can't tell you."

"Ah, he wasn't so bad. You had to know him. He had his good points too."

"Yeah, like being gigantic."

"Brendan!"

"What was it, Nikki? Come on, you can tell me. Some

kind of trick he did? Some technique? What? How did he get all these women so crazy for him?"

"He was a nice guy!"

"Nice guy, my ass. Nice guys finish last. Nice guys don't finish at all! They're always too worried about the girl finishing. 'Are you finished, dear? Is it okay for me to have my pathetic little climax?' Don't tell me!"

"Are *you* finished?"

"Yeah. I'm sorry. Go ahead."

"Anyway, I don't think Lorraine is a suspect. She lives for Jesus now. Although you never can tell with those people. But she isn't like that. You know how they sort of clobber you over the head with their humility? She isn't really like that. I don't see her as a suspect."

"All right, who else?"

"Ha! The main one! The Pender dame!"

"Why do you hate her so much? You don't seem to mind the others."

I sighed. "I hardly know where to begin."

"Try."

"All right, but do you promise not to interrupt, because it's going to be hard enough as it is, and if you interrupt every two seconds to *correct* me and tell me how *wrong* I am about everything, it'll just be impossible. I mean I just know you're going to take her side of it completely because, for one thing, she doesn't *sound* that bad if you just describe her and, for another, I think your natural bent will be to take her side *anyway*, because that's how you are."

"I forgot the question."

"Do you promise not to interrupt?"

"Oh. Yes."

"Okay. Well, the first time I laid eyes on Pender—because, let's face it, before she married Joe, she was not what you'd call your public figure. I don't care what her father owned, nobody ever saw her or heard of her until she married Joe, unless they were in the habit of reading the *New York Society Blue Book*, if there really is such a thing. I'm sure her usual crowd was that uptight, constipated, old-money bunch who—I don't care how much money they have—still look like they dress off the tables at Alexander's. But then she married Joe, and all of a sudden, she was welcomed with open arms into the artsy, literary set, which must have been quite a change from the zombie conclave she was used to; so all of a sudden, she's on Channel Thirteen every other day, holding forth on this and that subject, mostly on what it's like to be married to Joe Savanah, and she's on cable and in the newspapers and magazines and getting seated in Elaine's and ushered into Xanadu's, et cetera, et cetera, and having the time of her life, *for once*. I mean, face it, would 'Book Beat' want to know her if it weren't for Joe?"

Brendan gestured with his mouth that his lips were sealed. I gave him a dirty look and went on.

"Anyway, the first time I laid eyes on her, which incidentally was also the first time Joe laid eyes on her, was at this museum bash."

"Museums have bashes? That sounds a little incongruous. Like Happy Hour at the Morgue or something."

"Shut up. Her family had just forked over eighty-eight zillion dollars for some new wing and they tied it in with the opening of an exhibition of graffiti art, if you can believe it. I guess they had to do something to publicize this graffiti art exhibit, because what normal person is going to traipse into a museum to see graffiti when all they have to do is take the F train and see more of it than anyone would want to see in one lifetime? Anyway, there she was, Lady Bountiful, Patroness of the Arts, and Joe and I tooled in together. Joe was there by invite, of course, and for once, he brought me out in public! A real bona-fide date. I guess he figured it was an art thing and they had allowed for a certain number of zanies.

"Well, naturally, she was all over Joe, like white on rice, as soon as they were introduced. She just went all exuberant about how she LOVED his work and how thrilled she was to be meeting him in the flesh, so to speak, and how brilliant he was, et cetera. Meanwhile, completely ignoring the fact that her family's bread was now enabling these graffiti people to exhibit while real artists, who practically paint with their blood, are so poverty-stricken that they can't buy paint!"

"Well, if they paint with their blood . . ."

"I mean I could understand it if she really loved graffiti, but she did not strike me as the type of person who would have a canvas with *Blade* or *Paco* spray-painted across it in her living room. I knew where she was coming from, which was, 'Well, Art is Art, and we all have to be open-minded about these things, don't we?' Like that.

"So the three of us sort of strolled around looking at these masterworks of the subway art, and she kept saying things like, 'Now that *is* interesting, isn't it?' And Joe was nodding pleasantly just to be friendly and not argumentative and nasty. He put on his open-minded hat since he was dealing with such an open-minded person, and it was *not* because he was being an ass-kisser and browning up to Big Money in the person of Ann Pender.

"Anyway, I was beginning to feel like a fifth wheel and, also, whenever Joe went all reasonable like that it just brought out the brat in me. Plus, there was the way she kept looking at me. Terrified. Her eyes would open real wide and her mouth would clamp shut, like she was talking to some wild-eyed bomb-thrower who was about to demolish the place in some kind of frenzied fit. Somebody looks at you like you're crazy and suddenly everything you say *sounds* crazy. So of course, everything I said just sounded crazier by the minute! And she just kept looking at me cross-eyed. Ten minutes with this broad, and I suddenly sounded like the most spoiled, pampered, flighty, irresponsible brat who ever lived. Whiny, and I-want-what-I-want-*NOW*, you know? And there she was, Miss Cool-Reasonable-Rational-Moderation, gushing all this reasonable praise on Joe, because it was understood that any reasonable, intelligent person could gush over Joe, since he was already so well established in the art world, but *not* gushing over this graffiti, because the jury was still out on *that*. It was making me testy.

"So the next time we came to a painting and she pointed out how interesting it was, I asked her if she meant interesting in a Zen Buddhist kind of a way, you know: I love it because it's THERE. Which I knew goddamn fuckin' well she did *not* mean. She got all nervous and pishy-eyed, looking at Joe with this pleading look, like, 'Oh, help me, the bomb-thrower is going to beat me up.' Joe meanwhile was starting to sweat, which he claims is why he could never take me anywhere, anywhere like *that* at any rate, because I practically always start World War Three and leave everybody with plenty to talk about, such as what an unpleasant person I am. So Joe is starting to sweat, but who cared about him at *this* point?

"Then she eyes me real suspiciously, through narrowed eyes, I swear, and says, no, she meant it in the way that, even in the ghetto, there was a place for art. Which positively made me nauseous, since I know any number of black and Latin artists who would give their eyeteeth to be exhibited in a museum and nobody gives a flying fuck about their 'ghetto' art, since it is real and pulsating and vibrant and who cares about *that* stuff?

"I figured she had made herself look stupid enough with that remark, so I was willing to drop the subject. But *she* wasn't. She says how you have to be open to many new forms of art, and who really knows what's good art or bad art, and sometimes people don't know for a hundred years when something is good, and look at poor van Gogh. She actually said *'poor van Gogh.'* So I asked her if she honestly thought that this graffiti shit we were currently gaping at was going to be considered great art in a hundred years, and Joe coughed because I said *shit* and she looked about ready to drop, but she was showing how she wasn't a sissy and could stand up to the likes of me! So she says to me, 'Who knows? Who *really* knows?' And she gives me this nervous, twitching-all-over-her-face smile, like she was challenging me to say, 'I know.' Like she was positive I didn't have the gall to claim any such thing, so she was safe.

"So I said, 'Didn't you ever hear of any such thing as discernment?' And were we all supposed to give up discernment because in a hundred years we could be proven wrong? And if we did that, well, we might as well all go back to living in caves and grunting to each other like Neanderthals, because all of *life* is preference.

"Joe, meanwhile, starts hustling me toward the door, saying how we really have to go now, and I said, 'WAIT a minute! This is getting really *interesting*, and let's discuss this for a while.' Mainly because she gave this superior little laugh when I said the thing about caves, like how absurd I was being. She says, 'Yes, let's,' still all nervous and twitchy. She thought she was impressing Joe by showing what a brave little soldier she could be, but Joe hates an argument or fight of any kind. If she really wanted to score points with him, all she had to do was eye me coolly and say, 'Fuck off, creep.' He would have fallen in love with her on the spot. But of course she didn't know that.

"So I asked her what she thought of Pop Art a few decades back, and guess what she said."

"That it was interesting."

"Ohh, you're so smart sometimes. So I say, 'Interesting in what way? Interesting in that it showed the plasticity, the artificiality, the cloneness of American society? The lifelessness and predictability of it all?' We were talking about Warhol's Campbell's soup can, of course. And she looks at me and says, 'Well, I hadn't really thought of it in those terms.' So I say, 'Or was it because it showed the beauty of form, line and color in even the most mundane of the paraphernalia that permeates American life?' And did she think that that soup can was Warhol's version of Aaron Copland's 'Fanfare for the Common Man,' *celebrating* the *nobility*, the lonely and singular *strength* of the common man! Was that what Warhol was saying? Or was he saying just the opposite? What did she think he meant when he said, 'I want to be a machine'? Was he saying we are already machines? Is that good? Bad? Ugly? Beautiful? So, guess what she says."

"Fuck off, creep?"

"No. She said it was obvious I thought in terms of extremes of things. Ugly or beautiful. And that I thought in terms of value judgments and that she didn't think art should be viewed in terms of value judgments. So I said, 'Well, isn't that a value judgment?' And she said yes, she supposed it was, but at least it was a value judgment that allowed for an objective, moderate approach to things. And I asked her if she thought artists should take a moderate approach when they were creating this art, and she asked what I meant by that, immediately smelling a skunk.

"So I told her that moderation never yet had given birth to anything remotely worthwhile and that moderation, as a method of creating, wasn't worth a shit and that an artist had to be totally subjective about his work and then step back from it and walk away and then go back and see how far off the mark of objective truth, or how far on the mark for that matter, he had gotten, and try to maintain that objective truth while still being totally submerged in the work and *that's* how you got moderation, by experiencing the extremes of a thing, not by being deaf, dumb and blind to everything but moderation."

"So Joe said we really had to be going, but by then we were both so steamed that we practically both pushed him out of the way, and she said she didn't think it meant a person was deaf, dumb, and blind if they happened to value the Golden Mean of Moderation, which mankind has been striving for forever, since the Ancient Greeks and moderation-in-all-things, et cetera.

"So I quoted to her, too. I said, 'Moderation is my enemy.' Guess who said that."

"Hitler?"

"Blake. The poet."

"It sounds like something Hitler would have liked."

"Yeah, well. She said that much was very obvious to her,

about moderation being my enemy, which was probably a crack about my outfit or whatever. So I said an awful lot of people loved moderation because it really was just a form of suppression, and some people were very high on suppression, so if they could call it moderation, so much the better. And basically, such people were just fascists because what they really wanted to do was kill emotions because emotions are *always* extreme, even if the emotion is boredom or something, it's always extreme because man just is not a moderate creature, no matter what these fascists would have you believe.

"Then she says, all snotty-like, that she couldn't quite follow the connection between being objective, moderate and fascist. So I told her, that I wasn't at all surprised that she couldn't follow something, because that was apt to happen when a person had an inordinate fear of extremes, blocking out everything except this sliver of accepted thought and behavior which probably seemed very moderate to them but which was, in reality very *odd*, since it excluded so much.

"So she laughed her bitter, superior laugh and said she didn't have trouble following what people were saying, provided that it contained the barest thread of logic, and wasn't it funny how she couldn't make heads or tails out of what I was saying at all? So I said it was even funnier how often these moderate fascist types made a god of logic, too, because they saw logic as a way to *detach* themselves from things. Rather than as a way to involve themselves. And besides, any lunatic will be happy to explain to you how *logical* his insanity is.

"And she said maybe I should try to detach myself from things sometimes, if I found myself getting upset in difficult situations, such as discussing art or whatever, if I always took these things so personally. She said it might help me cope with situations.

"So I told her I never tried to cope with situations. I only tried to cope with myself in situations, and she said that certainly sounded like a full-time job, me trying to cope with myself.

"So Joe, said, 'Now, now, ladies. Let's not . . .'

"And I said maybe she ought to try coping with herself sometime, instead of standing around, coping with situations and saying things like, 'Who knows what good art really is?' and finding graffiti very, very interesting.

"And she said it sounded like I had some personal prejudice against graffiti artists and was *that* the problem?

"And I said it sounded for all the world like she was calling me a racist, in which case, for the first time in this conversation, she was making sense, since I do subscribe to the theory that some races are superior to others, intrinsically. And how the Indians, for instance, had it all over us two hundred years ago, and like all brutes, our only goal was to obliterate their far superior culture and replace it with our own. And how the blacks certainly have us beat as far as physical constitution goes, and some would say in terms of classic beauty as well, and there's a very strong possibility they may be a hell of a lot smarter than us too, not that we'll ever give them half a chance to prove that to themselves or anybody else. And I said if some kid up in Harlem can get five thousand dollars a throw from rich morons for this graffiti stuff, more power to him and maybe it'll inspire him to go on and paint something with some *content* in it someday.

"And she said it was obvious I was a racist, be it a reverse one, and how could she be expected to carry on a discussion with someone who judged people on the basis of their skin color or ethnic background?

"So then Joe said we REALLY DID have to be going anyway, and he sort of muscled me to the door and we left.

"As soon as we got outside, I was seized with the sudden desire to create some graffiti of my own, right out on the sidewalk in front of the museum. Something subtle and timeless, yet in keeping with the genre. Like, 'ANN PENDER SUCKS BIG BLACK COCKS,' in foot-high letters. Just to show all the world that she at any rate wasn't a racist. Unfortunately, I didn't have any chalk.

"Joe, meanwhile, was in a terrible snit, because he said I had practically called Ann Pender a Neanderthal and a fascist to her face and he should have known better than to bring me out in polite society and when would he learn? So I told him if he felt that way about it I'd just as soon go home alone and he shouldn't feel obligated to accompany me to my doorstep and he said, 'Back to your doorstep on classy Avenue B?' And why didn't I move out of that crumby neighborhood, for God's sake. But then how could I move out of that neighborhood, he said, when I was too proud or stupid to take money from him and meanwhile didn't know shit about furthering my own career, if I could shoot my mouth off to somebody as influential as Ann Pender and not even have the brains to know how dumb that was. What the hell did I think *he* was being nice to her for, if not for my sake and that's why he brought me there to begin with, to meet people who might do my career some good, but trust me to fuck it up. 'Good,' he said, 'stay on Avenue B, with the rats and the junkies, if that's what you want.'

"Then he said something about how I was one fuckin' joke of a prótege. I nearly fell down laughing over the *prótege* bit, and I kept calling him *de Medici* and *Duke* and stuff, and he said, all right, all right, maybe prótege wasn't the right word, but it was clear I knew nothing about the mentor—mentee relationship and how, when I made myself look bad, I made him look bad, too. I cracked up over the way he said *mentee*, all mad and everything. And then I said, why didn't he just go back there and ask Ann Pender if she wanted to be his prótege and mentee, as it looked pretty obvious to me she wanted to be his fuckee.

"So he just sat down on the curb for a while, shaking his head and real disgusted with everything, still saying it was no wonder I had nothing and would never have anything, since everything was a great big joke to me and I was such a stupid, arrogant, loudmouth.

"So I sat down next to him and waited for his mood to brighten a bit, meanwhile I was still looking around for a rock or a piece of chalk or something with which to inscribe my testimony of Ann Pender's nonracist attitudes. But I couldn't find anything and after a while he said, 'Oh, come on, I'll take you home. Back to the rats and the junkies.' And then he laughed a little bit and said, 'And all that very *interesting* graffiti.'

"So I laughed a little bit too and we mostly made up. But anyway, that's what happened the first time I met Ann Pender."

8

By then Bren and I had reached
the zoo part of the park and he suggested we stroll around and
take a look at the animals, which usually irritates the hell out
of me. All those wild animals, pacing back and forth in these
truly horrific little cages, just in despair really. But I hear
they're going to make the zoo better soon.

Anyway, Brendan generally eats his way through the park.
Being surrounded by all those trees and grass seemed to bring
out the omnivore in him. Right now he was chewing on an ice
cream cone. "I could go for a cold beer and a couple of pieces of
chicken. That would really hit the spot," he said. In spite of all
his relentless chomping, Brendan is built like a reed. So we
headed for the refreshment stand behind the bears.

Over his beer, he said, "So you and Pender didn't hit it off
real well at that first meeting."

"First and only meeting."

"Whatever. How does that prove she offed her husband?"

"Her estranged husband."

"The point is you can't call her a murderer because she
made a lousy first impression on you. It sounds to me like you
both brought out the worst in each other. You're nowhere near
as wild as you came across, and I'm sure she's nowhere near as
tame as she did. You were both really just fighting over Joe
anyway, so how can you judge a person's character in the middle of a cat fight?"

"What a sexist thing to say! We were discussing issues! Philosophies! This had nothing to do with any man."

"Yeah, yeah."

"Besides which, my first impression of her was right on the money. I know from what she's said since. Whenever I've seen her on the boob tube or read about her, she's still mouthing the same old song. My first impression of her was accurate, all right. She's a repressed, repressive, power-hungry, fa—"

"So, how come, if she's so repressed and repressive, she married Savanah, the Wild Man of the North? Why didn't she just marry some banker type and . . ."

"Boy! You really don't understand anything about human nature *at all*, do you?"

"Well, I thought I did. I mean my friends always complimented me on my understanding of human nature." He feigned foppish hurt pride. I ignored him.

"She married him to *destroy* him," I said heatedly. Some beer drinkers at the next table looked over at me fearfully.

Brendan laughed. "Isn't that a little melodramatic?"

"Maybe it is. It's also true. Listen. You gotta understand Pender!"

"Don't use *names*," Brendan said like a ventriloquist, looking down at his chicken.

"Sorry. But you gotta understand her. Her background. But it wasn't only her background that made her a dictatorial, autocratic, powerhungry—Even if she was born poor, she would have managed to stick herself in some situation where she ruled the roost entirely. She would have been a grammar-school teacher, for chrissakes!"

"How diabolical!"

"Don't you understand? She lived her life in a totally artificial environment. Like a really terrible first grade teacher. The kids can't just walk out. They can't over-throw her. Whatever she says goes. She gets used to that kind of power. She

70

thinks the whole world has to do what she says, you know? Pender had—"

"Shhhh."

"She had that kind of power all her life. And she didn't rebel against it, like Tish did at least, sensing that maybe there was something unfair about it. She pushed it in people's faces and she reveled in it. And since she's just a naturally repressive, life-hating type of a person, that's what she wants to make everybody else be, too. *But,* she is also an enormous egomaniac. I mean, what's the fun of bossing a lot of helpless people around? Where's the kick in that?"

"How true. I've spent some of the dullest afternoons of my life bossing helpless people around. It gets to be such a *drag.*"

"So she goes after the *best.* She goes after it coolly and rationally. She gives him exactly what he needs, exactly when he needs it, and,—*voop voop*—she's got him on her hook. Now, if she can make *him* grovel, she'll really be accomplishing something. Proving what she has known all along—that she is KING!"

"In other words, you don't have one tiny, minute shred of real evidence to connect her with you-know-who's death."

"Of course I do. She had a key. Whoever came into the apartment that day let themselves in with their own key. Nobody rang the bell."

"She had a key? You know for a fact?"

"I know for a fact. But that's not important. Listen. The crux of the matter is that she gave Joe what he needed most at one particular time in his life."

"Sure, let's forget all about the key that could maybe unlock this whole thing for us and go back to talking about fun Freudian things. What'd she give him?"

"Disapproval!"

Brendan smacked his palm to his forehead. "How obvious! And to think I didn't even see it."

"It's true! You mean to say you didn't even know that?

That people marry people who disapprove of them? Oh God. What *do* you know?"

"People marry people who disapprove of them? Are you shitting me?"

"Of course they do. It makes them feel comfortable. It reminds them of home. It reminds them of their folks."

"Oh. I see. And to think, all these years I've just been looking for a nymphomaniac who knows how to cook. Have *I* been barking up the wrong tree."

"Anyway, Pen—I mean you-know-who is no dope. She saw that he needed generous doses of disapproval and she gave it to him. And then she just reeled him in and let him flap around on her boat for a while."

"You don't know any of that. You only met her once and—"

"I read all about it! In *Playboy!*"

Brendan leaned back in his chair and laughed, nice and quietly. It was one of the nicest things I've ever seen him do. His usually brown hair was glinting gold in the sunlight, and his blue-green eyes were sparkling and misty, and his wide mouth was in a mellow smile. Then he leaned back across the table and whispered to me, "What a horse's ass thing to say."

"It's true! Joe gave an interview in *Playboy* and there was the whole story, right there. He said, 'Thank God for my wife. She keeps me down-to-earth and regular. She reminds me every goddamn day that I'm nothing special. All the time, she tells me, "Be HUMBLE. Be HUMBLE." I need that.' There it was in black and white. She didn't have to be any genius to figure out what he needed."

I leaned back in my chair, but I wasn't laughing or anything. The day I read that interview was one of the blackest days of my life. It was like a slap in the face to me. Oh, not that Joe did anything like that on purpose. I'm sure he didn't even *think* about me that much to say something in a magazine that I would take as a slap in the face. But that's how I took it. I guess because I knew he could never count on me to keep him down-to-earth and regular. And to remind him every-day to Be HUMBLE. I know I had a very big mouth with him sometimes, but I think he sensed I was pretty crazy about him and whatever he said or did was okay in my book.

"Could we talk about this key business? I know it's totally irrelevant, but humor me."

"What? She had a key. She killed him."

"Why'd she kill him if she had him flapping around in her boat? A landed fish."

"Because that part of the relationship was over. He was getting over being addicted to her disapproval."

"So she killed him."

"Right. If she couldn't control him anymore, she'd just as soon see him dead. She couldn't take losing this contest. So she killed him."

"Doesn't that sound a little emotional for somebody who is supposedly such a cold, calculating type?"

"Oh, this was no crime of passion. There were very real reasons why she'd be better off with him dead."

"What? She doesn't need his money, that's for sure."

"Status! He was about to divorce her. She would be just one more ex–Mrs. Joe Savanah. She would be the discarded one, not him. Who do you think all those artsy, literary people were going to side with, him or her? She'd be a persona non grata in that crowd once they got divorced. She definitely would not have been able to tolerate that. But if he's dead— well, then, she's his beloved widow. Her table at Elaine's is secure, you know?"

"Anybody else have a key?"

"What are you nitpicking? I'm telling you she did it."

"Who else had a key?"

"Well, Tish had one."

"I don't suppose you have any concrete proof of this, other than to give me a complete psychological rundown of her life from day one."

"She used to cook for him sometimes."

"So this makes her above suspicion?"

"No. I mean she used to cook for herself at home and sometimes she made extra and brought it over for him. Or sometimes, she'd make something special, just for him. Like Texas chili. He loved her Texas chili. So she'd make a big pot of it and bring it over and if he wasn't there, she'd just let herself in and out with her own key. I know because once when we went back to his place, there was a pot of it waiting on the stove and he said, 'Hey, look what Leticia brought over. Too bad we missed her.' Like that. So I know she was in the habit of letting herself in and out of his apartment."

"The guy must have been gargantuan, I don't care what you say. Women, tiptoeing in and out with pots of food . . ."

"Brendan, he let people *do* for him, that's all. Sometimes that's what people want, that you should let them *do* for you. In a way, you're giving *them* something. What are you complaining about? You'd break out in a cold sweat if anybody brought you over a pot of food. You'd say, 'Hey, baby! I think you're getting a little too involved in this. I mean if I eat this stew, does that mean we're engaged, or what?'"

"That's right! I like to set things straight. I'm not a user!"

"Oh, he wasn't a user either, you jerk. He just let people do for him."

"He was all heart, this guy. What wasn't dick was heart."

"Brendan!"

"All right, all right. Anybody else have a key?"

"Yeah. Lorraine Rice has one."

"Oh, right. Wife number two. The actor's kid. What'd she have a key for? To do his laundry?"

"No. She'd come into New York a couple of times a year, on business or whatever, and she'd stay at his place. He was living out in Bedford Falls by then, married to Ann, but he had this apartment in the city, so Lorraine would stay there instead of a hotel or something."

"Didn't Pender mind that? One of his exes, living in his apartment in the city?"

"No, no. It was all very aboveboard and proper. Lorraine got religion, I told you. Obviously, they weren't sleeping together."

"Okay, so let's see now. Joe's out in estate country with Ann. Tish is over in the Village, still being supported by him, and Lorraine is staying at his apartment from time to time. And now his third marriage starts to fall apart because he's getting over being addicted to disapproval. So he moves out of Ann's place and—"

"No, no, no! He didn't move out of his own volition! She *threw* him out."

"Why?"

"Because of the womanizing thing! Look, she was reforming him, right? She was teaching him how to become a Better Person. How to value moderation and humility, instead of whatever the hell else he valued. But no matter what else he changed about himself, he just kept right on catting around."

"Well, look, you gotta admit that could be a bitch to adjust to in a marriage. Your husband sleeping around. You can't really blame her for minding *that*. I mean I don't care how much you hate her, she was within her rights to demand fidelity from the guy, no?"

"See? That's what I mean about her. She sounds all right and reasonable and all, but that's not how it was. I mean I could understand if it was really tearing her up inside, him sleeping around. I mean that's a Big Thing, and a gut-wrencher if ever there was one. But that's not how she took it. It was part of her program with him and he was flunking it, you know? Like she didn't mind it on any gut level. She minded it because . . . well, she couldn't control it."

"How come you didn't mind it? How come you didn't mind the fact that he was sleeping with other women when he was supposedly having an affair with you? I mean, I am assuming you had a physical relationship with this guy, unless you're a lot more peculiar than I know and *all* your relationships are as sexless as ours is."

"Of course I minded! But there was nothing I could do about it. Besides which, our relationship was never really clearly defined like that. Like, 'Well, now I'm having an affair with Joe Savanah.' It was all very sloppy and unpredictable. We'd be seeing each other and then he'd marry somebody else and we wouldn't be seeing each other. With his occasional casual flings, it was getting too much to worry about, so I finally said to myself, oh, fuck his womanizing, maybe it'll just go away someday."

"Okay, so Pender throws him out for his philandering."

"Yes, but it was just to throw a *scare* into him. She tells him to move out and she demands a divorce. But it was all bullshit, as far as I'm concerned. She no more intended to divorce him than rocks intend to fly. She just wanted him to be more *obedient*."

"Well, she was taking an awful chance, wasn't she? Threatening? If she didn't really mean it?"

"I don't know. He was still pretty much under her thumb. I mean, totally cowed by his own capacity for selfishness, and clinging to her to save him from himself. There *is* something comforting about people who say they know the *real* you, and 'Yes, you're a terrible mess, but basically, I know you *mean* well and you *can* be saved. By me, of course. By my relentlessly pointing out your myriad faults.' I mean, none of us lack for self-hatred and Pender's type capitalize on that. And they go after the ones who do have something going for them, some self-esteem or self-respect or whatever. To make their victory that much sweeter when this formerly strong person bites the dust. Anyway, Joe had plenty of spirit and heart, and Pender's mouth was watering for this victory. But she wants him to know she means business. Promises aren't good enough for her anymore. She demands the divorce, but she lets herself be convinced to make it a trial separation. He'll go live in the city and come to terms with his problem. And when he's cured, he can come back. He was supposed to, meanwhile, be seeking professional help in overcoming his problem of promiscuity.

"So he does move back to the city and he even sees a shrink for a while, who, he told me, was one of the craziest people he's ever come across, even counting some of the wing-dings he ran into at various orphan asylums, and some of them were right out of Dickens, I swear. Which is another reason I tended to look the other way about Joe's philandering. He did not have what you'd call your happy childhood. He had to come out of it scarred in one way or another, and in his case it happened to be by having the conviction that the nicest thing you could do to another human being was have a little loving sex with them, which really isn't such a terrible idea, if you think about it.

"Anyway, he's going along with this austerity program of hers, seeing the shrink and living all alone, like a monk, no fooling, and telling her to drop in ANYTIME, announced or unannounced, so she can see for herself what a good boy he's being. That's why she had a key. He gave it to her to prove to her that she could charge in on him anytime and he'd be all by his lonesome. He *wanted* her to check up on him. He really did. He wanted this trial separation over and done with so he could move back to Bedford Falls and see her miserable, scowl-ing face around the house again. That's another thing he said in that *Playboy* interview. He said, thanks to Ann, he was learn-ing that love wasn't what the rest of us slobs call love at all. It wasn't happiness or the hots or being overjoyed. It was suffer-ing together for about fifty years and then and only then could you say you loved the person and not be laughed off the face of the earth by all the right-thinking people on the planet. So he was anxious to get back to putting in his fifty years of suffering with Ann Pender, so he could be entitled to say, 'I love you.' He tells her, come and check up on me, anytime.

"But she doesn't, of course. She wants the kind of power that's *so* powerful it doesn't even have to be checked up on.

"A couple of months go by, and it starts to dawn on Joe, hey, maybe he really can survive without her after all. Besides which, here he is, wasting all this self-control as far as getting laid is concerned, and Mommy doesn't even come around to tell him what a good boy he's being so he figures, what, am I crazy?"

"So the first one he calls is you."

"Well, I don't know about that, but anyway . . . He goes back to being his old self and he starts thinking this trial separation was really a very good idea. Like, maybe Ann is right and they really shouldn't be married to each other. Maybe divorce was a real good idea. So Ann now begins to get the gist of this. And this is not what she had in mind AT ALL.

"So she comes over to his apartment, letting herself in with the key, and what do you know, he's in the middle of a tryst. And is he begging her for forgiveness? Is he groveling? No. He's standing around, shooting the breeze, talking to her like he's her goddamn *equal* for once. I didn't hear her voice, it's true. Sure. She was probably talking through clenched teeth! She must have been furious! But I heard him, and he sounded relaxed and happy and just fine. Really at peace with the world, you know? It must have driven her crazy. So they go up to the roof to talk things over, supposedly, and she kills him."

"Just like that?"

"Just like that. Maybe she already knew he wanted a divorce. Maybe she didn't and he just told her that day. At any rate, she figures it's better to be his widow than his ex—also, she is not too fond of him at the moment, all things considered—so she kills him. She'd do something like that, don't think she wouldn't."

"But did she?"

"She did!"

"The only remotely convincing thing you've said is that she has a key. But then so does the Rice kid and so does Tish. My money's on Tish. Because of the paintings."

"No, you're wrong."

"And that's all who had keys?"

"Yes. Well, I had one, technically speaking, but that doesn't count because I was already there."

"Oh, yeah, that's right. Anybody else have a key?"

"Well, Shelly has one, of course. You know Shelly. Shelly, who this very moment is probably still asleep in my apartment . . ."

"Shelly? What's *she* doing there?" I looked at Brendan in surprise. For as long as I'd known him, this was the first and the *only* time he sounded like a jealous lover. He didn't even act that way about *Joe*. Then I realized why. Brendan accepted the fact that he and I didn't sleep together with good grace. After all, that was my prerogative and, I'm sure he thought, my loss. So we'd be platonic friends. But if *he* was my friend, what did I need Shelly for? He was jealous. "What's she doing sleeping at your place?" he said. I explained what she was doing sleeping at my place.

"Well, I hope she doesn't start making a pest of herself now," he said.

"Shelly? Not Shelly. She's usually a very self-sufficient person. This morning was an unusual circumstance, I'm sure. She's not the clinging type. She's like you. Another realist."

"Oh. So she has a key, too. But she was in Florida when it happened, so that lets her out. It could still be checked, though."

"Don't be ridiculous. It was Pender, I'm telling you!"

"Any more keys floating around?"

"No. Hey, listen, he was a little cavalier with his body, but his keys he was more careful with."

9

Traveling around with Brendan was a lot like hanging around with a little kid—he always either wanted to eat or to go to the john. He excused himself and left me sitting there alone for a while.

We were at the outdoor tables, the ones off to the side, where the outdoor bar was. They only served wine at this bar, wine from big jugs, and not mixed drinks at all, which was fine because who the hell was going to order a frozen daiquiri or a champagne cocktail when there was a trace of elephant dung in the air?

Alone with my memories, so to speak, I immediately remembered the occasion of my revenge on Joe for his *Playboy* interview, having had the incident so recently brought to mind.

It happened after our affair, if you could call it that, started up again. After he was separated, good and soundly, from Ann Pender and had started socializing again. I was naturally overjoyed that Dorothy here (Joe) had finally escaped from the clutches of the Wicked Witch (Ann), and it looked as if things were going to go back to normal, or as normal as they ever got, at any rate. So we were having a fine old time, having not seen each other for a while and getting reacquainted, so to speak. But I guess that, deep down, I was still somewhat put out about the whole episode of the Pender marriage, you know? Joe was oblivious to the latent hostility going on right under his nose practically, and he was having the time of his life.

That Pender dame must not have even *looked* at him all that often, because right now he was all gung-ho for the idea that I should look at him. I mean he kept inviting me to share in the spectacle of what lust hath wrought, which was fine with me and very exciting and all. But in between orgasms, I was still a little bugged by Pender in general.

I have to admit that he did look like some great, glistening god of maleness. With his arms outstretched and his head thrown back and that magnificent heart-stopping face of his. (His cheekbones alone were enough to drive me wild.) And him laughing like a madman and saying, "Would you *look* at this?" Not meaning his *face*, of course, and just in general feeling very proud of himself.

So he was just about to launch this debauchery on my person (I just looked up *debauchery* in the dictionary and it says "extreme indulgence of one's appetites, especially for sensual pleasure." That's the word I want all right), so he was just about to launch himself into this debauchery, when all of a sudden, I remembered that *Playboy* interview and did something terrible. I said, "Joe?"

And he said, "WHAT? Oh, God, would you look at *this?*"

And I said, "Be HUMBLE! Be HUMBLE!"

Man, did he get mad! I didn't care though. I guess I made *my* point. I was not only tossed out of bed but out of the whole damn apartment, all the while he was complaining about what a castrating *bitch* I could be when I set my mind to it. As I mentioned, Joe hated fights of any kind, so he wasn't yelling. He was speaking very softly (and carrying a big stick, oh, that's awful!) as he tossed out another item of clothing, mumbling to himself about what a certifiable lunatic I was. I just sat out there on the floor, in the little vestibule outside his apartment, laughing myself silly at seeing these clothes hurtling by. I think I may have mentioned to him, during one of his fleeting appearances at the door, that moderation in all things was really the key to happiness, and didn't he know that? He got real quiet for a while, then he opened the door with this real somber look on his face, and finally says to me, "Who would know it just to look at you?"

Who would know *what*, I wanted to know. And he says, "That on the outside, you're so beautiful, but on the inside, you're so mean and rotten and spiteful." Then, looking real disgusted with everything, he closed the door again.

Well, I was just floored. He thought I was beautiful? Since when? This was news to me. Listen, I *know* I'm not beautiful. When a person is beautiful, they know it, and I definitely *know* I'm not beautiful. Did he think I was beautiful? Wow! I couldn't have been more thrilled.

Oh, who gave a shit what he said about my character? Not me, you can be sure. But he did say I was beautiful on the outside! I went home on a cloud, I swear.

Fortunately, he didn't stay mad too long. I've found that if there's one thing you can count on in this life, it's lust. After a few days, we started seeing each other again. It was understood I should not mention moderation or being humble again.

Hey, listen. Don't think I don't know what a crazy thing that was to do, to choose that particular moment to even the score. And if I had been dealing with anyone even slightly weird in that situation, I never would have done it. (Not that I'm ever in that situation with anyone weird, if you don't count my ex-husband, that is.) Like Brendan, for instance. I mean, he's a fine friend and generally a wonderful person, but I am not always 100 percent sure that Brendan has all his marbles, sexually speaking. For instance, I have noticed on occasion that some of Brendan's girlfriends look like tarted-up nine-year-olds. Oh, not that they really *are* nine-year-olds or anything. He's not an out-and-out *degenerate*, for God's sake. But sometimes they just have this flaky look to them. Some of his girlfriends are completely normal looking though, and quite pretty, even. But those are the ones who always like him more than he likes them. The ones *he* really likes are the tarted-up nine-year-old-looking ones. Also, I sometimes wonder if Brendan is capable of rape. The reason I wonder and don't know for *sure* is that the one time I was about to find out, I fortunately remembered an old hockey injury of his and quickly reminded him of it, too. ("All right, Brendan, cut it out, or I'll kick you right in your bad knee, so help me God.") It wasn't that I considered Brendan vicious or anything. It was more like he was an overly amorous great dane from time to time. But maybe it was one of the reasons I always thought it best to keep our relationship on an entirely platonic level.

But anyway, with Joe, I knew I was dealing with an eminently sane person who would never lower himself to using any kind of physical force against a woman.

So things were going fine between Joe and me, better than they ever had. And now *this* happened. It still didn't seem real to me. Him not being in the world, I mean.

Brendan came back from the john. I got up from the table and we started walking. After a while, he said, "Well, all in all, I think we've had a very productive morning. It looks as if the police will have other people to investigate besides you, at least. Assuming, that is, that they don't write it off as suicide, which would really be the best thing. But if they do investigate it as a murder, there are at least other suspects. Women with keys. They had access, motive, and opportunity. You may beat this rap yet."

"Number One," I said, "nobody's charged me with anything."

"Yet."

"All right, yet. And, Number Two, we could be completely wrong about all of this."

"We? What do you mean, we, *kemo sabe?* If our little theories are wrong, that it was a woman with a key, you're in this all alone. If we're right, well, then of course I take most of the credit."

"Suppose, Bren, it's a random killer. Not someone with a key at all. Not someone he even knew that well. Suppose it really was a robbery and the murder was just a byproduct of the robbery."

"But if the doorbell didn't ring and the lock wasn't tampered with . . . ?"

"Still. Suppose this is what happened: He and I are in the bedroom together. He hears someone in the hall. I don't, because I am otherwise occupied. So I am not listening for somebody in the hall. But he hears them because he *lives* there. He's used to what sounds belong there and what sounds don't. You know how those things are, in your own place. You can tell right away when somebody's approaching your door."

"But you were both in the bedroom. Maybe sounds from the hall can't be heard in the bedroom."

"But they *can*. Later on, I very clearly heard him go up to the roof with this person. I heard their footsteps on the stairs. I could even still hear his voice a little bit. Because I was listening for it by then."

"Okay."

"Okay, so maybe he hears the elevator stop at his landing. I'm oblivious to it, but he hears it. So he says, 'Excuse me' and goes to see who's coming. He goes to his front door and looks through the peephole, recognizes the person, and lets them in. No key involved at all."

"But he's naked."

"Okay, so it's still a woman. A woman he's been intimate with. But even so, it doesn't jibe that he would open the door naked to her. *Unless,* unless it's some kind of emergency. So he looks through the peephole and sees somebody who is obviously strung out with some problem, and he opens the door right away."

"What kind of problem?"

"Who knows? So she steps inside, they talk a little bit, she finds out there's somebody else in the apartment and she wants to talk to him in private, so they go up to the roof. It has to be some kind of emergency, because if it's a regular friend, dropping in, they would ascertain the situation, get a little embarrassed, and beat a hasty retreat. Also, a friend would call before dropping in. Joe didn't like unexpected company. This person isn't a friend-friend. This person is just somebody who knows him, knows where he lives. Somebody in trouble, coming to him for help. *That* kind of stuff happened to him all the time. He knew a lot of subterranean types who were no stranger to trouble. Junkies, ex-cons. He used to help a lot of people like that. Get them jobs, give them a quick handout if they needed it.

Brendan yawned.

"Okay, so it's one of these subterranean types, there for an emergency of some sort. Maybe she's on cocaine and she needed money for her next fix. Or she comes there for the cocaine itself!"

"Joe was dealing coke?"

"Are you really crazy or what? Of course he wasn't dealing coke. But he sometimes had coke. He never had it for too long, but . . ."

"Who among us does?" Brendan was nodding in understanding, completely misunderstanding everything. For the first time, there was a note of compassion in his voice regarding something to do with Joe. What a shame I had to shatter the illusion.

"You don't understand, knucklehead. The reason he never had it for too long was that he would blow it away. I mean *literally*. He would blow it into the air, scatter it. Listen, people used to give him drugs all the time. Fans and stuff. He'd walk into a place, and instead of shaking hands, people would walk over to him and stick something in his pocket. And say something like, 'Here you go, man. Enjoy it in good health.' Like it was a little love offering or something. But Joe never used what they gave him. When it first started happening, that pain in the ass would actually lay a little drug lecture on them. 'You don't need that, baby. That poison could kill you.' But of course, nobody wanted to hear *that*. So they didn't. People are amazing, I swear. They would completely ignore what he was saying and act exactly, but *exactly*, as if he had said, 'Gee, thanks. I do appreciate it, man.' I mean they'd go right on nodding and smiling and saying, 'Don't mention it, buddy.' After a while, he finally realized nobody was listening to him anyway, and he stopped with the drug shpiel. He'd just accept what they gave him and smile and say thank you, and then, when he was alone, he'd empty his pockets and blow the stuff into the air. He never used it, but a lot of people wouldn't know that. People might think he'd have cocaine in the house."

"Fame must be so fuckin' wonderful, I can't stand it. People just walking over to you, handing you coke. You think it's too late for me to get famous? Maybe if I write a book? I could write a hell of a book. *Sex and Money*, how's that for a title? That's all people are really interested in, you know? Sex and money. How I would *love* being famous."

"Anyway, where we were? Oh, yes. I was hypothesizing. Okay, so some girl comes to see him at his apartment, either for money or because she thinks maybe she can get some cocaine right there."

"Yeah, but would she be so open about it? If she wasn't a real good friend of his, would she just go to see him and ask him directly for something like that? Make herself look so . . . uncool?"

"Listen, Brendan, I have a news flash for you. Not everybody on drugs is an upper-middle-class executive, worried about their reputation or their career. There's a whole other stratum of society that takes drugs."

"You mean *poor* people use dope? God, how can they afford it. Even on my income, it . . ."

"Very funny. Okay, so say she's a little bit of a rough character. She's not worried about her reputation or her career. She's in the apartment long enough to look around and see many fenceable items. This noted, they go up to the roof to talk. She asks for a quick handout or for dope. He tells her he has no dope. Also, if she wants money for drugs, she's going to come away empty-handed from Joe. She might get a little lecture on signing up for a rehab program, but she's not going to get anything else. Meanwhile, she's just interested in getting her quick fix. Remembering the valuables downstairs and also that the door isn't locked, she pushes him off the roof, the son of a bitch, zips back into the apartment, grabs something, and goes on her merry way. Don't think it wouldn't happen like that, because even junkies will tell you they'd push their *mothers* off a roof, if the situation called for it."

"So it could have been a random person after all."

"Why not? I'll tell you something. Even Shelly suggested that this morning. She said, 'I bet it was one of the low-life creeps he was always helping.' Maybe she's right. and I'll tell you something else. That living room *did* look different when I went in there. Just like Morrisey said. She asked me if I noticed anything missing in the apartment. Anything valuable. I pooh-poohed it at the time, maybe because my mind was set on it being Pender."

"And your heart set on it, too. I suppose you're going to tell the police all this too."

"Why shouldn't I tell them? If it's a possibility . . ."

"Watch my lips, Nikki. This will be important. I don't want you to miss this. Because, if you tell the police about how maybe it was this random person, they will *never* find her. Do you understand? She left no clues. They will never, ever find her. Police do not like murder cases where they never, ever find the killer. Especially not murder cases that are in the newspapers, like this one is. So they will focus their attention on you again. And if they focus on *you*, well . . ."

"Then *you'll* be involved?"

"I'm *already* involved," Brendan said. I was shocked by the anger in his voice. "Just by knowing you, I'm already involved." The anger in his voice became apparent to him, too, and he laughed, but it was a harsh, brittle laugh. "God! Can't you understand this, Nikki? If, by some miracle, the police don't actually charge you with his murder, the possibility they'll consider next is that it was a jealous lover of yours who—"

"So what are *you* worried about? We're not lovers."

"A minor point, you can be sure. I doubt very much the police will believe that. I'm not sure I believe it myself sometimes. Why I would put up with all your crap . . . ?"

Ordinarily, I might have laughed at such a comment. Ordinarily, he would have said it only to make me laugh. Oh, it wasn't that Brendan was even remotely in love with me or any such thing. It was just his wounded male ego that I heard now. Why *didn't* I sleep with him? Not really a question, but a demand. I didn't even have the excuse of a husband to justify keeping this relationship platonic, or even a steady boyfriend. I had known Brendan through Joe-less times. Through completely manless times. His pride was hurt. How come I never noticed *that* before?

"Right now," he said, "the police are investigating everything about you. Where you go, who you see. Can't you understand that? This isn't some joke that'll—"

"I still don't understand what you're so worried about. It happened on Wednesday afternoon. You were no doubt toiling in the vineyard of Abercrombie, Pierce, Fenner, and Fitch—"

"It's Livingston, Brown, Collins, and—"

"Whatever! You were at work! Nobody's going to blame you if you were at work while it happened . . ."

"I wasn't at work."

I was duly stunned. A weekday afternoon, and Brendan wasn't at work? "Well, where the hell *were* you?"

"See? That's exactly what I mean. Even *you're* suspicious."

"I am not! Don't be crazy. I'm just a little surprised, that's all. Where were you?"

"Where I was was home in bed. Alone! I went to work in the morning, but I didn't feel good, so I went home at about two o'clock."

I was again surprised. I have known Brendan to stay at

work with a fever of 103. I have known Brendan to wait until his coffee break to throw up and to be dutifully back at his desk within the alloted time. I mentioned this to him.

"That was in the beginning. I'm a little more secure in my job now. When I get sick, I go home."

"So, as they say in the movies, you have no alibi."

"As they say in real life, too. Which brings me to something I've been wanting to tell you all afternoon. God only knows how you're going to take this."

"What is it?"

"It's this. I think it really would be best, until this whole thing blows over, if you and I cooled it for a while. You know what I mean? If you and I maybe didn't see each other for a while. If you maybe didn't call me on the phone."

"Maybe?"

"All right, definitely. If you and I definitely didn't see each other . . ."

"That's what I thought."

"Damn it, I knew you were going to take it like this. I just knew you would get all excited and . . ."

"I don't believe this. I'm getting the kiss-off speech. We never even slept together and I'm getting the kiss-off speech! It's just too bad I don't have a watch to throw back in your face, that's all."

"And vicious! I knew you were going to get vicious about this." We glared at each other for a minute. The watch referred to an incident a while back. I was over at Brendan's for our Saturday morning bagel nosh when his mail arrived. In the mail was a manila envelope, and in the envelope was a very expensive ladies' watch that had apparently had some work done on it with a hammer. Also, a note, saying *This watch is like you—no damn good.* The note wasn't signed, but I knew it was from this girl named Diane. They had been going together for quite a while. I helped him pick out the watch for her birthday. She was one of the decent-looking ones.

Brendan insisted that she had known all along there was to

be no commitment on either side. The smashed watch hinted that her agreement may not have been wholehearted. Right now, I could understand exactly how she felt. Funny, I had never thought of our friendship in terms of commitments, but I suppose I did expect some sort of commitment anyway. Was that expecting too much? Brendan read my mind.

"You really do expect too much of people sometimes, Nikki. God! A murder case! And I'm supposed to get involved, just like that, just because we're friends. I have my *career* to worry about. Do you know how my line of work takes to scandal, Nikki? Not well. Not well at all. Do you think people are going to trust me with their life savings if I'm a suspect in a murder case? And what good is it going to do you if I lose my job, can you tell me that?"

This chickenshit speech did not deserve a response.

"You really expect people to walk through fire for you, don't you? Well, I've got news for you, now. There are not too many people willing to walk through fire. Not in the real world, Nikki. Maybe in Never-Never Land, where you live, but not in the *real* world."

I felt my throat constrict. *Joe* would walk through fire for you, if you really needed him to walk through fire. He was real, wasn't he?

"What are you so quiet about?" Brendan demanded. I felt my eyes beginning to tear up. I fought it, which had the stupid effect of making my bottom lip tremble. "What are you thinking about?" Brendan demanded again.

"Nothing!" Damn it, my voice cracked.

"You're thinking of Don Quixote there, aren't you? About how he stood up to all the Hell's Angels on your behalf? Yeah, well, maybe he just lived for the big grandstand gesture—"

"Shut up, Brendan. Just shut up."

"Maybe he just went out of his way to make himself look like a big macho man every once in a while, just to impress the natives. And, God knows, you were impressed!"

"You're DAMN RIGHT I was impressed!" I was blind

with rage. "What the hell is your problem anyway? What's sticking up *your* ass all of a sudden?" Then I knew. He was jealous that Joe didn't use drugs. "Is it the drugs? Is it that he didn't use drugs? That's it, isn't it? That's what's got you all perturbed. Well, relax. The guy had his faults, don't worry. The bastard went and DIED on everybody, didn't he?"

I burst into tears. Brendan didn't say anything. He just handed me a clean white handkerchief and we kept walking, me blowing my nose and crying and him keeping quiet for once.

After a couple of minutes I stopped crying. I looked over at Brendan. His face was a blank. I always thought Brendan looked like an angel. But not some pudgy, cherubic-looking angel. Some arrogant, smart-ass, uppity angel. Exactly the kind that would ask God for All Knowledge and then be puzzled when he got tossed out of heaven for his trouble. "What'd I say? I just asked a simple question! Jeez, He's so uptight!" A smart-ass angel.

"Ha!" I said, my voice heavily laced with irony. "I was just about to say I'll give you this handkerchief back the next time I see you. But then I remembered what a psycho you are. You're probably afraid the police will search my apartment and trace its laundry mark back to you, so I'd better burn it as soon as I get home. Ha!"

"You really do have a terrible temper," he observed coolly. "Really. A terrible temper. Can I ask you just one thing, Nikki?" I immediately felt a laugh beginning to percolate inside me.

"What is it?" I snapped.

"Are you absolutely, positively sure *you* didn't do it?" He made a shoving gesture with his hands, meanwhile raising his eyebrows. I bit my lip to keep from laughing. "I mean maybe you were discussing art at the time or something," he continued, "and he said something you didn't like and you. . . ?" He shoved at the air again, and I burst out laughing. "I'm sure, you jerk!"

We started walking again.

"Anyway, as I was saying," Brendan said, "it might be better if you didn't call me. Which is *not* to say I won't call you. Because I will. But from a safe phone. One that's not likely to be tapped or traced."

"Oh, Christ, I don't believe this! You mean to say you're going to call me from outside only? Will you be wearing a disguise when you make these mystery calls? A big nose and glasses maybe? Hahahahahahaha."

He ignored me completely. "And I will continue to help you. For instance, as soon as this lawyer friend of mine finds out about the will, I'll let you know."

"Bren! You could put a handkerchief over the receiver, you know, to disguise your *voice!* Hahahahahahaha. On second thought, maybe you better not do that. If anybody sees you doing that, in one of these public phones, they're apt to think you're making obscene calls. What with your big nose and glasses. Hahahummm."

"The will has to be made public within ten days anyway. But if he can find out something sooner, so much the better. But you will hear from me Nikki, all right? Don't worry. Don't feel abandoned, all right?"

I nodded, immediately feeling abandoned.

We had come to the end of the road, literally. We stood at the edge of the path that led onto the street at Fifty-ninth and Fifth. It was assumed we would now go our separate ways.

As we stood there staring at each other for a few seconds, I almost expected him to shake my hand. Instead, he leaned over and kissed me, awkwardly and abruptly, on the lips. Our front teeth bunked. We both pretended it was entirely normal for a gesture of affection to leave you with a throbbing upper lip.

"Okay," he said. "Take care."

Then he crossed the street and began walking down Fifty-ninth. Midway down the block, he started to jog. Energetically.

Actually, it looked for all the world as if he were running away.

When I got home, Shelly was gone, and I found a note propped up on the kitchen table: *Thanks for the tea and sympathy. A Lieut. Morrisey called. She wants to see you immediately.*

Immediately was underlined. My stomach flip-flopped. So Lieutenant Morrisey wanted to see me immediately, did she? I wondered what would happen if I didn't show up. If I never showed up at all.

10

What the hell did I have to be afraid of? I had nothing to hide. I was the one who wanted them to investigate in the first place. There was no way I was *not* going to go to that precinct. I wanted a few answers myself! Such as, were they closing in on the Pender dame, or what?

Also, it's not totally unpleasant to go to a police station, you know? I mean it's a famous institution, The Police, and it's interesting as hell to see it in real life. I guess it's the Yoko Ono thing of wanting to communicate with the whole world. I'm a big Yoko fan. It's like everybody knows about the police because of about a zillion movies and cop shows and all, so when you find yourself involved in some kind of famous setting like that, it's like you're communicating with the whole world, on some level. A lot of people put that instinct down, wanting to communicate with the whole world—"Yeah, yeah, everybody wants to be famous"—but I think it's a good instinct. (Actually, I think all our instincts are good. The trouble comes when our instincts are interfered with and they get perverted.) So, all in all, I was not that averse to going to the police station.

That's because I'm an *idiot!*

I FORGOT! I forgot all about The Bastards. Brendan is right about some things. I live in an isolated world, with my paintbrushes and my oils and my canvases. I forget what's out there! I forgot all about The Bastards. You'd think just dealing with my landlady would be enough to remind me, but anyway—The Bastards are this whole group of afflicted people. I'm sure I don't have to describe a Bastard to you. You've no doubt come into contact with one somewhere along the way, probably quite recently. It seems to me Bastardliness is reaching epidemic proportions lately. Brendan blames it on the economy. Oh, I know everything is supposed to be okay now, regarding the economy. At least that's what The Bastards in Washington want us to believe so they can get reelected. But everybody knows better. Oh, they act very cocky and sure of themselves, these Washington Bastards, because they were elected, weren't they? They claim they have some sort of mandate from the people. Well, it seems to me they're overlooking one thing.

Look. If *more* than half the people in the United States don't vote for anybody at all, even in Presidential elections, the mandate from the people seems crystal clear to *me*. The majority of people in this country vote for *nobody*. And that's who they want to be President. Nobody! They vote for nobody in the Senate or in the House. And that's who they want. Nobody! Majority is supposed to rule in this country, isn't it? So how come these dudes keep showing up for work? This country does not want a government! Now if only those blockheads would pack up and go home, we'd all be fine. No taxes, no wars. Do you think some strapping eighteen-year-old is going to take it into his head to gear up and go serve as target practice for some hotheaded foreigners? And shoot at them besides? Oh, there's bound to be a few teenagers who would come up with that idea on their own, but that's just the lunatic fringe.

Anyway, where was I? Oh, yeah, The Bastards.

I had an insight regarding Bastards recently. Regarding why we're reduced to such ineffectual idiots whenever they're around. It's all the Marquis de Sade's fault! He gave everybody a very cockeyed view of sadists, which is what Bastards are. I mean you hear something like, "I take torture out of myself by inflicting it on you," and what do you picture? Some nut in boots and chains and whips, right? But that's not what sadists (Bastards) look like anymore. They look like sweet little gray-haired ladies. They look like the Moral Majority. They look like anybody and everybody else. But they got the same problem as the fruitcakes in the rubber suits. They don't feel right if you're not suffering. If you're happy, they're miserable. If you're miserable, they're happy. It's you or them. They choose them.

Which brings me, finally, to the two Bastards at the police station. It was Morrisey, of course, and a cohort of hers named Reynolds. What a team! At first, I was completely offguard, because I am an idiot and that is my way.

So when they started out by asking if I was Joe's common-law wife, well, it was a jolt, but all right. They had to ask their questions, didn't they? I mean, it definitely had a grimy ring to it—common-law wife—but I figured maybe that's how the police would describe unmarried people living together. Common-law husband. Common-law wife. So I told myself not to take it personally.

I wasn't Joe's common-law wife, and I told them so. (They referred to him always as Mr. Savanah. I, on the other hand, became Nikki. They weren't being chummy. They were showing me they didn't have to be so careful about what they called me.) I wondered a little bit why they asked me this question. I mean, they already had a few days to investigate things like that. So how come they didn't know already?

So, then, what exactly *was* our relationship, they asked, all puzzled. Well, I told them already, didn't I? We were friends. Intimate friends.

Yeah, yeah, they weren't interested in what I told them before. They were only interested in what I was going to tell them *now*, understand?

I nodded, but I didn't understand at all, to tell you the truth.

This next part I'd just as soon skip over. I mean it was just too insulting and humiliating to even repeat. I mean if some people think *artist* is a euphemism for . . . for *prostitute*, that's *their* problem. Oh, yes, didn't you know that? *Artist* and *model*

96

and *actress* are all euphemisms for *hooker*—according to the Dynamic Duo, anyway. But, hey, listen, it wasn't my job to straighten them out. ("Vengeance is mine, sayeth the Lord." I always figured that means don't waste your time on low-lifes.)

"So Mr. Savanah didn't contribute to your support in any way whatsoever?"

"No."

"Just a little help with the bills every once in a while?"

"No."

"Hmmm. That's strange. A woman alone. An actress. What was it, a model?"

"An artist! I'm an artist."

"Oh, yeah, right. An artist! I knew it was something that's hard to make a living at. Sometimes, girls like you, they make a little something on the side . . . ?"

What they were doing here was setting the tone for the whole afternoon, which was going to be one of unrelenting sleaze. They were letting me know that they already put me so far down in their estimation that it was going to be an uphill fight for me all the way.

"So you never took any money *at all* from Mr. Savanah?"

Somehow they made this sound even worse. As if everything had been on the house.

"No. We didn't have that kind of relationship. We were friends. Our relationship didn't have anything to do with money." ("Why won't you let me help you? If you had money and I didn't, you'd help *me*, wouldn't you?" "Yeah, and if I kept marrying other people, would you keep taking it? Joe, don't take it personally. Money screws everything up. If you start paying my rent and I one day feel like telling you to go fuck yourself, right away I have to think about the rent. Money and love should have *nothing* to do with each other." "Money and love are the same thing! What the hell *is* love, if it isn't sharing money? Love *is* money!" "Yeah, well . . . I don't need it anyway. I do fine on my own." "Yeah, that's true. I forgot." He rolls his eyes.)

"What about loans? Did Mr. Savanah ever lend you money to be paid back at some future date?"

"No. No loans." (Brendan I borrowed money from. Brendan I still owed $35 from two years ago.)

"What about from other men? Any gifts or loans from other . . . ?"

"Listen. No gifts. No loans from anybody." (Brendan didn't count. In bagels alone I paid him back.) "I support myself. I'm an artist!"

I tried to explain about my work to them. Unfortunately, it all got filtered through the sludge and slime that coated what is laughably called their minds.

It all came out sleaze. Thanks to the paperback covers I had done, I became a porno artist. And my commissions for private portraits? That was a laugh.

"Oh, so you go to people's houses and paint them? What is is, mostly men? Are they in the nude?"

"Family portraits! The whole family!"

"Oh, are they all in the nude?"

Yeah, could you just see Mr. and Mrs. Braithwaite, of Sag Harbor and Sutton Place, and all the little Braithwaites standing around naked, posing for me. "No. They are never in the nude. Unless maybe I'm doing just the children. Sometimes, if it's the children, they might be . . .

"Ohhhh. The children? Really? But hey, listen. We're not the vice squad here." What was I worried about? They didn't care how I earned my living. They were just investigating a murder case.

I told them I wasn't worried about them being the vice squad. Why should I be worried about them being the vice squad? (You think I'm exaggerating about this? Get involved in a murder case sometime, God forbid, and you'll see if I'm exaggerating. I'm playing it DOWN, for chrissakes.) Listen, why didn't they ask Mr. And Mrs. Braithwaite themselves what sort of a portrait I did of them? I'd be happy to give them a list . . .

What was I getting so touchy about? Jeez. They just

wanted a few simple answers, that's all. Relax! Reynolds flashed me a wide smile. Right about then it began to dawn on me how much these two enjoyed their work.

We progressed on to the subject of the afternoon in question. We were alone when it happened, weren't we? Just me and Mr. Savanah on the roof. What happened? Had there been an argument? They had witnesses who could testify I was on the roof. ("But that was afterward!") Were we fighting? Had he already belted me a few times? Was that it? Listen, they had witnesses who could testify that we fought a lot. (This was pure bullshit. Joe and I had our set-to's from time to time, but ALWAYS in the privacy of our own homes. Joe would rather die than argue in public.) Who was telling them all this bullshit?

No, no, there was no argument of any kind.

Was it an accident? He pushed me and I pushed back, and before you knew it, there he went—right over the side. Listen, if it was an accident, just in the course of me protecting myself, they could square that.

No, no, I wasn't even there!

All right, all right. So it wasn't a fight. Reynolds leaned low over me. What were we two doing? Getting it on? And we got a little carried away with the fun and games? Listen, those things happen! They would understand. They were cops! They heard about all kinds of crazy thrills. They were liberated. What was I worried about? If it was an accident like that, why, I probably wouldn't even be arrested. They could arrange that, couldn't they, he asked Morrisey. Morrisey nodded, assuring him they could. *But,* I would have to start telling the *truth* about things.

I am telling the truth. Somebody else came there. Somebody came and they went up to the roof together and . . .

All right, then, who was it? Was it somebody I brought with me? Somebody who was maybe going to take part in the afternoon's festivities?

What festivities? Listen, I don't like the way you're talking about this. This was private. This was personal. You have no right to . . .

Reynolds's fist slammed down hard on the desk, and I jumped three feet in the air.

This was a MURDER CASE, GODDAMN IT. There was nothing FUCKIN' PERSONAL OR PRIVATE about it. When was I going to FIGURE THAT OUT?

(They're the police. They're just doing their job. Don't take it personally. Most people lie to the police. They're supposed to scare people, to confuse them. This helps them get at the truth. This helps them find the killer. Good. I want them to find the killer. I want it very badly. All right, so let them scare me. Let's get this part over with, so at least they'll know it's *not* me.)

No, I didn't bring anyone with me. Did I call someone from the apartment? To join us later? Maybe Mr. Savanah himself suggested calling in another party?

(They were determined to turn this into a ménage à trois one way or the other. What they didn't know, and I wasn't about to explain to them, is that such things are beyond my capabilities. I have dyslexia. I can't do more than one thing at a time. Even with *one* person I can't. Another person in the bed is definitely going to present a very big problem to me. I mean in fantasy, it's not without its attractions. In reality, I'd probably end up doing some real damage to somebody.

No. We didn't call anybody. Wouldn't the phone company have a listing of the calls made from a phone? Couldn't they check with the phone company and see that . . .

Why didn't I just leave the investigating to them? They'd handle that. Listen, if it was a ménage à trois, I shouldn't be embarrassed. They heard it all before. I could tell them anything! It was just like talking to a priest!

No, no, it was nothing like that! I didn't *see* the person. I didn't even hear them.

Why was I protecting this person? Was it a man or a woman? Didn't I realize that by protecting them, I was putting my own ass in a sling? And why protect somebody who left me holding the bag? Was I afraid of them? What was it, a jealous boyfriend? Hey, listen, a jealous boyfriend was a picnic compared to what the police department could do to my life if I didn't start cooperating.

I *am* cooperating. I have no jealous boyfriend. I have no boyfriend at all. (Joe was my boyfriend!)

I was divorced, wasn't I? What about my ex-husband?

How the HELL did I know? I hadn't seen him for about ten years. (We were married for all of six months, during which time he turned my apartment into a pigsty. Then he took off with my Water-Pic, my good luggage, and my bank account. Thank *God* they hadn't found him. He could give them an earful and a half. I could just imagine what that creep would tell them. "Yes, she always had a terrible temper. Terrible, really. She bit me on the arm once. I'm sure that if I had been standing by a window, she would have thrown me out." Thank *God* they hadn't found him.)

All right then, so who was it? How could it be I didn't hear them if I could hear Mr. Savanah? I must have some idea.

(Don't mention Ann Pender again. Brendan will murder me if I mention Ann Pender again.)

Why was I protecting them? I must have *some* idea . . .

I wasn't protecting anyone. I'd tell them if I knew. Maybe it was a robbery? Was anything missing? . . . It did seem to me that something was missing from the living room . . .

They smirked at each other. No, there was nothing missing from the living room. It wasn't a robbery. It was a little too late to try *that.*

I wasn't trying anything. There *was* something missing . . .

What?

I don't know.

(Did they question Ann Pender like this? Somehow, for the life of me, I could not picture them questioning Ann Pender like this.)

All I know is that it must have been a woman, I tell them. Because he was naked. A woman he knew very well. (Like the Pender dame, I don't tell them. Sure, he'd be naked in front of her. He was reaffirming his *manhood*, for God's sakes!)

Oh? Was it a woman friend of mine? An *intimate* friend? (Now I'm a lesbian.) I look into Morrisey's parboiled lobster face and tell her *again* I don't know who it was. Round and round we go, all saying the same thing, a million times, a million different ways.

It finally penetrated my thick skull: Bastards. I was shaking and sweating and crying from time to time, and this was fine with them. And it had NOTHING to do with police work! They were simply spending a pleasant afternoon, keeping their tranquillity on an even keel by scaring me shitless. IT HAD NOTHING TO DO WITH POLICE WORK. Or finding the killer or getting at the truth or anything like that. It was the look of satisfaction that passed across their faces every once in a while, when I would burst into tears or something. I had seen that look a million times, walking past construction sites and having my anatomy described in minute detail for me. There was that look. "I can say these things and you can't do a thing about it, sweetie." Like that. A lot of bosses have that look, in offices. And every landlord I've ever had, had that look: I feel better when I make you suffer, even when it isn't necessary. I'm just keeping my hand in it.

Ohhhhh. They were Bastards, these two. That's probably why they became cops, to have access to suckers like me. I thought they were the good guys! Wait a minute, this changes everything. I'm going home. My mother doesn't like me to sit around talking dirty, not even to the police, who are like priests, we know.

"Listen, we've gone over everything about a million times—(I didn't know you were Bastards)—and we don't seem to be getting anywhere. So I'm leaving. I've already told you everything I know and I can't think of anything else that would be relevant." (Who told you it was fine and proper to suggest I was a hooker, or Joe's common-law anything? Pender? Is she still pulling the strings in this case?)

I got up out of the chair.

"Sit down," Morrisey said.

"No thank you. I'm leaving."

They both laughed, like, "Get a load of this one."

"SIT DOWN!"

"No, thank you," I said again. "It was really very foolish of me to answer all these questions without my legal counsel present. But I honestly did want to help." (I didn't realize I was dealing with Bastards.)

"Where the fuck do you think you're going?"

"Home."

We all three fell silent. Will they arrest me or won't they? Am I going to be the patsy in this case or not? Did Ann lead you to believe that? Sorry. She was mistaken. Don't fuck with me, fellas. I can be formidable.

They hesitate a moment longer. "Wait a minute, would you please?"

Such a change!

"In other words, you are no longer willing to cooperate voluntarily in this investigation. In other words, in order to question you further, we'll have to charge you with something. Is that it, Nikki?"

"That's it."

"Do you think it'll be easier once we feed you into the system? Is that it? Do you know how long you can be detained, just for questioning, in this city? Days, Nikki. Days and days. Incommunicado."

Ah, but what stories I can tell when I get out, I think.

"And that's not even remotely related to anything like false arrest, you know?" Morrisey tells me. "It's all perfectly legal." They're getting hairy again. Do I put it into words for them? Joe was a famous man. Surely the media would be interested in this. "We could hold you up to three days, right here in this precinct."

"You people talk as if I'm keeping something back from you. But I've already told you everything. Up to and including my own personal opinion, which I mentioned last time. In my humble opinion, Ann Pender should certainly be asked where she was at the time of the . . ." They don't look up or anything. Nobody jumps. But all the same, a jolt of electricity goes through the room.

What's this? I am not shot on the spot? Nobody tells me to shut up? What have we hit on here? Do they already know about her? Do they already know she did it? Was this intended to be a coverup? And I was supposed to be the hapless fool they pinned it on?

Wait a minute. I'm being paranoid. Not everything is a coverup. So how come they both got jolted there for a minute? Let's run it up the flagpole and see if they salute again.

"I mean, far be it from me to cast aspersions on her character, even in the confines of this little room, with the confidentiality I'm sure you guarantee"—unlike the Six O'Clock News, who can't wait to blab to everybody—"but I certainly think you wouldn't be remiss in questioning Miss Pender, excuse me, I mean Mrs. Savanah, as to her whereabouts on the day in question. I mean, they were about to be divorced, and if it's jealous mates you're looking for, Ann Pender certainly . . ."

They seem to cringe a little bit, inwardly, every time I say the name. They look at each other very briefly, then back at me. They do not want to hear the Pender name mentioned again. Here or anywhere else. Especially not on the Six O'Clock News. Have we struck a bargain, fellas? Not yet. Not completely.

"Would you be willing to take a lie-detector test?" Reynolds asks me. "It wouldn't be admissible in court, but just to attest to the facts as you've told them to us."

No. Now you get nothing.

"A lie-detector test?" I said. "As I understand it, they're not always completely accurate. And I have dyslexia. Maybe that would affect it, too. I'm afraid you're just going to have to take my word for things. Maybe you should call in a psychic. The police department works with psychics now, doesn't it?"

Morrisey eyes me murderously.

"Don't leave town," she says.

"I wouldn't dream of it. I want to see this thing brought to a right and just conclusion. Just as much as you guys do."

"Get the fuck out of here, bitch," Reynolds spoke.

I got the fuck out of there.

11

I shaked, rattled, and rolled all the way down the block.

What THE HELL was *that* all about? You mean it really was Pender who did it? My goodness! Look at that, how I figured that out without one tiny little bit of real evidence or nothing.

What am I getting all gleeful about? If she really did it and she's determined to have it pinned on me, how the hell do I get out of it? This was no surrender on their part if the police are in on this coverup. This was just a temporary pause while they regrouped. But would the police really be that corrupt? (I heard the echo of a thousand voices in the background. They were laughing.) But surely, at some level, such corruption would not be tolerated. Some Kojak somewhere would say, "Wait a minute. Why are you pinning this horrendous crime on an innocent bystander? If Ann Pender did it, she must be punished. I don't give a fuck what her father owns." Kojak was a real person, wasn't he? I mean, he was based on a real New York detective. Yes. The Marcus-Nielson murders. "I kept expecting somebody else to do something. Nobody else did." So he did. He saved the innocent bystander and put the real killer behind bars. Did he still work for the New York police department? Surely there were others like him. Then how come he said, "I kept expecting somebody else to do something. But nobody else did"?

Maybe I should go public with all of this, the sooner the

better. With what? With all my half-baked allegations? So how come the police backed off when I brought it up? Judging from their reaction, going public was my one and only ace in the hole. But what if I tell the media everything, and the media doesn't like me. (Nobody ever likes me.) What if the media decides I'm guilty? I call in the cavalry and the cavalry shoots me. Maybe I'd best forget about the media for the time being. It is strange that the police haven't given my name to the press yet, though. They must be afraid for me to talk to them.

Oh, all this sounds like "real life" stuff, and I'm so bad at dealing with that. I wish I could talk to Brendan about this. He's the one who interprets real life for me.

I felt this barely controllable urge to stop strangers, to grab them by the lapels and ask them, "Would you happen to know if the real Kojak still works for the police department?" People would probably think I was crazy. When you crack up on the streets of New York you blend in with so many other crazies that people just ignore you. If the pod people had invaded Queens instead of that little town they invaded in *Invasion of the Body Snatchers*, and that guy ran out on the highway to tell people about it, he'd still be wandering around, trying to get someone to listen. And sleeping in Central Park probably.

I decided to go home and take a hot bath. Then I realized, what was I saying, hot bath? There was never any hot water in my apartment. There was lukewarm for two seconds, then there was ice cold. I'd be sitting in a tub with three inches of cold water lapping around my ass and I'd feel more like screaming than ever.

But I needed a hot bath. An emergency.

Hey! Shelly! I did it for her, didn't I? Now she could do it for me. A little soon to be calling in favors, but so what?

I called her from a phone booth. "Yeah, sure. Come on over." Wasn't it wonderful how all us neurotics understood each other? Shelly's apartment was in a nice, new, modern high-rise. It would be so nice to be surrounded by nice, new, modern things while I took my bath. No mice scurrying across the bathroom floor. I'd be sitting in a nice, new, modern tub, up to my chin in boiling water. Actually, Shelly did have mice once. Or should I say *mouse*. It was only one mouse, and it turned out to be somebody's escaped pet. I know because I called her when I discovered I had mice. A lot of them. And they were nobody's pet.

"I know," she said then. "It's very scary when you see one. But when I saw that mouse, I had just come back from the country." Shelly had a cabin someplace upstate. "I was in the country all weekend, so I was used to seeing things running in and out of the bushes and all."

It was a comfort just to walk into Shelly's apartment. It was so neat and orderly and tidy. So unlike mine. Listen, Picasso said dust is *good* for paintings. He said it preserves them.

Anyway, even Shelly's clutter was arranged in an orderly fashion, which turned it into a "collection" and not clutter at all. Her collection was actually memorabilia connected with Joe. The place was indeed loaded with memories. There was a large wooden bowl filled with matchbooks, pilfered no doubt from every restaurant the two of them ever sat in. Business lunches, he used to tell me they were. "I would always take a little something," she explained to me, "every time we were together. Just something to remember it by."

There were, on the walls, framed and hung, engraved invitations to every gallery showing of his work, which she helped plan. Every book review, every announcement, was dutifully represented, carefully arranged in their dustless frames.

The bookshelves were likewise sprinkled with mementos. A rock. Not just any old rock. A rock from the country, from the time Joe went up to her summer place to work on the final draft of one of his books. He stayed there alone, in isolation, but she drove him up (and took a rock), and she went back a few weeks later to bring him back (a wilted daisy marked that occasion).

The tiny dish filled with sand? Fire Island, quite a few years back, a house-warming party. Hadn't I been invited to that? Oh, no, of course not. He was married to Lorraine then. Too bad. It was a nice party. Lorraine was such a doll. A terrific hostess, really.

The seashells, too? No, that was something else entirely. That was Barbados, just last year.

"There are towels in the linen closet, right next to the tub. Help yourself."

"Okay. Thanks a million. You're a life-saver."

"Don't mention it. What are friends for? And there's bubble bath on the shelf over the sink. Rose-scented. Use all you like. That's supposedly the most soothing scent. Some scientists did a study on it and rose is supposedly the most soothing of all."

"Just what I need! Thank you."

"Okay. I'm going downstairs to the basement to do my laundry. Will you be okay here alone?"

"Fine. I'll be terrific. Thank you."

I sat in the steaming hot tub. It didn't help. Mentally, I was spinning my wheels. Emotionally, I was in some kind of paralyzed coma. And physically, I felt I was in the grip of some bizarre torture from the Inquisition, having my skin scalded by boiling, rose-scented water.

I felt bad Shelly had gone to do her laundry. I felt bad Shelly was not sitting in the next room, wringing her hands with worry over my distraught state.

Well, she did ask how things went at the police station. But you could see she didn't really want to know. She did offer tea. But she was relieved when I said no. No cups to wash.

Then again, I hadn't been very nice to her when she showed up at my place this morning, had I? What goes around, comes around.

I sat there in the tub, determined not to leave it till she came back upstairs. I didn't want her thinking I had spent this time snooping through her apartment. What snooping? She had everything on display.

So she had been to Barbados, had she? And Fire Island. Me,

he took to Coney Island. Well, sure—she was his friend. His *real* friend. What was I to him? His Coney Island baby. And she was so chummy with all his wives. Well sure, she was a nice, friendly chummy person. I had no friends! I was a total loser. PLUS I was worried about a murder rap now. I contemplated drowning myself in hot, rose-scented water.

"I'm back!" I heard Shelly call through the door. "I put the clothes in the dryer. I'll go down later for them."

"I'll be right out."

"Don't rush on my account."

I got out of the tub and looked around for a towel. Oh, yes—in the linen closet. How wonderful to have a linen closet. Such things made life worthwhile. What could go wrong, seriously wrong, in a life with a linen closet? My towels were all squashed in a—wait a minute. Some thought just flicked across my mind. What was it? Oh, well, it couldn't have been too important . . .

I gazed in at the linen closet. Beautiful rows of fresh, clean towels. What a gorgeous sight. All arranged according to color and size, even. My towels were usually thrown in a damp heap . . .

A TOWEL!!!

Oh my God! A TOWEL!

THAT'S what had been missing from the living room, Joe's living room, that afternoon. It was a towel! Not something valuable at all. That's probably what threw me off, thinking it had to be something valuable. It was just a towel!

We had taken a shower together. When we came out of the bathroom and into the living room, he had a damp towel wrapped around his pelvis. I did not have a towel wrapped around my pelvis, and before you know it, what with one thing and another, we never made it into the bedroom. You know how those things are. I mean, maybe if Joe didn't look quite so magnificent in a towel . . . He looked like a statue, I swear to God. Michelangelo's David. What a torso that man had. Every sculptor I know wanted to do Joe. Anyway, we made a stop in the living room. And the towel got dropped onto the couch. I remembered I was worried about the towel staining the couch's upholstery—I thought it was silk—but Joe was beyond worrying about the upholstery by then.

When we went into the bedroom afterwards, we were both naked. That towel should have stayed out there. It wasn't there when I went into the living room later, to look for Joe. I remembered thinking I would take it off the couch then. (I was Betty Crocker, all of a sudden.) But it wasn't there and I forgot about it with everything that happened afterwards.

I remembered it now. So how come that towel wasn't on the couch? Where the hell was it?

OH. MY! GOD!

It could have been a man! Joe, standing there with a towel wrapped around his hips, talking to a *man*. But who? And why do they go up to the roof? For privacy? Maybe Joe's voice wasn't so much calm as cool! *Hostile* cool. So they step outside, for a little altercation?

Was there a fight on the roof? During which time, the towel gets undone and Joe gets pushed off the roof. But who? Could it be Ann had nothing to do with it? I am reluctant to believe this. Maybe she hired somebody. Maybe she gave them her key. But Joe wouldn't stand around chatting with a hired assassin. It must have been someone he knew.

I wished I could talk to Brendan about this. Brendan was the one who was good at figuring out angles, at second-guessing—OH! MY! GOD!

COULD IT HAVE BEEN BRENDAN? They knew each other! No, no, that's impossible. I'm catching Brendan's paranoia. Just because *he's* terrified of being involved . . . Hey! He didn't have an alibi, did he? No, no, no. That's ridiculous. I've been hanging around with too many *policemen* all day. Why the hell would *Brendan* ever. . . ?

Jealousy? Now I'm *really* being crazy. Well, it's Brendan's own fault, actually. He's the one who keeps telling me that the first one they'll look for is a jealous lover of mine.

I pulled a towel out of the closet and began drying myself.

How crazy: Brendan, jealous! Although today, in the park . . . "He lived to make the grandstand gesture, didn't he! Just to impress the natives. And God knows, *you* were impressed!" His eyes looked reptilian then, when he said that. I told myself it was the way the light was hitting them. It was too much of a cliché—the green-eyed monster.

No. I'm being ridiculous. But there were other times, too.

"How long is this brother-and-sister routine going to go on between us? That's all I want to know. You mean to say you're not even curious?" "I'm curious. So what? I'm curious about a lot of things I'm never going to find out about. I don't have to know everything." "You're very bourgeois, you know that?" Snake-eyes says to me. "You think you're Miss Superhip, avant-garde artist. Meanwhile, you're very played-out, middle-class Bensonhurst." Brendan was not without his own supply of venom, on occasion.

Another time: "Nikki. I'm tired of sleeping with other girls and pretending it's you." He is a little drunk and a little stoned. "So now you want to sleep with me and pretend it's them?" He laughs. "Come on," he says, "loosen up. What is it? You find me grotesque?" "You? You're fine. It's me that's the washout. I'm nothing special. Believe me." (Did he think because I slept with a famous man I was something special? Probably. A man would think something like that.) "So let me find that out for myself!" "Ohhh. Boy! Thanks a lot!" "That's not what I mean and you know it." "I know no such thing." "Are you afraid I'll be disappointed? Oh, God! Don't tell me *that's* it. I won't be disappointed, Nikki, I swear. I promise! I'll *love* it." We both end up laughing hysterically. "You see why we can't sleep together, Bren? We laugh too much. 'Passion never laughs.' Guess who said that." "I don't give a fuck." "Dostoevski!" "Here. Eat something, Dostoevski. Get fat and ugly. Give me a break!"

And another time: He is staring at me, not talking. "What's the matter?" "I was just thinking. Wouldn't it be funny if it turns out you're the one?" "What one?" "The one for me. The one I end up falling in love with." "Don't worry. It won't happen." He laughs. Very nice. Very laid-back. "Naaa. I guess not."

Oh, God, not Brendan. This is getting so ugly. I finish drying myself, realizing suddenly that even with a linen closet things can go very wrong in one's life.

"Where're you going? I made tea for us!"

"I can't stay. I have to talk to somebody. Right away."

"Awww, why? Where you going?"

"I'm sorry. Is it very rude just to bathe and run like this? Are you very pissed off?"

"Well, a little bit. I thought maybe later we could go out and eat or something. It's going to be awful being all by myself tonight. I still feel very strung out by this whole thing, Nikki. Don't you feel that way too? I thought we'd be good company for each other. Not that we're going to spend all our time talking about Joe or anything," she added, setting things straight, "but I just thought we'd be good company for each other." (Brendan was even jealous of Shelly, wasn't he!)

"I'm sorry, Shelly. I have to go. I really have to talk to somebody right away."

"Awww."

"I'm sorry."

"It's just that this'll probably be *the* worst night, you know? My first night in my apartment." She was sitting there, and for the first time, I noticed she was wearing a black dress.

"The tags are still on that dress, you know?"

"What? Oh, yeah, I was just trying it on. I bought it this afternoon. It's for the funeral Monday."

"The funeral?"

"Yes. They couldn't have it before this, because of the autopsy. The autopsy showed exactly what they expected it to show: that he died from a fall. Anyway, so the funeral is Monday. Ann's had her hands full arranging things, but I told her it was probably a blessing in disguise, you know, having to make all the arrangements. The best thing for her is probably to stay busy right now. Of course, I told her I was here if she needed me for anything. It's going to be by invitation only, you know. Otherwise it would just be pandemonium at the funeral Mass."

"Where?"

"At Saint Patrick's. Eleven o'clock Monday."

"Oh."

"I don't suppose you got an invitation to that either."

"No."

"Do you want me to get you one? I could tell her it's for someone else. The security's going to be very tight. You're really going to need an invitation to get in."

"No, that's all right."

"So you're just not going to go?"

"I don't know. Maybe I'll try to crash. That's me, the old funeral Mass crasher."

"Why don't you let me ask Ann? I won't tell her it's for you."

"No. Really."

"Well, okay then." Shelly looked particularly dazed and forlorn. "I guess you'd better go, if you're going."

"Listen, Shelly, I'll try to call you later, all right? We'll talk on the phone, as much as you like." I hated the thought of her sitting there all by herself all night, in her black dress with the tags hanging off.

"Oh. Okay. It'll give me something to look forward to, anyway, if I know you're going to call."

"I'll call. Don't get up, I'll let myself out."

"Okay."

Then as I got to the door, she called after me.

"Nikki? Don't call after eleven, all right? I may be sleeping."

"Right." Go figure Shelly out.

"Or even after ten. I didn't get much sleep at your place. I'll probably turn in early."

"Okay."

"Maybe I should even say nine or nine-thirty, the latest."

"Listen, Shelly, I won't call at all if it's going to *disturb* you."

"No, no. You could call. Just don't call after about nine-thirty."

I could see she was debating about making it nine, so I thanked her for the bath again and left.

Maybe I was being crazy and maybe I wasn't. But when I left there, I was sure someone was following me.

12

My first intention had been to go straight to Brendan's, but if someone was following me, that was out of the question. And I wasn't even sure someone *was* following me. It was a sleazy-looking man I had seen, crossing streets when I crossed, rounding corners that I rounded. Maybe it was just a coincidence. Maybe it wasn't a cop at all. Maybe it was just your average New York pervert, stalking hapless women at random. Still, I didn't dare take a chance on leading the police right to Brendan's doorstep.

I was getting so nervous that I was even afraid to call him from a phone booth. Besides, what the hell was I going to say to him? "Uh . . . Brendan. By any chance was it *you* who killed Joe?" What did I expect him to say if it were? Was I expecting him to give himself up? That didn't seem likely, since doing so was just bound to affect his career adversely.

Maybe I should just go straight to Morrisey and tell her what I remembered about the towel. Ask her if it was found up on the roof, mixed in with the other stuff up there, suntan lotion and visors and stuff. Then at least the police would know it could have been a man Joe was talking to. But then she'd be sure to start harping on my case again, and if I was purposely trying to keep Brendan's name out of it, those two bloodhounds would pick up on it instantly, because whatever else you said about them, they were probably good cops. So it was practically like turning Brendan in, if I went there, and maybe he didn't do it. But so what? They wouldn't care about that at all.

No, I had to talk to Brendan first. So I had to "ditch the tail"? Is that the right expression?

I ducked into a doorway, and sure enough, old sleazebag rounded the corner a moment later, and I jumped out at him.

"What do you want, you?"

His eyes met mine and opened wide for a moment. I had obviously surprised him. Then a slight smile began playing on his skeeve mouth.

"I like your tits," he said. "I really do."

This clarified nothing. It could *still* be a cop. (I heard plenty of talk in that precinct, don't worry.)

"Ah, your mother's tits. Why don't you go haunt somebody else before I start screaming?"

For a moment, he looked betrayed. Were we having our first spat? Then he looked like he never saw me or my tits before. ("Whuh? I was just walking along, minding my own business, when this crazy lady . . ." Like that.)

He turned abruptly and walked the opposite way down the street. Fast. Thank God. It was only a pervert.

I walked a few more blocks just to make sure the tit-lover was gone, then I walked a few more blocks to find a phone booth that worked.

"Hello? Hah hah hah hah."

"Teehee tee hee hee hee."

"Brendan?" It sounded as if he had company.

"Who is this? *Nnn* . . . Is that you?"

"Teeheee heee heeeee."

"Cut that out. *Nnnnnn* . . . Is that you? I *told* you not to call . . . oh, Christ! Where are you calling from?"

"Relax, would you please? I'm outside. In disguise. In my big nose and glasses."

"What are you calling me for? Didn't I tell you that . . ."

"Teehee heee heee."

"Cut that *out.* This is important!"

"What do you have, company?" It sounded like one of the more lighthearted girls.

"Yeah. What are you calling me for? I *told* you that I'd . . ."

"Listen, I have to talk to you right away. It's important."

"Holy Christ! Don't come here! Don't come here, whatever you do. What's so important anyway? I told you they would try to scare you. Is that what happened? I told you to be prepared for . . ."

"Brendan," I heard his heart's delight whine. "Come on! Are you going to talk on the phone all night? Or what?"

"Wait a minute. Hah hah hah hah. Cut that out. Nnnnnn . . . Does it have to be tonight? It's Saturday night, for chrissakes!"

"Oh, I'm sorry, Brendan. I forgot that if you don't get laid on Saturday night, you can't function all week."

"That's right. I'm a normal person! I need sex. Maybe you could go for months without. . . . Men are different from women, *Ni . . . nn . . .* Women don't need sex all the time, but men . . ."

"Teehee. *I'm* a woman, Brendan. And *I* need . . ."

"I know, honey. Just a minute. Can't it wait till tomorrow?"

"Who you talking to?" I said. "Me or her?"

"You! Listen. I'll meet you tomorrow."

"Tomorrow? I have to talk to you *now.*" He didn't sound very worried about this. He didn't sound like a murderer at all.

"Yes. *Early* tomorrow. All right?"

"All right, where?"

"Don't say any places over the phone."

"Okay, where?"

"Who are you talking to anyway? Is that another girl? Are you making another date, right in front of me?"

"No, honey, no. It's my sister. *Eeoouu,* you devil! You lit-

118

tle devil. I'll get to you in a minute. *Nnnn?* Are you still there?"

"I'm here. So where?"

"Let me think. I got it. The Titanic. I'll meet you on the Titanic. At our usual time.

"Oh. Okay."

"The Titanic? Didn't that sink already? How could you meet your sister on the Titanic if it sunk already?"

"Now you're going to get it, you little devil."

"Teehee hee heee . . ."

"Hah hah hah hah . . ."

Click.

So I was supposed to meet Brendan on the Staten Island Ferry at ten the following morning. There was nothing to do in the meantime except go home and worry. Which I did.

13

The day broke dark and dreary and dank. I couldn't have been more pleased. All that sunshine and those balmy breezes were getting to be a real pain in the ass. My heart rejoiced when I thought I could detect the rumble of thunder in the distance.

Then I remembered. One of my worst recurring nightmares was about to come true. I would sink on a slow boat to Staten Island. Oh, why had Brendan chosen the ferry? I *hated* it. He loved it—Brendan's a Pisces, the fish.

For a while he even bamboozled me into having our Saturday morning food fests on the ferry. I have to admit that the charm of these excursions was mostly lost on me. Every once in a while, very rarely, you'd get a whiff of something that could pass for a sea breeze. Provided a garbage barge wasn't passing by. And the boat pitches and tosses like it's in a hurricane, believe me. The whole rest of the ocean could be calm as glass, but this one strip of it between lower Manhattan and Staten Island is always in the midst of a hurricane. And getting into the slip, that space between the rows of logs in the water, where the ferry is supposed to slide right in? Well, they ought to call it a *crash* instead of a *slip*. That boat would go barreling into those logs at five hundred miles an hour. I was always reduced to a quivering mass after one of these outings. And I used to have nightmares about it, too. I told somebody about my dreams once and they told me that boats, and ferries in particular, meant death. I said, You're telling me!

So here it was, early in the morning, with thunder and lightning flashing in the skies and I'm heading for the Staten Island ferry, because that's my life. Listen, the best quote I ever heard about God was "God is a comedian, playing to an audience that's afraid to laugh." Voltaire said it. Well, sometimes I think God gets particularly droll and witty when He's dealing with my life. I mean I see truly dazzling displays of what can only be an omniscient sense of humor at work. Sometimes I have to laugh myself. I was complaining about it once, to my sixteen-year-old niece, and she came up with a terrific quote about God. (The kid's a genius, I swear.) She said God's motto is "I made you and I can break you."

Anyway, the ferry. So I'm walking along, praying to God, "Oh, pull-eeze let them cancel the ferries on account of the weather. Or *You* could cancel the weather. One or the other. Please God!" I had already tried calling Brendan to cancel meeting him, but there was no answer. My only hope was to catch him before he actually boarded the *Bounty*.

No such luck. There he was, his equine, wide-mouthed face peering out at me from one of the passenger deck windows. Obviously, my face revealed my inner terror because he was smiling broadly, a real demonic grin.

I gave him the finger, then paid my fare and stepped onto death's deck. Already I felt seasick. Naturally, Paranoid's first question was "Were you followed?"

I ignored him. "Listen, I have to talk to you about something," I said instead. "Something important."

"This, I assumed. Why the hell else would you get me up at the crack of dawn on my only real day off and agree to meet me *here*? Actually, I'm glad you did. I've never taken the ferry in this kind of weather. I bet it'll be interesting as hell to see how this baby handles herself in a brisk wind."

"A brisk wind?" I bellowed. "This is a brisk wind to you? This is a typhoon!"

"Shhhh. We're going to start up."

I just moaned low for a while, hoping we would sink right

away, while there was still a chance I could make it to shore. All too quickly we were out on the open seas. Brendan decided, even though it was raining in torrents ("This little drizzle?") that we should go downstairs, where the cars were, so we could see the water up close.

Somehow, I made it down the flight of metal steps to the lower landing, Brendan preceding me on the stairs in order to break my fall. At the bottom was a man in some sort of ferry uniform. I immediately pictured the worst. He was there in order to direct us to life jackets. The call to abandon ship had gone out and I had somehow missed it.

"Is anything wrong, officer?" I blurted out, still midway on the stairs, over Brendan's head. He shook his head a definite no. "I'm just here to tell folks no one's allowed to walk around outside in this kind of weather."

"You SEE?" I said, smacking Brendan's back. "Even *they* admit it's bad weather." I sweated more profusely.

"I bet they were even thinking of *canceling* the ferries!" I yelled over the hurricane. "RIGHT? I BET YOU WERE EVEN THINKING OF CANCELING THE FERRIES, BUT YOU FIGURED, WHAT THE HELL, YOU'D TAKE A CHANCE."

The ferryman and Brendan exchanged smug smirks. Like, *Some people get so alarmed over impending death.*

"No. The weather'd have to be a lot worse than *this* for us to suspend ferry service," the old salt said. "We've taken 'em out in bigger blows than this. Right, fella? You look like *you* know." Brendan beamed him a big horse smile. Like, he sure did. How come all jerks recognize each other instantly?

In no time at all, Ishmael and Captain Ahab here were conversing only with each other and I was reduced to being the passive audience for this bullshit. This wasn't turning out AT ALL like I planned. My only hope was to broach the subject on the return trip.

Slipping and sliding into the slip at Staten Island turned out to be such an interesting experience that, for a while, it seemed certain that *I* was not going to make any goddamned return trip.

"What do ya *mean*, you're not going back?" Brendan screamed at me. "What are you going to *live* here? In Staten Island?"

"You know, Bren, I think even if we sunk, the last thing I would hear is your voice saying, 'Don't worry, Nikki. This is *supposed* to happen.'"

We both fell silent as we walked along, on solid ground now.

"I thought you had to talk to me about something. Something important."

"It can wait."

"Well, now I'm curious."

"Oh, all right. I was going to ask you if *you* killed Joe. I remembered about this towel and I started thinking that . . ."

He stopped walking.

"Are you kidding? Are you joking with me now?" He sounded incredulous enough.

"No. I'm very serious. I was thinking and it seems to me that . . ."

"You're asking me if I kill—Just because of that question I asked you once, right?

"What question?"

"Don't be cute, all right?"

"I'm not being cute! What fuckin' question?"

"When I asked you, if it wasn't for Joe, if you and I would be . . . closer."

"I forgot about that. I didn't remember you asking me that. I swear to God."

"But you're asking me *anyway*."

"Asking you what? I thought you asked *me*, if it wasn't for Joe, if you and I . . . ? You know, Bren, I pictured this whole big dramatic confrontation between us. And *as usual*, it's turning into an Abbott and Costello routine. Jeez. All I'm asking you is, was it *you* that killed Joe. That's all. That's my question."

"What a shitty thing to say. To actually come right out and ask me if I *killed* somebody. What a shitty thing to say."

"Hey, listen, Brendan, it was a shitty thing to *do*. I'd like to find out who did it, okay?"

"Oh. So you'll hurt your best friend's feelings by asking if—"

"Hurt your feelings? Brendan! We're talking about a murder here!" I sounded just like Morrisey. "Somebody didn't just hurt his feelings. Somebody killed him!"

"And you think it might have been me."

"It might have. You're the one who's always telling me everybody is capable of murder. You're the one who's always saying that anybody could commit murder if the situation—"

"Everybody's capable of it. That doesn't mean I did it. For what reason would I kill Joe?"

I shrugged, not wanting to sound conceited.

"Well?"

"Well, I don't know. Jealousy maybe?"

"Jealousy? Jealousy over you? Are you kidding or what? Don't flatter yourself, all right, Nikki?"

"*Eeeooouuu*, you're such an insulting bastard sometimes! It's a good thing I never slept with you. You're such an insulting bastard sometimes."

"Ha! I don't believe this! You just asked me if I committed murder and *you're* insulted. Amazing! The ego some people have. It's just amazing."

We eyed each other with mutual suspicion for a few moments.

"All right. No. It wasn't me. You asked and I'm answering. No."

"It really wasn't you?"

"No."

"Oh." It was only then I realized what a fool's errand I had been on. If Brendan was capable of murder, he was certainly capable of lying. It isn't that I was sure he did it. I just wasn't sure he didn't.

It was still raining a little bit, but the sun started to come out anyway. We walked back to the ferry. We spoke hardly at all on the whole trip home. Brendan just stood leaning against the metal railing, starting down into the water. For some reason, that's all I could do, too, even though it looked scary as hell. It was almost a relief to be looking at something so scary. I mean everything had looked scary to me lately, since this happened. Normal, everyday things looked scary, things that had always looked fine to me before. So it was a relief to be staring into that choppy, ferocious-looking water. I mean, if the ocean looked cold and cruel and chaotic to me now, well, maybe it, at least, was supposed to.

14

By one o'clock that afternoon, it seemed to me that I had already put in a full day, so I was content to go straight home, lounge around, cry uncontrollably, and listen to the radio. Well, I hadn't *planned* on crying uncontrollably all day. That came about because of the radio and because I never know when not to think about sex. (That's because I was raised Catholic. I spent the first twenty years of my life not thinking about sex. It was a full-time job, believe me, and it led to all *kinds* of strange behavior. Such as making sure all the shoes in my closet were lined up *very carefully*, side by side and pointing straight ahead, before I could fall asleep at night. Eventually, of course, I wised up. And I never wanted to fall into that trap of not thinking about sex again.)

However, that day I discovered it is not a good idea to think about sex when one's lover is not only out of town but out of this plateau of existence. It only depresses you. This I already suspected, but so what? I wasn't going to let that stop me. I was going to think about sex with Joe as much as I wanted. Isn't that what people meant when they said, "At least I have my memories"?

It all started out harmlessly enough. I wasn't thinking about sex at all. I was thinking about murder. About who was capable of it and who wasn't, and whether Brendan was right about everybody being capable of it. I knew I certainly was. Just let some arrogant S.O.B. get ahead of me on line at the cash register in Macy's and watch how I feel like wringing their goddamned necks on the spot. I knew that I, at any rate, was not only capable of murder but probably predisposed to it.

But was Brendan? That was the question. I don't care what he said about me flattering myself. I wasn't ready to discount him as a suspect. I don't say that Brendan was so in love with me that he coldly and calculatingly went there to kill Joe. But Brendan was capable of violence. If he went there to talk to Joe, as he had halfheartedly threatened to do a number of times in the past, and push came to shove, Brendan was very capable of the fatal shove. Brendan and Joe had met a few times in the past, and when they did, there was always an undercurrent of violence between them. The first time was at a street fair. I was with Joe, and I introduced them. You could see they hated each other on sight. Afterward, I asked Brendan, "Well? What did you think of him?" and Brendan said, "He's a prick. Just like I figured he'd be." I already know what Joe thought of Brendan because as soon as we walked away, Joe said, "You know more weirdos . . ."

Another time, I was with Brendan and Joe was with another woman, someone gorgeous. We all ran into each other waiting to get into Carnegie Hall. I cried all through *Die Fledermaus*. "I'd like to tell that fuck off, that's all." "Shhhhhh." *Sob, sniff, sob.* "I'd like to tell that fuck off, just once. *You* never will, right? Let me. Let me talk to him, just once." "Shhhhh! It's all right. It's nothing." *Sob, sniff, sob.* "Who the fuck does he think he is? I don't like his attitude." "What attitude? He didn't have an attitude." *Sniff, sniff.* "He was very nice and polite." "I'll give him polite. Don't tell *me*. He's got an attitude." "He's just on a date"—*sob, sniff*— "that's all." "I thought he was married. Isn't he supposed to be married? That's not her." "I heard they broke up. I heard they separated. I guess he's dating again." *Sob, sob.* "Nothing wrong with that. He's allowed to date. I'm on a date, aren't I?" "Yeah, but are you going to get *laid* after this date? You want to bet *he* is?" "Waaaaaaa! Did you see her? She was beautiful." *Sob, sob, sob.* "She had lousy teeth." "She had a slight overbite. Like, *waaaaaa*, Gene Tierney's! I always wanted an overbite like Gene Tierney's in *Laura*. When I was a kid I used to try and put my mouth like that. I looked retarded." *Boo-hooooo.*

Right up until the night before it happened. Brendan had asked me to meet him for lunch the next day.

"No, I can't make it tomorrow, Bren. I'm going over to Joe's." "So it's really in full swing again, isn't it? It's really going full force. Aren't you ever going to wise up to that guy? How many times does he have to step all over you before you realize . . . ?" "It's DIFFERENT now, Bren. It's altogether different. We're starting over from scratch." "Yeah, scratch, my ass. You wanna bet?" "No, it really is." "It's like you walk into a propeller blade every once in a while. With your eyes wide open."

"No, it's not going to be like that this time. Everything's different now." "Yeah? Let me talk to him. And we'll find out how different everything's going to be. Let me talk to him, just as a friend of yours." "Don't you dare!" "Go ahead then. Be his pussy supply. Sucker!" "BRENDAN! THAT'S DISGUSTING!" "All right, I'm sorry. Dope! Fool!"

Brendan could have killed Joe. And in a way, it had nothing at all to do with me. They seemed to have a natural animosity towards each other. It worked both ways.

"Who was that weirdo you were with a couple of weeks ago? At Carnegie Hall." "If you're referring to my good friend Brendan, I'd appreciate it if you didn't call him a weirdo. Besides which, you know damn well who he is. You've met him at least half a dozen times before."

"Yeah, well, I wasn't sure it was the same guy. So, he's still around, huh?" "Yes." "He looks like a fuckin' horse, I swear." "He does not. Everybody tells him he looks like Mick Jagger." "Him? Hahahahahahaha. He does not! I look more like Mick Jagger than he does!" "YOU?! Hahahaha. Are you crazy? You look nothing *at all* like Mick Jagger." "Yeah, well, neither does he. He just looks weird." "Do I say what *your* friends look like? Do I remind you that Lorraine Rice looked exactly, but *exactly,* like her father? It must have been like sleeping with Lincoln, I swear!" (Samuel Rice, the actor, was best known for his Lincoln role.) "So you do sleep with him! You always told me you were just friends. I *knew* you were bullshitting me." "I thought we weren't going to fight anymore. *That* didn't last too long." "Why couldn't you at least be honest about it, that's all. I never figured you were living like a nun. By why couldn't you be honest about it?" "I *was* being honest! I *am* being honest. I didn't sleep with him. I don't sleep with him. I don't sleep with anybody but you, you son of a bitch! Goddamn it to hell! And if this keeps up, I don't even sleep with you any more!"

So, of course, we immediately jumped into bed.

And afterwards. Afterwards, afterwards, afterwards . . . I am down on him, as the expression goes. I am loving his cock. I am using it as a lipstick, wet and slippery, running it slowly around and around my lips. Loving it, kissing it, using it as my lipstick, very, very slowly. I am too swept away to even moan in ecstasy. I am shocked when he speaks.

"Only mine, huh? Only mine you love like this, right?"

I can barely nod. I am too weak. I can only press my lips against his cock and kiss it slowly. Then use it as my lipstick again. Slowly, very slowly. I am shocked again when he speaks.

"No, Nikki. I don't think so. I don't think it's only mine you love like this. No, not you."

I ignore him. Who cares what *he* says. His cock loves me. His cock *always* loves me. That's all that really counts. I go back to loving his cock.

His hands are caressing my head, his fingers woven through my hair. But suddenly his hands stop moving, his palms resting on my temples, his fingers encircling my scalp. What's his problem now, I think, annoyed. His large sculptor's hands surround my skull. He's not going to do something stupid, is he? Like kill me? My lips withdraw from his cock's head. I look up at him. He looks weird.

"Joe? What's the matter?"

"Nothing."

"What's the MATTER?" I am very annoyed. I feel like telling his cock, "Who is this jerk?"

"Is something wrong?" I say to him. He shakes his head very slowly. Sadly, for chrissakes!

"Sometimes I just think I'd be better off with you dead," he tells me.

"Oh. I thought maybe it was something I should worry about. Something *serious*."

He smiles, so sadly. Like, how sweet of me to try to cheer up the King of Pain. Then his fingers start to slowly rub my head again, tenderly and gently. His murderous impulse has passed.

Oh, what is he carrying on about? I think. He's some genius, isn't he? *He's* the one who goes larking about, not *me*! And now he wants to kill me? What is he, kidding? Oh, who cares what *he* says. His cock loves me. Thank God for that or I would be totally unloved in this world! I go back to returning his cock's love. It's wonderful, heavenly, magical love. The only love that really counts.

This memory now reduces me to a heap of convulsive sobs. The radio is, of course, playing "Let My Love Open the Door," one of "our" songs, the Who. I shouldn't have thought about all of that. I shouldn't have let my mind dwell on it. I should try to forget about things like that for the time being . . . "You're so lucky I'm around . . ." YES. He should have killed me. *Yes*. It would have been better than this! Better than surviving him! At least I would have died happy! He should have *known* this would happen. He should have known that, one way or another, I'd be left here all by myself. I DON'T WANT TO STAY HERE WITHOUT HIM. Why *didn't* he kill me, that fuck? Because he didn't love me enough, that's why! That selfish bastard! Dying without me. I HATE him, HATE him. HE SHOULD HAVE *KNOWN* THIS WOULD HAPPEN.

And so it went, more or less, all afternoon. The radio didn't stay on long, of course, because THAT RAT had to like so many kinds of music. Everything was connected with him! Everything I liked, anyway. He always had to have a little background music. That bum!

I mean, I definitely could not listen to any classical music right now, thanks to him. All the biggies were out, like Beethoven, Bach, Mozart, Vivaldi, Strauss. Even all the other stuff, which I didn't even recognize was out now, because I figured he'd probably know whatever the hell it was, even if it was some obscure recording that got played once every other decade. So classical music was out completely. Why did sport have to take me to the Mostly Mozart Festival last year? Look how he ruined everything!

And Christmas! Christmas was just going to be a million laughs, what with the Nutcracker blaring out of every PA system in the city. (We took my niece to see it one year.) Not to mention the Hallelujah Chorus from *Messiah*. Well, I could forget all about Christmas from now on!

And rock! I might as well just throw all of my rock albums right in the garbage right now. (Did we have to fuck to *everything*?) Talking Heads! Dire Straits! And the Stones! *Ha*! Eric Clapton! Led Zeppelin! Robert Plant! The Police! Patti Smith! Bruce Springsteen! The Cars! ZZ Top!

It would all be banished now. Ditto for Gershwin, Glenn Miller, Louis Armstrong, Bix Beiderbecke, Duke Ellington, Billie Holiday, Django Reinhardt, Cole Porter and *anybody* doing "Stardust."

Well, I told myself, I suppose I could always listen to the cowboy station, provided they didn't play anything by George Jones.

But with or without music, I kept remembering everything. So I cried and remembered and cried some more, on into the night. I fell asleep with the strains of "Don't Fear the Reaper" running through my head.

And I whispered into the black void, "Come back for me, Joe. Come back and take me. I don't fear the Reaper. Honest to God, I don't. Come back for me. Please. Baby, you're my man."

I fell asleep.

15

The *Weather Bureau* promised
it was going to rain all day Monday. So the sun was shining
brightly when I was awakened out of my nightmare-ridden
sleep. Between the ferry and Joe, my subconscious was having
a field day.

Anyway, the phone woke me.

"Nikki? I woke you. Oh, shit!"

"Hello?"

"Nikki? Do you want to go back to sleep? Should I call
back later? I'll call you back in a half-hour."

"Hello?"

"Nikki. Wake up! Do you want to go back to sleep or not?
Should I call you back?"

"Hello? Who is this?"

"Hehehehe. Same ol' Nikki. Crazy as ever. How the hell
are you?"

It was the way she said *hell* that clued me in. She still had
a Texas accent. "Hail."

"Tish? Is that you, Tish?" This suddenly struck me as the
most poignant thing in the world that I should be hearing from
Tish.

"Yes! Yes, it's Tish!"

"Tish! Oh, Tish." I started to cry.

"Ahh, don't cry. We'll cry later. At the funeral. You are
going, aren't you?"

"I don't know. Hey, what time is it?"

"Relax. It's just after eight."

"I don't even have an invitation. Or a pass or a ticket, or whatever the hell you need to get in."

"Relax, honey!" (She pronounced it "honeh.") "I got you one!"

"You did?"

"Yes! I heard what that bitch tried to pull. Who the fuck does she think she is?" (Tish even managed to sound leisurely and mint-julepy when she cursed. Or should I say cussed? And she cussed a lot. It was mostly in front of Joe, and in relation to Joe, that she was the passive disciple. In all other aspects of her life, she was a firecracker. She continued: "I told that bitch, 'Listen, honey, don't pull that shit' (sheeat) 'with me.' I mean who IN HELL does this Ann think she is? Taking over all the arrangements and all? I felt like telling her, 'You were on your way out anyway, honey, so don't go getting all bossy with *me*.' Listen, Nikki. Should I call you back? Do you want to go back to sleep?"

"Are you kidding? I've never been more awake in my life. What *happened*?" I sat up and reached for my cigarettes.

"Well, she just took over everything. All the funeral arrangements and all? But I said to myself, oh, all right, let her. She looks like the type who gets her rocks off planning funerals anyway, don't she?"

I got hysterical. "Yeah."

"I did think I should have at least been consulted, but all right. I know we were divorced, too, but at least it was a friendly divorce. And there weren't going to be nothing friendly about her divorce. Believe you me."

"Whuh? . . . Who? . . . When? . . ."

"Oh, he was going to divorce her. Didn't you know that, honey? Didn't you two ever talk at all? I mean he should have told you *that*." (Thaaayet.)

"Well, he did tell me, but . . . I wasn't sure if it was true. I mean he just kind of hinted at it and . . ."

"Well, of course it was true. He told me. He told a lot of people. He even told Ann herself!"

"Are you sure? Are you sure she knew?"

"Sure, I'm sure. She knew she was on her way out. So who does she think she's bullshitting by taking over like this? I mean if anybody was going to do the arranging of things, I would have thought it'd be me and Bob. And you, of course, if you wanted, too." (Bob was Bob DeBenetto, Joe's best friend for years and years.) "But no, she just took over everything, like some kind of fuckin' queen mother. Tell me, is that woman a bitch or ain't she?"

"She is."

"She didn't call me or nothing after it happened. You think she would have at least called. She's such a cold fish! Anyhow, I get my invitation to this thing in the mail, no phone call, no nothing. And it's just for the church, you know? For the Mass? So I said, 'Well, what about the burial? I mean, what arrangements have been made for getting me to the cemetery? There was nothing saying anything about *that*." (Thaaayet) "So I just decided to give her a little ringy-dingy myself. Bob answered. He just sounds awful, you know? Just terrible. I feel so bad for him. Anyway, I said, let me talk to the Queen Mother there, and she gets on and she says she don't have neither the time nor the inclination to deal with *me* right now. How do you like *that*?"

"Humph!"

"So she puts Bob back on. It sounds to me like Bob has just been relegated to being her personal valet over there. And he just sounds too comatose to even know what's going on. Anyhow, I says to Bob, 'Listen, Bob, I don't want to go making a pain in the ass of myself over this, but what about the cemetery? And is there going to be a limo for me, too, or what? He said, 'Why don't I give Shelly a call, as she's handling that kind of thing.' So I said okay.

"So I called Shelly. What is that girl's problem, can you tell me that? She always sounds so *annoyed* with me?"

"That's just her way sometimes. She's very upset right now." I had forgotten about calling Shelly back completely. Well, she was keeping herself busy, helping Ann. She was probably happy as a pig in slop.

"Yeah, well, we're all very upset right now. Anyhow, I asked her about the limos and she's acting like her usual fucked-up annoyed self and I get the impression she also doesn't think I'm going to the cemetery and, oh, where can she put me and all, and it's all been arranged already and where can she put an extra person? And I said, what extra person? There's two extra people. Me and my guest! So she has another shit fit over that, and how is she going to find room for two people when she can't even squeeze *one* in? So I told her, 'Well, shit, Shelly, get another fuckin' limo! I'll pay for it myself. What are they all counting pennies over there now? Which wouldn't surprise me in the slightest, what with Ann in charge of the purse strings!' So Shelly says, 'Well, I'll have to check with Ann about that first.' And I told her to check whatever the hell she pleased, because I know damn well Ann is not about to start twisting my balls over this little matter or she'll hear plenty from me. I mean Ann knows she had no right arranging SHIT without consulting me in the first place. So then I said to Shelly, 'Where's Nikki going to be?' Thinking, probably Ann is giving you a hard time, too, and maybe you'd rather be in our limo. And Shelly says, 'Nikki wasn't even invited to the church, much less the cemetery.' And how it's going to be a very, very small group of people anyhow, going out to the cemetery, and they were trying to keep the number down. I was beginning to get the idea that even *Joe* wasn't totally welcome at this thing, you know? And meanwhile, who do they think they're shitting? I happen to know for a *fact* that they invited at least *half* of Washington!"

"Hummmph."

"So to make a long story even longer, I told Shelly that there better be an invitation with your name on it waiting for you at the back of that church in some usher's sweaty palm by ten o'clock this morning or Ann was going to hear plenty from my mouth! So now you've got your invite, honey!" I didn't say anything. "You *do* want to go, don't you?" she asked.

"Well . . . I don't know."

"What in holy hell do you mean?"

"I mean I sort of had it in my mind that I *wasn't* going. Inside the church, I mean. I thought I'd just go, and stand outside for a while, and . . ."

She burst out laughing. "Oh, Nikki, you are too much. Now that you can go, you want to be little Stella Dallas, standing outside the church with her nose pressed against the stained-glass windows. I swear! You *have* to go inside now, Nikki, if only to stick it to Ann." She stopped and considered a moment. "You *do* want to stick it to Ann, don't you?"

"Of course I do! I'm just not sure it would be worth it."

"Now what's that supposed to mean? Oh, I get it. I know what you're talking about. You're afraid to go inside the church, aren't you? You're afraid you'll be . . . affected by it. Is that it?" I didn't say anything. After a moment, she said, "It's going to be a closed coffin. 'Cause of the autopsy, I guess. Is that what you were worried about?" I still didn't say anything. "Are you afraid you're going to get hysterical or something?" she said. "Listen, honey, if you get hysterical, I promise to hold you up. If you faint or anything, I'll be right there to catch your falling body."

"Now, wouldn't that be cute?" I said.

"I personally think it would be a riot! In fact, I wish you would get hysterical! Wouldn't Ann just hate that, though? In fact, even if you don't feel all that hysterical, I wish you would fake it. Yahooo! That would just be a blast! But that's your decision, of course. I mean about going altogether. There is just one other thing, though. About your reaching a decision on this? What do you think Joe would want you to do? Have you thought about that?"

"Joe!" I said. "Joe would be terrified, but terrified, that I would show up wearing nothing but a black lace garterbelt, swinging a pocketbook, and clicking my chewing gum."

She really laughed then. "Ohhh, I love it! I just love it. He would, too. He would!"

"He'd be so fuckin' relieved if I just contented myself with just showing up and acting like a lady, I can't tell you."

"That's the truth," she said, still laughing. "Wasn't it a riot, Nikki, how he would be so super-straight about things sometimes? Hahahahaha."

I was laughing, too, but the truth was that Tish had hit upon the crux of the matter with her question. It was thinking about what Joe would want that made me hesitate at all. On my own, I would have decided not to go at all, feeling as I do about favors. If Ann considered this a favor to me, even if Tish did practically blackmail her to get it, Ann could just stuff it. But then I thought of Joe.

So Joe was planning on getting the divorce. He had already told Ann, and other people, about it. But judging from the day's scenario, all that would be swept under the rug. Ann would forever be etched as his grieving widow. And if she killed him for that? For exactly that motive? Well, then, she won, didn't she? She'd be getting exactly what she wanted. But what good would my presence in this tableau do? Maybe it would jar everything, just a little bit. And this tableau needed a little jarring.

"I'm going," I told Tish.

"Ohh, *goood*. And listen, don't you go stick yourself in the back of the church somewhere. You sashay right down that middle aisle, right up to the front. I'll save you a seat."

"Right."

"And look gorgeous, Nikki! Let's really drive her crazy. Look gorgeous!"

"I'll do my best."

"Yippeeeee!"

And on that solemn note, we hung up.

The church was, as Shelly predicted, Pandemonium. The crowd outside was enormous, and the streets in front of and around St. Pat's were packed with black limousines in an advanced state of gridlock. I was having no luck getting past the police barricades across the street from the church.

"Excuse me. Pardon me. I just want to get through here. Excuse me."

"Hey! Would you stop pushing, lady?"

"I'm not going to take your spot, Miss. I'm just trying to get *through* here."

"Would ya look at this one?" "Well, push her back!"

"I'm sorry, I didn't mean to push you. The man behind me pushed me and I . . . Hey, mister! You want to cut it out please?"

"Awright! Awright! What's going on here? Everybody calm down! There's room for everybody."

"Officer! I'm just trying to get across the street to the church . . ."

"You can't go over there. Nobody's allowed on that side of the street. You have to stay right here, behind these . . ."

"But I have an invitation! I have an invitation to the church."

"You do? Well, that's different. Let's see it."

"I don't have it with me. But somebody in the church will have it, if I could just go ask at the door."

"HA! Did you hear this one, Dot? Her invitation's in the church. Yeah, right. Mine too. Right, Dot? Yeah, officer. All our invitations are over in the church. How stupid does she think he *is*? Right, officer? First she tries to take my spot, then she tells the officer here . . ."

"Well, push her *back*!"

"No. It really is. If you could just go ask at the door, officer . . ."

"What, are you kidding, lady?"

"No. I mean it. If you could just go ask at the door for an invitation for Nikki Andrews. Nicole. It might say Nicole . . ."

"I'm sorry, lady, that's impossible." The officer and Dot's bunch all exchange knowing glances. "Well, it takes all kinds . . ." Dot says. To make this New York City, I guess, is the rest of that.

"No. Really!" Even I can see that it's hopeless. The steps outside the cathedral are packed with invited mourners, waiting as they file, one by one, past the security at the big front doors. Even I can't imagine this policeman elbowing his way through that distinguished crowd to fetch my invite.

I sighed deeply. Was I going to spend the while time out here after all? Just to make sure I wasn't getting too comfortable in her spot, Dot's friend leaned her two hundred pounds a little harder on my left foot.

"Lady, would you get off my foot at least?"

"Well, *move!*"

"In a minute!"

"What is she waiting for, a bus?" Dot inquired. "Hahahaha. Hey, Denise! Ask her if she's waiting for a bus! There's no buses running here today, dearie!"

"Yeah, so move it!"

"Would you just *wait a minute*?!"

"See? What did I tell you? She's here for the duration! I knew it! See why this city stinks? Everybody does just what they want! And the *police* don't care."

That brought him around fast enough. "You'll have to move, Miss. If this was that lady's spot . . ."

"But officer . . . !"

"See how nice he talks to her, Dot? I wonder why. Hahahahaha."

"Yeah. I wonder why. Hahahahaha. Could it be her big bazooms? Hahahaha."

"Let's not get vulgar, ladies, all right? You ladies get very vulgar sometimes and . . .Hey! Hey! What's going on back there? You! Hey! Yoauh! Stop that pushing back there! Move back. Move back."

"Officer, if I could just go ask at the door . . ." I was going to start to cry. I was either going to start to cry or I was going to choke somebody, probably Dot, right on the spot. My eyes frantically searched the crowd standing on the church steps. Where the hell was Tish? Or Shelly, even? Everybody looked alike in their mourning clothes. Not just the men, but the women, too. Groomed to the teeth, of course, but subdued. A few famous faces stood out in the crowd. Actors, writers, politicians, artists, celebrities in one field or another. Most of the onlookers were no doubt there to see them. A few faces I recognized from the old crowd, Joe's friends from our student days. There were a few people who stood out just because they were so noticeable. One such one was a girl, tall and willowy. Gorgeous. probably a model. She looked slightly familiar. I'd probably seen her plenty of times on magazine covers. Her hair was longish and honey-colored and silky. She was one of those people who look so well put together that, whenever you see them, you want to go home and do yourself over completely and never leave the house like a slob again. She looked pampered and perfumed and feminine. It was as if she had a spotlight on her. I couldn't hear her from across the street, but I had the impression she was talking louder than everyone else. Her mouth was working more energetically, at any rate. And she laughed every once in a while, not at all concerned with maintaining the proper mode of solemnity. The recipient of all this energetic emoting was a squat man standing at her side, at least two heads shorter than she. (She was very tall.) I thought it was a man, that is, until the crowd shifted a little bit and I saw the man was wearing a skirt under the man-tailored jacket. So it was either a very peculiar man or a very mannish woman.

"See? She's not moving. Having a good time, dearie?"

"Oh, all right!" I was about to give up and make my way back out of the crowd when I heard someone calling.

"Nikki! Nikki!"

My eyes found him as he wove his way through the stalled limos that filled the street.

"Bob! Oh, Bob!" In his formal mourning attire, he looked terrible. Shell-shocked. Those deep circles under his eyes! His skin, so sallow and wrinkled! As if he disguised himself to look like an old man. But of course it was Joe's death that had added the ravaging years to his face. "Bob!" I screamed, surprised by the sudden connection I felt for him. "Oh, Bob!" My arms reached out over the police barrier, as if we were separated by some enormous chasm that would take superhuman effort to bridge. His face shattered into a grimace of unfathomable grief. For one insane moment, I feared his face would crack and fall off. "BOB!!" His arms stretched out, too, and when he reached me, we clung, the wooden barrier still between us, as if we were two souls on the deck of a sinking ship, our grief and terror reawakened by the sight of it in each other's faces.

So this is what Joe's death looks like, I thought. It wasn't only that horrible image of Joe in that alley. It had other images as well. It was the image of Bob's face, now. We clung together, and his man's sobs were hollow and terrible to hear. I was crying, too. So it happens in waking life, too? Not just in nightmares? The bottomless, limitless, infinite realm of terror and despair. We hold on to each other, tighter and tighter, but the pain doesn't lessen. It keeps reaching new depths. No bottom boundaries at all.

We're incapable of saying anything but each other's names. Over and over again. We hang on.

We separate just long enough for me to scramble under the wooden barrier, and then we lock into each other again. Who expected this? To have it all brought home to me by seeing Bob? I hadn't even *thought* of Bob. But Joe is dead, isn't he? Joe is really dead? "Oh, Bob. Bob. Bob." "Nikki. Nikki." Shoulders muffle our sounds. I want to weep and wail and tear my hair. Joe's having the wrong kind of funeral, I realize. He should be having an old-fashioned black folks funeral, the kind we went to once. A black artist died. A suicide. How they wept and wailed, that black family. They tore at their hair. I want that now for Joe. I need that now. So does Bob.

How strange that scene across the street looks. Surrealistic. Magritte. Everything is made of stone, cement—the sidewalk, the steps, the church, the people. I'm afraid to go there. I hug Bob tighter. He hugs back. We hold on.

When we separate, Bob fumbles through his pockets for a handkerchief. He blows his nose, and this ordinary, guileless gesture breaks my heart all over again. So this is what Joe's death looks like now. Then he reaches into another pocket, childlike, worried, where is it? I'm sure I have it. I want to tell him, Bob, please, I can't look at you. You break my heart.

He finds my invitation and hands it to me.

"I'm so sorry about all this confusion with the invitations, Nikki. You should have gotten this days ago."

"Oh, don't be silly. What's the difference?"

"It's just been such chaos, you can't imagine. He made me executor of the will. Did you know that?" He starts to cry again, but he fights for control. I don't dare look at his eyes.

"No, I didn't know. But I'm glad to hear it. It should be you."

"Thank you. We had talked about it, years ago. But whoever thinks these things will really happen? I thought by now he might have changed his mind, picked another artist. Someone who knew about the paintings, how to handle all of that."

"He trusted your judgment. That's what he considered most, I guess."

"Yeah. Well." He smiles and I have to look away, there is so much love in his smile. "Anyway," he says, "it's just been crazy. There is so much that has to be taken care of right away. And I don't mean business. That can wait. I'm talking about a million other things that nobody knew about. Good things he did for people, without telling anybody." He's determined to keep on talking, no matter what feelings he has to battle. "All of a sudden, I start hearing from rehab places and hospitals and children's homes and everybody's in a panic. Should they kick little Johnny out of the rehab place upstate because you see the drug program costs a thousand a month and Mr. Savanah used to foot the bill, but what with Mr. Savanah gone, who's going to pay? I tell everybody that everything's going to continue, like usual . . . but anyway, I haven't had much time for anything else. Ann's been taking care of most of it. I'm sure she didn't mean anything with this invitation business."

"Would you stop? I told you. It's nothing."

"Okay. Well, shall we go?"

"Sure. Wait a minute! I must look awful. Is there mascara all over my face?"

"Yes."

"Well, I have to *fix* myself." I go through my pocketbook, finally find my mirror, and start scrubbing. "You go ahead if you want to. I don't want to keep you."

"No, that's okay. Take your time."

"It's just that I have strict orders to look gorgeous. From Tish. I have a feeling it's a hopeless—"

"Tish!" He sounds very annoyed. "Don't mind Tish."

"What's the matter?"

"Nothing. She's making a general pain in the ass of herself, as usual." He's not kidding around. He's mad.

I could count on one hand the times I've heard Bob say anything remotely unkind about anybody. It surprised me this should be one of the times.

"Don't mind her at all," he says in disgust. "And you look fine." I stop scrubbing my face, link my arm through his and we cross.

16

We no sooner reached the other side of the street than Bob was called away by somebody with a walkie-talkie in his hand and a worried look on his face. Left alone, on the periphery of the crowd, I looked around. It was not unlike a cocktail party, except everyone had been told to wear something requiem-ish. The crowd was divided into small clusters, each cluster clearly defining its territorial boundary in some invisible way. Since I didn't feel like muscling in anywhere, I stood alone.

There was plenty to look at, don't worry. Hey, is that . . . ? She looks different in person. She's got wrinkles? Since when? *That* doesn't show up on the silver screen. And who's that she's with? Is it . . . ? Yes! That's his *skin!* I have never seen a pimple on that man *once* in the movies! And look at that. There's what's-her-name. She's not fat. Where's all the fat? She's not fat at all. You mean she photographs fat? Now that's a tragedy. She looks terrific in real life.

The politicians, for some strange reason, all looked better in person. Taller, thinner, and tanner. Maybe because when they were on television, making speeches and lying through their teeth, my mind automatically ascribed ugliness to them. In person, they were a pretty good-looking bunch. For one wild moment I even thought I saw Lincoln in the crowd. I mean that's how illustrious this bunch was. But then I saw another Lincoln standing right next to him. A littler Lincoln, smaller and more finely etched, and I realized it was Samuel Rice and his daughter, Lorraine. The man on the other side of Lorraine I recognized as her intended groom. So they all came in for the funeral. Well, they were supposed to be nice people. Actually, I had met Lorraine once, and she did strike me as a very nice person.

It was in the furniture department at Bloomingdale's, in one of the model rooms, a week before her and Joe's wedding. She was with Joe. And I was with my mother.

We were all standing outside the little rope that showed a model room. The room was totally lined with mirrors. Everything, including the ceiling and the floor. Out of the corner of my eye, I was suddenly aware of the presence of a very attractive man at my side. You know how those things are. You don't even have to look. Your body seems to know it. The hunk alarm goes out. And this guy was definitely radiating hunkdom. My mother was saying she didn't like the room.

"Why not?" I demanded. I thought the room was great!

"It's silly, that's all."

"What's silly about it?"

My mother, St. Louise the Oblivious, thought we were alone and told me.

"For one thing, how could they have mirrors on the floor? You could see everyone's underwear! And then, the mirrors would break." She meant from the pressure of people standing on them, but it sounded like she meant "from the spectacle of it all." Well, everybody laughed, including my mother. So naturally, I looked up at the hunk at my side. And it was Joe, goddamn it to hell! So we were both duly shocked, of course, and then I saw Lorraine at his side and he saw my mother and introductions were made all around. And everyone was just as nice and polite and pleasant as could be, and Lorraine looked adorable and happy, about to become a bride and all, and I was of course praying for death on the spot. Mine, not hers. And then Lorraine announced, totally without guile and probably without thinking, that they were shopping, so help me, for a bed.

So I congratulated God on His latest hysterical coup, and Lorraine blushed and I blushed and even Joe blushed a little bit, and my mother thought it was just adorable, which it was, I guess, except for my death wish.

And there she was now, Lorraine, just like I figured all along, being a nice person.

It was about then that my attention wandered back to the model-type girl that seemed to have the spotlight on her. Their backs were facing me now, hers and the short stocky whatever at her side. And I could see they each had one arm wrapped around the other's waist. I told myself not to jump to conclusions. Wasn't I the one who was always saying people should touch more? It didn't mean they were queer. They were probably just good friends. And when they held hands, in between the hugging—okay, so they were very good friends. And when the taller one leaned over to kiss the shorter one, I nearly dropped my teeth. Because I got a good look at the taller one's profile and it was Tish!

Tish was kissing a short, mannish looking person on the steps of St. Patrick's Cathedral? What was going on? Tish was queer? Since when? This was news to me. Naaah, it couldn't be.

Also, Tish never looked better in her life. She looked terrific. What happened to the waif look? The hacking cough? I guess she got better. Well, that was good.

Since Tish was largely playing to the crowd with this performance, she kept looking around to see who was getting this and who wasn't, and in no time at all, she spotted me, probably with my mouth still hanging open.

"Nikki! Nikki! Over here! Over here!" She gestured broadly for me to join them. "Nikki! Oh, look, it's Nikki! Come here!" Heads turned to see the object of this joyful outburst. I was tempted to gaze off in the opposite direction, whistling an innocent-sounding tune. But of course it was too late to feign ignorance, what with Tish literally jumping up and down—unnecessarily, since she was already a head taller than anyone else around, and calling out persistently, "Nikkiiiii! Over here!"

Even going by the most circuitous route possible, I reached them in no time at all. She couldn't be gay. They were just good, good friends probably.

Tish and I hugged each other. ("See how open-minded I am, folks? I'm not afraid.") There was much patting and embracing. I was glad. ("She's not queer. She's just expansive, you small-minded, uptight people in this crowd.")

We separated.

"I want you to meet Alex," she announced. "My lover."

Well, that certainly settled *that*. (That, folks, in case you missed it, was the closet door slamming shut. They are out now and they won't get back in, no matter what we do. We could squirm and look embarrassed all we want. They don't care. Tish always did have a very rebellious streak.)

"Alex. Nikki," she said, completing the introductions.

I extended my hand. *"How,"* I said, "do you do?" and Alex here shakes my hand in a very butch manner and says hi. Actually, she had this terrible smoker's cough, so it was more like *"Cough, cough, uh, uh, uh, cough, cough, hi, cough, cough, cough!"* Which somehow made her more *likable*. I guess when you see somebody in that much pain, your heart just goes out to them a little bit. And then I remembered it was Tish who always had the terrible cough, but now Tish isn't coughing at all. It's almost as if she had given the cough to Alex and she could relax now.

Anyway, I'm just totally shocked by this new development. Did Joe know about this? Or is this very recent? Did Tish come out of the closet after Joe died? Or was this going on all along? Joe would just have been aghast. You know how men are. They're bound to take things like that very personally. "Oh, God! My wife left me for another woman. Take me now, God!" Or even, as it would have been in Joe's case, "My ex turned gay!" He'd definitely be super-straight about it.

I immediately wonder if these two live together, over on

the Mews, and how did Joe feel about paying the bills over there if they lived together. I betcha he wouldn't be too thrilled. I mean, it was one thing to support Tish, especially while she was still being his dutiful daughter, but it would be a different story if that meant he was supporting Carlo Ponti here too.

Meanwhile, while I am trying to sort all this out in my mind, Tish continues to give a performance right out of *La Bohème*. She does everything but sing an aria. I mean, she definitely did not want anybody to miss this relationship of hers. And don't worry, nobody was. She makes sure she mentions about a million things that would lead your casual bystander to conclude that they lived together. She even invites me to come visit sometime, so I could see how she and Alex had redone the place.

So I'm wondering if it was Joe that paid for all this redecorating and just how bugged was he by all these changes, and was he so bugged that he threatened to not support her anymore? I mean, it was her life to live any way she wanted. And he did promise to support her, no matter what. But I don't think, even in his wildest dreams, he imagined something like *this* happening. Even if he took it with a certain amount of grace, Ann probably died a thousand deaths over it. Her husband's ex? A dyke? Whooooaaaaa! Ann, that sicko, would probably want to have Tish *committed*. She would have bitched long and loud about Joe's money going to support *this* twosome. And Tish did complain about Ann being a tightwad this morning, didn't she! But she didn't care now. Because she had her *own* money, it sounded like.

And I keep remembering what Brendan said. About how Tish was one very rich waif now, what with Joe's paintings, regardless of who disapproved of her life-style.

So I'm looking at Tish with new eyes, so to speak, and wondering just how far this rebellious streak of hers goes, and does it extend right up to and including murder?

And off to the side a bit, talking to a group of gallery people, I catch a glimpse of Shelly's old gray head and I wonder if Shelly knew about this, too, although I sort of think Shelly would have mentioned it if she had. ("TISH is QUEER!") And if she doesn't know, well, I certainly can't wait to tell her, because I'm such a low-minded gossip sometimes.

And there's Lorraine Rice, doing the good Christian thing and coming in from the coast to attend the funeral, and giving the whole affair some genuine class . . . and what do you know? One of the big black stretch limos pulls up to the curb and deposits the bereaved widow into our midst. And the Pender dame is flanked on one side by a Senator and on the other side by the Senator's wife, and it's all so subdued and respectable that it makes me positively nauseated. And I'm thinking if it was Ann who killed Joe, how THE HELL do I begin to fight all that safely ensconced respectability and it just seemed like a hopeless cause.

It occurs to me that all the keys to Joe's apartment are right here on this sidewalk, save for the lone male rogue (Brendan) who could have pilfered it from me. So I look from one face (Tish!) to the other (Shelly!) to the other (Lorraine!) to the other (Ann!), and all I could think of, though I didn't say it out loud of course, was—

Okay. Which one of you bitches killed my lover?

17

I ascertained from Ann's appearance that there was not going to be any weeping and wailing at *this* funeral, unless it was over *her* dead body. And that she, for one, was certainly not about to tear at any hairdo that Kenneth had so recently finished laboring over. The bereaved widow descended upon the crowd, setting the *tone*. The *tone* was one of dignified restraint. The *tone* is ". . . what they mean when they say 'grace under pressure'. . . ." And ". . . one of the most courageous woman I've ever . . ."

In other words, the tone is pure bullshit.

Ann has now progressed way beyond being the brave little soldier. She is Patton. And we are the Sicilians. She cuts a wide swath and goes sailing through. In her wake, there is the sympathetic clicking of tongues. "A wonderful example for all of us . . . Dear, dear Ann . . . We're so sorry . . ."

I was a little surprised that all of this was making me not just figuratively nauseated, but literally. Now, wouldn't that be adorable, I thought, disgusted with myself, if I were to throw up at this particular point in time? But how could I throw up, if I hadn't eaten anything? So of course, I immediately commenced to feel dizzy, realizing I had skipped breakfast. I have a very suggestible mind sometimes. Or was this my body's way of telling me I wasn't going to make it through this and to get the fuck out of there? Well, too bad! I was going to see this through or bust.

God, never One to miss an opportunity for a few yucks,

was in fine form. As I passed through the massive doors of the cathedral, that enormous, soul-quaking organ was starting up. It took a few moments for me to recognize the tune. Even I had to laugh. It was a Missa Solemnis, Bach's B-Minor Mass, and the last time I heard *that* I was with Joe and we were fucking. (Listen, I mean no disrespect. What can I tell you? The man was my Priest of Love! And if you find sex blasphemous . . . well . . .)

Tish, meanwhile, had an iron grip on my right arm, determined to march me right down that center aisle NO MATTER WHAT. Alex was on my other side, equally at the ready to strong-arm me, should that prove necessary. It didn't. I wanted to do this, no matter how crappy I felt. I leaned on Tish a little bit and kept walking.

Thus, the Unholy Three made their entrance.

Well, the decent folk did the only decent thing. They pretended we didn't exist. Not too convincingly, of course, because they wanted us to *know* they were pretending we didn't exist. Marlon Brando's right. Everybody's a genius, when it comes to acting. He said he couldn't understand why everybody made such a fuss over his acting. He said everybody's an actor, and they're much better at it than he is. I think he's right, about everybody being an actor.

So everybody let us know they saw us but that, for all practical purposes, we didn't exist. They weren't going to let us spoil their good time.

And so it went. There were the appropriate sounds of sniffing and the blowing of noses, discernible only when the organ stopped. There were the eulogies, and the standing and sitting and kneeling and sitting again and standing and kneeling some more. Tish leaned over once to tell me I looked godawful. I apologized. She said that's not what she meant. She said I looked sickly-godawful, not ugly-godawful, thank the Lord. Apparently sickly-godawful was all right.

There was only one hairy moment, when Alex turned to me and opened her mouth to speak. I knew it was going to be trouble right off, for although her mouth was open, no sound was forthcoming, save for a faint hissing. A wheeze. If only I had spoken up sooner. If only I had been quicker with a cautionary warning. ("Don't talk, Alex. Talking'll do you in. Save your breath for breathing.") But it was too late. I saw her eyebrows shoot up in alarm and I braced myself.

"COUGH! COUGH, COUGH, COUGH, COUGH, COUGH, COUGH!" There was much chest-rumbling, a trembling and shaking of lungs. A veritable Tin Man, she was. Teary-eyed, her face red, her eyebrows crimped and worried. "WOOOOOOUGH, WAAAAOOOUUGH . . . ah-HA. Huh, huh . . . COUGH, COUGH, COUGH." She patted her chest hurriedly, all to no avail. "Wooooough! COUGH, COUGH, COUGH, COUGH. Uhhhhh." I watched her in alarm. "COUGH,cough, cough, cough, uhhh, COUGH, COUGH! . . . wrong pipe!" she told me in a Louis Armstrong voice. I was about to ask her if there was anything I could do. She read the message in my face and began shaking her head no. It was trying to *say* no that kicked up the next attack. "COUGH, COUGH, COUGH, COUGH, COUGH." This time, she kept hitting the pew in front of her with the flat of her hand, as if it was the pew's fault all this was happening and she was feebly trying to admonish it for its cruelty. "COUGH! COUGH! (*Smack, smack, smack, smack*) COUGH, COUGH, huhhhh, COUGH!"

EMI prayed for the organ to begin again. When it did, it didn't matter. Alex was louder. Tish looked so pleased, I can't tell you. I could almost hear her thinking—if I could hear anything besides Alex, that is—"Let them try to ignore *that!*" "COUGH! COUGH, COUGH, COUGH, WOOOOOUUUUUGGHH, WAAAAAAA, *uh-h-h-h-h-h,* COUGH, COUGH, COUGH." I began patting Alex's back furiously. Tish leaned over us both and said, "Do you want a glass of water?" We both looked at her like she was crazy. Where the hell was she going to get this water? In time to do Alex any good with it? No, Alex signified, newly alarmed. I kept patting, my pat relaying the message. "Nobody's going to make a big commotion about getting you water, don't worry. It's all right." Alex and the choir reached their crescendos simultaneously. Sometimes she sounded like *two* people coughing, but I told myself it was probably just a trick of the acoustics. Eventually, there were a few weary *ah-hem, ah-hem, ah-hems,* followed by another flurry of violent activity, and then, at last, peace.

The whole church seemed to sigh in relief.

As we filed out of the church, Tish was already twittering about the limos, about how she wasn't going to stand around waiting forever and she should, by rights, be in one of the first limos leaving, and I was going with them, in their limo, wasn't I? And she hoped Shelly didn't intend to stick any strangers in their limo because if there was one thing she could go for right now, it was a little weed. On and on she went. Alex had the good sense to conserve her oxygen and not speak. I felt that anything else that happened that day was bound to be anticlimactic, so I went home.

18

There's nothing like a good loud knock on the door in the middle of the night to bring on cardiac arrest. Unless it's seeing the silhouette of a man crouched on your fire escape.

Funnily enough, both those things happened to me on the same night, within moments of each other. It was Monday night, the day of the funeral, and I was awakened from a deep, nightmare-laden sleep. It began to look as if I would never again awaken naturally from sleep. From now on, it would always be the DOOR BUZZZZER, or the PHOOOOONE, or the DOWNSSSSTAIRS INTERCOM jolting me back into a panicked wakefulness.

This time a loud, purposeful rapping of knuckles on wood sent my heart pounding and my pulse soaring. Obviously, it was a madman! Someone too deranged to even notice there was a doorbell to ring. Perhaps he was such a basic, primitive type that he considered doorbells newfangled and frivolous. I stared at the door, fully expecting it to splinter. Who knocks like that? Except madmen. Or the police!

Did the police have a change of heart? All right, all right, I wouldn't talk to the media, if they felt that strongly about it.

Maybe this had nothing to do with that. Maybe this was a drug bust and they had the wrong apartment! I read about that happening to a perfectly innocent nuclear family. The FBI just charged in on them and shot up the whole place. They had the wrong address. And they never even apologized! I thought of running down the fire escape.

So that's when I looked over at my kitchen window, where the fire escape is. And I saw the silhouette of the crouched man on the shade. Oh, God, they were coming through the windows! Just like they did with that family! And there I was, naked! So I looked around for something to wear, of course. I mean how could I let the police in if I was naked? It was probably against the law to sleep naked. Also, it wouldn't be appropriate for me to be naked if I was going to be target practice for a SWAT team. So I looked around for something to wear. Something a little revolutionary looking. I always like to dress appropriately. (When I was twelve years old, the *Andrea Doria* sank, through no fault of my own. My father said it was a good thing I wasn't on it because while people were being rescued, I'd have been locked in my stateroom, trying to decide on an appropriate going-over-the-side outfit. My father's pretty sardonic sometimes, for a welder.) I was pulling on a khaki T-shirt and jeans when the second barrage of knocks came. It was only now I noticed they were not coming from the door, but from the window! Obviously, it was only a burglar, demanding entrance.

Now I loved the police again. I wanted the police all around me. Whatever made me think it was the police, scaring me like this? Policemen are wonderful people. (Morrisey and Reynolds aside.) The police don't terrorize people, they save them. That business with the FBI and that family was just one in a million.

I was positively palsied as I made my trembling way to the phone. What the hell was that number—911? Or was it 411? No, that was Information. Or *was* it? Then what was 911? Was that long-distance information? No, that was 555-1212. Then what was 212? Listen, when you're really scared, plus half-asleep, these things are very confusing. I was dialing 911 and hoping for the best, when suddenly I heard a muffled voice from the other side of the windowpane.

"Nikki? Nikki! It's me. Let me in."

"GO AWAY!" I yelled back, realizing a moment later that I had been called by name. "Who is it," I said, "anyway?"

"It's me. Brendan. Open the window."

"Brendan!" I whispered back, just as hoarsely. "What the hell are you doing on my . . . ?"

"Would you open the fuckin' window please?"

I opened the shade and there he was, looming in at me. Then I had to go get the hammer because that window is *always* stuck. I let it stay stuck because it's my version of a burglar alarm. (It worked!) So after much tapping and prying, the window was opened and Brendan was in. He looked awful.

"What the hell do you want at this hour? And why did you . . . ?"

"I have to talk to you."

"Why didn't you just come up the stairs, like a normal person?" Then I remembered with whom I was dealing. "Oh. You were afraid the police were watching."

"The police aren't watching you. I know. I watched for a long time. Nobody's watching you."

"Except you. So why'd you come up the . . . ?"

"Why take chances?"

"It seems to me that's a surefire way to *attract* a little police attention! Crawling up fire escapes in the middle of the night!"

"Nobody saw me. That's why thieves use fire escapes, Nikki. Nobody *sees* you."

"Oh." I sat down at the kitchen table. Brendan paced. I gestured for him to take a seat. He ignored it. "So? What is it?" I said.

"About the other day. About something you said the other day." So *that* was it. He had a little time to ponder the fact that I had practically accused him of murder outright. He must have been really pissed because he looked absolutely awful.

"Hey, listen, Brendan, nobody accused you of murder. All I said was that it *might* have been you. Might! Might!"

"Not about that. Although that was quite a jolt, I can tell you. But all right, I needed that. To wake me up to a few things."

Boy, he really was mad! Now I was going to hear all about what a lousy friend I am and how he's not going to take this abuse anymore. Oh-oh.

"But that's not what I'm here to talk about," he said. We both continued whispering. I don't know why. We certainly didn't have to worry about waking up the other tenants. Not at this hour. The place only comes alive after midnight. Nobody has to get up early to go to work, that's for sure. And they have a lot to do at night. They have to drink, blast the radio, and fight!

"So about what, then?"

"About something else you said. I wasn't really paying attention, at the time. You were babbling something about a towel?"

"Oh, right. That's what made me think it could have been a man. There was a towel in the living room. Joe could have had that on when he was talking to whomever. So it could have been a man."

"Did you tell the police any of this?"

"No. Not yet."

"Not yet? In other words, you intend to."

"Well, yes. It could be important. Especially considering the fact that I was the one who kept insisting it could only have been a woman. It turns out they actually believed me. Well, a little bit anyway. Shelly told me they asked her about it, too. If she thought Joe would have been standing around naked talking to another man, and she told them the same thing I did. No way. She told me they even asked Ann. Ann, of course, said Joe wouldn't stand around naked in front of a man *or* a woman, and it was a suicide, but that's *her* story. So now I definitely have to tell them about this towel, because that changes everything."

I had seen Brendan's face devoid of humor before. When he was discussing the impending collapse of the world's monetary systems. When he was talking about his knee operations. When he was out of coffee. But never had I seen his face look more serious than it did right now. It was almost ferociously serious.

"You can't do that, Nikki."

"Why not?"

"Because it'll look bad for me."

"Brendan! No one has even been around to *talk* to you. To question you, or anything. I don't know what you're so worried about. The police don't even know you exist! Your name hasn't been mentioned by anybody, least of all me. They haven't been around to talk to you, have they?"

"No. I know. At first I thought it was a good sign, too. Now I see it isn't."

"Why not? Would you sit down please? You're making me nervous, pacing back and forth like that."

"And how come they're not hassling you? You went there for questioning, right? How come they let you go so fast?"

"So *fast*? I was there for hours!"

"They could have kept you there for *days*. Just for questioning. How come they let you go so fast?"

"We reached a little understanding, the police department and I. I don't talk to the Six O'Clock News, and they back off for a while. Besides which, they know damn well I had nothing to do with Joe's death."

"Oh, really? You reached a little understanding? That's interesting. Because we're going to reach a little understanding, too. You and I."

"Oh, are we!" I laughed, but it was a nervous laugh. He wasn't kidding around. This wasn't going to be a little friendly argument. I felt like I had somehow wandered into the cage of a very high-strung panther. And now I was locked in, too.

158

"You're damn straight we are!"

"And what, pray-tell, is that?" The *pray-tell* was a mistake, I saw instantly from the rage in his eyes. He wanted me to be *afraid* of him. Amazing! How far would he go to scare me? Would he hurt me? Who was this stranger, pacing back and forth in my kitchen? Why didn't I recognize him for the stranger he was all along?

"The understanding is this—you don't tell the police anything about the towel. About how it could have been a man or anything like that."

"And?"

"And what?"

"What's the rest of it? I don't tell the police and you don't—what? Hurt me? Kill me? What's the rest of this threat?"

"I'm not threatening you, Nikki. I'm just telling you that I'll do whatever I have to do to protect myself."

"*Why?* Nobody's bothering you!"

"They must know about me by now. They *must.* It stands to reason. Even if you didn't tell them, they have to know about me by now."

"Know *what,* damn it?"

"Don't underestimate them, Nikki. Don't make the mistake of underestimating them. They talked to Shelly, right? They probably asked Shelly all about *you.*"

"She didn't tell me that."

"Well, she's not going to tell *you* that. So they ask her about you and who you pal out with, et cetera, and she tells them about me. Shelly knows me. My name, my address, where I work, everything. So maybe they ask my boss or the people I work with where was I last Wednesday. And what do you know? I have no alibi. And they *still* don't come and talk to me. And you still can't figure out why, right?" He was almost a parody of paranoia. He must have been brooding about this constantly for the last two days.

"No. Why?"

"Because! They don't want to tip me off! They're afraid I'll bolt! That I'll run away!" I understood suddenly that it was a real possibility. Brendan was thinking of it. He was seriously considering running away. We had talked about the subject before, in jest, I thought. ("If you ever committed a crime, what would it be?" "A robbery." "A bank?" "No, diamonds. The Diamond Exchange." "A big heist, you mean?" "No, a small heist. A one-man operation. That'd be my first rule. No partners." "Shucks!" "Just a few big stones. I'd swallow them and head for the border." "Which border?" "South America. One good bowel movement and I live like a king for the rest of my life." "Yeah, but in South America." "So? I'd like South America. I like Latin women. Hah hah hah hah.") Now he was actually thinking of running away. Even without diamonds in his intestines.

It didn't mean he killed Joe. It didn't mean he didn't. It only meant he was scared enough to run away.

"They're waiting for some stronger evidence. When they arrest me, they want to make sure it sticks." Brendan was cracking up from fear. "And if you tell them about this towel crap, it's one more nail in my coffin."

"All right, I won't tell them."

"I don't believe you. And that's not what I came here for, anyway. To hear your bullshit. I came to warn you."

"To threaten me."

"All right, to threaten you. Call it whatever you want. I came to tell you that if I'm implicated in this, seriously implicated, I'll cover my precious ass. You were right, Nikki. I don't want to run away. I want to stay right here, in the good old U. S. of A. So I'll protect my ass in the most direct way I know how."

"Which is?"

"By blaming you."

I was struck speechless.

"I'll tell them you told me you did it. People saw you on the roof. It doesn't matter that they only saw you afterwards.

Eyewitnesses get everything fucked up. Somebody'll swear they saw you there before it happened, too. The police want to blame you anyway. All they need is my testimony. You told me you were having an argument. You pushed him. You told me all about it."

I still didn't speak. There was nothing to say.

"And don't think you can turn it around and blame me, once I do that. I have an alibi now. A girl I know. She'll go along with it. She was in bed with me all day Wednesday afternoon. You weren't the only two fucking the day away."

"I see."

"I hope you see. I don't want it to come to that, but if it has to, it will."

"Okay." I want him to just get out. Leave!

"Now, what you do is up to you. What you tell the police or what you don't tell the police. It's up to you."

"Okay."

"And I want you to know one thing. Whatever you tell them, I'll find out about it. I know a lot of lawyers, Nikki. And lawyers know a lot of cops. So I'll find out what you tell them. One way or the other, I'll find out."

I nodded and he walked to the door, then turned, his hand on the knob.

"I'm sorry, Nikki."

I nodded again and he left. I got up and locked the door. What's that expression, about closing the barn door after the horse has escaped? I locked the door, but it was too late. I had already been violated. So violated! Right here, in my own kitchen, in the middle of the night.

So, I thought. It seems Brendan really is capable of rape. One way or the other. One way or the other.

19

The next day brought—whad-dya know!—good news. I found out I was going to be getting Joe's painting back. *Eros.*

Bob called and told me. I always thought the "reading of the will" was some big deal you had to go to a lawyer's office for. Apparently not, because Bob told me all about the will right on the phone. Joe had left me the painting! I can't tell you how happy I was about it, because the truth was I always felt bad about the way I sent it back. I mean I know Joe *deserved* it and all at the time, but it still bothered me that I sent back such a personal thing to him. It was like I was rejecting him totally, as a person. But the fact that he left it to me showed that he knew I didn't mean it like that, that I sent it back because I was in a terrible snit and that deep down I really still wanted the painting.

Bob apologized about a million times over the fact that, other than the painting, I wasn't mentioned at all in the will. I kept telling him that was silly and that I certainly never expected anything like that. After all, I was perfectly capable of taking care of myself. (Even if I did, at the moment, have turn-off notices from both the phone company and the electric company. But I *was* expecting a check any day now for one of the book covers I had done.) Still, Bob just kept right on apologizing about it, saying how Joe had made up the will a few years ago, when he first married Ann. Bob told me Joe didn't want to make up any will at all, because he was a little superstitious about it, but Ann insisted, because of the size of her estate and his estate, to keep everything straight.

"If only he had revised it, any time within the past year even, I'm sure he would have provided for you in it," Bob insisted. But I kept telling him that was silly, and what, was he trying to demoralize me? and he said, no, no, no, and I finally convinced him I was independently wealthy and that I was just pleased as punch about getting the painting back, because that was something emotional and it showed that even though Joe and I were on the outs at the time, he still wanted me to have it and that meant a lot to me.

Bob told me Joe left just about everything to charity. Children's charities, mostly, all over the world. His paintings were going to be sold at auction over the next two years. There was a trust fund for Tish and for a few dozen other people that he helped, some kids he knew personally, orphans like himself, and some older people, too—artists who didn't quite support themselves on their art. Some paintings were going to be donated to museums, both here and in Europe. And there were grants to art schools and writers' colonies and stuff. And that was the will. Ann wasn't left anything in the will, because that would have been like bringing coals to Newcastle, and neither was Lorraine, probably for the same reason.

Then Bob asked me if I could do him a favor and help him with figuring out the dates of some of Joe's paintings. The year, at least. So we agreed to meet the following afternoon over at Joe's studio in Hoboken. Joe had a big loft there. Most of his paintings had already been taken out because the security wasn't too tight, but they had all been photographed and the slides were still over at the studio. The paintings had been transferred to someplace here in the city, under lock and key. Bob said it would be a while yet before *Eros* was sent to me, because of legalities and stuff, but I told him that was fine, and that I'd see him tomorrow afternoon, about two.

Then I got dressed and went to the precinct to tell Morrisey about the towel.

Look, I'm sorry. I thought it was a pertinent fact in the case. It might turn out to be really important. Brendan would just have to take his chances with the police. And I'd just have to take my chances with Brendan. So I gussied up and went over to the precinct.

Morrisey couldn't have cared less. I explained all about this towel and she barely looked up from her desk. It looked as if she was still pretty annoyed at me from our questioning session. She was not what you'd call friendly. Also, it looked as if she didn't give a good shit about this towel business. Anyway, I did my part and told her about it, and she thanked me, her voice loaded with sarcasm, for my "continued interest in the case."

So that all turned out to be a big nothing.

I wondered if it was really true, what Brendan said about finding out what I told the cops and what I didn't. Or if he was just bluffing.

I feel about the smell of paint the way Elizabeth Taylor felt about the smell of horses in *National Velvet*. I can't get enough of it. So when I walked in the next day, Joe's studio smelled its usual delightful way. Bob was already there to let me in.

Joe's Hoboken studio was four rooms, more or less, in this big loft. There was the big main room, which was enormous and had the good lighting, what with the skylights and one whole side of it made of big windows. Then there was this kitchen-type affair off to one side. It wasn't really a kitchen at all, but it had a sink and some cabinets. No stove or refrigerator or anything, though. If you were *truly* desperate for a cup of coffee, Joe had this thing you stuck in a plug and put the other end in a cup to warm up the water. It made grotesque coffee. When we were both painting there, Joe would have the milk delivered every day. Now, that was a horrendous spectacle. Because sometimes we wouldn't go every day, and then when we did go, there'd be this spongy-looking milk in these little glass bottles outside the door, waiting for us. Joe always

164

insisted it was perfectly good milk. He said that's how they make cheese. Did you ever see chocolate cheese? (The chocolate milk was for me.) It's not pretty. Anyway, I always passed on it because I told Joe I didn't like any milk you had to get out of the bottle with a knife and fork.

At the back of the studio there was another little room, a long narrow one that we hardly ever used, and then there was a bathroom off to the side of that. Bob had all the slides and stuff set up on a big table in the main room.

Well, it seems the dating-the-canvases business turned out to be a lot harder than I thought. There were about two hundred slides there, and it got really confusing. After about three hours, I had dated only about fifteen of them, and four of those were *circas*. The process went like this:

"This one was done in seventy-four. The end of seventy-four, the beginning of seventy-five. Wait a minute! Wait a minute! He did this one *after* he did that other one and I know he did that other one in seventy-five. So it must have been the end of seventy-five, the beginning of seventy-six. You better say *circa, circa* '75. And I would never call this impressionist. Maybe *e*xpressionist. Who made this list like this for you? First of all, this one is upside down! Is the slide in upside down? No? Well, then they photographed it upside down. No! I'm not kidding you."

Finally, Bob got up to make himself some instant coffee, leaving me alone to play with the slides and his lists. I used the time to goof off, naturally. I wandered around the studio, sticking my nose into this and that. Eventually, I made my way into the long narrow room in the back. It had a skylight, too, but there must have been something blocking it on the outside because that room was always too dark. Too dark, too cold, and too dreary. I never felt comfortable in that room.

There was a long table along one wall of it—more like a wide shelf, really—and it was smeared all over with globs of old paint and cluttered with rusted cans that held discarded brushes and rags and used-up tubes of paint. Sometimes, when we ran out of stuff, we'd be forced to scrounge in there among the leftovers. There was always a water bug hiding out somewhere.

In the midst of the ancient stuff on the table, one thing stood out because it was new and crisp and clean-looking: a sheet of parchment paper, folded over in thirds, like a letter. It wasn't old parchment paper, it was new, the kind they sell in art stores, in pads. I had one such pad myself, Aquabee Antique, which I used for calligraphy.

So there was this sheet of paper, sort of folded up but pretty much opened. I picked it up and looked at it. Read it, actually. It was in Joe's handwriting. It said:

I, Joseph Savanah, being of sound and disposing mind, and considering the uncertainty of this life, do make, publish, and declare this to be my last Will and Testament as follows, hereby revoking all other former Wills by me at any time made.

First: I direct that all my just debts and funeral expenses be paid as soon after my death as may be practicable.

Second: I give and bequeath to Leticia Hassel Savanah the sum of $50,000 (fifty thousand dollars).

Third: All the rest, residue and remainder of my estate, of whatever kind or nature it may be, of which I shall die seized or possessed or to which I may be entitled at the time of my death (including any property over which I have power of appointment), I do hereby give and bequeath to Nicole Andrews, of New York City, New York, absolutely and forever, to be used in any way Nicole Andrews deems desirable.

In witness whereof I have hereunto signed my name this 6th day of February 1982.

(Signed) Joseph Savanah

What?
My voice, the embodiment of bafflement, laced with an-

166

noyance, called out, "Bob." Then, "Bob!" almost angrily. He came strolling into the room behind me, a coffee mug in hand.

"Bob," I said. "What's this?"

"What?"

"This."

He took it from my hand and read. He looked up for a minute, then he read it again. Then he looked up again, then he looked at me, and then he read it again. And then he said, "Where'd you *get* this?"

"Right here." I gestured to the place on the table, not daring to touch it, however, as if it were contaminated.

He took another swallow of his coffee, leisurely, in no hurry at all. Then he gazed off into space again, then back at me, then back at the paper. He read it again, while taking another drink of his coffee. Then he said, "Right here?"

"Yes!"

For some insane reason, both of us seemed determined to blame this—this whatever-it-was—on the table.

"You're kidding!"

"No-oh."

"Right there?" I nodded, yes, definitely, yes. "But Nikki," he said, "you couldn't have. This is a will."

"I know!" Like, how do you like the nerve of this goddamned table?!

"Nikki." Now he was getting angry, too. Annoyed, like me. Even at me, a little bit. "This is another will."

"I know!" *I* didn't do it. The table did!

"But this is another *will!*"

"It *sounds* like it."

"It is! I know. I've been reading the will for a week now! This sounds like another will."

"Doesn't it?"

"And you found it right here?"

"Yeah! There!"

"Well. I'll be darned."

"I know!" Like, I'll be darned, too. Then I laughed a little bit. Like, is this some crazy world or isn't it?

"I'm gonna go lock the door," Bob said. "Don't move."

I wasn't going anywhere. I just stood there thinking what a crazy thing life is. Where people can fall down from high places, KA-BOOM, with a bang, and that's it, they're gone for good and how can that be? One minute this man is all over you, inside you and outside you, just all over you, and you're all over him, so much so that for a while there, you don't know where he begins and where you leave off, and all of a sudden, KA-BOOM, he's not there anymore and he's not anywhere that you can go and put your finger on. Somebody else can *push* people off high places and then just walk away and continue to go about their business, like they had every right to push someone else off a high place; and *they* still wake up in the morning and go to the bathroom and eat, drink, and be merry, for yesterday they killed somebody, but that's okay, because nobody knows or cares; and they're safe to go about their business, and only Joe is dead, not them.

And you can still feel his presence in your heart because that lasts for a while after you've been together; and you still walk around with this doper's look in your eyes because your body remembers, even after your mind forgets; and then pretty soon you want another ecstasy fix and, miraculously, he does too, so you seek each other out and continue right from where you left off; but where the hell will he be now, when the glow from last time wears off and I want to go looking for him again? He just won't be anywhere, because, naaaaaa, it can't be, is Joe dead? And you always said that man had a death wish, right from that night he wanted to go walking on the beach in the middle of winter just to show you what a storm looked like, what it did to the ocean, and you told him there'd be nobody on Coney Island beach now except muggers and crazies, but he wanted to go anyway, so you went because you could never tell that man no. So you both stayed under the boardwalk and watched what the storm did to the ocean, and it was something to see, all right, and then the storm was over, and it was nighttime and the sky just looked so clear, and he wanted to go down to the shoreline, *take a little walk* he said and you knew what *that* meant and you said the sand's all wet, so Crazy ran back to the car for a blanket, a regular Boy Scout, he, always prepared, so you both went tooling down the beach and then you spread out the blanket and you said we'd probably both get arthritis, and he told you sex was very good for arthritis and about how it had to do with hormone levels and before you know it there's unzipping and unsnapping and what do you know? passion *does* laugh once in a while, because you're laughing and fucking at the same time and it's terrific, and you see his beautiful face surrounded by a zillion stars and the stars aren't just shining down, they're radiating love, like van Gogh saw, and they're not just indifferent things up there in the sky, they're these loving God-existences and they *love* you, they're shining out there, shimmering and beaming, because they love you so much and they're telling you, We love you. You're what makes our sun come up in the morning! And all of a sudden it's just crystal clear that the *last* thing this universe is, is indifferent and that the whole beautiful universe loves you and why not? you're their own, aren't you? And Joe suddenly decides that the most important thing in the world right now is for you to tell him if you know that he loves you. It's all of a sudden urgent for you to say if you know he loves you and he doesn't even care if you love him or not. That's not important, he says, all that's important is that you should know he loves you. But you can't lie, you have to tell him the truth, he says, and, "Do you really know I love you?" And you tell him "Yes, I know." Because you do, and then you say, "Hey, what about me? Do you really know I love you too?" and he says yes. And you both keep asking each other, "But do you *really* know?" And you both keep saying, "Yes, *I* know." And he says, "Thank you for really knowing I love you," and you say, "Thank you, too, for really knowing."

And then he's dead and you don't believe any of it anymore. He never really loved you or he wouldn't have died, and you must not have loved him very much, to allow this to happen. And nobody loves anybody anymore, and people don't act or look friendly and loving anymore, like they did when he was around, and it wasn't only that he was famous that made people act like that, to him and to you and to each other, because you knew him before he was famous and people *always* acted like that around him because he made everybody feel soooo happy all of a sudden. And even when he was aggravating the shit out of everybody, being so damned irresponsible about some things and then so damned fanatical about others, the worst, the absolute worst thing you ever heard anybody say about him was, "He's such a goddamn *cheerful* son of a bitch, isn't he?" Then they'd laugh, because there was no winning against him. He took you over, 'cause he loved you. No bullshit love—real love—and you were defenseless against it, like a newborn babe. And maybe it was the ferocious intelligence in his eyes or the way he had of smiling, so beautifully, with a million laugh lines around his eyes, eyes that saw everything and understood everything, eyes without blinders on that *loved* everything. Because he always knew what was behind the last veil, even if he didn't know he knew it—and it was love, pure love. And *that's* what cheered everybody up, for goodness sakes. Because everybody thought, "Well, if Joe's happy (and Joe doesn't miss a trick!), then it must be *all right!*" But then he's dead and nobody's happy anymore and the stars in the sky don't love you and whatever made you think a crazy thing like that in the first place? And you can't even blame it on drugs or liquor or anything, because all it was was the magic of another person that made you think things like that and he's gone now and you can see very clearly that the stars don't love you and never did. They don't even like you much. They don't even know you exist!

And is that why brother Theo, beloved Theo, died in a madhouse six months after Vincent went out into a field and shot himself? The van Goghs. The poor van Goghs. He shot himself in a field, then went back to his house and lay in his bed with his face to the wall and waited for Theo to come. And he did, of course, being Theo, and they held hands for a while, and early the next morning, he said, "I wish I could die now," and he did. And Theo must have realized that the magic went out of the world with Vincent, and that the stars didn't love him anymore. Is that what killed Theo? Would it kill me too? No, no, because I knew all about craziness. I knew you just had to let it be there and it would go away eventually. You just had to persevere and persevere and it would go away. I read a book about it once, good old *Peace From Nervous Suffering*. Why wasn't she more famous than Freud? She ought to be, that Claire Weekes. Freud just described insanity. Claire Weekes cured it. Why wasn't she more famous? Because she was a woman? A middle-aged M.D. from Australia. She ought to be more famous. She knew everything. She could have cured van Gogh. Let the voices be there, Vincent. Don't cut off your ear. Let the voices be there. Learn to live with the voices. "What are you worried about?" Joe yelled at me. "You're not van Gogh." "Why, you dirty—" "For one thing, you're a woman!" "*Ooooo*, you chauvinistic—" "And for another, you're *crazier*." "Oh," I said, consoled. I wasn't afraid of craziness. But now I'm afraid of the stars not loving me. Can I ever learn to live with this?

And wasn't it strange how everybody knew exactly how much to cry at the funeral? To just sniffle and cry nicely, and not open their mouths wide and go WAAAAAAAAAAAAAAAAAA.

And isn't it strange how peculiar everybody's been acting since? What with Brendan climbing in through kitchen windows from fire escapes and Tish not being in love with Joe anymore but being in love with a woman instead? And Ann saying it was a suicide and not a murder at all, and Shelly saving piles of sand and me being not less crazy but more, because I actually got jealous of all that stuff in Shelly's house and wishing *I'd* saved stuff, too? But that was impossible, because everywhere I went with Joe became sacred ground and you couldn't take anything from there, just put it in your pocket and bring it home, because every good Indian knows you don't mess with sacred ground. And that would mean there was sacred ground and unsacred ground, and safe places and unsafe places, and I refused to feel that way about things and who is this guy to make me think such a thing? And I was determined to believe the *whole world* was sacred ground and everywhere is safe. But I know better now, don't I?

And now here's this parchment paper, trying to fool me again. Another joke from God. Come on, Nikki, believe it! Joe did love you, and love is money, just like he said—and see? He proved it. He made you rich, rich, rich. But I know better about that, too, and good things like that don't happen, not to me, and I won't be fooled again. Because I know what this paper is really saying, and it's: Go to jail. Go directly to jail. Do not pass Go. Do not collect $200. Much less an estate. Go directly to jail. Well? What are you waiting for? GO GO GO!

"Nikki! Nikki! I locked the door."

"Oh. Okay, Bob."

"Now what?"

"I think we should leave it right here. Leave it right there on the table and go home. Let somebody else find it. Let *their* mothers worry." I laughed.

"Are you all right?"

"I'm fine. Don't worry, I'm not hysterical or anything. I just need a little drink." I went into the kitchen and searched frantically for hard liquor, to no avail. Bob was right behind me.

"Don't get scared, all right? Just stay calm, Nikki, all right?"

"What do you mean, don't get scared? You know what this means, don't you? You went to lock the door! This means I have a motive! This wasn't a will. It's a death warrant! Do they still have the death penalty in New York?"

"No."

"I'm sure there was a bottle of something in this cabinet. *Whiskey* or something! AAAAIIIII! Did you see that? That was a water bug, I think. Did you see it? It looked pretty big, didn't it? *Ahhhh,* who cares. I'm sure there was a bottle of *something.*"

"Nikki! Stop it! Just stand still for a minute. Just stop and stand still!"

I stopped slamming cabinet doors and stood still. Bob started talking but I was busy thinking. Inside! It must be inside. "Maybe it's in here," I said, going back into the studio proper. "It must be in here. I'm sure there was a bottle of something," I said, my eyes scanning the shelves and tables hurriedly.

"Would you look at yourself? It's like you're an alcoholic! You're like Jack Lemmon in *The Subject Was Roses.* When he was in the greenhouse."

I guess it was the skylights that made him think of greenhouses. "Boy, are you confused, Bob. That wasn't Jack Lemmon. That was Martin Sheen!"

"Nikki! I'm going to smack your face, I swear! Unless you stop this right now, I'm going to smack you right across your face."

"What? Why?"

"Because you're getting hysterical."

"I am not! I'm just looking for a little drink. God! Didn't you ever want a little drink?" But when I found myself seriously considering a swig of the turpentine, I rethought my position. Maybe Bob had a point. I was getting hysterical. He stood in front of me, one hand raised ominously in the air.

"You're right," I said. "I am hysterical. But don't hit me. I know it now. Does it help if you know it?"

"I don't know."

"Ohhhhh, Bob. I should be hysterical. I have a right to be hysterical. I'm going to be sent to jail for murder! Oh God!"

"Maybe you should drink a little something. To calm you down."

"That's what *I* thought."

We couldn't find any goddamned bottle. I had to settle for instant coffee. Black, no sugar. I was surprised. It was sort of good.

20

"*All right, now*, let's just think things through calmly," Bob said, sitting across from me at the table.

"Okay."

"One, is it a real will?"

"How the hell do I know?"

"I'm not asking you. I'm just listing all the things we'll have to consider."

"Oh."

"One, is it a real will? By which I mean, did Joe really write it? It looks like his handwriting. Do you agree?"

"Yeah, it looks. But so what? It could be a forgery. If it was Brendan that did this, which I think it was, he could have gotten somebody to forge it. Brendan's a lawyer and lawyers know a lot of cops, he told me. Lawyers also know a lot of criminals."

"Wait a minute. One thing at a time. Where was I? Oh, yeah. One, is it a real will?"

"Are we going to stay on one forever? Where's two?"

"*Two*, if it is a real will, is it valid?"

"Are you kidding, or what? Of course it's not valid! Wills are big deals! You can't just write on a piece of paper, this is a will, and—"

"Yes, you can! In some situations. If you're in the army or the navy or the merchant marine, I think, too. I was in the navy, and I could have written a will on a piece of paper if I wanted to. It would have been valid. Joe was in the navy with me. He would have known about a will like that. It's called a holographic will."

"That sounds reverential."

"It means entirely written by hand. It stays valid even after you get out of the navy. For a whole year, I think."

"Yeah, well, neither of you were in the navy *last* year."

"It could still be valid. In certain states, you can have a holographic will. It's legal. But not in New York."

"Well, there you are!"

"But we're not *in* New York."

"We're not?"

"No."

We said it in unison. "We're in New Jersey."

"A holographic will might be valid in New Jersey," Bob said. "I'll have to check."

"You're not checking anything. We're going to burn it. I don't know what you think we're plotting and planning here because I can tell you right now there's no way I'm going to be made beneficiary to all that money. No way! Things like that don't happen to me. All it's going to do is get me convicted of murder. That's all it was meant to do, by whoever put it there. Which was Brendan."

"Wait a minute. Wait a minute. Let's take this a step at a time. Where was I?"

"Ohhhh, would you please?"

"Two: Is it valid? Maybe. We'll have to see. Okay, three: How did it get here? It wasn't here last week or the police would have seen it. They were over here, too, last week, after it happened. They would have seen it just lying there on the table like that. It was just on the table? Are you sure?"

"Yes!"

"All right, so somebody's been here and they put it there. To be found probably by me."

"Brendan put it there. He broke in and put it there. He

176

came up the fire escape through the bathroom in the middle of the night and put it there."

"How do you know that?"

"Because he came up *my* fire escape one night. He's getting proficient at it, I'm telling you."

"I never did like that guy. Do you really think he killed Joe?"

"I don't know. All I know is, he's terrified of being blamed. So`he's blaming me. He threatened to do something like this. I guess he wasn't bluffing. I think he's just gone *crazy.*"

"Okay, did I have a three? Yes. How did it get here? Okay, four: What do we do now?"

"Burn it, just like I said."

"And if it's valid?"

"So what? If it is valid, I get convicted of murder because it gives me a motive. PLUS, I was the only one positively absolutely there when Joe got killed. And if it isn't valid, I get convicted of forgery, too. Besides murder. Any way you look at it, that will does not bode good things for my future. Let's burn it already."

"Wait. We can't do that. What if Joe really wrote that will? Maybe it was there all along and the police missed it for some reason. If it's what Joe wanted, we can't just destroy it."

"What Joe wanted! Would Joe want me to spend the rest of my life in jail? No! Let's burn it. Fast! *That's* what Joe would have wanted."

"I think you may be right."

"Halleluljah!"

"We'll hide it somewhere."

"We'll burn it."

"In a safe deposit box somewhere. Here in Jersey. No one'll know about it till this blows over."

"This will *never* blow over. This is going to be my life from now on! We have to burn it. Fast!"

"We'll investigate on our own in the meantime. We'll find out who put the will here. We'll find out who killed Joe."

"We'll find out what idiots we are trying to find things like that out. We'll burn the will, that's what we'll do."

"Wait! Nikki! Where are you going? Stop! I *forbid*—I forbid you to touch that will! Nikki!"

We both ran into the little room in the back. Then we wrestled around there, half-kidding, half-serious. He was surprised at how strong I was. I told him I'm a horse. He suggested we talk about it some more first. I told him, "What's to talk about? I'll never know a moment's peace while that will is in existence. It's very incriminating, and it always will be. It has to be destroyed. It can't be hidden."

"What if they catch the murderer someday? What if they have absolute proof that you're innocent?"

"They'll never have absolute proof. There were no clues, no nothing, in this murder. There'll always be a doubt. I'll always be suspect. Especially if this will comes to light. Besides which, even if that happened, do you really think Pender is going to let me be beneficiary to all that stuff? You know her lawyers. Do you really think they wouldn't contest this will?"

He thought. Then he admitted, "They'd probably claim 'undue influence.'"

"Thank you for your honesty. So we agree. There's no way this will is going to do me any good, and there's a thousand ways it could do me real harm. Let's burn it."

"Listen, Nikki, if we do, I want you to know that I'll try to arrange something so that Joe's estate goes to you. I'm the executor, aren't I? Of the other will? There's got to be something I could do . . ."

"With all those banks and trustees breathing down your neck? Don't be ridiculous. Listen, that other will was a fine will. Even if Joe did leave me all his money, I'd do the same thing with it that he did. Give it all to kids' charities. That's what should be done with it anyway. Besides, I don't need that money. I have my own money."

"Oh, that's right. How could I forget? Did you pay your phone bill yet?"

"Tomorrow."

"Shall I or shall you?"

"Let's both." We went into the bathroom and stood over the sink. He held the will, and I struck the match. The parchment paper caught right away. I recited a poem.

> "My candle burns at both ends,
> It will not last the night.
> But ah, my foes, and, oh, my friends—
> It gives a lovely light."

"Why do I have the feeling this is the dumbest thing we could possibly do?"

"Yeah, me too. Maybe that's a good sign. It's always when I think I'm doing something smart that I get into trouble."

"Yeah, well, in that case—ouch! There now. It's gone. I hope you're happy. Feel better?"

"Much."

We turned on the water and the ashes went down the drain.

21

We left the bathroom and went back into the big room, over to the table that had all the slides on it.

"Now that it's gone, I can think more clearly," I said. I did feel better, too. I wasn't just saying that.

"Now tell me you're sorry we burned it and, so help me, I'll—"

"Of course, I'm not sorry. We did the only sensible thing. Nobody in a million years would have expected us to burn the will."

"Least of all, me."

"But we foxed 'em."

"Now why don't we kill ourselves and *really* confuse the hell out of them?" he said. I got hysterical. I wasn't used to Bob's wit. In fact, I didn't think he had any. Bob always seemed so serious in front of women, the kind of guy who thought it was disrespectful to crack jokes to women. There was a strain of propriety in him that I always found distancing. I guess that's because that's how he treated me in the past—distancing. Like, God forbid it should ever be thought he was making a play for a female connected with Joe. I could see Ann turning him into a valet, because his manner was already so respectful and acquiescent. He's put up with something like that, either out of affection for Joe or because he had the idea that a real man put up with a certain amount of bullshit from women. It was the gallant thing to do. Gallantry like that always confuses the hell out of me. When someone is being a "real man" like that, I never know how to be a "real woman" in response. I'd find myself being forced into this stereotype—the best friend's girl. I could never talk to Bob about anything that didn't relate directly to Joe, lest, God forbid, it should look like Joe's girl was making a play for *him*. No matter how hard I fought against this stereotype, just trying to be my regular self, Bob's gallantry knew no bounds. It would just keep expanding to include any outrage. "Oh, look. Joe's girl is dressed as a Nazi. Real women are so cute sometimes." Like that. (I'm exaggerating, of course.)

I think Bob was always a little puzzled by me, too. Like, if Joe could have anybody he wanted, why Huckleberry Finn here? Why not some gorgeous blonde? I was sure Bob thought Loni Anderson was the ultimate "real woman."

Anyway, seeing Bob cry at that funeral was a real revelation to me. Like, there was a person behind that gallantry, wasn't there? A terrific person, too. And the fact that he went along with this burning of the will was another shock. See, Nikki? You should never categorize people. They're way more complex than they ever let on.

Anyway, with one thing and another, Bob and I had spoken more to each other in the last half-hour than we had in all the years previous. I think we were both a little relieved at what we found.

"I guess you don't feel like looking at any more slides today, huh? We'd better call it a day," he said.

"No, no. That's all right. I'll work a little longer. You can go home if you want, though."

"Noooo. I wouldn't leave you here alone." Of course not. How could I think *that!*

"I just realized I've been doing this all wrong, though," I said. "I shouldn't be looking at them one at a time. I should look through the whole lot of them, all at once, a couple of times, and then eventually, some order will make itself clear to me."

"You want to put them on the projector? It'll be faster. It changes the slides automatically, right? Set it for a high speed. We'll look at all of them fast the first time."

"Okay."

He set it up and the machine began clicking, flashing pictures onto the screen. I got hysterical laughing because the speed was a little *too* fast. Bob smiled, his form of hysteria, I guess.

"Not that fast!" I said.

"I know. Wait a minute. I'll fix it."

The pace a little less Charlie Chaplin-esque, we watched the pictures flashing by. *Click, click (The Night Watchman). Click, Click (Waterfall). Click, click.*

"BOB!"

"WHAT?" He stopped the machine, as if he thought I had made some amazing discovery about the picture being shown.

"No, no, not that!" I said. "It's about the murder. I think we could use this to catch the killer! This will business."

"Nikki, we're not going to catch anybody. The police are handling that. We burned the will—God, I can't believe we did that—to keep you *out* of trouble. Let's not go looking for any *more* trouble."

"That's exactly what we should do. Go looking for trouble! Listen!" I told him all about my key theory. I told him all my suspects. I was shocked when he didn't drop his teeth at my mention of Ann. So maybe I wasn't so crazy after all. If even Bob thought it was possible that Ann did it.

"So we use this will business now to stir things up a little."

"How?"

"Well, first of all, they'll have expected you to find the will. You, or somebody else who would have given it to the police. So they'll be expecting me to get arrested. When I don't, they'll know something went wrong and be puzzled, worried. Let's capitalize on that. Let's make the most of that. We'll get the word out, to the suspects at least, that instead of incriminating me this will has incriminated them somehow. Their plan has backfired. The police know about the will, but I'm not arrested because the police also know it was a setup. And instead of me, *they* will be arrested, any minute. You get it?"

"No."

"Look. When I'm not arrested, they'll know something went wrong. Let them think you gave it to the police. Let them think that the police didn't arrest me because, in leaving the will, they left some enormous clue about themselves. Something so incriminating that the police knew right off who did it and they don't even bother arresting me."

"What if the person who left the will isn't the killer? What if it was this Brendan who left the will, like you said. Just so he doesn't get blamed."

"All right, so that's one chance in—how many? One in eight? The odds are that the person who put the will here is the person who killed Joe. And now they'll think that the police have some valuable clue to their identity. They'll do something. Maybe something stupid, but something. They won't just sit back and wait to be arrested."

"Why not?"

"Because this person is not playing with a full deck! They've already committed murder. That's not a rational act! This person has already behaved irrationally and they will again. At least I'm betting they will. A mystery writer told me that. I did the cover for one of his books. He told me that you have to remember that a murderer is an irrational person, and that's how they get caught. They already tried to solve one problem by committing murder. They'll most likely do something else irrational to prevent being caught. Sometimes, they commit a *second* murder."

"Now, that is good news. So if one of us gets knocked off, we'll know we're on the right track."

I cracked up. "Nobody's going to knock us off. Is it our

fault the murderer fouled up, leaving this clue? We've got nothing to do with it. It's the police's fault."

"What if they found out it's a gigantic bluff? That there was no clue."

"Now how are they going to find that out? They can't verify it, one way or the other. What are they going to do? Call up the police and say, 'Well? What'd you think of that will I planted?' And even if they do have some sort of an in at the police department, it won't help. That's the beauty part of this! Nobody will know a damn thing about it!"

"Why don't I find that a comfort?"

I got hysterical again.

"You know," Bob said, "you remind me of Joe sometimes. You're just like him. Disaster strikes, and you laugh. We had a flood one time out in Bedford Falls. The whole basement was flooded. Ann nearly had a nervous breakdown. You know what Joe did? He went swimming! In the flood in the basement! I think that gave Ann a whole new perspective on Joe. Watching him do the backstroke through all those floating cartons and all." He demonstrated with flying arms.

I was rocking back and forth, holding my sides and laughing, smacking the table.

"Yeah," he said. "Another lunatic. I should have figured. But okay, I get it. The odds are it was the murderer who left the will. But what if he or she *knows* they didn't leave any clues?"

"They could never be sure of that. A stray fingerprint. Somebody who saw them in the neighborhood around here. If the will was a forgery, the police would find that out right away and trace it to the forger. Whoever did it will think of a million ways they could have screwed up. That's why I hate to lie or do anything on the sneak. Because if you do, you must always be thinking you loused up *somewhere*. They'll get antsy and do something."

"Okay. So we start spreading the word. I could tell Ann and Tish, probably."

"And I'll tell Brendan, somehow, and Shelly. You could tell Lorraine, although I don't seriously think she had anything to do with it."

"You never know. She had a key. All the 'keys' get the story. But it'll have to be subtle. I'll say something like, 'It looks like there's been a break in the case—nothing I can discuss, of course—a new development that revealed the identity of the killer. Even Nikki is pleased with the way the police are handling it.' So they'll know it's not you being blamed. 'An arrest is imminent . . .'" He supplied the appropriate body language.

"Look at this. He's an actor!"

He blushed. To cover up his embarrassment, he harped on me. "Well, we'll have to act a little bit, Nikki. You too, you know. Don't just walk in and make an announcement! Let them know this is all on the QT. 'Very few people know about this.'" He rolled his eyes. "*Very* few. Just hint at it, really. Subtlety. That's what we're after here."

"But what he really wants to do is *direct*."

We both laughed. Things were looking up.

22

We *went right about* our nefarious deeds as soon as we returned to civilization.

I dropped Brendan a note—not through the postal service; I didn't want this to take a year. I stuck it right in his mailbox. A friendship card. It was a movie still, a picture of Bogie in *Casablanca*, looking longingly out a window with that wonderful sad Bogie face of his. Inside the card it said, "Do I miss you? Hell yes." And I *did* miss Brendan too, that mother-fucker! It better turn out he had nothing to do with this murder! And that he was just being his usual paranoid, psychotic self, worrying about the police arresting him. But back to the matter at hand—setting traps. Ineptly, probably. I inscribed:

> Just wanted you to know I'm all better. The doctors diagnosed everything expertly. You were right. I was underestimating them. But it seems they do know their business after all. I understand they're all set to cure somebody else with the same thing I had, only much worse. I don't know who though. But at least we don't have to worry about little *me* anymore. They tell me it was *my* cure that's going to help them cure the other person, but good!
>
> Fondly,
> Attila the Hun

I knew he'd recognize my writing.
Well, I don't know how subtle that was, but when I called

Shelly as soon as I got home, I knew subtlety wasn't going to get me anywhere. She was already so subdued that I'd have to hit her over the head with a mallet just to get her attention. I dropped a million hints that went right over her head. "I heard the police are making real progress with the case." "Really? That's nice." "I heard there's been a real big breakthrough." "That's good." "Don't dare mention this to anybody, but I heard—" "Did you see Tish at that funeral? Honestly! That girl! Laughing and carrying on like it was a party! Do you think that's right? *I* don't. And that—*person* she was with! Did you hear that cough?! You think she would have *left* instead of *disrupting* everything like that. I mean, really! Wouldn't you have left? I certainly would have left. That wasn't right. I know she wasn't doing it on purpose but . . . It *was* a woman, wasn't it?"

"Yes! Shelly! I meant to ask you! Did you know Tish was queer?" (Well, my dear . . . !)

"I kind of suspected, to tell you the truth. I kind of had my suspicions."

"You *did?* You never told me!"

"Didn't I? Didn't we talk about this once already?"

"No! Never!"

"I thought we did. You know what must have happened? I must have been *planning* to talk to you about it. You know, practicing what I was going to say? Fantasizing the conversation, in other words. Do you ever do that? Well, sometimes you almost think you already *had* the conversation. Afterwards."

"Well, we didn't."

"Oh. Well, let's have it now. I've already got my part all planned. Hahahahaha."

"Yeah, so?"

"Well, it started about a year ago. Joe mentioned a few things to me about Tish's 'friend.' 'Tish and her friend are going to be away for a couple of weeks, so don't send the check yet.' That kind of thing. The last thing was 'Tish and her friend are going to redecorate, so if there's bills from department stores, that's why.' So I finally asked him. 'Who's this friend of Tish's?' He told me her name. What is it, Harold or something?"

"Hahahahahaha. Alex!"

"Right! Alex! So I said, 'It's a man, you mean?' And he said, real disgusted-like, 'Sort of.' So at first I thought it was a queer guy! Tish would live with a queer guy, don't you think? She's the type. Spend all their time decorating together. She's such a waste, that girl. Anyway, eventually I came to the conclusion that Alex was female. I think we got a GYN bill of hers. So right away, I said, I betcha Alex is a *girl*."

"Very clever."

"Hahahahahahaha. So it's true? Alex is a girl?"

"I'm pretty sure."

"Hahahaha. Yeah. She probably is. A queer guy would look more feminine. That Tish is such a lost cause. Okay. So now I'll remember we definitely had this conversation and I didn't just imagine it."

"Shelly, you are too much."

"Really? Heh, heh, heh, heh. Why? Oh! I forgot something! See? I must still have it in my mind we *talked* about this already."

"What?"

"*What* what?"

"What did you forget?"

"Oh. I think Tish is *bi*."

"Bisexual?"

"No, bicoastal! *Of course* bisexual!"

"Why do you say that?"

"Because we got another GYN bill and it was for Tish! It said D and C, but I think it was an abortion!"

"Why do you say that? It could have been a D and C."

"No. Because this bill didn't just come to Joe's office, like all the rest of her bills do. She *handed* me this bill, personally. Asked me if it was possible to have it paid without bothering Joe about it. So how come all of a sudden she doesn't want to bother Joe? She bothers him for everything else! It was an abortion, trust me. I think what she really wanted, accidentally on purpose, was that Joe should find out, from me. Make herself look more pathetic. Well, she got fooled, because I never told Joe. I mean why should I hurt him like that?"

"Hurt him?"

"Yeah. If it was his kid?"

"You think she got pregnant from him?"

"Well, she didn't get pregnant from Alex, I don't care if she does smoke cigars. And besides, I'm not naïve, like some people I could mention, *Nikki!* I never had any illusions that I was the only one Joe was sleeping with. And Tish was always so accommodating to him! After all, he was a *man*. Why shouldn't he let himself be seduced? No skin off his teeth. But I didn't tell him about the abortion. First of all, it was told to me in confidence, sort of, and much as I dislike Tish, I wouldn't break a confidence."

"You just told me, didn't you?"

"That's different. You're not going to tell anyone, are you?"

"No."

"See? And second of all, I think abortions are criminal! At least they should be. People talk about them so lightly now, as if it's nothing. I would never have an abortion. Would you? Killing your own child! It's just crazy!"

"Now, this conversation we *did* have."

"We did?"

"Yes. When you were trying to get me to vote for Reagan."

"You didn't, did you?"

"No. I don't vote at all. As someone smarter than I once said, it only encourages them."

"Oh, I love to vote. It's one of the most exciting days of the year to me. I vote in all the elections, not just the Presidential ones. So anyway, that's why I think Tish is bi. Now that really *is* the end of this conversation. I said everything I planned."

"Wait a minute! I was telling you something."

"Really? What?"

"About the police case! About new developments. About how it's all very hush-hush."

"Ohhhhh, right. So? Go ahead."

"Well, there have been new developments. But it's all very hush-hush."

"Uh-huh." She was humoring me, giving me a chance to talk now.

"I think an arrest is imminent. I think the police are really closing in on the killer now."

"Uh-huh."

"Uh-huh?! Don't you even want to know *who*?"

"Oh, all right. Who?"

"*I* don't know."

"Well . . . isn't that what you were telling me?"

"No! I was just *hinting* . . . I mean I was just saying . . ."

"Ohhh, you want *me* to find out? Gee, I don't know, Nikki. Nobody ever tells me anything. But I'll keep my ears open in case I hear anything, okay?"

I sighed deeply. I was some lousy interrogator.

"Okay."

"Well, thanks for calling. And call again soon. It'd be nice if we could get together once in a while, you know?"

"Yes, Shell. We will."

"Okay. Bye now. And thanks for calling and telling me all about the police. I'll never get over the way that girl coughed like that. She should have left if she knew that was going to happen. I hope we get together soon. I'm still so depressed over this. Well, look, I can't spend all day talking on the phone. I have *work* to do. Bye."

And then they tell me *I'm* crazy.

A little while later Bob called to tell me that he too had spread the word, to Ann and to Tish and even to Lorraine, who was already back in California.

"I think you're right about Lorraine," he said. "I think we can safely eliminate her as a suspect. All my teasing little hints fell on deaf ears. She seemed oblivious."

"Shelly, too. What about Ann and Tish? What was their reaction?"

"Guarded. Yeah, I would definitely say guarded."

I told Bob I had left a note for Brendan.

"Well, there's nothing to do now but wait," he said. "For what, I don't know. We're expecting this person to explode like a volcano and I have a feeling we won't even hear a firecracker pop."

"Time will tell," I said, and we hung up.

By nine o'clock that night, the ground began to quake. Faint tremors only, but encouraging. Tish called to invite me to lunch the following day. And to pump me for information, no doubt. I agreed happily.

"I can't wait to see you!" she enthused. "I have so much to tell you about the burial!"

Oh, spare me, God!

"Did you hear what Ann said?"

"About what?"

"Why, about you, silly!" How come she still had that lovely Southern drawl when she'd lived in New Yawk for almost twenty years? Some people have all the luck. "You mean you didn't hear yet?"

"Hear what? WHAT'D SHE SAY? WHAT'D SHE SAY?!"

"Ooooouuuuu. Hahahahaha. I'll tell you all about it tomorrow. This ought to be a real *hoot*, this ladies' luncheon. I love superstraight things like that, don't you, honey? Ladies' luncheons and such."

"In that case, how 'bout if I invite Shelly, too? Would you mind if I asked her along? She sounds a little lonely."

She thought for a moment. "All right. Why not? She can corroborate what I'm going to tell you, and it's an earful, believe you me. Honey, you are just going to want to kill that Ann. About twoish?"

"Fine."

"Shall I call Shelly or will you?"

"I will."

"Okay. And wear something ladies' luncheonish, all right? Let's go all out. We'll dress up, too. Me and Alex. It'll be a hoot!"

We hung up and then I called Shelly.

"At Tish's house? Tomorrow? What time?"

"Around two."

"Gee, I don't know."

"Why not?"

"Because, why would I want to go there? I *hate* Tish."

"Ah, come on. We're going to talk about old times."

"Oh. All right. I'm supposed to go help Ann with a few things, but that's just in the morning. She's going out in the afternoon, too. Why don't you pick me up here and we'll go over by taxi. It'll be cheaper."

"Okay. Oh, and look proper."

"What?"

"Look proper. Tish wants us all to dress like ladies. Even Alex."

"That Tish! She's such a moron."

When I picked Shelly up the next day, we both said, almost at the same time, "You look *nice*."

I wore a navy linen suit with a matching straw hat that had a ridiculously wide, stiff brim. Also, navy and white spectator pumps and a fake red carnation in my lapel. St. Agatha's Ladies' Auxiliary would have been proud of me. I looked like someone who would buy at least two raffle books.

Shelly wore a dark brown print dress that would have felt completely at home on Dame Edith May Whitty. Fortunately, Shelly's figure was so zaftig that the outfit wasn't a complete disaster. It was, like everything else she wore, a little quaint. Genteel, old-lady quaint.

She was carrying a dead cat.

"Oh!" she said. "You're wearing a hat! Should I wear a hat too? Although I have my stole. I don't want to look too 'done.' What do you think?"

"I think the stole is plenty," I said.

"Well, come in for a minute, while I put it on." I followed her into the apartment. While she primped in front of the mirror, situating the dead—cat—stole this way and that on her shoulder blades, I looked around. There had been some changes since I last saw the place. At least half the memorabilia collection was gone.

"You thought it was strange, didn't you?" she said, smiling almost shyly. "Peculiar. Me saving all that stuff."

"No!"

"Oh yes, you did. I could tell. I guess it did look a little peculiar. Like a shrine or something! I didn't realize it myself till I saw it through someone else's eyes. Yours, as it turned out. It probably looked so eccentric."

"So you just threw it all away?"

"No, not all of it. I do, after all, want some mementos. And there's other stuff I still have around the house, too, things that I use, though. Like I have a beautiful pillowcase from the Ritz Hotel in Paris. I use that all the time, so I'm certainly not going to throw that out. I guess I'll keep things like that. But all the rest of it, the knickknacks and stuff . . . well, it's probably not that healthy to keep that stuff around."

Pillowcases, eh? Pillowcases! From the *Ritz!* That bum! That fuck! And when I think of how I *believed* that lying bastard. . . !

"Well, shall we be off?" Shelly inquired, the picture of innocence, knowing *damn well* she had just zapped me one.

"Sure."

We took a taxi and split the fare. I wondered what it cost to spend a night at the Ritz. And he told me they were there for museum stuff. Well, then, how come she took the pillowcase, huh? Huh?

23

So we sat around Tish's new dining room table—the house looked very nice—and had our ladies' luncheon. Vichyssoise and little finger sandwiches. We were ripping everybody apart and having a fine old time.

"So that's who she's going to marry. He looks kind of insipid in person. I thought Lorraine had better taste than that."

"Ah, why? He's cute. Did you think he was cute, Nikki?"

"Yeah. He's cute. And she's cute. They're such a cute couple."

"Oh, come on! A little too cute. They're both so short!" Tish said. "They're going to look like the little bride and groom dolls on top of the wedding cake."

Cackle, cackle, cackle.

"And did you see What's-her-name? Don't tell *me* she's not still on the sauce. Did you see those eyes?"

"Ahh, they're all loaded half the time, that whole Washington bunch. That's why they don't want cameras in the Senate!"

"But did you see that young one? *Oooooo* Lordy! What is he, a Congressman or something? What a bod!" (This, from Tish. Apparently, she *was* bi.) "Is that legal to have a body like that?" She bit her lip in frustration and proceeded to make appreciative sounds.

"Yeah, he's a Congressman," Shelly offered. "I voted for him last year."

"I don't blame you, honey. I vote for him, too."

"Was he too much? Those shoulders!"

"And he knew it, too. Did you see the way he moved? Stud city!" Tish again. "And that suit was just tailored to perfection," she drawled. "Those pants? You just couldn't help but notice that de*light*ful bulge! . . . Ohhh, baby!"

"*Tish!*"

"Oh, Tish!"

"Hehehehehe. Well, could you now? Admit it, ladies. How could you *help* but notice? I mean, the man was blessed, let's face it."

"Well, *I* certainly didn't look!" Shelly blushed. "I mean I saw a little but . . ." We all laughed. At least three of us did. The fourth didn't look any too happy. I guess she was jealous. Alex opened her mouth to say something but only got as far as, "Are we? . . . ah-hem . . . ah-hem . . . ah-*hem* . . . a frog! . . . Ah-hemmmmm . . . cough, cough . . . a *frog!* . . . Cough . . . woooah . . . Woooah . . . in my *throat* . . ." Oh-oh. Her eyebrows looked very worried.

We braced ourselves. The storm struck.

There ensued the clatter of silverware, the rattling of china, and the shattering of glass. Oh, I know she apologized for knocking over that wineglass when she was pounding the table, but don't tell *me*. It was breaking the *sound barrier* that shattered it. When the storm passed, Satchmo said, "As I was about to say, are we going to discuss *politics* all day or what?" And we all keeled over laughing, including Alex.

Then Tish said, "Hey! No one's told Nikki what Ann said yet, right?"

"Right," I said.

The three of them all of a sudden got quiet.

"Well? So tell me! What'd she say?"

They all exchanged glances.

"Well? Out with it!" I looked at Shelly.

"Don't look at *me*," she said. "I'm certainly not going to tell you."

"Tish? Come on! Tish'll tell me. Tish? Let's hear it."

"Oh, why even bother?"

"TISH!"

"Oh, all right." She told me. I heard it and pondered. Then I said, "I'm sorry. I don't believe it. I don't believe any female over the age of twelve could use the word *slut* with a straight face! I just don't believe it."

Tish gasped. "You don't think I could make that *up*, do you?" Outrage. Raising her right hand. "May God strike me dead! . . ."

"You mean she actually . . ."

"Shelly? You were there. *You* tell her. I don't know why you'd think I made something like that *up* . . ."

"I don't think you made it *up*, I just find it hard to believe that a grown woman would . . ."

"Tell her, Shelly!"

Shelly nodded solemnly, not looking up. "It's true."

"What'd she say, exactly! Let SHELLY tell me."

"Just what Tish said she said. She said, 'I don't understand how a slut like that has the nerve to walk into a church.' Oh, and weren't you afraid of getting struck by lightning, considering your disgraceful, degenerate life-style."

"*Oouuu*, that's right!" Tish enthused. "I even *forgot* that part. The *disgraceful, degenerate* part."

"I didn't hear her say that," Alex offered. "I heard the *degenerate* part, but I didn't hear *disgraceful*."

"Well, she said both," Tish said. Let's get this very clear.

"It's true," Shelly verified.

"Wait a minute! Wait a minute!" I said, "Maybe she wasn't even talking about me! Maybe she was talking about somebody else entirely! I mean there were enough there that it could *apply* to." It was understood: present company excluded.

The three of them shook their heads purposefully.

"She meant you, all right, Nikki," Tish said. "Names were mentioned."

"She mentioned my *name*! She called me a degenerate by *name*?"

"It's true," Shelly said.

"*I'LL SUE HER. I'LL SUE! I'LL SUE!*"

"She asked the good senator's wife, 'Did you see that awful Nikki Andrews person?' Et cetera, et cetera."

"*OOOOUUUUUU. I'LL SUE!*"

Tish giggled merrily. "And she made sure we were in earshot before she said it. Didn't she, Shelly?"

"It's true."

"She turned around and looked at us both, right in the face, and then she said it like she wanted to make *sure* we heard it. She *wanted* it to get back to you."

"It's true."

"*WOULD YOU STOP SAYING, 'IT'S TRUE,' LIKE SOME KIND OF BROKEN RECORD?*"

Shelly gasped. "Well, what *should* I say? It *is* true."

"Aw. She's upset, Shelly."

"*I'LL KILL HER! I'LL KILL HER!*"

They all gave cynical chortles, like that was a desire devoutly to be wished, but they knew I was probably full of shit.

After a moment, Shelly said, "You shouldn't say something like that. Even in jest."

"Who's jesting?"

"No, you really shouldn't, Nikki. I mean, God forbid something should happen to *Ann* now. We *see* how peculiar things can happen in real life. It's nothing to say things like that in front of us, but if you go around saying things like that in front of other people, and then something happens to Ann, people will think . . ."

"Aw, fuck people!" Tish opined. "She's got every right to say whatever she damn pleases. After what that bitch said about her? Right, Nikki?"

"I'd just like to tell her off. Just ONCE."

"So? Why don't you?"

"How? Believe me, she's going to make sure there's plenty of distance between her and me from now on. I'll never get anywhere *near* her."

197

"So, surprise her!" Tish said.

I immediately thought, like you surprised Joe? Was I actually accomplishing what I set out to do at this luncheon? Finding things out?

"Sneak up on her somewhere," Tish continued. "Take her by surprise."

"Where? I don't know where she goes. What am I supposed to do? Lurk in the doorways of Saks indefinitely and just leap out at her one day?"

"No, silly. Go to some social occasion she's at. Tell her off in front of everybody! Humiliate the shit out of her!"

Tish would definitely enjoy it if that other will had been found and made public, with Joe leaving everything to me and thereby humiliating Ann. Tish would definitely get a charge out of that. So much so that she had written it herself? She might have pulled it off. Forgery was probably a lot like drawing the person's handwriting. Tish was an artist, wasn't she?

"I don't want to humiliate her," I said.

"We know," Shelly said. "You want to kill her. We thought maybe you'd settle for just humiliating her." Laughter all around.

"No, really, I don't. I'm willing to tell her off all by her lonesome. I just want *her* to know."

"I think that was a good idea about suing her. Right, Alex?" Tish asked. "As long as you don't really have your heart into making a terrible public scene. Sue her. That's more refined, anyway."

"And then Nikki would have some money *too*," Alex pointed out. Like they both did now, from the paintings?

"That's right!" Tish said. "Sue her for a bundle! I'll testify! We both will. Right, Alex? We both heard her. Defamation of character! *We'll* testify!"

"Well, I didn't hear her say *disgraceful*. I only heard her say the slut part and the degenerate part."

"Oh, would you stop nitpicking?" Tish turned back to me.

"And she certainly could afford to pay off a lawsuit *now.* With what Joe's probably left her?"

Was Tish baiting *me?*

Dopey Shelly jumped for the hook.

"Joe didn't leave anything to Ann! Don't you know that? The whole will was practically in the papers. Didn't you read it?"

"I don't read that establishment crap! All I know is *my* part of the will, which Bob told me about. Which I think we'll all agree I have every right to?"

Well, we wouldn't all agree, but Shelly let it pass. Instead she said, "Joe left almost everything to charity, Tish. Other than your allotment, I mean. He didn't leave anything to Ann."

"Well, she could still afford to pay off a lawsuit! And don't you dare settle out of court, Nikki! The whole point is to humiliate her publicly!"

Was Tish merely being a good actress? I could swear she wasn't bluffing, that she knew nothing whatever about that other will. I decided to test it out.

"But what about that *other* www—" fumble, stammer, look around embarrassed. "Oh, dear . . . uh . . . never mind."

Sorry, Marlon, there goes your theory. Not everybody knows how to act.

"That other *what?*" It was Tish. She *was* baiting me.

"Hmmm?"

"You said, 'What about that other . . .' That other *what?*"

"Oh. Er . . . nothing. Something the police uncovered. I don't really know that much about it. All I know is *I'm* not a suspect anymore. Thank God! But somebody else sure is. I don't know who. But I have a feeling they're going to arrest somebody very soon."

"Bob said almost the same thing yesterday," Tish said. "I must say, you're both being very mysterious about it. What's going on?"

"I really don't know. I shouldn't even talk about it."

"To us?" Tish said, incredulous.

"All I know is they've found something, or they've traced something, or something! I wouldn't be surprised if they arrested someone *today,* from what I heard."

"Really?" Shelly said, as if waking up from a long sleep. "They're going to arrest someone?"

"I told you! Yesterday!"

"Me? You told me? You did not. You must have imagined it. You never told me—ohhh, wait a minute. I remember. You were talking about the police, weren't you. I thought you wanted *me* to find out . . ."

"Go back to sleep, Shelly."

She laughed and blushed a little bit, as was her way when kidded about her vagueness. "That's because I really don't care about that whole part of it. Who did it or why or whatever. Bad enough it was done. Most of the time it's some lunatic who just wants to get his name in the newspapers anyhow. That's why they do it. Just to get famous. So I make it a point not to follow up on things like that. At least *I* won't know their name. I think we should do what they do in Canada. When that guy killed John Lennon? They never even published his name in Canada. They told all about the case, of course, but they never printed his name. I think that's what we should do here, too, instead of making celebrities of them."

"That's right!" Alex said.

"Oh, who cares about all that," Tish said impatiently. "Let's go back to talking about Ann. So what are you going to do? Sue her, kill her, or tell her off?"

"Tell her off. Hide in Bendel's and pounce!"

"As it happens, girls . . ." Shelly said, leaning forward in her seat. (Well, my dears . . .) "I happen to know where Ann is at this very moment. Where you could go and pounce, Nikki."

"WHERE?" Tish demanded.

"At Rutece. Having lunch. With the girls. Just like us."

"REALLY?"

"No, Tish. Forget it," I said.

"Why THE HELL not? Oh, I always knew you were all talk and no action, Nikki. I knew you'd be chickenshit to tell her off, ever."

"I would not."

"Well then? Come on! What's the matter? We're just going there for a few drinks! That's all. Women go out in the afternoon for a few drinks, don't they? Why can't we? I'll *treat*, damn it."

"Count me out," Shelly said. I could see Tish already did. But I didn't.

"Well, that settles it," I said. "Either we all go or nobody goes."

"You mean you'd really go?" Tish practically squealed in anticipation. "I knew I could count on you. I knew you were a ballsy dame. Well, Shelly, you have to come now. You heard her. If you go, she'll go."

Shelly thought. "I don't know. That's going to look like a very funny coincidence, us showing up there when I knew she'd be there. She's bound to think we did it on purpose."

"So? Who cares what that old fart thinks?" Tish inquired. "What do you care what Ann thinks—now?" She meant, with Joe gone.

Shelly pondered that for a moment. She took so *damned long* for everything. Finally, she said, "You're right!" She sounded as if she surprised herself. "I *don't* care what Ann thinks anymore!"

"Fantastic!" Tish said. "So? What are we waiting for? Let's go!"

So, after much freshening up and reapplying of lipsticks and repowdering of noses and recombing of hair and re-straightening of skirts, and amid the loud clatter of high heels on newly polished floors, we went.

24

The restaurant looked exactly the way a good restaurant ought to look. Totally intimidating. At least to poor slobs like me. The aura of money was everywhere. I tried to make myself comfortable, regardless. Tish wouldn't let me.

"Well? What are you waiting for? Go ahead!"

"Wait a minute, would you please?"

"These are *good*. What are they called again?"

"Black Russians, Shelly. Black Russians. They've been 'out' about ten years now."

"Really? That's a shame. They're delicious."

"What are you *waiting* for? She's going to be finished taking her crap and be out here again! Would you hurry up?!"

"*Wait* a minute, would you please? Let me practice what I'm going to say."

"See? You do it, too! And you acted like it was so strange when I told you I practiced conversations ahead of time. These are so *delicious* that . . ."

"She's going to come walking out of there, I know it. Would you go?!"

"Oh, all right! I'm going."

There was no one in the john when I went in there, except the attendant. That's because the john was a whole apartment of rooms. I went past the entranceway into the powder room. The attendant smiled at me and I smiled back. I worried if I already owed her a tip. I went into the toilets. Surprise! It was just *another* powder room, this one with full length mirrors. I guess so you could make sure there wasn't a stream of toilet paper stuck to your shoe when you came out of the toilets. There was no one in there either. I opened one more door, thinking there better be toilet bowls in here or I'm giving up.

There were. Nice big cubicles, too. I guess rich people give themselves a wide berth. I stopped and listened. Not that I expected to hear Ann Pender "grunting out a large turd," as Erica Jong once so aptly put it. I just listened for regular ladylike sounds. I heard humming! That looney-tunes was humming in there! Boy, was she crazy! Sure! Why shouldn't she hum? She committed a murder and everything was turning out just like she planned. Well, no more now! I peeked under the partitions and saw a pair of sensible shoes. It had to be the Pender dame. I went back into the outer-outer powder room and handed the matron a $10 bill.

"I'd like to speak privately to my friend in there for a moment. Would you mind waiting outside? It won't take but a minute." The matron hesitated for a moment, then decided, why the hell not? and left.

I waited.

She was still humming as she passed the full-length mirrors. I sat at one of the little chairs in front of the mirrored vanities, performing my toilette. I would be able to see her enter the room behind me in the reflection of the mirror.

When she came in and saw me sitting there, she jumped visibly. She regained her presence of mind a second later. I could see her debating. Should she walk right past me? Why give me that satisfaction? She had lipstick to put on! No need to change her plans because of *me*.

She sat down a little bit aways from me and started primping.

"Hello, Ann."

Again, a visible jump. She hesitated. Should she ignore me altogether? No, I was a crazy person. Ignoring me altogether might stir my insane wrath. She gave me the barest minimum of a nod.

"How ya been?"

"Fine." Not looking at me. Making it very clear she is not hot for any little chitchat.

"No *and you*?" I said. Listen, I was chomping at the bit for a set-to with this one. Subtlety was gone with the wind. "Humph!" I said.

She was getting really nervous. Maybe I wasn't just walking-around-crazy. Maybe I was *crazy*-crazy. She looked even more pop-eyed than usual. Discretion being the better part of valor, she said, "And you?"

"Me? Oh, same as usual." Slut, eh? Afraid to be hit by lightning, eh? I'll give her *slut*. "I must say, you're looking well though. Downright foxy, if you ask me." She gave me this so-who-asked-you? look, then remembered I might not have all my marbles and said, "Why, thank you." She got up, about to leave.

"*Wait* a minute. Where you running off to? Don't you like to shoot the breeze with an old friend every once in a while?"

Old friend! She looked aghast.

"I'd love to," Acid Annie said, "but I really have to be going. Perhaps some other time."

"*Wait* a minute," I said, the epitome of joviality. "I wanna *talk* to you." That last part didn't sound quite so jovial. It sounded like I wanted to punch her lights out. Good! Let it sound like that.

She laughed slightly, her bitter, superior-sounding laugh. I was being *such* a child. Like that.

"Listen, Nikki, if you're looking for some sort of unpleasant scene, I'm afraid you're going to be disappointed. I have neither the time nor the inclination to indulge you in that sort of thing. I'm sure that's your forte, but—"

"You want to talk unpleasant scenes? *I'll* give you unpleasant scenes! Like Joe, in that alley. That was one hell of an unpleasant scene."

"Oh, Nikki." Like, how low could I get? "Is this necessary?"

"I'm afraid it is, Ann. I'm afraid it is. You see, I know it wasn't suicide. I *know* it was murder."

"I'm sure you do. In fact I'm really very shocked that you're still at liberty. I didn't know they let murder suspects walk around unleashed."

"I guess you'll find out soon enough. When they come to slap the cuffs on you."

She really laughed then. "Now, why on earth would they do that?"

"Because now I'm not the only one who knows you did it. The police know it too."

"Yes, I heard all about what you told the police. Did you really think they would put any credence into anything someone like *you* would tell them? Someone who makes her living in a very questionable manner, someone who has no respect for the legal institution of marriage, someone who—"

"Was it you who told them all those terrible things about me? I knew it! How could you *dare* to—"

"I told only the truth!" I stared at her in amazement. Could it be she actually believed that? Could it be she actually thought she told them the truth about me? A more horrifying thought crossed my mind. What if she wasn't the murderer? What if she was just someone who was a little big priggish and not too bright? That would mean I was bullying an innocent person. A not-too-bright innocent person! Oh God, how awful. But I couldn't just give up now. Oh God, no wonder police get so callous! It's awful trying to find stuff like this out.

"Okay, so you told them the truth," I said. "And I told them the truth. And then they went and found out the truth all on their own. And somebody's about to be arrested. And my money's on *you*." Oh, how I'd hate myself if it turned out she was innocent. But how come she was hanging around for this whole rap? Why didn't she leave five minutes ago?

The door opened, and a sweet little silver-haired lady

walked resolutely into the powder room. It was then I discovered what three hundred mil in the bank could do to the human voice.

"Leave, please! We want privacy."

You had to hear that pompous, arrogant voice! Like that old woman had some goddamned nerve wanting to use the bathroom in the *first* place. Without even hesitating, that lady turned on her heels and walked out, without so much as a backwards glance. I was sure Ann had been issuing such orders since birth, right from her little bassinet. I looked at her. Yeah, she was dumb, all right, dumb like a fox. When she looked back at me, her eyes were as hard and lifeless as a doll's.

"Now, what is this you're running on about?" she said.

Yeah, she did it all right. Don't tell *me*. Otherwise, I'd have been left standing there talking to my own reflection by now.

"I was running on about your imminent arrest. And *this* time, Annie, old bean, not all the king's horses and all the king's men are going to be able to—"

"Nikki, Nikki, Nikki." A superior, bitter laugh. "Your allegations didn't make any sense two weeks ago. They make even less sense now. I would strongly advise you to refrain from saying such things to the police in the future. I overlooked it the first time, but I assure you I will not overlook it a second time. If you bother the police with any more of your absurd 'theories'—and we *do* know why you're doing it, don't we, Nikki?"

"Doing what?"

"Pursuing this so relentlessly! Showing up almost daily with some sort of 'clue' or other. Lieutenant Morrisey thinks you're quite amusing, actually, in a depressing sort of way."

"No. Why am I doing this? You tell me!"

"At first I thought it was yet another manifestation of your very unhealthy narcissism. And I'm using *narcissism* as a psychiatric term here. Those who suffer from it feel they must deal effectively with absolutely every aspect of their lives, the basic neurosis being a dangerous overestimation of their capabilities." (I was getting interested.) "It's fairly common among artists and so called 'creative' people," she said. "It generally requires in-depth analysis for a number of years under the care of a proficient psychiatrist. Although I doubt in *your* case, considering the severity of the problem, even in-depth analysis—"

"Oh, goody! We're going to talk about *me*."

She sighed. Was it worth her time to even explain it to me? Apparently, it was, because she continued.

"However, I have come to realize it is more than that. More than your simply feeling responsible for everyone and everything. What it actually is, Nikki, is that you are making a very feeble, very pathetic attempt to convince yourself that my late husband had some real feeling for you."

Wow! She was good! No *wonder* Joe was so addicted to her criticism. She was positively masterful! It's always a pleasure to watch a master at work. Wasn't she terrific at it? Right to the jugular! My mouth dropped open in admiration. She knew a captive audience when she saw one and went on.

"You don't really care who murdered him and who didn't. You're snooping into everyone's business and sticking yourself in places you have no right to be because you're trying to unravel *another* mystery. Did my late husband have any feelings at all for you? Well, that's one mystery we can solve right here. With a loud, resounding, and definite *no!* A moment ago, you accused me of telling the police, quote, terrible things, unquote, about you. Perhaps my impression of you *is* wrong, I really don't know. But I do know this. It is an impression based totally and completely on things I heard Joe say about you many, many times. I didn't fabricate this impression of you out of thin air, Nikki, although I'm sure that's what you'd like to believe."

"Naaaa," I said—sarcastically, I hoped. "You got it from *him*."

"That's exactly right. Now if you'll excuse me . . ."

WHY DID I BURN THAT DAMNED WILL? WHATEVER
MADE ME BURN THAT WILL? It would have been WORTH a
prison rap—it would have been worth THE CHAIR! WHY DID
I BURN THAT DAMN WILL? Oh, if only I had it right here in
my pocketbook to throw in her self-satisfied face right now!
Hey, wait a minute. *She* didn't know I burned the will.

"So how come—" I singsonged.

She stopped in her tracks and turned around, bored but tol-
erant.

"So how come," I continued, "he made me sole beneficiary? In that other will? In that other will that nobody knows
about yet."

Now what was she going to say? "*I* wrote that will,
sucker?"

As it turned out, she didn't say anything. She was laughing
too hard. It's a good thing she had already been to the john or
she might have had an accident. When she caught her breath,
she just kept saying, "Sole beneficiary? Hahahaha. Sole beneficiary!" Then she said, "I'm sorry, Nikki. But you really do get
a little too ridiculous sometimes. But I shouldn't laugh. I'm
sure you take all this very seriously. *But*, be it known that if
you *dare* to submit some sort of bogus will, you'll find yourself
in some very serious legal trouble. So why don't you just go
home and forget all about *that* idea. I suspected right from the
beginning you would claim some sort of common law status."

"It *was* you who told the police!"

"I'm sure, Nikki, that cleverer minds than yours will attempt the very same thing. Joe's proclivities in regard to
women have long been a source of embarrassment to me. I
have no doubt there will be many such claims regarding wills.
And they'll have no more success at it than you would have
had. Hahahahahahaha." She was still laughing when she got
outside.

The matron came back in and asked if there was anything
else she could do for me. I told her, "Yeah, shoot me and put

me out of my misery." She smiled sweetly and backed away from me.

When I rejoined my group at the bar, Tish said, "Well?"

"Well, what?"

"Did you tell her off?"

"Of course! Didn't you see her crying when she came out of the john?"

"Crying?!" Alex said. "Shows you how much *I* know. I thought she was *laughing.*"

"She was only trying to cover up," I said.

"Oh."

Shelly was sitting there with a happy drunken smile on her face, swaying ever so slightly to and fro.

"This calls for another round, ladies!" Tish announced.

"I guess I'll stick with the Black Russians," Shelly slurred, a paragon of cooperation.

"Don't you think we'd better call it a day?" I said to Tish, gesturing with my head toward Shelly.

"Awwwww," Shelly said. "Why? I'm not tired. All's I need is a little nap. Just about five minutes or so. That would feel *sooo* good. Just let me take a little nap. Right here." She meant on the bar. Her head began to lower.

"No, Shelly. Come on. We're going home."

"Yeah," Tish said, "we might as well. God knows what this fuckin' clip joint is going to rook me for as it is. *Garçon! Le billet, s'il vous plait.*"

On our way out, Tish couldn't bring herself to leave well enough alone. She stopped at Ann's table and said, "Well? I guess that settled *your* hash, eh, Ann?"

The senator's wife looked up inquisitively. Ann said nothing but covered her mouth demurely with her hand in order to laugh up her sleeve.

I held on to Shelly, who had a noticeable wobble. "Hey! There's Ann!" she enthused. "Didn't you want to talk to Ann,

Nikki? 'Cause there she is. Didn't you want to talk to her about something? Or did I just imagine it?"

That night, Bob called. We had been checking in with each other periodically. "Well?" he said. "Did you learn anything today? At lunch with the girls?"

"Yeah. I learned just what I suspected all along. That I need in-depth psychoanalysis."

"Aaah, Ann tells that to everybody. What else happened?"

I told him. When I finished, he said, "Don't worry, Nikki. Something'll break soon."

The next day, it did.

25

First thing in the morning, I went out for some groceries. I was in the mood for salami rollups, with cream cheese and pimiento-stuffed olives in the middle. Coming home from the supermarket, I saw the headlines at the newsstand and nearly dropped my bags. The *Daily News* headline read: SAVANAH DEATH—MURDER OR SUICIDE?

The *Post* was a little more direct. It showed the picture of a black man, just his face, in closeup. It covered almost the whole front page. The man's eyes were closed. But it didn't look like he was sleeping or meditating or something. It looked like he was dead. He was. The caption said: SAVANAH'S KILLER FOUND DEAD. I bought both papers, plus the *Times*, and began reading right there on the street, my grocery bags at my feet.

"An unidentified source in the police department today revealed," the *News* said, "that new facts pertaining to Joe Savanah's death have come to light, facts that indicate his death may have been murder, and not suicide, as was previously believed."

To make a short story long, they were going to pin it on this poor dead black junkie, is what they were going to do. The police, that is. It was a robbery, the theory was, and Mr. Savanah had apparently caught the junkie in the act and got killed for his trouble. Possessions belonging to Mr. Savanah were found in said junkie's apartment. Said junkie met his demise by means of an OD, having recently acquired the bread for this fatal dose of dope by fencing other valuables stolen from Mr. Savanah's apartment.

When asked about these new developments, Mrs. Savanah, the former Ann Pender, wife of the deceased, offered no comment. Asked if this altered her previous conviction that the death had been a suicide, Mrs. Savanah replied, "I'm very grateful for the wonderful work being done by the New York City Police Department. Their handling of the case has been thorough and exemplary." It is expected that Mrs. Savanah will release a more detailed statement later today, through a spokesman.

The provisions of the Savanah will have already been made public. It is not expected that these new findings will in any way alter those provisions.

I high-tailed it right home, as fast as my short little legs could carry me.

"Well?"

"Well?"

"Well, something *happened*, Bob!"

"Yeah, but what?"

"I don't know!"

"What the hell does *this* mean now?"

"*I* don't know."

"Neither do *I*."

"It must mean something!"

"Yeah, but what?"

"I don't know!"

"Man! Between the two of us . . ." Bob said into the phone.

"I know!"

"Well, let's *think*."

"Okay, let's *think*."

We thought.

"Well?"

"Well, *what?*"

"What'd you think?"

"Nothing!"

"Me too. All right, we take it one at a time," Bob said. "One way or another, at least this will cut down on our suspects. Right? Not too many people would have the clout to engineer *this*, right?"

"Right!"

"Okay. The most obvious one. Ann."

"Yeah!"

"All right, you talked to her yesterday and she laughed so hard she almost peed in her pants. Excuse me. You know what I mean."

"Yes."

"Okay, regardless of the laughing, she was very freaked out when she got back here yesterday. I thought it was just from *seeing* you, but okay, maybe your message did take effect." (Bob was living out in Bedford Falls right now, at Ann's. He had his own apartment in Queens somewhere, but he used to live with Joe and Ann when they were married. After they split up, he moved out, of course. But he'd gone back there after it happened, because it was just easier to deal with the lawyers and the will and everything else from there. And also to help Ann in her time of need.) "Okay, so the message hits its mark, let's say, and she doesn't waste any time. She gets on the phone right away, with some bigwig somewhere and says, 'Solve this damned case *fast.*' So the order goes out, and presto, changeo, what-do-you-know, how-do-you-do, it's solved by this morning."

"But does she *really* have that kind of pull?"

"Are you kidding, or what? You know who was just on this phone? Not ten minutes ago? The Secretary of—"

"*Don't* tell me! I don't want to get involved in all political things! I don't even want to *think* if that junkie was already dead when they found him, or if they maybe decided to treat him to the overdose, to maybe make sure his mouth stayed nice and shut."

"Naaa, listen, there's so many dead junkies every day. All they had to do was match one up with the crime and take it from there. All I know is she's got the pull, believe me."

"Okay. So the police accommodate her and make up this story about the bro. That's one possibility. The one I personally like best myself. But let's be fair. Could it be anybody else?"

"All right, how 'bout Tish?"

"Go 'head."

"She'd know people who could fence things for her."

"You're kidding!"

"She already swiped quite a few things out of Joe's apartment, way before this."

"She *stole*, you mean?"

"Yeah, she'd walk off with a knickknack every once in a while. Joe knew. He laughed about it, that idiot! She'd leave her pot of chili and put a gold cigarette case in her pocketbook. I told Joe he ought to tell her to cut it out, but he said, 'Believe me, in Tish's mind, it's a fair swap!'"

"Gee, I always thought her cooking was good, but not *that* good!" Small joke. Bob ignored it.

"Tish never stopped cashing in on that two-year marriage, so help me God. She still felt like he owed her everything. Her motto was, 'If it's his, it's mine.' She didn't even want the stuff half the time. She was just being a ballbuster. Excuse me. A pain in the ass. The butt."

"Would you stop censoring everything you say? You're making me nervous!"

"She used to sell the stuff! We know because once somebody tried to sell Joe back his own cigarette lighter!" I laughed. "Only to him, things like that could happen," Bob said. "He bought it back, too. That jerk." We both laughed.

"Who tried to sell it to him?"

"Heyyy! A junkie!"

"Heyyy! That's interesting!"

"Yeah! Heyyy, so Tish definitely is a suspect here! This is very discouraging. We got *two* very possible suspects."

"Okay, so let's say, just for the sake of argument . . ."

"You don't have to keep saying things like that, Nikki. 'Let's say . . .' We both understand this is just possibilities. Nothing definite yet."

"Okay. So Tish kills Joe. And maybe lifts a few things from his apartment. Maybe not even that same day. Maybe from before that day. She already has some of his stuff."

"Okay, so then you give her your little speech, new developments, et cetera, and just like we hoped, she gets scared and does something. Sells the stuff to a junkie, maybe even supplies him with the fatal dose, and then calls the police. 'Go look in apartment 3B at such-and-such an address on West 132nd Street and you'll find a nice surprise.' An anonymous call, of course. Did you know that's how most crimes get solved? The ones that do get solved, that is. Plenty don't. Somebody calls up and tells the police who did it! Or even walks right into the precinct. That's a fact. You could look it up."

"I believe you."

"Okay, so that's how she could have pulled this off."

"Well, at least we narrowed it down to two. That's better than the twenty-seven we had before . . ." I said.

"*Wait* a minute. Let's do 'em all."

"Shucks!"

"What about What's-his-face? Bradley?"

"Brendan. Gee, I don't know. He was bragging about some kind of an in he had in the police department. I don't know if he could have engineered this, though he is supposedly some kind of fantastic wheeler-dealer. Financial things, though. Financial finagling."

"So? The cops don't use money, like the rest of us? If he goes to the one corrupt cop in the whole system"—I got hysterical—"and suggests some sort of financial deal that might make it worth this cop's while to plant a little evidence on a dead junkie . . ."

"I don't know. I can't see Brendan doing that. He's afraid of the police. He's very paranoid. He'd be afraid of getting arrested himself. Standing up in front of the Knapp Commission and . . ."

"He's a lawyer, isn't he? He told you himself lawyers know cops. Maybe he came across the one crooked cop in the whole system who he knew damned well wasn't going to arrest him."

"Still. He'd never be *sure.*"

"All right, so maybe he did it surreptitiously. That's the word, right? On the sneak. Like Tish might have done. Planted the stuff himself."

I gasped. "You're right! Brendan knows drug dealers! Boy, does Brendan know drug dealers! He could have gone up to 125th Street and wheeled and dealed a little bit. He's done it before. He definitely could have planted the stuff, up to and included the fatal heroin dose. But wait a minute! Where'd he get Joe's valuables to begin with?"

"This is the second-story man, right? The one who likes to climb in fire escapes?"

"Yeah!"

"So he robbed Joe's place after the murder! The apartment isn't sealed anymore. By the police, I mean. And the security there was always lousy. That's how the killer walked in and out the first time. Most of the time, the front door's not even locked. Although now those tenants are being a little more careful!"

"I bet. Okay, so he went through the fire escape or the roof or whatever, stole a few things, et cetera, et cetera. He would have known the layout of the place, having already been there. Goddamn it!" I didn't want it to be Brendan.

"I know. Another possible," Bob said, misunderstanding me.

"It's just that he was a friend!"

216

"Oh. And also, this list is still staying long, Nikki. We're supposed to be eliminating people. Not proving how they could have *all* done it."

"Could that be it? They *all* did it?"

"Now we're really getting desperate."

"But this is getting impossible. Did you ever see so many people all look so guilty of the same crime? What does this mean?"

"It must mean we mix with a bad element."

"That's just it! They're all such pillars of the community. With the possible exception of Tish. But Ann! Brendan! Lorraine Rice! We didn't even *talk* about Lorraine yet."

"Let's eliminate her, eh? She didn't have anything to do with it."

"You're prejudiced because she's so cute." I just knew Bob thought of Lorraine as a real little doll.

"That's not why! When I called her the other day to set our traps, she offered to pray for me. She started telling me all about the Lord."

"So what? Didn't you ever hear of the Crusades? People do strange things in the name of the Lord! Look at the Moral Majority!"

"I'm Catholic, Nikki. I'd appreciate it if you didn't say anything against religion."

"Ahhh, relax. I used to be Catholic, too. A long time ago, though."

"Hey, that's right. You used to be Italian. I mean I guess you still are. It was the name that threw me off, *Andrews.* It sounds so WASP. What was your real name?"

"DeGeorgio. I kept my married name after my divorce though."

"That's right, DeGeorgio! Now I remember. I bet I know why you kept the WASP name though. 'Cause when people hear a wop name, right away they think Mafioso, right?"

"No, that wasn't it."

"That's what happens to me all the time. People hear De-

Benetto, and right away they think . . . But I never wanted to change it. Let the dopes think what they want. At least that was my real name."

I suddenly remembered where it was that Joe and Bob first became friends. At the Upper Sandusky Home for Orphaned Boys, as they not-so-affectionately called it. The Upper Sandusky part was a joke. That was the fictional name of the hometown in the old Laurel and Hardy flicks. The second part of the name was real enough.

So Bob at least had a birth certificate. Joe didn't. He was literally left on their doorstep when he was about three years old. Which I always considered an enormous pain in the ass, because it meant I could never do Joe's astrological chart! And Joe wasn't too thrilled with it either, although I could never really sympathize that much over the fact that he was an orphan. I mean considering *my* relatives, it didn't strike me as any great tragedy not to have any relatives *at all*. Anyway, Joe picked out his own name when he was eighteen, had it legally changed and all, from whatever the orphanage had given him. He picked Savanah, not because he particularly thought he might be Spanish or anything, but because it reminded him of Africa. You know, the African savannas? I think he was thinking of Tarzan. The Lord of Greystoke. Another orphan.

After Joe started making money, he got all obsessed with finding his mother. Bob was against it. "I figure if a woman leaves a kid in an orphanage, it's a sure sign she don't want to be bothered," he said. I, asshole that I am, was all for it, though. "Maybe she was very young when it happened. All alone and frightened in the world? Maybe she gave you up because she really loved you. Maybe she's been looking for *you* all these years too!" I was picturing St. Teresa. Or at least Teresa Wright. Bob was picturing Sadie Thompson. Joe ignored both of us. He said he'd settle for a regular normal person.

He found a regular normal person in the advanced stages of alcoholism. And she didn't want to be reformed, either. So it turned out to be one big heartache, just like Bob predicted. I turned out to be one big heartache, just like Bob predicted. I could have just kicked myself for encouraging Joe to look for her in the first place. Not that he listened to me, of course, but still, I should have been against it, like Bob was. Because, no matter what Joe said, he was expecting some idealized version of a mother, too. So for two weeks after he found her, he didn't even tell anybody about it. He just acted fucked up. Very morose and preoccupied. Finally he spilled the beans and told both of us he'd found her. I was all overjoyed, because I'm such a smart person. "So? What is she like?" Joe gave me this real disgusted look and said, "Well, she doesn't look like Teresa Wright." Bob stood up and said, "I don't think I want to hear this," and walked right out of the room. But me, God forbid I should know when disaster's struck. I keep trying to twist it and turn it every which way, so it'll come out not too bad. I kept telling him, "Ah, come on, it can't be that bad," and he said it was worse than I could imagine. So then I kept insisting that I wanted to meet this dame and see for myself. He wouldn't hear of it at first, of course, but I finally made life so unbearable for him that he agreed. So I went with him up to the Bronx, where she'd been all along, and met her. My God, but it was a shock.

You know, when you're around twelve years old, you always thought your parents were okay, maybe even a little better than most people, and then you introduce them to somebody, and all of a sudden, you see them through this other person's eyes and you think, "Who *are* these strange short people? These are my parents? How deeply embarrassing!" And you try to disassociate yourself from them completely. You try to imply to this person you've just introduced them to that you hardly ever even *talk* to these strange short people, let alone *love* them.

Well, multiply that feeling by at least a hundred and you'll get an idea of how Joe felt about introducing his mother to anybody, even me. I mean, I tried to pretend everything was very fine and normal, of course, as the three of us sat there, talking about the Bronx, of all things, but I kept looking over at Joe and I could just tell all he was thinking was, "This is my *mother?!*" Which is what I was thinking, too. "This is his *mother?!*"

So we had our little visit over in this little apartment on Gun Hill Road, which Joe had set her up in, and then we left. And on the way home, he said, "Well? What'd you think?" And I said, "She's all right. No better or worse than anybody else. A regular person, just like you said." And he burst into tears! I swear! I *tried* telling him that all kids feel that way about their parents at one time or another, and that you get over it. But the fact is I felt like warmed-over shit, too. Because she wasn't no better or no worse than anybody else. She was worse, much worse. And I could just see Joe thinking, "What does this mean to *me?* How does this pertain to *me?*" Maybe that's one of the reasons the Pender dame had such a hold on him, with her self-improvement program. He was still trying to disassociate himself from that mean, ugly sot of a mother he found over in the Bronx. I mean she did look a little bit like him, and it must have been a very heavy trip to come face-to-face with that whole thing. Anyway, she died last year, this so-called mother of his.

"Where were we?" Bob said, calling me back to the present. "Oh, yeah, talking about suspects."

Oh, yeah. So who else? "You want to cross Lorraine off the list, right?"

"Well, let's just say she's a possible, but not a probable."

"Okay. One more. Shelly. I think I'd say the same thing about her," I said. "I mean I know she comes across as a little flaky sometimes, but actually she's very intelligent. She belongs to Mensa. It's only because she's so slow moving that people think she's dumb. But she isn't. Basically, I think she's just what she's always claiming she is. A realist. Murder is just not in her repertoire of real things to do. I don't think she could live with herself if she committed a murder. And I'm sure she knows that about herself, too. I'm sure she would say, in her very realistic tone of voice, 'Some people could live with that sort of thing. I couldn't.' So I think we could pretty much eliminate her as a suspect, too."

Bob, like Brendan before him, wasn't interested in psychological profiles. "Yeah, but *could* she have done it? Planted the evidence on the—"

"Shelly wouldn't be caught dead in Harlem, now. And unless the valuables they were talking about were seashells and ashtrays swiped from hotels and little dishes of sand or some other memento of happy times with Joe . . ."

"She kept seashells and little dishes of sand?" he said. I would have thought Bob would think that was adorable. Instead he said, "You know what? They were all crazy. All the women Joe knew were crazy. I'm just beginning to realize it. Except you. I always thought you were the craziest one and it's turning out they were all even crazier than you."

Was I supposed to thank him for this compliment?

"Yeah, well," I said. "Anyway, I don't think Shelly had any valuables of Joe's to plant on anybody."

"Okay, so she's another possible, but not probable. I hope to God that's *it* now."

"I think so. Now what?"

"Now we do what we did before," Bob said. "It worked the first time, didn't it? We kick up a little dust and see who gets scared. I tell everybody I'm not satisfied with the way the police are handling this th—"

"*You?* Where the hell do *you* shine in here? *I* tell everybody . . ."

So we were both thinking the same thing, were we? That this time it could be a little dangerous to start kicking up dust. The murderer had already played their ace, with the junkie business. If somebody started making trouble again, they might decide to shut up this pain-in-the-ass troublemaker once and for all. That second murder that sometimes accompanies the first?

"Listen, Nikki, you stay out of it this time . . ."

"Hey, listen, Bob! Don't bust my chops! We keep on doing just what we've been doing. I open my big mouth and you work in the background."

"In the *background!*" You had to hear that macho indignation. "Hey, Nikki, be a woman, all right? You're a woman? Act like a woman! From now on *I* take over and . . ."

"*One!*" I stuck my finger up in his face, even though he wasn't here to see it. "You're not going to scare shit out of anybody. Everybody knows you already. They know you're a nice, reasonable, sane guy. They figure you'll voice your complaints to the police and then go make a novena. People already know you got all your marbles, unfortunately, whereas with *me*—"

"Yeah, well. Maybe they'll figure I'm not so sane anymore, since my best friend got knocked off! Which is the God's honest truth. And besides, I'm Italian! Let the dopes think I'm Mafia."

"Nobody thinks things like that anymore, Bob. Everybody's enlightened now. Where was I? *Two*, people never know what I'll do. They always expect me to do something crazy, so *I'll* go around saying . . ."

We finally compromised. I would be the one with the big mouth and he would work in the background. But I'd have to check in with him every five minutes, practically. He even suggested moving in with me, for the duration, but I told him people would talk and that shut him up fast enough.

"One more thing, Bob. Are we very sure the junkie didn't do it?"

"Listen, Nikki, lousy security or not, do you think the bro could have been seen walking around that neighborhood without somebody calling in the cavalry immediately?"

"No." I thought of Brendan, of the first time I went to meet him at his office for lunch. What a shock it was to see him in his Brooks Brothers three-piece suit instead of his usual torn jeans and Grateful Dead T-shirt. (It was a miracle he didn't get arrested for exhibitionism sometimes, considering the places those jeans were torn in.) In his elegantly tailored gray suit, however, he could have walked into that townhouse and looked right at home. Damn!

"Are you having second thoughts?" Bob said. "Do you want to just leave it as it lays? If you do, I'll go along with that. It's up to you."

"No."

"I know. They're still walking around free, right?"

"Right. Besides which, we owe him one. At least one. You never should have encouraged him to go looking for his mother that time . . ."

"Me?! *I* encouraged him? *I* didn't encourage him! I was the one who—oh, I get it. You're kidding. Very funny."

"Hmmmm."

"Listen, Nikki, don't feel bad about that time. You didn't know . . ."

"Yeah, I *never* know. Well, this time, I'm gonna know."

"Okay, see you later. Let me ask you something. Maybe you have some relatives? Relatives who could help us out here a little bit?"

"Oh, Bob! That's terrible."

"Just thought I'd ask. Hehhehhehhehheh."

I had to admit, though Bob didn't laugh often, he had a terrific laugh. Loaded with machismo. I hung up before I started giggling back girlishly in response.

26

So then I called Tish to thank her for the wonderful lunch yesterday and to say, how do you like these establishment newspaper rags and how stupid do they think we are, claiming this black guy killed Joe and I certainly wasn't satisfied that this case had been settled at all and I had every intention to keep right on digging and digging and I was going to find out how those particular valuables came into the possession of that particular black guy, no matter whose toes I stepped on; and what was this, a coverup to protect the Pender name or what? *Whatever* it was, I'd find out!

I hung up, leaving her to contemplate that.

Then I called Shelly and told her not to even bother learning this guy's name because he didn't do it, and maybe I had been a little too gullible at other times in my life but not this time, and surely a pragmatic person like herself could understand my wanting to get to the truth of the matter. But then I felt a little bad, because ole gullible Shelly, who thought she was such a cynic, believed every word I said—even cautioned me, in fact, saying the same things Bob did about how it could be dangerous to keep making a commotion about this, and apparently the police were happy with this explanation and maybe it wasn't such a good idea to keep bucking their opinion, not to mention the fact that if I was right and there really was a murderer out there on the loose, he—or she, she supposed—might come looking for *me*; and sometimes, even when I thought I was being smart, I was *still* being too naïve, because there *are* murderers in this world and it's a real thing, and I should worry about my own safety a little bit now. And what was the difference anyway, it wouldn't bring Joe back. She's just as soon not think anything about the crazy person who did this. So then she asked me how did her stole look yesterday, and I said fine, but she said she thought it was beginning to look a little worn out, as she had bought it used to begin with, and maybe it was time to invest in a new one, and what did I think? And I said, well, maybe, and she said did I want to go with her tomorrow to Bloomingdale's and maybe she'd treat herself to a brand-new fur, maybe a jacket this time, just to cheer herself up because God knows she could use some cheering, considering what's been going on lately, and she still felt extremely depressed about everything and now was a good time to buy fur, this being spring and furs being on sale. So I told her, sure, I'd go to Bloomingdale's with her the following day, because the going was getting tough now, and we both said in unison, "And when the going gets tough, the tough go shopping," and laughed hysterically.

I tried to get Brendan on the phone, figuring by now the ban had been lifted on calls from me, but there was no answer. That's because I ran smack into him a few minutes later as I was running down the steps of my front stoop and he was running up, carrying a bouquet of flowers! And in the rush of happiness of the moment, I said, "Heyyyy!" all overjoyed at seeing him again, and he said, "Heyyyy!" back the same way, but then I remembered a few things and calmed down. And he handed me the bouquet, which was really very lovely, and I said, "What's this supposed to be for?" and he said, "Because you're off the police shit list!" So I took them, in a sort of surly manner, and said, "Oh." "And to make peace," he said. So I just said thank you, since I still didn't know if I was talking to a murderer or what, and we went for a walk. He was on his lunch hour, (dressed in a nice suit and all), he said, but he had to run over and talk to me after he heard they caught the murderer; and I said, well, if he believed that, he wasn't as smart as he was always bragging he was, and I had a nice bridge I could sell him, connecting Brooklyn and Manhattan, and he could collect tolls and everything and make a fortune in no time and, did he want to buy it from me, cheap?, as my grandfather had bought it when he got off the boat and now it was mine. So he laughed and said, "*Now*, what's the matter? So I laid the shpiel on him, "Digging and digging . . . whose toes I step on . . . something very fishy about this stuff turning up on some poor dead junkie, etc. etc. . . ." But he just said I was getting to be a real drag, living in the past all the time now, and I said, "*That's* the past? Two weeks ago is the *past* already?" But it was just a regular friendly argument with lots of yelling and calling of names. Then he asked me, how about meeting him for dinner, but I told him I already had a previous engagement and he said, "Ah! It begins . . ." and who was *this* one now, and that was fast, and I said, no, no, it wasn't like that, it was just with a friend, and he said what's this friend's name and I said the name, and he said, "Oh, I get it, now you're going to fuck Joe by proxy," and I told him to keep his filthy mouth shut, and why didn't he just go back to work *right now?* So he told me to take it easy and, well, how about lunch tomorrow then, but I told him I was meeting Shelly in Bloomingdale's to go fur shopping, and, hey, maybe he wanted to come along and have lunch together. But he said no, he wasn't that crazy about Shelly, and I told him *again* that I didn't understand how come they never hit it off with each other because they were really a lot alike in many ways. He got insulted because he thinks Shelly's crazy, and in any case he didn't want to have lunch with her, as she had a sloppy way of eating, which was sort of true because she was always so *relaxed* that she didn't even bother closing her fuckin' mouth while she was eating and he *hated* that. (Meanwhile, Brendan eats the same way, but never mind.)

226

So we had already walked back down to Wall Street by then, and just as I was beginning to relax and think how absurd it was to suspect Brendan, he of course said something to put him right back on my suspect's list. He said he couldn't understand why I was still so puzzled about the case, since it turned out exactly the way I thought it would. Or one of the ways, anyhow.

"You're the one who said it could have been a junkie, don't you remember? You're the one who said it was probably some junkie who went there for a handout, got turned down, and decided to rob the place instead. You're the one who said a junkie would throw their very own mother off a roof. So why make a stink? Forget about it and get on with your life."

I immediately got worried that he remembered all those things I said, and maybe he just went ahead and made it all come true, just like I mapped it out for him. So when I didn't answer, he just gave me one of those snake-eyed looks of his again and said, "I might as well save my breath though. You're not gonna let up on this, are you?"

I got a little scared again. Like, maybe without even knowing it, he was giving me a veiled threat. I had by no means forgotten all the other threats he had so recently doled out to me, threats about making sure I got blamed for it if things looked bad for him. (You'd think he would have realized that, if things really *were* back to normal between us, I would have been bitching about *that* plenty. Unless he really thought that little bouquet of flowers was really going to make me forget such abuse.) Anyway, I didn't say anything right away and he asked me *again*. "*Are* you going to let up on this?"

So I looked off into the distance, very dramatically, and said, "No." He didn't say anything right away, but then he said, "Well, all right. Listen, give me a call when you've got some free time. When you're not so booked up." And I said I would, and he walked into the building, back to the offices of

Leon, Aimes, Fierce, Lender, and Smith, or whoever the hell it was he worked for.

Still not being sure about anything, as soon as I got home, I called the main one, the Pender dame. To my great surprise, she actually came to the phone. Probably to gloat. So I laid the whole rap on her.

". . . just going to keep right on digging and digging . . . maybe bigger than *Watergate*, for all I know . . . So the NYPD found some stooge they could pin this on for you . . . *still* talk to the media . . . maybe Joe's body ought to be *exhumed* . . . by no means satisfied with . . ."

She listened to it all and then she said she had neither the time nor the inclination to listen to my mad ravings, et cetera, et cetera, and hung up. But I left her with plenty of food for thought.

All in all, I felt as if I'd put in a good day's work. So I called up some other friends of mine, artist friends who had nothing to do with any of this, just to give myself a break. They sounded real pleased to hear from me and said what was I going to be a hermit from now on? and why didn't I go down to the café anymore and everybody's been asking for me, and I said, yeah, I'd probably take a walk down there this weekend some night, just to hang out for a while, and they said, good, take your mind off it for a while, meaning Joe's death, since a lot of them knew him, too.

And I felt a little better, thinking I had friends who missed me, at least a little bit.

So, that night, I met Bob for dinner, like we planned, over on Kenmare Street, and as we were munching on bread sticks waiting for our veal parmesan to arrive, I told him I had notified all the notables and did he think something would be turning up soon, or what?

Bob asked me if I happened to have heard what a certain party said about Joe on the David Susskind Show the other night and I said no, and he said just as well because morons like that were just jealous and they always had been, but they were shooting off their mouths now because Joe was no longer here to go feed them a knuckle sandwich. So I said, what'd he SAY? And Bob said it wasn't anything too terrible, just that Joe was, in actuality, a very ruthless, ambitious S.O.B. I was duly aghast at somebody badmouthing Joe like that as this seemed a bit soon to be stomping on the grave, so I told Bob that this certain shithead's only problem was that he once came on to Joe and Joe not only told him to go fuck himself but that, if he didn't get lost, he was going to rearrange this guy's face into a cubist portrait. Which I thought was very funny—you know, an eye here, a nose over there, another eye someplace else. Joe wasn't usually nasty like that in those kind of situations, but this guy was a real mean bastard and deserved exactly that kind of response. So Bob said, how do you like that S.O.B. now, calling Joe ruthless, and I said he had some nerve and Joe was never ruthless that *I* could recall, which wasn't exactly the truth, because I myself on one occasion had called him ruthless, but—well, that was in a different context entirely. It was a sexual matter.

You see, what it was, was I didn't use to like to have this certain thing done to me. I mean, I didn't mind doing it (I actually didn't mind doing it AT ALL), but I just didn't want it done *to* me. I just didn't think I'd like it. And it wasn't necessary. I mean there were plenty of other ways to keep ourselves occupied. I was just as happy without it.

All right, I was afraid of it. I didn't think I could handle it. *Him*, going down on me? It would be too much. I just didn't think I could cope with it. I mean, I was afraid I might actually *die* of bliss! Have a heart attack or something. So I always told him no, when it came to that. And usually, he listened. But this one time . . .

I thought at first he was just messing around near my belly button. All right, let him, I figured. But then it looked like he wasn't coming back *up* again. If anything, he was going down lower! *Well*, naturally, I tried to stop him. I mean, I said, "Eh . . . Joe. Eh . . . no, Joe. Don't . . ." And it looked like he was *ignoring* me. Well, I couldn't believe it, so I got a little more forceful about it and said, "Joe! You *know* I don't like that! What are you going to do?!" But he just kept right on ignoring me! So I was in a real pickle! I mean I wasn't about to really *hurt* him or anything, to stop him, but I kept trying to make him stop, just by hitting his shoulders and all. Well, it suddenly became crystal clear to me that I *couldn't* stop him. Without getting violent about it, I mean, which I certainly wasn't about to do. (It's not as if it was a stranger doing this.) So all of a sudden, I realized, looking at that vast expanse of his shoulders and his big muscled arms, how the hell was I supposed to fight *that* off me. So I just resigned myself. Let him, I thought, he'll get bored. Meanwhile, I'd just ignore everything that was going on. Put my mind on something else entirely and wait for it to be over.

Well, Joe, no dope, soon figured out what I was thinking, so he looks up at me and says, "I got all *night*, Nicole," and he laughs this sexy laugh and goes right back to doing what he was doing. So I got mad and said, "How could you be so *ruthless!*" But he just laughed again and went right back to doing what he was doing, and finally I gave up. And that's the night I found out what multiorgasmic really means.

So much for Joe's ruthlessness.

So now I looked across the table at Bob and I guess I was blushing a little bit, remembering these things while sitting here with Bob, and Bob misunderstood, because he said, "Oh, don't let yourself get upset over things like that, Nikki. Anybody who knew Joe knows he wasn't ruthless. Unless it was for a good cause."

And I nearly burst out laughing.

Which, of course, made me immediately want to burst out *crying*, realizing as I did that things like that wouldn't be happening to me anymore. Not with Joe, anyway, and who cared about anybody else? Oh, that guy just *ruined* me for sex with anybody else, don't worry—him, with all those IQ points of his, all busy working on ways to pleasure my body? Who the hell was I supposed to sleep with after *that?* And it wasn't just a question of technique. At all. It was that he *wanted* to please me. I can't tell you what that used to do to me, that he wanted to please me. Ah, the guy used to leave me breathless with joy, no matter *what* he did.

So, I'm sitting there now, thinking of these things, and I actually *did* end up getting a little teary-eyed. So Bob starts apologizing about bringing up the whole subject of the David Susskind show in the first place, and what's wrong with him, telling me what some creeps on T.V. said about Joe. So I just let him apologize about a million times, and I didn't say anything. I mean, what was I supposed to say? "I'm crying because I was remembering how Animal went down on me the first time and now that won't happen anymore?"

Finally, thank God, he changed the subject. He told me that, just to make sure we hit all the bases, he had even phoned Lorraine Rice out in California and laid the shpiel on her but that she sounded pretty oblivious to it all. She said all those terrible things that happen are really just Satan loose in the world and that we should all pray to the Lord constantly, and would Bob like her to send him some literature about the Lord's love and Satan being loose in the world? But Bob told her no, because he was already Catholic and he already prayed to God with the Catholics. And I made such a face at that that Bob said, what's the matter? didn't I even believe in God anymore at all?

And I said no, I didn't, and what was praying but talking to a lot of cold dead stars up in the sky who never gave a shit about you to begin with? And what about all the starving babies in the world, and wars and people with terrible diseases, and I bet they prayed plenty and what good did it do *them,* nobody was out there to hear it! And he said maybe I was just saying things like this now because of what happened to Joe, and he could understand that, because he felt the same way, when it first happened. But that I shouldn't lose faith. He said maybe I'd start feeling more optimistic about things again when something good happened again.

But I told him not to hold his breath.

27

The next day, when I woke up, I was pleased to see it was raining. I met Shelly at our designated meeting place in Bloomingdale's—the Famous Amos Chocolate Chip department on one of the ground floors. You see, Bloomingdale's has any number of ground floors. It's got at least three or four. And you can't just say, well Ground Floor must be the one above the basement, because it has about five floors that are supposedly the basement, one of them starting right down in the subway, even. *All* the floors are like that. They've got sublevels and midlevels and midsublevels and balconies and . . . It's impossible to know where the *first* floor is! I asked a saleslady once, "Where's the first floor?" because I was lost on one of the submidlevels? And I followed her instructions *to the letter,* and I still couldn't find it. All I know is that Bloomingdale's still owes me $15, from my deposit on a dress in a department that completely disappeared off the face of the earth.

That's what I love about New Yorkers. Nothing throws them. They get in those Bloomingdale elevators and they push those buttons like they know exactly what they're going to find when those doors open! If they push Number 3, they get *out* at Number 3, damn it! So what if they were aiming for the restaurant and they ended up in the beauty parlor? They'll get their hair done! Anything is better than letting on that Bloomies has thrown them a curve by switching departments around again. People might think, God forbid, that they're from Out of

Town. Meanwhile, all of New York is from Out of Town. Over-achievers from the Midwest, as somebody once said.

Anyhow, Shelly and I agreed to meet in the cookie department, if it was still there. Fortunately, there she was, in Famous Amos, and we went up to one of the fur departments. Shelly drove some poor, frazzled saleslady crazy, looking at furs. Then, by accident, we found ourselves in the restaurant, so we had lunch. Then, when we were looking for the shoe department, we found another fur department, so she drove another saleslady crazy in there, pricing everything and trying everything on. I mean, if it took her twenty minutes to decide if she wanted Coke or Pepsi with her lunch, you can imagine how she was carrying on over a fur jacket! Once I thought she was actually going to buy one, but she handed it back with this very sorrowful look on her face, and told the saleslady, "This is all wrong for me." And then she whispered to me, "Come on. I can get it wholesale for half the price. Let's go down to Delancey Street."

So what the hell were we fotsing around in Bloomingdale's all day for, I wanted to know. So she'd know what to ask for, she explained reasonably. We tooled around in Bloomingdale's a little while longer. "God!" she says to me, "do you see all these homosexuals? Isn't there *anybody* straight in this city anymore?" It certainly didn't look like it.

A couple of times, I thought I saw Brendan. But doesn't that always happen? When you miss somebody or have a fight with them or something? Don't you keep thinking you're seeing them all over?

Finally, we left and went down into the subway. Always an interesting experience.

We had to take the IRT downtown, which is really tempting fate. It's really like playing Russian roulette. Would the switch box explode? Would we be derailed? Would we be asphyxiated by the cyanide gas released when the foam in the seating went on fire? (I don't know why I listen to the news. It just makes me a nervous wreck.)

So we're standing on the platform, waiting for the train (where *is* it?), getting jostled, as that station is always pretty crowded, even in the best of times, *plus*, it's getting closer to rush hour. And there's this big black dude standing next to me. But I mean right next to me, and I also mean BLACK. You know when blacks are really pitch black? When it's really kind of amazing to look at them and see someone so totally *black* black like that? Like Miles Davis. That's how this guy was. Except he was a giant! Also, he wasn't dressed too sharp. His clothes looked a little shabby and frayed. He had on a plaid polyester jacket and a—all right, so, if it had been a white guy, I would have figured it was a working-class hero coming home from a hard day at the garage or something. But he was black and I got leery. So I tucked my pocketbook more securely under my arm. Since I was not the only prejudiced bastard in the crowd, Shelly leaned over to me and said, "Watch your bag," her eyes and eyebrows indicating the black mountain at my side. "*I* know!" I said back.

We both looked down the track, into the tunnel. Where *is* this train? So we're standing there, breathing in the hot, musty, rusty, corroded smell of the subway, and looking down the track. Where *is* it? And you can almost taste all the rust and soot, I swear. The rain outside had turned the subways into one big steambath. Plus, the air was heavy with the smell of hot dogs, mustard, pretzels, potato chips and Dairy Queen ice cream, all of which is sold down there for the edification of the travelers, although how anyone could eat anything down there, in the bowels of the earth like that, was beyond me. It's all so subterranean in a "Nineteen Eighty-Four" kind of way. I mean I'm sure everything could look beautiful if you know how to look at it. You can find beauty of form and structure and color in anything. But, believe me, in the subways, you really have to bend over backwards to not be *repulsed* by everything you see. The spit and the gum on the floors, the stink of the urine, and the RACKET! Ehhh! That godawful racket down there! And it's all so dark and otherworldly.

We finally see the train pulling into the station ahead of us. Thank God. Although sometimes it sits *there* for half an hour, anyway. So everybody starts jostling a little closer together, jockeying for a more advantageous position on the platform from which to storm into the train, if it ever *gets* here, that is, and the black guy and I kind of get pushed a little closer together, and Shelly pokes me in the side and signals with her eyes again: "Black guy! Pocketbook! Watch it!" "*I* know!" I signal back.

And finally, here comes the damn train now, barreling through the tunnel. The crowd tightens up around the edge of the platform. And suddenly, it happens. The briefest moment of the feel of a hand at the small of my back and then a push. So light and neat, I'm not even sure it's happened. But all of a sudden, I'm flying through the air. I can't even say in slow motion. In that other kind of motion. What is it, stop-frame? You move a little bit and you stop, you move a little bit and you stop. I feel like I'm moving so slowly through the air that I actually stop once in a while.

I hit the tracks but good. HEYYYYY. Who did that? HEYYYYY. I'm on the *subway* tracks here. This is *really dangerous*, you know? HEYYYYY. Ohhhhhh, Gawd! I start to cry.

So *that's* what all those nightmares are for! Little shadow plays! To prepare me for this! Oh, *that's* what nightmares are for! Now I get it. To show you what's really, really, *really* behind the last veil. It's this. Terror. Horror. Total chaos and evil and pain and the unrelenting, unremitting wailing of lost souls in the throes of bottomless agony. Oh, I know it's really only the sound of metal on metal, steel on steel, the hellish rumble of the train, but it *sounds* like souls screaming in agony. And there I am, down in the muck and the filth, with the rats and the mice and the cans thrown on the tracks, and Joe falls off roofs and babies are starving to death and people get diseases like Muscular Dystrophy and Cerebral Palsy and cancer of the esophagus and that's what's behind the last veil. Unending horror and dread and fear! And Terror so real it has weight and substance and volume. It's *tangible,* terror is.

So I'm scrambling like a trapped mouse. My legs are working, not at all like in a nightmare, when you want to run but your legs won't work? My legs are working fine. They're going every *which* way. *Where's the train! Where is it! Oh, God, God, God, help me Please. Where's the train! I hear it, so loud. Don't look. Don't look. Just go. Just go. I hear it. It's in the station already, isn't it. Oh God. Please.* I hear it. Horror has a heavy thudding cadence. Heavy as the bottom of the ocean. Horror is a machine no one can turn off, a machine run by Evil. A heavy dead cadence that no one can turn off. You wanna not think about the train right now? You wanna not think about how you skinned your palms on the wooden planks between the tracks? How about you just think about not slipping on all those fuckin' little rocks between the wooden planks? Think about not doing that for a minute, all right? Why must I always be such a klutz? *Where is it! WHERE IS IT! Boy, do I hear it. What an insane roar! Oh, God.*

She's right. Satan is loose in the world. Satan owns it all. The whole world. It's his domain! I've been praying to the wrong guy all along! It all belongs to Satan. It's all rotten and evil and horrible and terrifying. That's what's the stuff of the universe. And that's why we're all running so scared all the time. I start to scream. And then I wet my pants because my foot is stuck under the track because I slipped on the little rocks again. I don't care, God. I don't care what the bastard owns or he doesn't own. I don't care what he rules, I'm sticking with you. *Help me please. I'm asking for a miracle here. That's right! A miracle! (Where's the train! Where is it!) I can't help it. I look. Oh-h-h-h-h. There it is. Those headlights are really bearing down on me, now, aren't they! It's not stopping. The train's not stopping and my shoe won't come off my foot!*

An animal could chew the foot right off and just leave it there, stuck in the trap. I'd do it. I don't have the time. Here's the train. (At last. It's about time! These damn trains . . .) I look up at the crowd lining the platform. Their faces are twisted into horrified expressions. Some of them are yelling but I can't hear a word. Some are turning away, afraid to look. *Oh, God, how awful. They can't even bear to see what's going to happen to me. This thing is going to happen, actually, to me. Moi!* The girl with the nightmares. The girl with the white knuckles from trying, for years and years, to climb out of some pit. The one with the skinned palms from clawing up some mountainside. And it's all going to end right here, isn't it? I don't blame them for turning away. It's going to be gruesome as all-get-out.

And suddenly, the big black monolith of a mountain is on the tracks with me. An unbelievably oversized King Kong of a hand reaches out and covers the whole of my chest, tightens on the front of my raincoat (I hear the back seam *ripppp*), and with my lapels bunched up in his massive fist, he picks me up and flings me. I land with a thud on my ass, and my head bunks into the cement wall in there—*ouch!*—into that little recessed place under the platform. I never even *noticed* it before and to think, I was just now thinking of chewing off my foot to get to it. Well, I'm here now. How the hell is *he* going to fit in here? He's so goddamn big! He'll never fit his whole big self into this place! *But I'll keep looking, honey. I won't turn away. I promise. I won't leave you all lonely like that out there alone. I'll look. Oh, God. Come on. Skrunch up. Come on. There's room. Get that tree trunk of a leg in here, Mister! He's in!*

We both sit like twisted up pretzels, squashed into the little space. And the beast is upon us. ROARING by, mad as hell. And then there is the deafeningly loud screech of brakes and the beast stops in its tracks. We are cheek-by-jowl with the underside of the train. *Don't look. Don't look.* I look. "Ohhhhhh, Gaaawwwwwd!" I swear I hear my echo. "Sweet Jesus!" the black man says. And "Praise the Lord."

Little by little, sounds resume their normal pitch. We hear the hubbub of voices over our heads. "Two people! Down there! In there! Yes! Under the train!" Screams. Yelling. "Yes! Under the train!" "Step back. Step back!" "In there, Officer!" "Oh my God! Watch out, there, Watch out!"

I can't see the black man's face. The wall of his back is facing me. He speaks, sounding exactly the way you'd expect a mountain to sound. A Blue Ridge Mountain. Something southern and honeyed and rich.

"Are you okay?"

I say, "Fine," and nothing comes out. Look at that. No voice. Try again. "Fine." It comes out. For some reason, the word sends me into fits of hysterical crying. It has exactly the same reaction on him. The polyester wall in front of my face shakes and quakes and the two of us bawl like overtired three-year-olds. ("A little too much excitement today. They're overtired, that's all. They'll be fine after a little nap.")

It was decided, finally, as long as we were snug as two bugs in a rug down there, that instead of derailing the train and lousing up every rush hour from here to next Tuesday, what they'd do instead is let the train pull out of the station very slowly. But we had to make sure we didn't move a muscle. We made sure. The train pulled out. We told each other not to look, but we both looked. Those great big ugly, sooty, rusty wheels, churning by until, finally, the last of them passed.

I was fine and Lamont Miller was fine, but Shelly had to be hospitalized. She fainted when she thought the train was rolling over me, grinding my body to a bloody pulp, and she hit her head when she fell onto the hard cement floor. She had to get six stitches on her forehead. Plus, they kept her overnight to make sure she didn't have a concussion.

Only Shelly and I went to the hospital. Lamont Miller said he was okay and just wanted to go home to his wife and six kids. The police questioned him a good deal, just on general principles, but everybody swore long and loud that Lamont had his arms folding across his massive chest at the time of the shove. "There was another man here though . . ." "Where'd *he* go?" "It was a woman! There was this *woman* here who . . ."

"Wasn't it a kid? There was this *teenager* standing here and . . ."

Finally, they told Lamont he could leave. I got his name and address before he left, though. I told him the least I could do was to try to help him find a job. (Maybe Bob could do something.) He said he'd been looking for a job for almost two years now.

Shows you what kind of assholes are running the personnel offices in this country!

28

I decided not to tell Bob about any of that train business. He'd just get all alarmed over it. And probably tell me he *told* me so, which—let's face it—he did. But I had to call him because the plan was that we'd check in with each other pretty frequently.

"Where *were* you?" he demanded. "It's almost eight o'clock. You were supposed to call at five."

"I forgot," I told him. "Listen, do you think you could get this friend of mine a job? A really good job that pays a lot? No window-washer shit or anything."

"Oh, it's a black guy, huh? No skills?"

"Well, I wouldn't exactly say that! He's very good at saving people's lives. At great risk to his *own*."

"*Nikki*! What *happened*?"

"Nothing! What are you getting excited about? He saved a friend of mine's life once. In the war."

"*What* war?"

"How do I know? I don't know about military things like that. I'm a woman! Alls I know is that he saved somebody's life and he's having a very hard time finding a job now. *Joe* would have been able to get him something," I threw in for good measure, "but, well, with Joe gone, I figured I'd ask you."

"All right, all right. I'll see what I can do. What'd the guy do before? Does he have any experience at all?"

"Yeah. He was a window-washer. But that's not the kind

of job he's looking for now. He needs something that pays good."

"You're a riot, I swear. How am I supposed to find a job . . ."

"How 'bout as a bodyguard? Hey! Maybe you could ask Lorraine if she knows any movie stars who need a bodyguard? She knows all those movie stars, doesn't she? Like Cher. Isn't Cher one of her clients? Maybe Cher needs a bodyguard!"

"I don't know. But could he do that kind of work?"

"Are you kidding? You have to see this guy! He's all muscle! And he's about seven feet tall!"

"I guess I could ask Lorraine. But hey, I don't even have to go that far. I'll ask Ann. She's got a security team right here in Bedford Falls."

I hadn't even thought of that. But now that I did, I remembered the army of musclebound guys I saw at the funeral, all in three-piece suits straining over their bulging biceps. It didn't occur to me that some of them were Ann's full-time employees. Was it one of them that pushed me in front of the train? She'd pay somebody to do something like that, don't think she wouldn't.

"All right," I said, "ask Ann." So what if she was going to be in jail soon, for murder. At least Lamont would have a good reference, guarding the Pender estate.

"Okay. She's got a big security staff out here," Bob said. "In fact, one time, she and Joe had a fight about it."

"Oh, really?" I said, all ears, always happy to hear about a little discord between them.

"Yeah. A couple of local kids climbed over the fence once. And those guys really went into action. Fortunately, Joe was here at the time. He had a fit and a half. He fired the guys on the spot. And then Ann had a fit about *that*. She said, well, didn't he want any security on the premises *at all?* and Joe told her if her idea of security on the premises was having half a dozen goons around who liked to give their muscles a workout on a couple of thirteen-year-olds, she ought to rethink her priorities. And she said you could take liberalism just so far, but when it came to protecting your very own property, she didn't see what was so wrong about it, et cetera, et cetera." (Didn't it sound like one hell of a happy marriage, though?) "The goons disappeared after that," Bob said. "But they're all back now, in full force."

"Are any of them black?" I asked.

"Yeah. A couple. Why? You worried about this guy fitting in?"

What I was worried about was, could one of them have blended in on that train platform, that's what. "No, that's not what I'm worried about," I said. "Because it would really be better if you tried to get him to head the whole staff. He'd fit in if he was the boss, wouldn't he?"

"And why should he be the boss? If he doesn't even have any experience . . ."

"He has valor in the presence of great danger! Shouldn't that be the main thing?"

"Are you *sure* nothing happened to you?"

"I'm sure. And listen, don't tell her it's through me that you heard about this guy. Tell her it was a friend of Joe's. She'll like doing a favor for a friend of Joe's, her being the *widow* and all."

"Okay. So nothing's happened yet? No reaction from anybody?"

"Not a thing."

"Okay. Make sure you lock your door. Don't go out any more tonight. And don't answer any knocks at the windows. Call the police right away if anything seems fishy to you and—"

"Good night, Bob. I'll talk to you tomorrow."

But it was only a couple of hours later that he called me again.

"A war, eh? It was in a war, right?"

"Who told you?"

"He saved somebody's life in a war! Some war! The Number Six IRT War is what it was."

"Who told you? Shelly? That bigmouth! Shelly told you? She is such a twit sometimes that . . ."

"Why didn't you *tell* me, Nikki? What the hell's wrong with you, you should excuse my French. Was the reason for us setting up this whole thing so that we could see who reacted?"

"Because it proved nothing! It didn't reveal beans! The fact is, it could have been *any* of them." I had been thinking about it, of course, since the moment it happened. "One: Ann hired a hit man."

"Possible."

"Two: I thought I saw Brendan a couple of times in the store. If I was right and it was him I saw, he could have followed us into the train station. In any case, he knew where I was going today."

"Another possible."

"Three: I understand the gay community is a very tight-knit group. And if two of their members are about to be fingered for murder, maybe they got a little community action going."

"Farfetched. But, okay. Tish—another possible."

"I am assuming Lorraine is still in California?"

"She is."

"Thank God. She's eliminated."

"What about Shelly? She was right there! In fact, she's the only one we know for *sure* was right there. It seems pretty obvious to me that if she was the one *right there* when it happened—"

"Bob. That's what people said about me, when Joe died. I was the one right there. The only one who was positively, absolutely right there. And I know *I* was innocent. You can't accuse Shelly, just 'cause she was there." I kept picturing Shelly's sickly white face in that hospital emergency room, with a great big square of gauze covering her six stitches. The gauze covered part of her eye, because when she fainted, she fell flat down on her face. They still didn't know if her nose was broken or if the bump would go away. If her eyes got black and blue during the night, it was broken.

"All right, but she's still a possible."

"So there you are. We learned nothing from it. What was there to tell you about?"

"What was there to tell me about? I'll tell you what was there to tell me about! What was there was that I'm moving in with you. You're not going to go walking around alone anymore. You're not going anywhere alone! *That's* what there was to tell me about."

"You know, Bob, you remind me a lot of my father."

"Do I? Thank you."

"That's not a compliment, Bob. My father is a very stubborn, dictatorial—"

"I'm moving in, Nikki. It's settled."

"—who never should have left the hills of Sicily—"

"I'll be over in about an hour and a half. Don't even stand in front of the windows in the meantime."

"I'll hide under the bed. But even in Sicily, by now, he would *still* stand out as one of the most thickheaded, autocratic . . ."

He hung up.

I called him right back.

"What about my reputation?! You know what people will say, don't you? You know how people's minds work.They'll say something was going on *all along* between us. They'll say Joe's best friend was making time with his girl and now that Joe is gone, we couldn't even *wait* to—"

"Since when are you so worried about your reputation? You never gave a damn what anybody thought!"

"Yeah, but *you* do!"

"No more now, Nikki, no more now."

"Why the hell not?"

"Because Joe's death taught me a couple of things. Such as, we do not live forever. Such as, I've wasted too much of my life thinking about what other people think. Your way was right all along. Live for yourself. Don't give a damn about what people think. From now on, I'm going to be like you."

I got worried. "Bo-ob!"

"Don't worry, I'll sleep on the couch."

He hung up again.

Good to his word, that pain in the ass showed up an hour and a half later. It turned out not to be a total disaster. He made *excellent* potato and egg sandwiches. He brought over fresh Italian bread, too.

I fell asleep with a full stomach and the knowledge there was a thick-headed wop on the premises who would keep me alive till morning.

I felt like I was ten years old. It felt great.

The next morning, of course, the phone woke me. I fully expected it to be somebody who would say, "*I* didn't know you and Bob had a thing going. How long has *this* been going on?"

Instead, it was Shelly.

"I'm home," she said. "Don't go pick me up at the hospital, because I'm home." It sounded like the tranquilizing shot they had given her still hadn't worn off.

"How's your nose?"

"Okay. My eyes didn't turn black and blue."

"I'm *sooooo* sorry, Shelly!'

"*You* didn't do it. What are *you* sorry about?"

"I feel responsible." It was true, what Ann said. I had a dangerous overestimation of my own abilities. I felt responsible for everything. Why shouldn't I? Everything usually was all my fault.

"Well, you weren't responsible, so stop apologizing. What are you whispering for?"

"Bob's inside. Sleeping on the floor. The poor dope thought I had a couch. He didn't know my couch was my bed. So he's sleeping on the floor in the kitchen. Behind all the plants. I feel sooo baaaad."

"Bob is there? Good! You *should* have somebody with you. Didn't I tell you, right from the beginning? Didn't I tell you it would be dangerous to go around telling everybody you were going to keep digging and digging . . ."

"All right, you told me so."

"I don't mean to say I-told-you-so, but it happens that I did. Well, anyway, I'm glad he's there with you. You shouldn't be by yourself."

"Well, that's why you *told* him, isn't it? I should have figured Miss Blabbermouth would—"

"Who's that you're on the phone with there?" a gruff voice asked me from the archway. So help me, he sounded just like my father!

"It's Shelly! What are you worried about? Nobody's going to kill me over the phone! Jeez! What are they going to do, hypnotize me? 'Walk over to the medicine cabinet,'" I intoned. "'Remove a bottle of sleeping pills.'" Shelly and I got hysterical.

Bob made a face and walked away. I was a little surprised he didn't say, "Well, hang up!" That's what my *father* would have said.

"Where were we?" I said into the phone. "Oh, yeah. *Why* did you tell Bob—"

"Breakfast is almost ready," a voice from the kitchen told me. "Hang up."

"How do you like the nerve of this guy?" I asked Shelly.

"That's okay. I want to hang up anyway. I'm going to get into bed and sleep all day. They kept waking me up every twenty minutes in the hospital."

I apologized for that, too, before we hung up.

29

Bob turned out to be pretty reasonable about things. He agreed we weren't going to get anywhere by staying in the house all day. And I agreed that if I was going to be out baiting suspects, Bob would be close behind, keeping an eye on things.

I called Brendan, but he wasn't free for lunch. Bob said he was going to have a private detective agency check into Ann's security men. The only luck we had was with Tish, who said she might stop by the café later that night as long as I was going to be there. The plan was that Bob and I would go to the café together and if Tish and Alex showed up, he'd leave me alone with them.

I was a little surprised to see how spiffed up Bob got for this outing. He looked like a narc. I told him I thought he looked a little overdressed and gave him a T-shirt of mine which said, "Whoever has the most things when he dies, wins."

"What does that mean?" he said. "Is that dirty?"

But once we got there, I must say, he fit right in. Plus, he seemed to be having the time of his life. I think he completely forgot about our reason for being there. His *raison d'etre*, for the time being, seemed to be to get Belinda Lenox into the sack. Which wasn't that much of an impossible dream.

As we sat there with all my artist friends, it was easy to get caught up in the café-artiste milieu. There were only eight of us at the table, but somehow there were twelve conversa-

tions going on simultaneously, and at least three of these spo-
radically threatened to break into fisticuffs.

"Magritte??! Surely, you jest. He is so overrated . . ."

"So I said to him, 'The vaginal orgasm is a myth. Wishful
thinking on the part of the male-dominated psychiatric establishment.'"

"Sold out? How *dare* you! The fact that one has removed
the safety pins from one's nose in no way signifies that one has
sold out! When *I* wore them, they meant something. Now
Macy's probably stocks them in the accessories department,
right along with spiked wristbands and heavy duty chains."

"It was Dali who showed the world of the nightmare with
an accuracy that was chilling! Magritte was little more than a
clever technician who cashed in on . . ."

"I think I heard both are recognized now. Belinda, didn't
you read in *Reader's Digest* or something where both the vaginal and clitoral orgasm are considered valid now?"

"If you're going to *talk* like an asshole, you're going to be
called an asshole. Magritte dealt with the *waking* nightmare.
You asshole."

"I beg to differ with you. Society hasn't coopted anything
in this case. Madison Avenue hasn't been pushing sadism. It's
the people themselves that have created the demand. There's
too much pain in the world and . . ."

"Well, in that case, I owe Nikki an apology. Nikki! You
were right. It seems there *are* vaginal orgasms."

"Pain so saturates American life that it has become the
medium of love. Does the world beat you up daily? Then let
your lover abuse you at night and you will have both tran-
scended pain. Turned it into ecstasy."

"It is not just a question of semantics. I'd be very happy to
tell you what the waking nightmare is. It's the sudden, unexpected, terrifying realization that you know nothing. That your
whole life has been based on a system of beliefs, prejudices,
and notions that don't amount to diddly. That you're as vulnerable as a newborn babe and, this time, there's no one to

take care of you till you grow up. You're stuck, with your infantile terror and your adult body. That's the waking nightmare. There is nothing more terrifying."

"Great artists and great thinkers have always paralleled each other. Dali has Freud. You can't say that about Magritte. Who's Magritte's great thinker?"

"Claire Weekes!" I opined and got ignored. I didn't mind though. I was too busy being fascinated by two things. One was Bob's attitude toward Belinda Lomax. She was talking mostly about sex and Bob was clearly all ears. Ordinarily, I would have thought he'd be shocked, but this was a new gusto-grabbing Bob I was seeing. When Belinda confessed to never having experienced a particular kind of orgasm, Bob all but saluted. ("Reporting for duty, *Sir*. Ready when you are, C.B.") And when someone suggested that perhaps a particularly kind and patient lover might bring about the desired response in her, Bob's whole demeanor screamed out, "ME! ME! ME!"

Which explains why they left together when the evening ended. Tish never did show up, so there really wasn't any reason for Bob to hang around protecting me from suspects.

The other thing that fascinated me was this guy at the bar. Talk about your nightmare blind date. He was almost totally encased in black leather, with enough chains around his torso to sink a small island. Ordinarily, I laugh at such people. Suddenly, I wasn't laughing. Suddenly, I was visualizing Joe in such a getup. He looked adorable.

What a pair of dopes we had been! Did we ever do anything really wild? Not us. We were too healthy. Retards, that's what we were.

Sometimes just a look would do it. If he *stared* at me in a certain way, I'd climax. He'd sit there, smoking a cigarette and staring at me through half-closed eyes, and before you knew it, I'd be moaning and groaning and writhing, and telling him to stop before I passed out and he'd say something cute like, "Go ahead. I know how to revive you." And I'd climax! Or "Let's both pass out." And I'd climax! Or he wouldn't say anything.

He'd just exhale the smoke. And I'd climax! Two morons. What did we know from variations? Not a damn thing. Ohhh, what I wouldn't have given for one more session with that man, now that I'd seen the light.

I wondered if this meant I was getting weird. Ahhh, with my rotten luck it was probably just a temporary condition. It probably happens to everybody who sees their boyfriend die a violent death and then nearly has their tonsils and their appendix removed in the fraction of a millisecond by a subway train. Already I could feel the appeal of excruciating pain lessening.

The Marquis de Sade at the bar apparently misinterpreted my blank expression as a come-hither look. He sauntered over, rattled his chains in my face, and suggested we leave together. But I told him, "Oh, grow up," and he left me alone.

My phone is ringing when I get home. It's Shelly. She's crying.

"Nikki? Thank God! Nikki? Don't say anything."

"Shelly? What is it? Is it your head? Does it hurt? Ohhhh . . ."

"Nikki! Shut the hell up and listen to me! Where's Bob? Is he there?"

"No. He'll probably be back later. He took Belinda Lomax home and . . ."

"*Listen* to me, goddamn it, Nikki! You have to get out of there right now! Do you understand? NOW!"

"Why? What's wrong?"

"Nikki?" She's crying and I start to cry too. A chill runs through me, head to toe, and suddenly, before she says it, I know what she's going to say. "Get out of there now, Nikki. I didn't tell Bob about the train."

30

I ran down my tenement stairway, taking the steps almost two at a time. But no wobbling-turkey sound came forth from me now. I was sure the frantic beating of my own heart, the fevered intake and outtake of my breath were audible enough as it was. I was positive, *positive*, as I rounded each and every corner of those landings that I would find Bob, slowly, patiently trudging up the stairs, on his slow, patient way to my apartment and to the sitting duck inside. But each landing contained nothing, save an occasional strolling cockroach, perusing the environs for a neighborly bag of garbage left outside an apartment door.

I made it down into the street and didn't stop to look around. I ran, *ran* to First Avenue and jumped in a cab. A few minutes later I was delivered at Shelly's door.

"What made you realize—?"

"I was thinking about—!"

"When did it first . . . ?"

"I didn't *speak* to Bob—!"

"Thank God I mentioned that—"

"So how did *he* know—?!"

"He must have been afraid I'd mention it—"

"He *couldn't* have known. It wasn't on the news. I know, because I listened for it in the hospital. It wasn't on any news. We didn't even tie up the rush hour long enough for that—"

"Remember? He *told* me to hang up. He must have been *afraid* you'd tell me—"

"How could he possibly have known, unless he was the one who pushed—!"

"I can't stay here, Shelly! He'll *know* where I've gone. He'll start to think, and he'll put two and two together! He'll know where I am. I can't stay here."

"But where can you go? To a hotel?"

"No." Bob has become omniscient. "He'll know where I am, no matter where I hide."

"Do you want to go to the police?"

"And tell them what? I have no proof of this. Of *any* of it! Oh, how could I have been so stupid? All along! He'd have a key! He'd had a motive! He'd have access to the valuables to plant on the junkie. And he was right there in the studio *with* me when I found the will! Oh, God! For once the person right *there* at the scene *was* the guilty one, and I was too stupid to know it! I can't stay here, Shelly. He'll know where I've gone!"

"How 'bout back home? Back to Brooklyn, I mean. Your folks' house, I mean."

"No, no. He'll think of that too, just like you did."

"It's a big city, Nikki. There's got to be someplace . . ."

"All of a sudden, it's very small, this city. All of a sudden, it's so small that it's *walkable,* from any one point to the other. I feel as if I'll walk right into him on any streetcorner. Ohhhh, God, Shelly, where am I going to go?"

"Out of state, maybe? Do you have any relatives that live out of state?"

"No, goddamn it to hell! They all live within ten blocks of each other. They're a very close-knit family. Except for one uncle in Staten Island. And I don't want to be stuck in *Staten Island* for this." We both stop and think. "Shelly!"

"What?"

"The country! Your place in the country! Do you think?"

"Wait a minute. Wait a minute. Let me think! Let me think if Bob knows about it."

It takes her forever to think about it. In between thinking about it, she bursts into tears every once in a while.

"Oh, Nikki, Nikki! When I realized what you *said!* When I realized you thought *I* had told Bob . . . !"

"Forget about that now! Does he know about your country place?"

"No. I don't think so. How would he know? I don't remember ever saying anything about it to him. We never really talked that much, me and Bob. I think he was afraid people would think he was getting too familiar with one of Joe's girls."

"I know what you mean. So he doesn't know about it?"

"I'm pretty sure."

"Would you mind if I went there? You don't have to come with me, if you're afraid. I wouldn't blame you if you didn't want to come with me."

Shelly thought. "He's already killed one person. And he's tried to kill you."

"I won't blame you if you don't want to come. I think he's very dangerous, too. I won't blame you . . ."

"How will you get there?"

"Shit! I'm afraid to go to any bus depots. Or to even call a car service! He'd find out. He's like a *cop*, that Bob, I swear to God! He always reminded me of a bull!"

"I'll have to come with you. I'll have to drive you."

"No, Shelly, it's all right. I'll think of something else . . ."

"Don't argue with me, stupid! We're wasting time. Let's go."

Without even stopping to pick up a toothbrush, we went.

Shelly drove like a maniac, but I didn't care, for once. The faster and farther we got away from the city, the happier I'd be. We took turns crying and rehashing it all. At one point, Shelly turned on the windshield wipers because she was crying and she thought it was raining outside.

"He was always very repressed," Shelly says. "Didn't he always strike you as a very repressed person? One of those people who goes along for years being Mr. Nice Guy, then goes on a shooting spree one day and kills twenty-one people? I asked him once what his favorite color was and he said blue. A sure sign of a repressed person!"

"Now, all of a sudden, he's shining. Did you notice? Oh, no, that's right. You haven't seen him. All of a sudden he's shining. Like he's gotten rid of some horrible burden. Talking about how we don't live forever and we might as well really live it up now. Just tonight, he was maneuvering Belinda Lomax into the sack. Or she was maneuvering him."

"Belinda Lomax? The girl in search of the better orgasm?"

"That's the one."

"She doesn't seem like his type at all!"

"Well, she is now. He's *free* now. He's *liberated*. His little light is no longer hidden under a bushel! He is no longer over-shadowed by Joe!"

"I would have thought it was for the money!"

"What money?"

"The inheritance. In the will! Joe left him a bundle!"

Now I'm the one who bursts into tears. "I didn't even know that. He told me Joe left most of it to charity."

"Well, he did. I suppose you could put it like that. But Bob was one of the charities he left some of it to."

"Oh, God! And to think I spent so much time alone with him. All last night, I slept like a baby, knowing he was in the next room. *Protecting* me."

"Well, thank God you found out when you did. Think of it. You could have been sleeping *right now*, with him in the next room."

"He was the one I went to for help. He was the one listing suspects with me!"

"Was I on that list?" Shelly asked nonchalantly, taking a curve at almost seventy miles an hour. I didn't say anything. "Listen," she said. "I'd be offended if I wasn't. I was a big part of Joe's life. I'd be offended if I wasn't at least a suspect."

"Well, in that case, relax. Brendan seemed to think—oh, my God! Brendan! I even accused innocent Brendan of—"

"You thought it might have been Brendan? I never would

have thought of Brendan. Why would he? He certainly wasn't in Joe's will. He's sort of wealthy, isn't he?"

"Sometimes he is and sometimes he isn't. He goes from being a millionaire to a pauper every other month, depending on the price of soy beans and gold. But I didn't think it had anything to do with money, when I suspected Brendan. I thought it was . . . emotional reasons."

"What emotional reasons?"

"I thought Brendan was in love with me."

"What? Oh, Nikki. No reflection on you! But you certainly don't seem like Brendan's type. Brendan always struck me as the kind of man who went for younger women, not *older* women." (Wasn't this terrific? First, a school teacher. Now I was just too darn old. Boy, the things people tell you right to your face sometimes.) "What ever made you think he was in love with *you*? Did he ever say anything?"

"No, not really. It's just that we never slept together. And you know how some men are. You tell them no, and it's like waving a red flag in front of a bull. As soon as they find out they can't have you, they fall instantly in love with you. Some guys are so damn in love with rejection, it's not even funny."

"I supposed it's the old thing of not wanting to join any club that would accept you as a member."

"I'll give them members! They're all so crazy, every last one of them. I never want to look at another man as long as I live."

"Who else was a suspect?"

"Tish."

"Really? Why Tish? Ohhh, I get it. Because of the paintings." The squeal of tires accompanied her insight. Another curve. "Yes, yes!" she said. "I would have thought of Tish, too. She always likes to take the easy way out. She'd commit murder in order to stay rich. She didn't ever want to go back to work again."

"Did Tish ever steal anything from Joe?"

"What? Of course not! Who told you that?"

"Bob! He said she used to swipe things. But I suppose that was all part of the plan, to keep me off course, to make me think it was—"

"Wait a minute. I do remember something now." The blare of a car horn punctuated that. Shelly cut someone off on the Thruway. "Ahhhh, same to you, mister!" she yelled out the window. "Did you see that guy? Giving me the finger? I signaled! What's he griping about?"

"What do you remember?"

"Oh, yeah. Tish stealing things."

"You mean it was true?"

"Would you wait a minute? And let me finish what I was going to say? You're so hyper, Nikki! You're a real Type A personality. Or is it Type B? Whichever one it is that's the candidate for a heart attack. You are definitely a candidate."

Shelly would never die of a heart attack. She would die because someone choked her to death, because their nerves snapped while they were waiting for her to get to the point.

"What it was," she continued slowly, "was that Tish told me something once. In confidence, of course. You won't tell anybody, will you?"

"Of course not."

"Well, she told me that Bob came on to her."

"WHAT?"

"That's right! That's why I didn't even believe her at the time. But maybe she was telling the truth. Why would she make up something like that? She's not smart enough to make things up. Anyway, she turned him down, of course. She wasn't about to risk Joe finding out about it. I personally think Joe couldn't have cared less. But anyway, she turned Bob down and you know what a bitch she can be when she wants to."

"Type A."

"At least. So she told me that she told Bob, 'Listen, Bob, super-straight can be a kick in some things, but in men, it's positively deadly.' She told him she'd probably fall asleep while he was doing it."

"Tish, the diplomat. And how did Bob react to all these compliments?"

"She said he got really nasty."

"I wonder why."

"She said he called her a lousy dyke and said he only suggested it because he felt sorry for her, because she walks around looking so horny all the time. He thought he could cure what ails her—better than Alex, anyway. So Tish told me, 'Don't be surprised if he starts spreading all kinds of stories about me now.' I thought she meant about being gay. I told you I already had my doubts about her. I thought that's what she was afraid of Bob blabbing about. I never heard anything about her stealing things, though. Listen, if Tish took anything from Joe, she'd take it because she thinks she's entitled to it. I wouldn't call that stealing, really."

We rode along in silence for a while. Strangely enough, I was already beginning to feel relaxed. Just getting out of the city was performing miracles on my nervous system. We turned off the Thruway, taking Route 17 instead, the scenic route. The enormous knot that had been in my chest began to loosen a little. It was being in the country that was doing it. The country cures everything. It's like sex. It restores your spirit and makes you whole. That's one belief Joe and I shared completely—about sex curing everything. ("You have a sore throat? You know what cures that, don't you?" "Yeah, hehhehheh. Who says?" "It's a fact! You could ask anybody in Algiers! It's the protein! It's very healthy." "Yeah, for *you!*" "I swear! Try it! It'll clear up your sore throat like *that.*" He snapped his fingers. "Oh, all right, you bullshit artist, but don't think you're kidding anybody . . ." Damned if he wasn't right. Or maybe I still had the sore throat and I just didn't care anymore. Of course, then he said *his* throat was feeling a little scratchy, too, and what was good for the goose was probably just as good for the gander. Lunatic. Meanwhile, we were two naive idiots. Never *once* a little torture. Dopes!)

All right, so I'd let the country purify things now for me,

like sex used to. I breathed deep, greedy breaths for that intoxicating country air. Grass! Horses! Was life getting bearable again?

Shelly hit a cruising speed of about eighty, and we went sailing headlong into the peaceful country night. She put a tape on the tape deck. Mantovani. I was in heaven.

As to what we would do about the current problem, neither of us had a clue. But like that guy in *God's Little Acre,* we had the land to comfort us now, and we'd think about problems tomorrow. Isn't that what Scarlett O'Hara used to say, too?

The cabin was terrific. Exactly what you'd expect a country cabin to look like—ramshackle, lopsided, and decidedly rustic. Nestled in about fifty feet off the dirt road, it was rimmed with a semicircle of lush trees. I loved it.

"I want to live here," I told Shelly. "If you ever want to sell this place, and I, due to some miracle, have the money, I want to buy it from you."

"You'll get first choice. But I'll never want to sell it. Isn't it fantastic?"

At the door, Shelly extricated a ring of keys from her pocketbook that would do Mrs. Danvers, that housekeeper in *Rebecca,* proud. But Shelly wasn't Mrs. Danvers. She was the nameless, hapless heroine, trying hard to cope. The square of cotton gauze was still over one eyebrow. God, but I was certainly bringing this girl a passel of trouble. We *were* good friends, weren't we! It turned out we really were good friends. Since grammar school. ("How could you, Nikki! You're supposed to be my friend! You're just a traitor, that's all! How could you sleep with him when you're supposed to be my friend?" But how could I not?) So we're not just acquaintances, after all. We're friends.

I was trying to hold the flashlight steady for her, its beam the only break in the darkness. She finds the right key and slipped it into the lock. "There!" I wonder how dark it would be without the flashlight. I flicked it off, and we both screamed so loud it was comical. So, of course, I fumbled trying to turn it on again, but eventually, I did. "I just wanted to see . . ." "You asshole!" The door was open and she was feeling along one wall for the light switch. "Wait a minute. Wait a minute. It's right here somewhere. Don't you *dare* turn that flashlight off again or, so help me, I'll wring your neck!" I started to cry, overwhelmed suddenly by her kindness.

"Oh, Shelly. You really are a good person to be doing all this for me. I'm so sorry for everything that's happened. For you banging your head and for turning out the flashlight."

"Retard. Wait a second. Here it is!" Click. Nothing happened. "Shit!" she said. "I forgot. The main fuse is off. We'll have to go around to the side of the house and turn it on."

"I'm afraid."

"Oh, grow up! Would you stop blubbering like an idiot and hold that flashlight steady? Come on. Let's go."

"I really couldn't help myself, Shelly. I mean I know it sounds stupid, but I really couldn't." She knew instantly what I was talking about. "I know it's a cliché," I continue crying, "but it really was like it was bigger than both of us. I mean, I knew you were going out with him, but I couldn't—"

"Yeah, yeah. Would you hold that thing steady? Shine it over here. Over here, where I'm walking! Watch out. I think that's poison sumac." Kreek and Kroak made their way along the outside of the cabin, rounding the bend, Shelly feeling for the fuse box. "In other words," she says, "if you had it to do all over again, you wouldn't."

"Of course, I would! That's what I'm telling you. It was unavoidable! It was something that just had to be!"

"That's what I figured. Some friend!"

"I'm sorry."

"Here it is!" She took another hour looking for the key to unlock the fuse box. Finally, she found it and threw the switch. The light inside the house went on. "There! Thank God. Let's get inside fast. It's creepy out here."

When she got to the front door and looked inside she screamed. "Oh, my God!"

"WHAT IS IT?" Shelly was wrong. I would never die of a heart attack if I didn't have one then.

"I left this place in such a mess! Oh, God, I'm so embarrassed. I don't suppose you'd consider waiting out here for a few minutes while I straighten up?"

"You're kidding, right?"

"I didn't think so. All right, well, just ignore the mess then. I'm so embarrassed."

Shelly's mess, as I already suspected, was no big deal. There was a large sketch pad on the couch with some loose pages torn out of it scattered around here and there, on the coffee table, on the floor next to the couch, on the couch itself. There was a coffee mug on the table, too, with the residue of a green murky liquid inside. And there were charcoal pencils and shading stubs and assorted drawing things around.

She immediately started gathering up the sketches. They were of clothes, of course. The usual Margaret Dumont fare. In her sketches, Margaret was a lot thinner though.

There was that musty, damp cabin smell in the room, which I thought was terrific. But Shelly kept going, "Peuw!" and "Open the windows. Open the windows."

"Could I use the bathroom first, please? If I don't pee I'm going to burst." I pushed against one door. "Is this the bathroom?"

"DON'T."

I froze. "WHAT IS IT?"

"I probably left that room a mess, too. Just give me a minute to straighten up."

"Oh, okay. But would you please stop screaming like that? I keep thinking you're catching a glimpse of Anthony Perkins in drag somewhere in here."

She laughed. "Oh, I'm sorry."

While she was straightening out the bathroom, I finished gathering up the sketches, tapping them against the coffee table to align them. Content with doing that much housework, I sat on the couch and fanned through them. Hmmmm, not bad. Hmmmm. Very nice. But there was only one I really liked a lot. For once, pre-1935 looked appropriate. It was a wedding gown. A wedding dress, really, as it was midcalf in length. (As were all Shelly's designs, anyway.) All very lacy and drapy, like it was a starched and ruffled white organza graduation dress that got a bucket of water dumped on it. The result was streamlined, if a little downcast. As graceful as a swan's neck though. I really liked it. This sketch had the face drawn in. The face looked a lot like Shelly's.

"Okay," she said from the doorway. "The coast is clear."

"You're really ridiculous, you know? You know what *my* place looks like."

She shrugged as I passed her in the doorway. Then I closed the bathroom door and peed for at least a full five minutes.

31

The mess gone, the windows opened, and my bladder emptied, everything began to take on a cozy warm glow to it. Shelly made tea.

This was really very nice.

Two spinsters, living a genteel spinster life. Maybe she'd be willing to sell me half the place. I had some more book-cover commissions coming up. I wondered what she'd want for half the place. I could really paint in peace up here. Maybe we could get some cats, for the yard. Sipping my Darjeeling, I asked, "Don't you ever get lonely up here? Coming up here, all by yourself? Isn't it kind of isolated?"

"That's why I love it! I *love* being isolated, not seeing another person for three or four days at a time. If I want company, I just take a walk into town. About three miles from here. People are so friendly up here. When I'm in the mood for company, I invite a few friends over for a game of Scrabble or a card game. The rest of the time I'm very happy to be alone. That's why I got this place. So I could be all alone."

So much for *that* idea.

After tea Shelly said she was exhausted and she was going to bed. And that she'd leave me some sheets and blankets on the couch. And did I want the electric heater, but you'd be surprised how, once you were under the covers, how you warmed up.

And I said, "On the couch? I don't want to sleep on the couch!"

"Well, I hope you don't expect me to sleep on the couch! There's a limit to the extent of my hospitality here."

"Of course I don't expect you to sleep on the couch. I thought we would sleep *together*."

After innumerable cracks like "First Tish, now you too?" and assorted wise-ass remarks, it was established that no one was looking to feel Shelly up in the night and that I was just afraid. (Dostoevski observed you should never say "only passion." Well, you should never say "just afraid" either.)

"But I hate to sleep with somebody else in the same bed," Shelly whined. "I don't feel comfortable. Except with Joe of course, but that was a different story." (Want to bet I was going to hear the whole story?) "With Joe, I'd sleep all cuddled up in his arms," she said, "just like a little child. I'd feel so safe."

"*Must* we go into that now?"

"Oh, all right. I just hope you appreciate what I'm doing. I probably won't sleep a wink all night!"

She loaned me a pair of her old lady pajamas, and I changed in the bathroom.

As to the matter of the lights staying on or off, she was absolutely adamant. They had to be off. All of them. "But why?" I whined. Apparently she was too tired to argue about it all night. She settled the issue with two brilliant sentences.

"What do you want to leave a light on for, Nikki? It'll just make you a clearer target if Bob is out there with a gun!"

Within sixty seconds of her head hitting the pillow, I heard her slow, even breathing. She was either already asleep or pretending to be. I certainly wasn't. I was lying there with my eyes wide open and my brain wide awake, staring into the black void in front of my nose.

"What was *that*?" I said.

"Hmmmm?"

"That *noise*! Didn't you hear that noise? You *must* have heard that noise."

"There's a lot of noises up here, Nikki. You're in the country now. Go to sleep."

"It sounded just like . . ." A chill ran through me. "Just like . . ." I gasped, ". . . someone stepping!"

"It was probably a little animal . . . stepping," she said wearily. "Tiptoeing from bush to bush. Go to sleep."

Boy, was she stupid for a smart girl. If she thought I was even going to so much as close my eyes, let *alone* go to sleep, she was sadly mistaken. I had every intention of staying awake all night, wide-eyed. With the patience of a saint, quietly waiting until morning. Uncomplaining, no matter *how* long it took getting here.

I fell asleep.

Morning arrived way too soon, as far as I was concerned.

"NIKKI! I'M GOING SHOPPING! DO YOU WANT ME TO GET YOU ANYTHING?"

"Arghhhh."

"NIKKI! WAKE UP FOR A MINUTE! DO YOU WANT ANYTHING FROM THE STORE?"

Where the hell did she get the megaphone, that's what *I* couldn't figure out.

"What are you *yelling* like that for?" I inquired reasonably, although frankly, I felt quite annoyed. "I'm right here, goddamn your eyes!"

"WHO'S *YELLING*?" she bellowed. "I'M *WHISPERING*. DO YOU WANT ANYTHING IN *TOOOWWWWNNNN*?"

"Yes. Ear plugs."

"I'M GOING. BYYYYYE."

I had almost dozed off again when I remembered. Leaping out of bed, I ran to the front door, but it was too late. I was just in time to see her car disappearing down the road, out of sight. The single word *COFFEEEEEEE* echoed through the mountainside, rousing all the little animals and flushing several large flocks of wild geese or vultures or some such birds from the treetops. I wondered if she heard me.

Well, I was up now, and there was no coffee in the house. I needed something to occupy my mind, lest I run amok. I decided to contemplate ways in which it might be possible for me to save my life, when and if I ever got back to the big city.

One. Throw myself at the mercy of the police. Tell them I was only *kidding* that time about going to the media.

Two. Get all the people I had previously suspected of murder to speak up on my behalf.

A. Tish: "Yes, Lieutenant Morrisey, he made a pass at me. And any man who would betray his best friend by making time with his best friend's ex is capable of any treachery, including murder. Also he spread stories that I stole things. Now how could I steal things when everybody knows they were my very own things to begin with? What was Joe's was mine."

B. Brendan: "Seize her, guards! She's a lunatic! None of us are safe to walk the streets while she goes unfettered. If she's saying this fellow Bob did it, don't believe her. Just a little while ago, she was telling everybody *I* did it. Also, she was telling people that I was in love with her. The woman's deranged, I tell you!" Okay, forget Brendan.

C. Shelly: Shelly's testimony was obvious. She never told Bob about the train, etc., etc. Shelly's testimony was by far the most important.

D. Lorraine: "He refused to let me send him any literature on the Lord." Lorraine's testimony was iffy, at best.

E. Ann: "I always liked Bob a lot, Lieutenant. He's always been a valued and trusted friend. If that awful Nikki Andrews slut is accusing him of murder now, pay no attention. She accuses everyone of murder eventually. That's what she *does*. It's a symptom of her paranoid, schizophrenic, manic-depressive psychosis. Also, it's probably a case of sour grapes, too. She probably lunged for his private parts once and he no doubt expressed disdain for her immoderate behavior."

All right, so it all depended on Shelly's testimony. I still had nothing to worry about. When Shelly knows she has right on her side, she's dauntless!

"Tell the police? Are you mad?" Shelly asked, unpacking groceries.

"Well, what else can we do? I can't hide out forever, living like a refugee."

"Moving to another state and living under a different name isn't exactly living like a refugee. Women do it all the time when they get married. Just pretend you got married. You really won't have to wear a babushka and travel in steerage the rest of your life. You'll settle in very nicely. In Oregon or someplace. They have artists in Oregon, don't they?"

"Very funny! Shelly! I don't believe you're refusing to do this!"

"Believe it!"

"But why?"

"Because I don't want to end up dead in some swamp out in Staten Island with a dead canary in my mouth."

"What the HELL are you talking about?"

"The 'boys,' the Mob. I'm not about to squeal to the 'screws' on one of their own. No matter *what* you say. So just . . ."

"HAHAHAHAHAHAHAHAHAHA. You think Bob has Mafia connections? How could you be so naïve? Bob doesn't have any Mafia connections!"

"How do *you* know?"

"Because . . ." I said lamely, "he told me."

"Oh. Pardon me. And what makes you think my talking to the police would do any good anyway? Neither of us have any proof whatsoever that it was Bob who pushed you. I certainly didn't see him on that platform, and you didn't either. So I'd just end up risking my life for nothing.

"Nikki, I really don't see that you have any choice in this. I'm sure it must be very traumatic to realize that you have to pull up stakes and start your life over somewhere else, but what else can you do? And it isn't as if you have some world-famous reputation as Nicole Andrews, Artist, to worry about. So what if you have to change your name? You might actually get *more* work." She laughed maliciously.

"Aren't we the soul of wit this morning," I snarled. "All right. Don't squeal on Bob. I'll handle it myself. As soon as we get back to the city, I'll go see Morrisey. What are you doing with that bag there?" It was the last grocery bag.

"I'm folding it. Why?"

"Isn't there anything else in that bag?"

"In this?" she inquired innocently. "No. Why?"

"Let *me* see that!" I whipped it out of her hands and stared down into the bottom of it. I did everything but turn it upside down and shake it. "Oh! My! God!" I said.

"What's the matter?"

"You didn't get any coffee," I said, massaging my temples. The massaging wasn't helping. Maybe if I pulled at my hair, very gently at first?

"I asked you if you wanted anything, didn't I?"

"Yeah, I know," I said, close to sobbing. "It's not your fault. I tried calling after you but . . ." It was then I noticed a particularly sadistic gleam in her aquamarine eyes. And a slightly arrogant grin on her face.

"It's in my pocketbook," she said, laughing, referring to that feedbag of a purse she carried with her all the time. "How could I *not* hear you? You could probably be heard in Brazil!"

I found the can of coffee in her purse.

"Happy now, you night person?"

My mood brightened considerably, and I laughed, too. I forgot about that side of Shelly's personality, the merry prankster side. Like everyone else, I was taken in by that newborn chick look of hers. It always amazed me in junior high how she got on so well with the toughest boys in the class. The ones who would call up the teachers' lunchroom during lunchtime and breathe heavily into the phone. They'd always tell her about their exploits (knowing she could be trusted not to squeal), and she'd always fall down laughing. Then she'd tell me and I'd be duly horrified, chickenshit that I was. While she'd never take part in any such exploits herself, she always had a healthy appreciation for somebody else's devilment.

I started to wonder if she and Joe ever played little games

involving old socks and four-poster beds. Maybe he wasn't as deprived as I thought!

Later that afternoon, we were sitting in the backyard. Shelly was reading *Pride and Prejudice* for the two-hundredth time. I was brooding.

"Shelly," I said, "I've been thinking."

"I *thought* I smelled wood burning."

"Whuh? Oh! Oh, God. That is so old. I didn't even laugh at it the first time I heard it, in the second grade." I looked at her, disgusted, and then we both proceeded to laugh hysterically.

"But seriously," I said at last, "it's possible that Bob could find out about this place, you know? We're still in New York state, aren't we?"

"No. Just over the border, in Pennsylvania."

"Same difference. He could go to some kind of hall of records or something, where deeds are registered. I mean, once he realizes you've disappeared, too, he might think of that. It's possible he does know you have a country place somewhere."

"You really think he might come here?" She looked concerned.

"He might."

"So what do you want to do?"

"Go back to the city."

"I still think you're being very reckless about this. I still say you shouldn't go back to the city at all. Just take off. Disappear altogether. Don't even tell *me* where you're going. This way, when they break both my legs, I won't be able to tell them anything."

"What a pal!"

"I could even tell them you held me hostage! Against my will! That you had a *gun* or something." She wasn't kidding. I ignored her.

"Nobody's going to break your legs! I'm going back and telling Morrisey . . ."

"I could let you have a little money," she said hopefully. "Not a lot, but I always keep a little cash stashed away up here. For emergencies. Would seven hundred dollars be enough? You could give me a personal check to cover it. I trust you."

"Yeah, well, don't. It would bounce. I have about a dollar twenty in my savings account. Besides which, I'm not running anywhere."

She sighed deeply, abandoning all hope.

"Okay, so what do you want to do? Go back now?"

"How 'bout we leave tonight?"

"All right. I don't mind driving at night. Less traffic. We can leave right after dinner. Around seven-thirty?"

"Very good." But it wasn't very good. In fact, everything looked very bad. And I couldn't help thinking it was only going to get worse.

The two condemned idiots ate a hearty meal. Shelly insisted she wanted to clean up the kitchen by herself. I'd only put everything back in the wrong places, she said.

"And I bought groceries!" she remembered.

"Take 'em back to the city, why don't you?"

"Oh, yeah, all right."

I went for a little walk in the meantime, to gather some wildflowers to bring home, too. When I came back, Shelly was sitting on the porch, reading in the fading light.

"How was your walk?"

"Terrific. I only got lost twice. And that was on the road. And then, while I was happily picking wildflowers, I realized I was standing ankle deep in something that looked like poison ivy. In my open-toed sandals."

"Sometimes it helps if you wash it off right away. Use the brown soap in the bathroom. Everything's all packed. I'm ready to go when you are."

"Okay. I'll be right out."

I stood in the tub, letting the water rinse the brown soap from my hands and feet. Then I looked around for a towel. It was a shame to use one of the new clean ones hanging there, just for my feet, so I opened the hamper, a wicker basket behind the door. I opened it hesitantly, afraid a field mouse would leap out at me.

I was in luck. No leaping mice. I peered into the basket cautiously anyway. And then I saw it. Not a mouse. A dark maroon towel, with the familiar gray monogram in one corner: *JS.* I pulled it out of the hamper slowly, as if it were somehow contaminated. There was the frayed spot at one end of it, just like I remembered it. Where the terrycloth had been worn away from repeated washings. I knew without a doubt it was the same towel. I sat down on the edge of the tub and tried to think.

The sketch of the girl in the wedding dress. The only figure that had a face. Shelly's face. As recently as her last visit up here, she was still making sketches of her wedding gown, as she had so many years ago. She still had hopes of marrying him. Was that so crazy? So did *I*, in a way. I mean, if I was going to marry anybody, it would have been him. But did something happen that made her realize, once and for all, that this marriage between them was never to be?

Yes, she could have come there that day, letting herself in with her own key. Yes, they could have stood there talking for a while. I wouldn't have been able to hear her voice. She always spoke in such a whisper when she talked to Joe. Shyly, demurely, respectfully. Yes, they would have gone up to the roof to discuss things in private. Discuss what? An ultimatum? At long last?

Her whole adult life was built on one belief. "Someday, he'll marry me. I'll have his children." I myself had heard her say it a hundred times. Through all his marriages, through everything, she continued saying it. She firmly believed that someday she'd be the suburban housewife, more affluent than most, but otherwise not unlike her older sister in Ramsey. Three sons, a station wagon, and a husband who came home from the office every day at six. She lived her whole life believing that.

("The scariest thing in the world is realizing you really

don't know anything. That the beliefs by which you've lived your life were really just so much illusion all along.") Shelly, the realist! Shelly, who prided herself on knowing life, on knowing human nature. Finding out, with the utterance of one word—*no*—that she really doesn't know anything at all. What would such a realization do to her? She would want to deny it at first, certainly. One doesn't live twenty years of one's life in an illusion and then watch it shatter, with calm and grace. One would deny it had been shattered, at least at first. Was pushing him off the roof her denial? And with him gone, she might even make herself believe in the illusion again. "He'd have married me eventually. But he died."

And Bob! I ran away from Bob, because of what *she* told me. It wasn't Bob who pushed me off that platform. It was Shelly. The person at the scene *was* the guilty one. The will! Her doing. She could have forged it. She was the only one who could make out his writing at its worst. She could have copied his writing. She was an artist, after all.

And why not do it? Let me get blamed for the murder. Perfect. I was the one who stole him away from her all those years before. At least I'm sure that's how she felt about it. Why shouldn't I suffer for that now? I was supposed to be her friend, back then, and I wasn't. I turned out to be a traitor. Why not pay me back now? "Tish, I could understand! They were married! But *you!*" She could forgive Tish. She could forgive Lorraine. She could forgive Ann. She just couldn't forgive *me.*

Prison, or a life underground. Oh, she'd be settling a *lot* of old scores by having me blamed for it. Like my work. "Everybody falls in love with oils, Nikki. But you can't make that your life's work. You have to be realistic(!). Sure, we'd all like to be, quote, serious, unquote, artists. But do you know what the odds are against making a living at that? Don't let Joe's success fool you. The odds are one in a million. And you're not another Joe Savanah! Why don't you get into something practical—full time, though, not half-assed, the way you do it now? Commercial art. Joe could probably get you into an ad agency, full time. Why don't you ask him? You want me to ask him for you? Maybe I could even get you into designing, as an assistant or something. But you'd have to take it seriously, Nikki, if I *do* get you something. No goofing off or anything. You'd have to show up on time, every day! Nine to five! Do you think you could do that?"

And when I'd tell her not to bother, it would sound as if I couldn't do it. Which was probably the God's honest truth after all! Even if I wanted to do it, I probably couldn't. And I didn't want to! But I'd tell her not to bother and it would sound as if I couldn't hope to accomplish what she did so effortlessly—support myself with a certain amount of comfort and security. Only she could do that. It sounded as if it was understood she was stable, serious, capable. And yes, yes, I knew I was just being stubborn and stupid, and worst of all, unrealistic, but I was going to stick with what I was doing, holding out for the big juicy plum—oils on canvas, success and recognition as a serious artist, no quotes around it. I must have sensed her real fear wasn't that I'd fail as an artist, but that I'd succeed! That I'd stand as a reminder of her own lost dreams. Because, even then, when she had the nice apartment and the country place, the clothes and the car, and I had nothing, she was still jealous! Jealous of the *nothing* I had. Because it meant I still had hope, and she had given that up long ago. Given it up only because it wasn't her real true hope. Her real true hope was Joe. "I don't think a wife should be more accomplished than her husband. Or even as accomplished. Oh, I know this makes me some kind of Victorian throwback, but I really don't. The husband has to be more successful than the wife, or else there's bound to be competition between them. Even if it's subconscious. I'd be very content to let my husband have the limelight all to himself."

And now, the solution she hit upon was almost too perfect, to settle the score regarding my ambitions. It was better than having me in prison, even. Because how could I make a name for myself as an artist if my one concern from now on was remaining anonymous? What better way to annihilate my goal once and for all? It would no longer be a question of the odds being against me. It would become a complete impossibility.

The whole thing had just the right quality of cleverness and devilment to brand it as her own. Still, I couldn't believe she would actually carry it through. Maybe long enough to scare the bejesus out of me, yes. But not long enough to make me live my *life* like that.

Or was I holding on to *my* illusions now, about her? Was I the one denying reality now? I held that reality in my very own hands, the reality of this towel. She killed Joe. But she wasn't going to ruin my career? Come on! She pushed me in front of a train, for chrissakes! How stupid could I be?

But even that. If she really meant to kill me, all she had to do that day was wait a few seconds longer and push me when there was no chance I could get away. Was it simply a miscalculation on her part? But no one could ever accuse Shelly of acting too quickly. No, she'd timed it right. Her intention was to scare me into running away, not to kill me. She just forgot what a hopeless klutz I am. (Thank God for Lamont Miller.)

Why am I so reluctant to believe she is capable of a cold, calculated murder? What makes me so sure that killing Joe was a crime of passion? Maybe that was a cold, calculated murder, too. And what the hell is the difference anyway? Murder is murder. Why should she hesitate about killing me? No doubt her first crime had inured her to the taking of human life. Was murder like everything else? You get used to it?

In any case, what do I do about it now? Go out there with a kitchen knife and make a citizen's arrest? Or take off into the woods on my own? Or simply go out there, get in the car, and calmly drive back to the city with her. And then tell Morrisey of yet another turn in the case. Apparently, Shelly doesn't consider this towel a particularly incriminating bit of evidence. Or did she just forget it was here? Or is she counting on Morrisey's not considering it incriminating either? But why take a chance on my finding it at all? It doesn't make sense. Yet in some strange, unfathomable way, it does. In some way I can't figure out—literally, for the life of me—it sccms Shelly's style.

I get up from the tub edge, planning to walk outside. I realize suddenly that I'm not at all afraid of her. Why the hell *not?* Because she's a woman? If it was a man I was stranded up here with, a man I knew for a fact had committed murder once, and attempted murder once, I would probably already be dead of a heart attack from fear! Maybe because she's a woman, I feel equal to the threat now. I'm on guard now. It wouldn't be so easy to kill me now. Besides, there is no reason to believe she has some sort of weapon. Through all of this, she hasn't used a weapon. She's pushed! We'll drive back to the city. I'll talk to Morrisey. I'll just have to be very careful where I stand!

"Nikki? Come on, let's get going, if we're going."

I put the towel back in the hamper and flush the toilet to justify my stay. "Okay," I call back. When I emerge, we look at each other a second longer than seems totally natural. Is it because she remembers about the towel now?

"I'll lock up," she says, and I wonder if I imagined the look of apprehension in her eyes. "Got everything?"

"Yeah." I go out to the car to wait for her. It is just beginning to get dark as we pull away.

32

The trip up took almost three hours. Shelly asks if I would mind it very much if the trip back took a little longer. "I'd rather take the scenic route," she says. "The *really* scenic route, not just the smaller highways—the country backroads this time. There's hardly anybody on them and I can really drive. I feel like I'm in the Indy 500."

"Fine," I tell her. I'm still not afraid. I'm hip to her now. It won't be so easy this time.

"And it's really much, much prettier."

"Fine with me."

Neither of us seems to have much to say. I'm still too busy trying to figure it all out. If it was a cold, calculated murder—why? Why force an ultimatum now to begin with? The will? Could it have been a real will I found that day in the studio? Put there by her, yes, but taken from somewhere else *before* the murder. From Joe's safe, of course. She had access to that. By accident, she comes across the will. How can she continue to believe he'll marry her if he's just named me beneficiary in his will?

So, in a jealous rage, she confronts him with it that day on the roof, etc., etc.

Wait a minute. Wait a minute. That's what I *want* to have happened. I want to believe the will was real. Ann was so right. All through this, all I'm searching for is proof that he loved me. Oh, yes, I believed him when he told me that he loved me. But even then I didn't ask the question I should have. I didn't even think of it then. But I've thought of it since. "More than anybody else?" That was the mystery I was trying to solve. Did he love me more than he loved anybody else? Wasn't that the only love worth having?

So, now I'm putting my illusions on events. The will was real? Don't make me laugh. Wise up!

"You're very quiet, I must say," she says after a while. It is completely dark by now. Her speed has slowed somewhat, the Indy 500 out of her system, apparently. We are cruising along comfortably.

"Just enjoying the ride."

Her laugh is cynical. Then she sighs. "You know what he was like?" she says. No need to ask who.

"No. What was he like?" We both laugh. It's the game again. The I-knew-him-so-much-better-than-you game.

"Did you ever hear the story of the blind men and the elephant?" (I used to love to hear Shelly tell a story. Her voice takes on a lovely, lilting quality when she tells a story.) "Six blind men," she begins, "are asked to describe an elephant, through touch. One reaches out and embraces a leg. 'An elephant,' he says, 'is like a mighty tree in the forest.' Another blind man stretches out his arms and feels the wide expanse of the elephant's body. 'No,' he says, 'an elephant is like a mountain, vast and solid and immovable.' The third man feels the trunk of the elephant and says, 'You are both mistaken. An elephant is like the python, long and graceful, its whole head a huge mouth.' And so it goes with each of the men. 'An elephant is no bigger than a lizard,' one says, holding the tail, 'with skin like rope.' The one who touches the ear says, 'No, no, the creature is a great bird, with wings of leather, smooth and flat.' And the last man touches the tusk and says, 'An elephant is a sharp curved spear, made of hardest marble.'

"Joe was a blind man's elephant. And we were all the blind men. Each of us reached out and touched a different part of him. And we were each so sure that ours was the real part, the only part. But we were blind men, fumbling blindly." She laughed a little bit. It wasn't a happy laugh. "What finally 'tipped you off,' as the saying goes?"

"The towel in the hamper. If I hadn't stepped in what I thought was poison ivy, I never would have looked for a used towel. Did you forget it was in there?"

"No. And I didn't forget about the sketch of me in the wedding dress either."

"But you ran around so furiously to clean up when we first got there. I thought for sure you didn't want me to see . . ."

"The place was a mess," she says, laughing again. "I was embarrassed to be caught being such a sloppy housekeeper. I wasn't trying to hide any evidence."

"But, why not?"

"Because I thought, well, this'll settle it once and for all. If you figured it out, well, then, you figured it out. If not, not. I was leaving it in the hands of fate, I guess. All along, I've been leaving it in the hands of fate."

So that was it. Yes, that sounded like something she might do.

"I never expected fate to let it go this far, to tell you the truth," she added. "I thought at first of turning myself in immediately. I hadn't meant to push him. Not really. It was as if another pair of hands reached out suddenly and shoved him, not my hands at all. And then he was gone. Just like that. I almost couldn't believe it. I think I actually leaned over the railing myself, as if I could somehow catch him and bring him back. But, of course, that was impossible. He was already dead by then."

I didn't say anything.

"Don't you want to know why?" she asked. "I'll tell you anyway. I'm in an expansive mood. I'd waited so *long*, Nikki. So long! But unlike you, I had no intention of waiting forever. I wanted *children*. How long have I been talking about wanting t was no phantom's hands that took possession of her own when she pushed him. They were her own angry hands, engaged by all those years of timid waiting. "So I told him. In my shy little voice! I never seemed able to speak to that man in a normal tone of voice. I was always so intimidated by him. I don't know why. He was just a *man*, after all. Anyway, I told him about the doctors and about time running out. I more or less proposed to him.

"It wouldn't have been so bad if he had said no. Just a nice direct *no.* I would have been able to handle that. I'd gotten so good at handling things like that through the years. I rationalized everything that happened between us. It was a very lovely dreamworld I inhabited." ("There's nothing so scary as realizing you don't know anything. That you've lived your whole life in an illusion.") "If only he'd said a simple no, I'd still be in my dreamworld, and, incidentally, he'd still be alive. I would have understood! 'He's been married three times!' I would have told myself, 'All of them ending badly. Small wonder he doesn't want to get married again. Perhaps in time . . .' I would have made peace with that. I'd even give up the hope of having children. It would probably be better as far as my health was concerned anyway. Yes, it would all be for the *best* that he didn't want to get married and have children. See how good I am at rationalizing these things? But he didn't give me a nice, clearcut *no.* He did something far worse."

Oh, God, I think, he didn't laugh! ("Disaster strikes, and that idiot would laugh.") Shelly reads my mind. She laughs a little bit herself. "It sounds as if I'm about to say he laughed. He didn't laugh. Although I think even that would have been better. A little cruel, maybe. And he'd never be cruel, not openly anyway. And not to me. After all, what had I ever done to deserve his cruelty? But his *pity?* That was something else entirely."

So that's what she found so unbearable. His pity. But wasn't it his compassion that she always found so admirable?

children? Since the sixth grade? Remember? '\
up . . .' You were going to live in Paris and be ar
going to get married and have *at least* six children
Well, it looks as if there was hardly time for si)
one? I did go to visit my mother that week. But I s
that visit in the hospital down there. 'Female tro
called. For years they've been chipping away at m\
moving just a tiny part of the ovary, 'Don't w(
won't affect your ability to have children. It reduce
ity but maybe all of one percent.' And a little whi
'The whole ovary should be removed. Don't won
still have the other one.' But then it began to be, 'I
to have children, you'd better hurry up.' By now th\
ing me I needed a radical hysterectomy, but I wou.
it. I didn't care what risk I was in. I wanted a child
the hospitals for abortions and there I'd be, despera'
ically, trying to hold on to my female plumbing lon
get pregnant and bear a child. It was almost five ye
they first suggested the hysterectomy. As you cou
by now, they were growing more insistent about it
them I needed just a little more time. I'd put u
monthly hemorrhaging. We struck a deal. If I wasn
within six months, I'd let them take everything o\
have tumors in your uterus and still carry a healt
term, did you know that?"

"No."

"Anyway, I thought it was a risk worth taking. I
hysterectomy done right after I gave birth, if neces
needed was a little more time.

"And he was free now. He was leaving Ann.
knew that. There was no reason why he shouldn't
now. He always wanted children, too, did you know \
laughs slightly. "Shades of our old game, I guess.
know that about him? *I* did.' But none of us knew h
of us knew him at all!" The bitterness in her voice sl

Was it that it applied to her this time? Did it necessarily mean he demeaned her by feeling pity for her? I could never understand the difference between pity and compassion. Why was one an insult and not the other?

Shelly continued talking. "The look on his face!" she said, "when I finally finished stammering out my tale of woe: 'If I'm ever to have a child . . . if we're ever to have a family.'" She made a grunting sound. "Even now it embarrasses me to think of the things I said. Anyway, he looked stunned! Absolutely stunned! As if he never in a million years thought of marrying me. As if he couldn't understand whatever made me come up with such an idea! His face! It was almost comical. A parody of surprise. The mouth dropped open, the eyebrows raised. I remember thinking it was *he* who was absurd and pathetic, not me. I think that's when it finally dawned on me, he's just a man, what the hell am I *whispering* for? He looked almost ugly to me. A stupid, ugly man. And he was pitying *me?* I had reached out, inadvertently maybe, and touched another part of the elephant, a part not nearly as attractive as the part I'd touched before.

"Can you understand any of this, Nikki? Anything of what I was feeling?"

I hesitated to answer her.

"Come on," she coaxed. "I want to know. Tell me the truth."

"Let me think," I said. "Let me put myself in your place. Did he ever pity me? Yes! Yes, he pitied me. Because of where I lived, because of all the disappointments in my so-called career. Yes, he pitied me. And I felt totally entitled to that pity. He damn well better pity me, I thought. He damn well better know what I have to contend with in this world. I have to say I didn't feel insulted by his pity. I'd earned it. It was the least he could do!"

She laughed. "But that was different. I wouldn't have been insulted by that either. I would have been just like you. I would have been glad that he understood so much about my life, understood the pain in it. Because he didn't cause that pain. But he *was* the cause of all *my* pain. And then to pity me for feeling it? It just struck me as the cruelest thing he could do.

"He reached out for me suddenly, all kindness, all maudlin compassion. His touch was unbearable suddenly. I actually recoiled from it. But he was insistent. He held on to my shoulders, drawing me closer to him. I could just imagine what he was thinking. 'She needs the human touch now,' or some such bullshit! I let myself be pulled into his arms, almost fascinated by the repulsion I felt for him suddenly. He started talking. If only he'd known . . . he had no idea I felt that way about our 'friendship' . . . why hadn't I ever told him any of this before? But how could I? I was always such a timid little mouse around him. I didn't dare force him into taking a stand in our relationship. He thought I *liked* being single. Having my career, my independence. He didn't know I wanted to get married, have children with him. Or he would have told me long before this—that there was no hope of that ever happening! The feel of his arms around me was making my skin crawl! And suddenly, I felt as if I could see the whole elephant!

"And what a beast it was! A selfish, greedy beast that took and took and took, and hurt everyone in the taking. It was so *clear* to me suddenly. All he ever did was *hurt* people! He reduced Tish to a silly frivolous woman who spends the greater part of her life in department stores and boutiques. She needed someone who would force her to be independent, make her grow up! Instead, by supporting her all those years, he pushed her deeper into her dependence and weakness. Lorraine? He was famous by then, so of course he had to marry someone famous, someone who had been reared in fame from the first day of her life. No unknown for him *that* time around. He left his mark on her life, too. Now she walks around expecting Satan to jump out of the bushes and grab her any minute. But

Satan already grabbed her, a long time ago, and tossed her away when he was finished with her. And Ann—he used her, too. You think she married him to get into *his* world? As usual, Nikki, you misunderstood everything. He married her to get into *her* world. The respectability and status of generation after generation of wealth and power! He had no ancestors, that nameless orphan! So he married into them. He used everybody! Me included! Maybe me most of all!

"For years and years, I ran his errands. I typed his manuscripts. I did everything but wipe his nose! Ol' reliable Shelly! Why did he think I was doing those things? Did he honestly think he was deserving of all that? Out of friendship? Did I have to actually tell him I was in love with him? Couldn't he have figured that out on his own? He was supposed to be a genius, wasn't he? The Renaissance man? Did he need it spelled out for him?"

I think, yes, he did. He was not one for assuming he was loved. She goes on. "He used me. And Bob. And you! Admit it, Nikki. Didn't you ever feel used by him?"

No. I never did. I don't answer her.

"If you didn't, you're just kidding yourself. But I can't blame you for that. I kidded myself for years, too. But know this—you were just another victim of his."

"So if you see me as another one of his victims, why have me blamed for his death?" I said.

"That came about by accident. I had no idea you'd be there that day. I drove back from Florida and went straight to his apartment. I used my own key to get in, because I always did that. Sometimes he'd be sleeping and I hated to wake him. He'd be up writing all night, or something, and he'd take a nap during the day. That's why I had a key. So I wouldn't wake him when I went over there, doing my happy little errands. What a fool I was! They always say that, don't they, in the movies? 'What a fool I was!' I guess because it really is a very dramatic feeling, when you realize that.

"Anyway, I let myself in, and there he was, in a towel. That's why I was so shocked when you told me he was naked when he answered the door. It never occurred to me that you'd think such a thing. I assumed he put on the towel in the bedroom and you'd seen him leave the room with it. So we stood there talking for a few minutes. I'd come back from Florida a little early, he realized. Was everything all right? He asked about my mother's health! Always so considerate! I began to get the impression that there was someone else in the apartment. I didn't know who. I realized suddenly that I'd interrupted something. Naturally, my embarrassment showed. He thought it was because he wasn't dressed. He was about to go back into the bedroom to put some clothes on! I had already told him there was something I wanted to discuss with him. My whole future, as it were. But I told him it wasn't necessary for him to get dressed. After all, we were going to be talking about something so intimate, why shouldn't he be half-naked? Just think, if he did go back into that room, you would have known it was me right from the beginning. I wouldn't have had the nerve to push him, what with you able to identify me to the police.

"Anyway, sensing someone else's presence in the apartment, I asked him if we could go up to the roof. Always so accommodating, he complied. And then we had our grimy little scene up there. And then it happened. I intended to go straight to the police. It was an accident, I thought. He was leaning against the railing, and I felt this moment of total revulsion for him. Without meaning to, my hands reached up and pushed him, as if they had a life of their own. In a way, I didn't feel responsible for what happened. In my confusion, I imagined the police would view it the same way! Now I realize how insane that was, but I wasn't exactly thinking clearly at the time. I did intend to go to the police. I'd left my pocketbook in his apartment. I went downstairs to retrieve it. And that's when I heard your voice, calling out from behind the bedroom door. 'Joe? Joe!' So self-contained. Light-hearted, almost. So sure he'd be there for you. And I suddenly thought, what's my big hurry? Eventually, I'd turn myself in. Why not postpone that for a while? Just to see what would happen in the meantime. I guess, in your eyes, I was being sadistic, leaving you as the prime suspect. In my eyes, I was simply being fair. Besides, you always acted as if you could get away with bloody murder. I was curious to see if you could. That was part of it, too. But mostly, I thought I was being fair. Care to guess why?"

It would sound like we were two fourteen-year-olds, but I said it anyway: "Because you saw him first."

She laughed. "No, Nikki. I am not that petty. I had long gotten over that early infidelity on his part. And yours. He'd been sleeping around with plenty of others back then. I didn't blame you in particular for that. It was something more than that. It was what *you*, in particular, did to him. You *changed* him, Nikki. You changed him so completely. Do you remember what he was like back then? He was everything I thought he was. *Truly* kind. Truly selfless. Noble! You laughed at me when I told you that, but it was an accurate word to describe him. He *was* noble.

"He wanted to be an architect, remember? A fine goal. A reasonable goal. I have no doubt that if he'd never met you, that's just what he would have become. He would have been an architect, and he would have married me, and life would have turned out exactly as it should have. A home in the suburbs. Children. But none of that happened. And it was totally because of you.

"Do you remember how you carried on the first time you saw his paintings? Like a madwoman, an absolute madwoman! 'But Joe! These are great! These are fantastic! These are better than half the stuff already hanging in museums! You can't go to school anymore. You cannot sit through one more engineering class. If I have to chain you to an easel, you are going to

285

paint! And that's *all* you're going to do.' You inflated his ego so much that he thought he was another Da Vinci."

He was.

"And little by little, everything changed. He did start cutting classes. To stay home and paint! I told him it was insane, that he was throwing away opportunity with both hands, going after some impossible dream. But he didn't listen to me. Tish, of course, took her usual wishy-washy stand. 'Well, if thay-et's what he wants to do . . .' And you, of course, drowned everyone out, with your rallying pep talks. He never would have had the nerve to show his work to a dealer without you goading him on."

I disagreed completely. Eventually he would have. Maybe after twenty years of quiet desperation, living a life he didn't want to live, he would have. But I remained silent.

"Painting would have stayed a hobby with him. He would have been an architect who painted on Sundays. And would that have been so terrible? So much worse than what actually happened? Can you honestly say that all that fame and recognition and money brought him one minute of happiness? I would have given him a happy life. I can honestly say that with certainty."

It was almost as if Joe wasn't a person at all. As if he had no identity of his own. *She* could have given him happiness. *I* changed him. As if he were a mannequin with no heart beating inside its chest! No dreams or nightmares of its own. No life force within it. Ruled only by the life we inflicted on it from the outside. But that wasn't Joe! It wouldn't have taken him twenty years to decide he was a painter. What was I thinking of a few minutes ago when I thought that? Had I already forgotten the ferocious force within the man? It would have taken him twenty *minutes* to break out of that little niche he'd gotten himself into. He was ready for it back then. You only had to look at his eyes to see it. Some change was coming. Laughing, reckless—he was about to shed some old skin. I just gave voice to it, because I saw it so clearly in his own eyes.

Who was this lifeless docile creature she thought Joe was? Who had she been loving all these years? Not Joey. Try to manipulate Joe into anything and you'd find yourself trying to push around a brick wall! She *didn't* know him at all. I knew him so much better than she!

But she seemed so taken with the sound of her own voice now, melodious and supple, still weaving out a tale. She went on. "His life brought him nothing but misery. Three failed marriages. Endless pressures. Endless demands."

He thrived on it. On all of it. Who was she kidding? Herself? Like Ann—"I hope he's finally found the peace that eluded him so long in life." More bullshit! If either of them knew, for one second, the peace that Joe felt in his heart, even in his most tumultuous hours, they'd shut their stupid mouths. What did they think peace was? Deadness? What happiness did Shelly envision herself delivering to him, along with her casseroles, out in the 'burbs? Numbness?

Didn't they know that peace was a living, vibrant thing? The opposite of something static and dead? The vibrating string of a harp, emitting a sound of almost unbearable beauty. The mass and volume of the ocean, tickled silly by its own forever-breaking waves. The whirling, giddy sounds of the planets in space. (How Joe and I laughed when we heard a recording of that. Some capsule brought it back, from Jupiter, I think. Ridiculous sounds. Pops and whizzes and explosions. A big happy clown out there, making the most riotous racket! How unutterably sweet it sounded.) Did they think the universe was silent and dead in other ways as well?

"Here, suddenly," Shelly was saying, "was an opportunity for me to get even with you. In ruining his life, in a very real sense, you ruined mine. Why shouldn't you be blamed for the murder? At least for a time. So I took my pocketbook, but instead of leaving the building immediately, I ran back up to the roof—to get the towel. It had come off while he was groping frantically for something to latch onto before he fell. If he was naked when he died, they'd *have* to blame you. I was sure you'd insist he was wearing a towel. But with the towel gone, they wouldn't believe you. I took it as an omen that God was on my side when you didn't even remember about the towel."

"He put it on in the living room, not the bedroom. I forgot it was out there."

"Well, it worked in my favor. You couldn't have looked more guilty. So I took the towel and put it in my pocketbook and left the building. I went straight to his office. No one even knew I was back from Florida yet. The office was empty, as I knew it would be. The secretaries were on vacation. I'd decided I'd come up here for another day or two, watch the proceedings from a distance. I'd have an alibi, if I should be questioned. I was still in Florida. My mother wouldn't be sure what day I left. She is sure of so little nowadays. She'd have no idea if I'd left on a Monday or a Wednesday, or if it was two days ago, or five minutes ago. So *I* was safe. But I needed money. I was completely out of cash, having spent it on the trip home from Florida. Which turned out to be another good thing. I hadn't paid for anything with my charge cards, so there would be no record of what motel I stayed at on what night. But I wasn't about to start using a charge card now, up here, since I was still supposed to be in Florida. So I needed cash. Joe always kept some in his safe at the office. I certainly knew the combination. Why shouldn't he trust me with the combination? I handled all the business details he couldn't trust anybody *else* to do. So I went to his office for some cash. And I found the will."

It took a moment for it to register. She found the will. She *found* the will? She didn't *write* the will? Which will is she talking about? The real one, or the phony-baloney one that left me everything?"

"Which will?"

Shelly laughed. "You know very well which one! The one you found in his studio—you and Bob. At least I'm assuming you found it. I put it there and then it was gone and you were the only two there in between. I suppose you have it hidden somewhere, waiting for all the furor to die down before you go and claim your inheritance! You wouldn't want to look guilty of murder. I took it out of the safe because I was afraid Ann would be the first to find it after his death. I was sure she would destroy it instantly. I'm sure she'd rather see you get away with murder than have it revealed that she was no longer the light of Joe's life. I had no such concern.

"So I took it and waited a while and then put it in the studio, expecting Bob to find it. But you turned up there, too! You kept popping up in places I didn't expect you to be. How did you ever convince him to hide the will? I supposed you used your so-called feminine wiles."

I actually laughed. Whatever gave Shelly the idea that men were such pliable creatures? Most of the ones I came into contact with were such stubborn lunkheads! One sure way to get them *not* to do something was to try to manipulate them into doing it. I began to think that the reason she had so much faith in the powers of female manipulation was because she had used those powers to manipulate Joe for so many years. Maybe he didn't want this "friendship" to go on for years. Maybe it was her quiet devotion and unfailing loyalty, her timid voice, her cheerful, eager willingness to help that manipulated him into keeping this friendship going so long. Who really used whom?

"So I assume," she said, "that you have the will tucked away in a safe place."

I burst out laughing again. She was going to try to kill me, and I was going to be laughing! I was going to die laughing, just the way Joe always predicted I would! ("Everything's a fuckin' joke, right, Nikki? So help me, someday you're going to *die* laughing.")

"What's so funny?" Shelly said.

"Nothing. Everything. The will. The will, Shelly, is in such a safe place that nobody'll ever find it."

"Well," she said, "I don't suppose it matters now." I know

I should have gotten scared. I'm sure she meant it to be a very dramatic moment. But I was just too overjoyed suddenly to worry about my death. The will was real! He loved me. More than anybody else. Love is money. Money is love. He loved me.

And there we were, riding along in this metal contraption through some winding country roads, talking of schemes and plots and turns of events. And it was all so weird and strange and unpredictable that I wonder why anybody ever even *tried* to figure it out. And Shelly looked over at me, as I was still shaking my head and laughing slightly.

"This is funny to you, Nikki? Sometimes I think you're weird. *Really* weird," the murderess said.

33

"Sorry," I said. "A private joke. Between me and . . . fate."

"Fate? Don't you believe in God anymore? In your own strange way, you used to be religious. What happened? How come all of a sudden it's *fate* and not *God?*"

"I don't know. A lot's happened. I don't know about God anymore. My faith came back, there, for a while. With that train roaring down on me. But you know what they say: 'No atheists in the trenches.' Now, I don't know anything anymore. I suspect there's nothing out there overseeing it all. Not fate, not God. Just us. The lunatics in charge of the asylum, so to speak."

"Funny, you, of all people should say that. All through this whole thing, it was as if you had some sort of supernatural protection! I really began to think you had a guardian angel! Imagine my surprise when I realized your guardian angel was Ann."

"Ann?!" Her surprise was nothing compared to mine.

"Of course. Why else do you think you were never seriously considered a suspect? Ann wanted you kept out of it, right from the beginning. Why else was your name never even leaked to the press? Why else didn't the police pursue you as their one and only lead? Because Ann made it very clear that she wanted your name kept out of it at all costs. For her own reasons, of course. The image to be maintained was that the marriage was intact right up to the time of his death. She didn't want you raising any doubts about that. What she wanted was for the case to be closed as quickly as possible. So she arranged for that very convenient 'solution' to the crime. She had help, of course. But not from the police department. They can be a very stubborn lot when they want to. The help she had wasn't from them. No matter. The link between organized crime and politics has always been a mutually beneficial one. What was one more favor, either way? And then, how could the police overlook such a preponderance of evidence? The evidence was conclusive. Ann made sure it was. All it took was a few phone calls on her part. Or on the part of her father, I should say.

"True, it would mean you'd get away with murder, because Ann didn't doubt for one moment that it was you who killed him. But so what? The important thing was to have the case settled, with no ugly rumors surfacing. And Ann's a great believer in expediency. I overheard her once at a cocktail party, talking to some general. She was shocked and horrified to find out that the army no longer put saltpeter in the troops' food. How could the army let all those young men walk around in a state of perpetual sexual excitement, she wanted to know. Was that wise? Yeah, Ann's a great believer in expediency."

I begin to realize that Shelly has nearly finished spinning out her tale. If she has any intention of doing something distasteful, such as trying to kill me, this is the time.

We haven't passed a car in either direction for miles now. Where the hell has she taken us? I also deduce she no longer has any intention of turning herself in. She seems to have outgrown that idea. Fate has let her get away with it for too long. Why shouldn't she get away with it forever? I am the only obstacle now.

So when will the big move come? I look over at her and there is still a smile on her face, the last remnant of the laugh we shared about Ann's expediency.

She looks almost saucy, but her expression of gay mischief is marred somewhat by the fact that she still has the square gauze bandage over one eyebrow. Huey Duck–van Gogh. But the bandage is in the wrong place. By rights, it should be covering the side of her head from which an ear has been recently severed. Like everything else that is happening, her image now is strangely out of kilter. Off-center, lopsided.

I should be frightened of her, but I'm not. She should be looking more menacing than Huey Duck–van Gogh, but she isn't. What the hell is wrong with this picture?

"I'm sorry about the train, Nikki," she says. I very nearly laugh. So I'm supposed to forgive her now? For making an attempt on my life? Right before she makes another one?

"Now, *that's* funny," I tell her.

"But I *am* sorry," she insists. "I just wanted to scare you. I forgot about how uncoordinated you are. Jeez! A *cripple* could have moved faster than you did."

"Gosh, I'm sorry. I was nervous."

She laughs. "That's okay. I forgive you."

"Gee, thanks."

"Do you forgive me?"

"You? For what? For pushing me in front of a train? For killing Joe? Or for the attempt you're going to make on my life now?"

"Attempt? What attempt? Nobody's going to make any attempt . . ." Her voice is full of good clean sadistic fun.

"It won't be so easy this time, Shelly! I'll have you know that I'm not by any means nearly as out of shape as I look. Also, I have a *lousy* temper, and when it comes to brute strength, I'm a horse!" I'm getting bugged now. Snorting, I turn my head and look out the side window. "There's a limit to what I'll put up with, goddamn it!"

"I must say, for someone who's about to have an attempt made on her life, you don't seem very frightened."

"Yeah, well! Who should I be frightened of? You? A skinny little twerp like you? Yeah, well—ha!"

She laughs. Absurdly, I find myself laughing, too.

"I don't know," I admit. "Maybe I've just known you too

long. I don't know what the hell it is. I just don't seem able to get deeply terrified right now. I think that train cured me. I'm immune to fear from now on." She is laughing so deliriously that she is actually holding her side. I'm not far from such hysteria myself. "Maybe there's something really wrong with me, Shell?" I say between guffaws.

"That's what everybody's been *telling* you for years and years!"

"Could it be they were right?"

"HAHAHHAHAHHAHAHAHAHA."

"HAHAHAHAHAHAHAHAHAHAHAHA."

"No, but seriously, hahahahaha," she says, "you're not afraid?"

"Noo. Unless you have some sort of a weapon! You don't have a weapon, do you?"

She clicks her tongue. The very idea. "Of course not!"

"Well, then I'm not afraid. I could take you out in a minute. I just wasn't prepared last time."

"Yeah, that really wasn't cricket on my part. You were totally unprepared."

My mood suddenly sobers. "So was he. Totally unprepared."

"I didn't mean to do that, Nikki. Not consciously anyway. Maybe *sub*consciously."

"That's what I like about prisons. Where all you people who let their subconscious solve their problems live together, and worry about each other's subconscious knocking you off."

"I guess I'm not forgiven, huh? If only he hadn't—"

"Yeah, if only. If only pigs could fly, we wouldn't need birds. Whatever he did or didn't do, it didn't warrant the death penalty!"

She's silent a moment. Then she says, "I see." Did she really think I was going to say, "We'll just keep this our little secret?" Is that what she thought? I still can't figure out what's wrong with this picture!

Why shouldn't it remain our little secret? He's dead already. Nothing'll bring him back. Her spending the next twenty years, maybe the rest of her life, in prison won't bring him back. And other than that one mad moment of her life, she had never hurt anyone before. True, there was the little matter of her pushing me in front of a *train*, but she actually ended up more hurt than I was. There was nothing phony about her dead faint, face first, onto a cement floor. She doesn't have the stomach for murder. Who does? Should she really spend the rest of her life in prison garb because of one mad moment's aberration, the one single moment of her life when repulsion ruled her, ruled her so completely that it was as if her hands were not her own and suddenly they were simply pushing repulsion away? The flood of self-hatred that must have filled her when she was within Joe's embrace. "You mean it hasn't been a coy act all along, me playing the faithful friend and loyal, unquestioning ally? With both of us knowing in our heart of hearts that we are destined for each other? You mean, you actually bought the act and that's all I am to you, the faithful friend?" And most horrifying of all, "Is that what I really *am?*" In a sense, Joe's death was simply a byproduct of what she did. All she really intended to do was stop the flow of self-loathing.

I picture her in prison garb. Eating prison food off prison plates. Year after year. No delicate painted china here, no antiques garnered from a grandmother's booty. The sadistic games they'll play in prison will leave *this* merry prankster pale and dazed, destroying her in no time at all. Will that be justice?

Why *don't* we just keep this our little secret? I'm furious with myself for even thinking it.

"It doesn't sound so bad, you know?" I say. " 'Died of injuries sustained in a fall.' It doesn't sound that bad. Once, when I was working on a cover for a crime novel, I thought I'd be a real hotshot and actually do some research. Nice friendly research, of course, nothing involving hours in libraries. Something involving cups of coffee and the endless puffing of cigarettes. I'd ask a friend for the information I needed. That's my idea of research. As it happened, I had a friend who was a photographer. He was starving at it, of course, so he finally said 'Uncle' and got a civil service job. As a photographer for the police department. Yeah, sure he could help me out, he said. He had lots of photos of crimes, real crimes, photos they don't even show in the *Post*. He brought them over one night and I made coffee. Stab wounds that aren't treated often remain open. Did you know that? They heal into neat tears of the flesh. Long oval windows into whatever lies beneath the skin's surface. Muscle, bone, whatever. Wherever the knife was plunged in and out, a little oblong window remains.

"I thought the pictures of the burn victims were a fluke. A person could burn to death and not be left looking like *that*. I was sure the pictures he had showed the one-in-a-million case of a body being burned to that extent. But then I read *The Right Stuff*, and I found out that's what they *always* mean when they say 'burned beyond recognition.' The pictures I saw? That's what that *means*.

"It doesn't sound so bad, injuries sustained in a fall. It doesn't explain the internal explosion that shattered bone and wrenched organs and ripped muscle. It doesn't describe what the impact felt like to the brain as the skull cracked. It must have been deafening, really. An A-bomb exploding in the cranium. If you threw a watermelon off a rooftop you'd hear and see what the impact could do a lot more clearly. With a person, they just lie there, like they're sleeping with their eyes open."

"I know," she says. And the way she says it tells me that she *does* know. That she has been thinking about it constantly, too, since it happened. "I know." Horrified. Amazed. "You know I'd never do anything like that again." *Like that.*

We pass a lonely outpost of civilization. A gas station, but not much of one. A single pump and a small shack a few yards behind it. The shack is boarded up and looks as if it's been boarded up for years. "Where the hell are we?" I say to her.

"You don't have to know," she says almost playfully.

"Only I have to know." That sounds a trifle menacing, so she softens it. "I'm the one who's driving."

The road we're on now is little more than a dirt path. The trees that have lined our way are beginning to thin out. The path apparently cuts across a wide, open stretch of land. A meadow? Is this what they call a meadow?

"You didn't have to put up with it, you know. For years and years. If you saw it as emotional abuse, you didn't have to put up with it. He never held a gun to your head."

"I know." Again. "But I didn't *see* it as emotional abuse. Not then. Not until that day on the roof. Then suddenly, I saw it very clearly."

Now, I say it. "I know."

There are no trees on either side of the road now. And certainly no evidence of man. It looks like an uninhabited planet. We might as well be on the moon. For miles we haven't passed a house or seen a light. Off in the distance, on one side of the road, I see the dark outline of trees in the murky moonlight. A lot of trees, their heavy tops swaying in the night breeze, the beginning of what looks like a bona-fide forest. On the other side of the road, across the open space of the meadow, there are other trees, but sparsely spaced. It looks too rocky there to grow another forest. It's hard to make out in the darkness, but it looks as if there are big boulders tossed around back there. A real moonscape. Beyond the boulders, I can see nothing. Heavy clouds keeping passing across the face of the moon, throwing everything into blackness. Is that a mountain back there, black in the darkness? Are we in a valley? Is that what this is called? A valley? Can there be a meadow in a valley? I don't know anything about the country.

Shelly's voice shocks me when she speaks, breaking the silence.

"I just want you to know one thing," she says.

"Yeah?" I'm cynical, defensive. ("You know I'd never do anything like that again? You might have done the same thing in my place? Why don't we keep this our secret?") "Yeah? What should I know?"

"That I love you. I really do."

I am so taken aback at this that I make a stupid, half-assed joke.

"First Tish, now you, too?"

Shelly laughs slightly. "Come on. You know what I mean. As friends. We're friends, aren't we? Through it all, we've been friends. Since we were little girls, right? Since kindergarten."

"Yeah. Right."

"Okay."

What's wrong with this picture?

The car slows down. Then stops. She turns off the motor.

"Get out," she says.

"What?"

"You heard me, Nikki. Get out."

"Here? For what reason?" It looks as if I'm not immune. I start to get nervous.

"Because I said so."

"Make me."

She sighs, wearily. "Just get out, Nikki, okay?"

"No! Why should I? What are you going to do, pull away? Make me walk for miles? All I have to do is walk back . . . *eventually*, I'll come across some store or house or some—"

"GET THE FUCK OOOUUUUUUUT!" Her shrill scream also takes me unaware. What's this, a temper tantrum? I seem willing to watch it, indifferent. Let her scream, the brat. I'm not going anywhere.

"What the *hell* is wrong with you? I'm sorry, this is one little prank you're not going to pull off. Start the fuckin' car again, Shelly, before I give you a good smack!"

Such a bully! And I used to be such a chickenshit kid.

Her feed-bag pocketbook has been resting on the seat at her side. Not between us, though—on her side by the door. She reaches into it now. My heart starts to pound. She withdraws a small gun. A small, delicate gun. An old lady's antique. She points it at me. "Now get out," she says flatly.

"Where'd you get that?" I say absurdly.

"You want the name of the store, or what?"

"I'm just curious."

"In Georgia, all right? Feel better? To protect me when I'm on the highway, back and forth from Florida. Now get the hell out."

"You lied to me, you son of a bitch! Why is everyone always *lying* to me?"

She sighs again, disgusted. "Come on," she says. "Move."

I get out and slam the door. I'm mad. The windows of the car are open. "All right, you rotten liar! I'm out." We are both eight years old, having a fight in the schoolyard. "You stepped over that line before I said go!" "I did not, you lousy cheat!" "Did too!" "Did not!"

"Is this your idea of cricket, Shelly? You gonna shoot me in the back, or what?" Am I really saying this? Or is this another childhood game that has gotten out of hand? (They're overtired, that's what it is. They'll have a little nap and be fine.)

"Nobody's going to shoot you in the back. I just want you out of the car. Now take off."

"Take off? You mean run?"

She has patience. She'll explain it to me. "That's what I mean," she says, singsong.

"Oh, I get it," I say, furious. She cheated! She lied about the gun. "I get it. You're going to try to run me over. Very baroque. Not exactly the Indy 500, but maybe a little demolition derby. That would be your idea of cricket. Gonna give me a head start and everything, I bet. I'm supposed to try and make it to the trees with the grill of your car yapping at my ass. And then I'm supposed to wander around in the woods for a while, terrified, and be found in a couple of weeks, all emaciated. Maybe. And if I don't make it to the trees and you get me first, well, then, it'll be settled *that* way. Either way, you're leaving it to fate, right, sicko?"

"No, I'm not leaving it to fate, *this* time," she says. Her unbandaged eyebrow is cocked, a superior smirk on her face. ("I *saw* you step over that line. Don't argue with *me*.") "You didn't think I'd do this, did you?" She's having a fine old time.

"This time it'll be different. This time it's a premeditated murder."

"Start running," she says, getting bored.

I start to back away from the car. "Come on, Shelly, cut it out." I see her profile, cast in the green light of the dashboard dials. She looks like a pilot in the cockpit. I wonder how I'd paint that light. Not too difficult. Reflected light. Cadmium yellow, prussian blue, raw umber. Just a drop of rose madder. No, I am not going to die laughing. I'm going to die mixing paints!

Her image still doesn't scare me as much as it should. What's wrong with this picture.

Another loud, warbling shrill fills the air.

"MOOOOOOOOVE!"

I start running, tiredly. This isn't really going to happen, is it? This isn't actually going to come off like this, is it? She hasn't started the motor yet. Any second I will hear her up-roarious laugh. "Nikki! I really scared you, didn't I? Come back, you dope." I keep running, halfheartedly. The motor starts.

Holy shit, she really means this. She's really crazy. What the fuck is she doing!

She guns the motor. My pace quickens. She's giving me a nice big head start, really being cricket about things now. I'm still not as afraid as I ought to be. My running is flawless. I am a fuckin' marathoner, knees pumping away at a nice even tempo. Even when I step into a small incline, I remain upright. I might actually *make* it to those damn trees. What'd ya know! *Just keep going now. Forget about the goal. Live in the present. One step at a time. Otherwise, you'll fuck up.* She guns the motor one more time and I hear the crunch of gravel and dirt and little stones under her tires. Oh God, she really means it. She's really going to mow me down like grass. I hear the loud hum of the motor, then the choke as she changes gears.

I am running furiously, FURIOUSLY, gulping air, sweating from every pore. How far away is she? *Don't look back, something might be gaining on you.* Hardy-har-har. What's wrong with this picture?

And suddenly I KNOW. A few more bumpy steps as I try to stop myself instantly. I remain facing straight ahead as my mind's eye focuses in on the flaw in the picture. I am transfixed to the spot. Petrified. I scream, openmouthed at the top of my lungs, "SHELLLLLYYYYYYY! DOOOOOOOOON'T." ("SHELLLLL-YYYYY! Oh, Hello, Mrs. Donat. Can Shelly come out and play?")

I turn around and begin running toward the car, screaming as I run. "OOOH, GOD, SHELLLL . . . PLEASE DOOOOON'T"

But it's too late. The car is beginning its swerve across the open field, swerving away from me, from my side of the road, hurling itself toward the amorphous blackness in the far distance.

It's not a meadow. Or a valley. *Plateau*, I think it's called. A wide, flat space, a step in the mountainside. It's a cliff she's heading for, not leaving it to fate anymore. The long graceful arch of the curve completed, she's heading straight for the cliff's edge now. That blackness is the sky beyond. The starless, clouded sky.

My view of Shelly from the rear is my last. I can just make out the silhouette of her ancient Afro.

"SHELLY?" I scream again. "I LOVE YOU, TOOO. YOU'RE MY FRIEND. I LOVE YOU TOOO. WE WERE *ALWAYS* FRIENDS. SINCE KIN-DER-GAR-TEN!" My voice breaks off in bumping sobs. A rubber ball thumping down a staircase, the car has disappeared into the black void. Sucked up by some black hole in space. Maybe that's where all the stars have gone. Sucked up into black holes.

A second later, the sky is light with the hellish glow of the explosion. The car has found its mark. ("You don't have to know where we are. Only I have to know. I'm the driver.")

I fall to my knees and cry tears that have no comfort in them. The gas tank explodes a second time.

After a while, I get up and start walking. Morning will have to come eventually. Eventually, I'd reach a home.

34

It *is* the *following morning,*
and I am sitting in Lieutenant Morrisey's office. I have just
finished giving her my statement, and we are waiting for it to
be typed so that I can sign it and be on my way.

It was Bob and Brendan who retrieved me a few hours earlier from the sheriff's office in a small town in Pennsylvania. I
have already given Morrisey the sheriff's name, and he has con-
firmed the events as I told them to Morrisey. All about the car
and the cliff. All about the car's single inhabitant being burned
beyond recognition.

The case is at last closed. All that remains is for me to sign
my statement. We both sit and wait as it's being typed. Morrisey is shuffling papers on her desk, already reading other
folders, other crimes. I am staring off into space.

Finally, the paper is brought in, and she tells me to read it
over before I sign it. I read it over and sign it. It stays on her
desk.

"Well?" she says to me.

"Well?" I say back.

"You can go now." She has remained the tough cop
through it all. Annoyed, put-upon, disapproving. Distancing.
What is it I want from her? Some kind of absolution? "Con-
gratulations, you found out the truth?" What is it I'm waiting
for?

"Miss Andrews? You're free to go now."

"I know." But I still don't get up.

She looks at me. As usual, annoyed, disapproving. "Was there anything else you wanted to say?"

"The case is closed now?"

"Yes, I would say so. Was there something else?"

"We . . . uh, found out the real murderer and the case is closed, right?"

"Yes, that's right. Now, if you'll excuse me, there are many other matters I have to attend to and—"

"He's still dead."

"What?"

"I said, he's still dead. Somehow I had it in my mind that . . . if I could only find out the truth, he wouldn't be dead anymore. He'd be alive again."

She makes a sound that conveys the sentiment *What nonsense.*

"Well, be that as it may," she says. "I'm afraid I'll have to ask you to excuse me now. I have a very busy day ahead of me and . . ."

"Oh. Yes. I'm sorry." I get up and leave.

Bob and Brendan are waiting for me downstairs, and they drive me home. They ask if I would like to stop for breakfast somewhere first. When I say no, Brendan feels my forehead and takes my pulse. Small joke. I must be getting sick for me to turn down food.

We say good-bye, and I go up to my apartment alone. I undress and climb into bed, feeling not unpleasantly tired. Outside my window, down in the street, I hear some children singing: "Row, row, row your boat, gently down the stream. Merrily, merrily, merrily, merrily, life is but a dream."

I marvel at the unexpected feeling of peace that comes over me. Why peace, now? Because a circle has been closed? Something began and now it's ended and the circle is completed. That's supposed to be perfection, isn't it? The circle? The perfect form? Isn't that what death does? Completes the circle? Was it witnessing the closing off of two lives that makes me think of completion and peace now?

Outside, I hear their young voices, singing. They're doing it well now. They've gone past the giggles and they're singing it in perfect rounds now, coming in when they should. "Row, row, row your boat, gently down the stream. Merrily, merrily . . . row, row, row . . ."

How nice, to hear them singing rounds. Something with no clear closing off. Instead, something beginning even as something else ends. That seems truer. Because life is not a circle, but a spiral. I wrote a poem about it once. The day I heard that some scientists discovered that DNA was structured in spirals, not circles. "The Secret of the Universe," my poem was called.

> I heard the secret of the Universe is not a circle, but a spiral.
> And when I heard the secret of the Universe is not a circle, but a spiral, it made me so happy, I laughed out loud.
> Because, if the secret of the Universe is not a circle, but a spiral, it doesn't mean the rules don't fit the game, it just means I should have allowed for more.

And now the children's words strike me as profound.

Gently down the stream. Merrily, merrily, merrily, merrily. Life is but a dream. Row, row, row.

I begin to fall asleep, being rocked gently down the stream . . . merrily, merrily, merrily, merrily, life is but a dream. I should have allowed for more. *Shhhhh.* Allow for everything. Accept and accept and accept again. Life is but a dream. A beautiful, peaceful dream. A dream full of wonder. *Shhhh.* Gently. Merrily. Gently down the stream. Merrily Merrily Yes Gently Merrily.

35

Guess what! You'll never guess. I had a baby! Yes! Almost nine months to the day after the last time I saw Joe Savanah. A little less, actually.

What an experience! Well, it just changed everything! It's a *miracle*, as far as I'm concerned. The whole business of people having babies is just a miracle, as you no doubt know if you've ever had one. Isn't it just *amazing*? I mean that little face, looking at you with all that wisdom and innocence and love? Is that something to knock your socks off or what? I just couldn't believe it. I just couldn't believe I could be that *lucky*. I mean *me*, the world's biggest foul-up? Actually pulling this off? Having this beautiful, wonderful baby? Wow! I was just so *honored*, you know?

One thing was very, very clear, as soon as I saw her face. I knew instantly that she was an ambassador from some far, far superior place in the universe. I mean that was just crystal clear, instantly. She was an ambassador from this very superior place and she's my guest on the planet, you know? I guess I am not the first person to ever realize this. Otherwise, where did the expression "bundle from Heaven" come from, huh? Because it's so true! Bundles from Heaven, that's what they are, all these newborn little Buddhas! So amazing.

Actually, I've been finding out that all those clichés are true, about kids. The patter of little feet around the house? My heart just soars! There is no sound on this earth sweeter than the patter of little feet around the house. I can say that unequivocally. She's almost two years old now. Every day is another bliss! Ah, but I could go on forever about her. What a kid! I'm learning everything from her. I mean I'm really learning everything important from *her*.

Oh, and we live in the country now. In one of those little houses that looks as if it should belong to a French peasant but actually costs a king's ransom? Look, there's no place like the country for kids, I don't care what you say. Close to the soil and all that. For a while I thought I was going to have to sell *Eros* in order to finance this. But then, all of a sudden, my own stuff started selling. The art world is crazy, I swear. My same stuff that has been hanging around for twenty years is all of a sudden valuable. Who knows how they figure those things. All I can say is thank God, because you have to be loaded to raise a kid. I mean, toys alone! I definitely think kids should have everything they want. That's very important, you know? That they shouldn't grow up thinking that life is one big "no." They should have the complete run of the place, and they should have everything they like. I mean, it seems to me that ought to be the first priority the world should have—that all the kids have everything. All kids should be spoiled rotten, as far as I'm concerned.

I tell you, I give those mothers at the sandbox plenty to talk about, don't worry. I think at first they thought I was some sort of retired rock and roll person, what with all the flashy cars that come zipping up this road on weekends. Brendan's DeLorean. (He says it's a good investment and the value can only go up.) And Tish's Rolls. Yeah, Aunt Tish and Aunt Alex visit us every so often, bringing half of F.A.O. Schwarz with them. One thing you have to say for Tish, she really knows how to shop. And Bob's Mercedes. He's given himself some sort of uncle status around here, which is fine with me. I mean, the more loving people around a kid, the better, right? I'll tell you, I definitely think there is something going on between Tish and Bob. I mean, people just could not have that much animosity toward each other unless there is something else quite the opposite going on. But who knows? Bob did tell me something sad about Ann, though. And Miss Reardon drinks a little? I was just stunned. Tish, of course, howled with delight, but I really hope Ann takes the cure. I mean, that's sad.

Which led Brendan to say something very profound, for once. He said that maybe it's true that man is a creature of extremes, because even when man was being moderate, he was moderate in the extreme. Extremely moderate. Which is really a point worth pondering, as far as I'm concerned.

Another point we all sat around pondering one night was love. What is it exactly that makes you fall in love with a person? I think, what you fall in love with, actually, is the person's frame of mind. You fall in love with the way they see the world, more or less. Which is probably why Joe is going to be such a hard act to follow, in my life, anyway. He was just the happiest person I ever met. A real cheerful son of a bitch, as someone once described him. I mean, if I ever have a choice as to what kind of man to fall in love with, I think I'd pick a happy man over anything else. I don't mean some kind of laughing idiot. I mean a happy man. They ain't that easy to come by!

Brendan's reading this book now and driving everybody crazy with it—*The Fourth Way*, or some such thing. He keeps asking everybody if they're conscious or unconscious. Asleep or awake. He says the book says everybody's sleeping. That history was made by sleeping people, and sleeping people wage wars, et cetera, et cetera. Which I definitely could agree with. Of course, Brendan likes the book because the book keeps saying how *impossible* it is to wake up. So he would love that dreary message. I keep telling him Claire Weekes has this guy beat. She has all these mystical dudes beat, what with her little stories about tea cakes and the village shoppe. But people don't like things if they're too easy to understand. They want everything to be hard! Crazy, I swear.

Anyway, along with the usual bunch, most of our friends are the local folk up here. They know me now and I know them. I think they pretty much accept me. At any rate, they know that this is as normal as I'm ever going to get. So all in all, me and lollipop are having a fine old time. I don't even paint anymore because I'm doing something much more important right now. I don't want to miss a minute of it. Later for the painting. My idea of a pleasant afternoon is sitting around in the park, watching our kids, and talking about who broke out in a little rash from her orange juice.

Hey, I didn't even tell you my daughter's name, did I? Well, look, if you were more or less working under the impression that you were never going to have children, and then one day, you had this beautiful baby, what would you name her? And also, if this baby taught you that all those beautiful, loving stars you were always searching the skies for? That the same stuff as those stars was right down deep inside you—what would you name her?

Well, I named her Joy. You should hear her laugh. You should hear that sweet, giddy giggle of hers. Well, you've probably heard kids laugh. Of course, she's got a pretty good *howl* too, but that's all part of it, right? Here she comes. She wants her bath. Dragging all her stuff with her. What a corker!